MOTH TO THE FLAME

"Why do you even care if I stay? You did your good deed for the year—saved poor little Cactus Maxie from a life of crime. Why should you care what I do?"

Aaron stared at her, examining with horror the answer that had suddenly surfaced in his mind. "Because I'm a goddamned idiot," he said, more to himself than to her. A goddamned idiot, and even worse. So much worse that he was afraid to say the words, even to himself.

He reached out and pulled her to him. Startled, she hadn't the time to resist before he brought his mouth down upon hers. The kiss was not gentle. He wasn't in a gentle frame of mind: he was in a desperate frame of mind. Wanting to make her feel what he was feeling, and knowing it was hopeless, he plundered her sweet mouth to salve his wound. Passion flooded him in hurtful force, and insanity—it had to be insanity—seared his brain and burned its way through his heart as she responded, a moth to the flame. . . .

Cactus Blossom

EMILY BRADSHAW

A DELL BOOK

Published by
Dell Publishing
a division of
Bantam Doubleday Dell Publishing Group, Inc.
666 Fifth Avenue
New York, New York 10103

ISBN: 0-440-20871-8

Printed in the United States of America

Published simultaneously in Canada

November 1991

10 9 8 7 6 5 4 3 2 1

Cactus
Blossom

Prologue

"**Y**ou're just a goddamned chicken-shit girl, Maxie! That's what you are!"

Ten-year-old Aleta Maria Maxwell—dubbed Cactus Maxie by those who had to live with her prickly temper—narrowed sky-blue eyes at the taunting smirk that spread across her twin brother's face. "Chicken" and "girl" used together in the same insult was an invitation to a fight, and Dirty Jim knew it.

"I ain't chicken!" Maxie replied, the gleam of battle in her eye.

"Are so."

"Ain't!"

Dirty Jim scooted back from the lip of the ravine where they both lay prone on the dusty ground. A robbery was in progress below them—their brothers Blackjack, Tom, and friend Aaron Hunter against two gringo silver miners. A hundred feet from where the two gringos stood with hands raised, a mine portal yawned like a dark door into hell. Deep underground, other miners labored, unaware that the fruit of their labor would soon be in Maxwell saddlebags.

"I say we go down so we can get a closer look," Jim declared in a bold voice.

"I say you're nuts. Blackjack'd whip our butts."

"You're just chicken!"

Maxie's temper reached the end of its short fuse. She'd gone to a lot of trouble to follow Hunter and her brothers this morning. It hadn't been easy slipping away from the hidden camp where her father and brothers reigned over a little kingdom of lawbreakers. But she wouldn't miss much of the fun below in the few minutes it would take to pound on her twin.

"We'll see who's chicken!" she told him, giving him a push. "And it ain't me, shitbrain."

Dirty Jim pushed back as they both scrambled to their feet. "Maxie's a girl," he singsonged, "a chicken-shit girl." He darted forward, grabbed one of Maxie's fat black braids, and yanked. Maxie responded by pummeling her twin's head, neck, and shoulders with her hard little fists. Soon they had forgotten the drama in the ravine below and were tussling on the rocky ground, scratching, biting, kicking, and flailing.

Finally Maxie managed to get her brother in an armlock. She squeezed without mercy while heaping upon his head every insult and curse she knew, combining English, Spanish, and a few phrases of Apache as well. Jim's face grew a very satisfactory purple. He flopped and bounced like a landed fish—until one of his fists connected with Maxie's small nose. Suddenly it was Dirty Jim on top, sitting on Maxie's bony little rump and joyfully twisting her arm behind her back.

Maxie sputtered angrily into the dirt. She wasn't about to surrender, in spite of the pain shooting through her arm and shoulder. She figured if she could just roll a bit and throw him off-balance . . .

A rifle shot cracked through the air. Maxie and Jim both froze, then scrambled frantically back to the edge of the ravine to see what was happening.

"Goddamn!" Jim whispered.

The robbery had erupted into chaos. From somewhere up the ravine a rifle shot had plowed into the midst of the bandits. Tom was fighting to control his horse; Blackjack was trying with shouts and curses to calm the mule he had loaded with silver bullion; Aaron Hunter held a steady pistol on the two miners, who looked ready to flee.

"Tom! Come help me with this goddamned mule!" Blackjack shouted.

The hidden rifle cracked again. Hunter's horse reared, squealing in pain, then toppled and fell to one side. Hunter went down with his mount, one leg pinned beneath the heavy body. His pistol arced through the air and landed in the sand twenty feet away.

The miners sprang forward. They grabbed the weapons they had earlier been forced to drop and let loose a random spray of bullets that plowed up the sandy creek bottom, rattled through the brush on the side of the ravine, and ricocheted off the rock walls.

Blackjack's pistol roared in answer. He let loose of the crow-hopping mule and headed for his horse, firing as he ran. One miner went down, a neat hole between his eyes. The second miner ran for the cover of the mine shack, but before he had gone five steps Blackjack's second and third shots lifted him off his feet, spun him around, and sent him sprawling into the dirt.

"Get outta here!" Blackjack yelled as he swung aboard his horse.

"But Hunter . . . !" Tom objected.

A rifle bullet pinged off a boulder at the edge of the ravine.

"Leave him, goddamn it!"

Rifle fire followed the brothers as they spurred their horses down the ravine and disappeared around a bend. Suddenly all was quiet except for the squeak of the mine shack door swinging in the breeze.

"Shit!" Maxie said, releasing her breath in a great whuff.

"What do they think they're doing? They can't leave Hunter like that!"

Dirty Jim tugged at her sleeve. "Come on, Maxie! We gotta get outta here. There's more miners down in that shaft." He pointed toward the mine portal. "When they come out and find those dead hombres, they're gonna be lookin' fer blood."

"Now who's chicken?" Maxie spit to emphasize her point. She had just recently learned to spit—it wasn't that easy a thing to do—and liked to use her new talent at any opportunity. "We've got to help Hunter!" she declared in her best heroic tone.

"What're you talkin' about? We go down there, we're gonna get drilled!"

"Not if we use our heads!"

"Your head's gonna get blown off! And mine too! I'm goin'!"

"Oh, go on! Go on and hightail it! You're no damned help anyway!"

Maxie didn't watch her twin brother run down the slope toward the little shaded wash where they'd tethered their horses. She didn't need help from him. How long had she waited for a chance to show her father and brothers that she was good for something other than hauling water, washing dirty clothes, shoveling horse shit, and carrying firewood! She'd just been handed the perfect opportunity.

A wink of light from across the ravine caught Maxie's eye —the sun bouncing off a metal rifle barrel. The rifleman might stay where he was for a few minutes to make sure the Maxwell brothers weren't coming back. And if he did . . .

Maxie's grin was so wide it stretched every freckle on her face. If these gringo miners thought the Maxwell brothers were tough, wait until they tangled with the Maxwell sister!

A few moments later Maxie had circled around the head of the ravine and crouched Apache style thirty feet from where a lone man squatted behind a boulder—a miner, from the look of him. A horse and a supply-laden mule were tied to a nearby mesquite. What rotten luck that the miner had returned from town just in time to turn the Maxwells' fun into a bloody mess. The horse flicked an ear and turned its head to look at Maxie, but the miner's eyes were locked on the ravine below, his ears tuned for the hoofbeats of returning outlaws. He didn't hear the littlest outlaw as she crept up behind him, picked up a fist-size rock, and raised it high.

The rock came down on the miner's head with a meaty thunk. For one awful moment the man continued to squat behind his boulder. Then he slowly toppled. His rifle clattered to the ground as he hit the dirt. Cautiously Maxie nudged the sprawled body with the toe of her boot. The guard didn't move except for the slight rise and fall of his chest. Maxie drew in a shaky breath. Committing mayhem on someone was a bit more unsettling than she had thought. Outlawing was a fine lark, but some parts of it were less fun than others.

But now the hard part was over. All she had left to do was pry Hunter from beneath his horse, grab the silver-laden mule, and ride home a heroine. She stepped gingerly around the body of her victim and clambered up to the edge of the ravine.

"Shit!"

Hunter was gone, and even at this distance she could see the trail of blood he'd left dragging himself away. At any moment the day shift would end and the miners would pour out of the mine portal to a nasty surprise—a dead crew boss and paymaster. They'd likely follow the trail of blood, find Hunter, and fill him so full of holes that what was left of him wouldn't make a decent meal for a vulture. Or they might get really nasty and hang him. Unless, of course, she could find him first.

Maxie sighed. Being a heroine wasn't easy.

Fifteen minutes later—five minutes after the first of the day shift emerged from the mine, discovered the bodies, and started passing out weapons and ammunition from the crew shack—Maxie found Hunter. He was hidden, sprawled in a bloody heap behind a mesquite thicket, his face ashen, his left side crimson. At least one of the miners' bullets had found a target.

"Wake up!" Maxie poked at his uninjured side. "Dammit, Hunter! Wake up. This place is crawling with shit-faced miners and nervous trigger fingers. They're gonna blast anything that moves."

"What?" Hunter croaked.

"Quiet! Couldn't you crawl any farther than this?"

Hunter slitted his eyes open and looked up at her, then groaned. "What're you doin' here? No"—he shut his eyes again—"don't tell me."

"Get up, Hunter! We gotta git! Here—" She slung his good arm over her small shoulder and tried to pull him to his feet. "Are you all right?"

"Hell no, I'm not all right! Leggo!"

"Come on! I've got a horse tied in the next ravine."

"The next ravine," Hunter gritted out between clenched teeth. "Forget it!"

"You can make it! Come on!"

He did make it, leaning his tall, whipcord-thin frame against her sturdy little shoulder. Maxie's bay mare stood waiting for them.

"Lightning's a good horse," Maxie told him. "Just give her her head and she'll take you right home to Stronghold. And don't let any of those shit-assed miners follow you."

Hunter grunted but somehow managed to pull himself into the saddle as Maxie propped a bony shoulder against his rear and pushed. He swayed for a moment, then straightened and reached down a hand to help her up. "Get on," he croaked.

"Lightning cain't outrun those miners with both of us on her back," Maxie said. "And they're yippin' and hollerin' over there like they've found our trail. You'd better git, Hunter."

"Get on!" he growled.

Maxie slapped the horse smartly on the rump. Lightning took off with a lunge that almost landed Hunter back on the ground. A string of curses trailed behind man and beast as they took off toward the mountains.

"And I thought I could cuss!" Maxie said with an admiring grin.

By the time a troop of irate miners rode out of the ravine and whipped their horses in the same direction, Hunter and Lightning were merely a dust cloud in the distance. Safe behind a screen of mesquite and acacia, Maxie watched the miners pass, then stood up and brushed the dust from her shirt and trousers. It was going to be a long walk home. If she was lucky she might get there by breakfast tomorrow, or maybe lunch. Already her tummy was rumbling a complaint.

Maxie sighed. She hoped saving Hunter's hide had been worth the trouble.

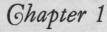

Chapter 1

June 1868
Just south of the Mexican border
Sonora, Mexico

The crack of a rifle echoed off steep canyon walls. At the same instant a bullet whined past Aaron Hunter's head and plowed up the sandy creek bottom two feet behind his horse's hind legs.

"Holy Mary!" Close beside Aaron, Simon Curtis vaulted out of his saddle and took cover behind his mount with an agility that belied his gray-streaked hair and finely seamed face. Before his feet hit the sand a pistol was in his hand. "I told you we ain't gonna get outta here alive!"

Two more reports of the rifle rumbled around the canyon; two more lead slugs sprayed sand a mere foot in front of the horses' front feet. Simon raised his pistol and looked desperately for a target. Aaron didn't move except to rein in his dancing horse.

"Hold off, Simon. That was just a warning. If he'd wanted to hit us, we'd be dead men by now."

"That's a comfort!" Simon commented wryly.

"Hey, you up there!" Aaron yelled at the towering canyon walls. "Peace, friend! I'm a compadre of Maxwell's."

The silence that answered was deafening. The birds had lost their voices in the heat of the day, and not a breath of a breeze stirred the scraggly brush that littered the dry streambed. The only sound in the whole vast canyon was the nervous creak of saddle leather and the agitated wheezing of the horses. Both men listened to themselves sweat and imagined an eye sighting down a rifle barrel, a finger tightening on a trigger—tightening, tightening. . . .

At the sound of a scrabbling along the canyon wall, both men jerked their heads around. The lookout, rifle poised and ready, was making his way down a precarious path.

Simon raised his pistol.

"No!" Aaron commanded quietly. "Wait! We're supposed to be friends here, Simon. *Comprende?*"

Eyes never leaving the rifleman, Aaron lifted his battered hat and ran one hand through the dark brown waves of his hair. Sweat beaded on his scalp, trickled down over sculptured cheekbones, and ran in rivulets down his stubble-darkened jaw. The heat was making him sweat, he told himself, not fear. He had planned too well and waited too long for something to go wrong now.

The lookout had scrambled halfway down the scree and now crouched behind a boulder not fifty feet away. "State yer business." He punctuated his demand by lifting the carbine to his shoulder.

"I came to see Maxwell," Aaron said.

The lookout gave them a wicked, gap-toothed grin. "Lotsa folks would like ta see Maxwell. Two 'r three lawmen I could name. Probably some I cain't."

"We're not lawmen."

"Yeah?" The grin disappeared as the lookout fingered the carbine's trigger. "How do I know?"

"My name's Hunter. Aaron Hunter. I rode with Maxwell awhile back. I just want to join up again—along with my partner here."

The lookout stared at them for a long moment. "I heard o' the name," he finally conceded. "Boy named Aaron Hunter was the fastest gun around here fer a while, so they says. They also says he was kilt in a mine job over by Tubac a long time ago."

Aaron shrugged. "Shot. Not killed. Eight years ago."

The lookout's eyes narrowed suspiciously. "Eight years is a long time, amigo. Where ya been?"

"That's my affair—amigo."

A tense silence stretched between them, and Aaron could almost see the wheels turning in the other man's mind, weighing the consequences of shooting him down if he really was a friend of Maxwell's. "I guess you c'n go," the lookout finally growled. "But leave yer guns here. That rifle, too." He pointed to the Winchester on Aaron's saddle.

Simon's mouth opened to object, but Aaron silenced him with a cautioning hand.

"I'd hate to part with these for very long." His black eyes narrowed as he handed over his pistol and pulled the rifle from its scabbard.

"Oh, you'll git 'em back, hombre. If yer still standin' on yer two feet when I get to Stronghold tonight. Now git— before I change my mind."

They hastened to obey, feeling the guard's carbine track their every move as they rode. The better part of a half mile and several bends in the trail passed before either drew an easy breath.

"Right friendly fella," Simon snorted.

"What'd you expect?" Aaron replied with a twisted grin. "Sunday school teachers?"

The canyon ahead narrowed to a steep-walled gorge, just as Aaron remembered. Eight years had passed since he'd last ridden through this defile, a cocksure, arrogant kid ready to flip the world on its ear. Since then, life had beaten

a little sense into him. Over the span of years he'd survived
a miner's lead slug in his side, gotten another slug in his leg
during the war back East, learned the value of peace—the
hard way, fallen in love, and been robbed of all his life's
dreams. He'd grown up, become a bit wiser—not much, but
a little. He had enough sense to know he was riding into
trouble, but not enough to keep him from doing it.

They were challenged three more times. None of the
lookouts were men who had ridden with Aaron in his lawless years, but two had heard of him. The third simply
passed them on with a careless wave of his rifle when Aaron
invoked Maxwell's name.

"Hope you remember where these lookouts are posted."
Simon urged his horse to trot up beside Aaron's, looked
around nervously, and wiped sweat from his face with a
kerchief. The dust had turned his skin almost as gray as the
stubble of his beard. "You're going to have to take every one
of them out when you come back. If those bastards get any
warning of what we're up to, I'm a dead man."

Aaron grinned. "You worry too much, compadre."

"That's how I've stayed alive such a long time." He gave a
doubtful look to the canyon walls that were pressing ever
closer. "Hell! I'd rather tangle with Cochise and his cut-
throat Cherrycows than this bunch of sidewinders."

Just as the canyon walls seemed to be drawing together in
a narrow dead end, the dry creek bottom took a sharp turn
to the left. For fifty feet beyond the bend they rode through
a narrow slot between sheer walls of granite, then suddenly
emerged into open space and light. Before them was a
spacious amphitheater ringed by towering cliffs. Incongru-
ous in the midst of nature's spectacular handiwork, human
footprints desecrated the sandy floor, ramshackle human
dwellings littered the canyon borders, and human voices
disturbed the stillness of the air.

"This is it," Hunter said as he reined his horse to a halt.
"Stronghold. Hidey-hole for every bandit in the border
country."

Simon glanced up at the granite walls that flanked the canyon's entrance. "Ain't a real careful bunch, are they? Anybody and his brother can ride in here."

"Yeah. But they won't ride out. Not unless Maxwell wants them to. You can bet at least two guards up on that ledge have rifles aimed at our backs. Wouldn't take more than one wrong move to make them pull the trigger."

"There's a thought to cheer a man's heart." Simon cleared his throat, then spat into the sand. "Cain't tell you how glad I am you brought me along, amigo."

"Don't mention it," Hunter replied with a smile.

Stronghold was much the same as Aaron remembered. Smoke from a dozen cookfires clouded the air and added its pungent aroma to the odor of garbage, dust, and frying tortillas. On the far side of the amphitheater, horses milled in a corral constructed of long, tough stalks of ocotillo cactus woven between poles of mesquite. Behind the corral a large adobe shed kept the sun and infrequent rain from saddles, bridles, and bins of grain.

At the base of Stronghold's cliffs squatted an ugly assortment of adobe huts, tents of skin or canvas, and lean-tos made of twisted mesquite branches or ocotillo stalks. Some of the sturdier dwellings sported ramadas, and a few were bordered by small gardens. But for the most part the settlement looked as disreputable as the refuse of humanity it sheltered.

Aaron and Simon sat uneasily on their mounts. Few people were about, and those were mostly women, several with children clinging to their skirts. A handful of men sat in front of their dwellings or leaned against the corral. Two more lounged in the shade of a huge cottonwood tree that grew where a spring gushed from the cliff, bubbled for a few feet over sand and rocks, then disappeared into the ground.

A few uncertain moments passed before one of the men beneath the cottonwood tree squinted their way, then lumbered to his feet. Black-bearded, with hair the same color straggling over his shoulders, the bandit fingered the butt of his holstered pistol as he strolled toward them.

"Who might you be?" he growled.

"I'm Hunter. Aaron Hunter." Aaron held his arms well away from his sides to show he was unarmed. "This here's my partner, Simon Curtis. We came to talk to Maxwell."

Beardface eyed them suspiciously, then grunted. "Maxwell, is it? You friends of his?"

"You might say that."

The man shifted his gaze to their horses, tack, and full saddlebags. At sight of the saddlebags, his eyes lighted with interest.

Aaron returned the man's greedy gaze with one as cold and black as steel. "Forget what you're thinking, compadre. These bags are for Maxwell. If I were you, I'd fetch him before you do something you'll regret."

They locked eyes, but only for a moment. Beardface's gaze flickered, then dropped.

"Stay put," the outlaw muttered. "We'll see what Maxwell has to say about this."

The one-man welcoming committee stalked off, and Simon snorted. "Not what I'd call a rousing welcome home."

"I've been gone a good while," Aaron explained with a frown, "and things can change. Keep a lively eye out."

He watched Beardface disappear into a shallow cave in the canyon wall directly across the amphitheater from the corral. Partially curtained off with threadbare canvas, the cave served as saloon, meeting house, and whorehouse. Aaron remembered it well, for in the two years he had called Stronghold his home, he'd spent a large portion of his time there.

"Where the hell is everybody?" Simon asked uneasily, looking around.

"Out somewhere raising hell, or in the cave. Only ones you'll see out working this time of day are the women."

"Yeah." Simon looked around with a frown. "I didn't expect to see women here."

Aaron chuckled. "You expect men to live without women?"

"Nah. Guess even the Devil's got a wife."

"Most of these women aren't exactly wives."

"Didn't figger they was."

The men who had witnessed their conversation with Beardface continued to stare at them. The wolves were beginning to circle, and if Maxwell didn't show soon, Aaron thought, he and Simon were going to have more trouble on their hands than they could handle.

Finally Beardface emerged from the cave, followed by a man whom Aaron immediately recognized. The height and arrogant carriage couldn't be mistaken. Aaron's spine grew a bit straighter and his hand instinctively drifted closer to his empty holster as the bandit chief stopped on the stone stairs that descended the cliff wall from the cave. Maxwell stared. Aaron stared back. Finally the outlaw's mouth tugged up in a smile.

"Now here's a face I didn't expect to see again this side of hell." He finished the descent and strode toward them, Beardface following in his wake. "Hunter, boy, we thought you were dead."

"Nope," Aaron replied. "Not yet."

"Where you been keeping yourself, lad?"

"Here and there."

Maxwell hadn't changed much, Hunter noted. It was a crime when a man could be so evil and show so little outward sign of it. He stood tall and straight, broad shoulders and slim hips belying his age. Tightly curled blond hair and cobalt-blue eyes set him apart from his mostly Mexican comrades. With his fancy back-East clothes and clean-cut looks, Maxwell seemed respectable enough to hobnob with the territorial governor at Tucson, except for a certain something in his eyes that made a man think of a rattle-snake.

"This here's my partner, Simon Curtis." Aaron tilted his head toward his companion. "We've been pulling jobs together for a couple of months. We're doing all right, but I figure we'd do better if we joined up with your bunch."

Maxwell frowned and pulled at his chin. "Well, now, boy, it has been a right long time since we've seen you around here. I don't know . . ."

Aaron reached in back of his saddle and untied the saddlebags that had drawn Beardface's covetous attention. With effort he hefted the bags and dropped them to the ground in front of Maxwell's feet. They landed with a thud and a metallic clink.

"That's your share of our last job. A mine over by Arrivaca is poorer by some four hundred pounds of silver bullion."

Maxwell squatted down, opened the saddlebags, and peered inside. He smiled up at Aaron, one blond brow arched skyward. "And where's the rest?"

Aaron smiled back. "Somewhere safe." They looked at each other for a few tense moments before Aaron broke the silence. "I'm not that much of a fool, Harrison. Not anymore."

"So I see." Maxwell stood and motioned to Beardface to pick up the bags. He regarded Aaron with thoughtful eyes, taking in the changes that eight years had wrought—not only the taller frame and broader shoulders, but a new look in the eyes that bespoke a man not easily gulled, nor lightly crossed. "I see you're not a boy anymore, either, Hunter. I think we can find a place for you and your friend in our little brotherhood. Provided you're willing to take orders."

Aaron nodded agreement. "We'll get along."

Maxwell stared at him for a seemingly endless moment, then his mouth slanted into a half smile. "See that you do, Hunter. Just see that you do."

As Maxwell walked away, Beardface following with the heavy saddlebags like a faithful mule, Simon lifted his hat and wiped a forearm across his sweating brow. "Holy Mary Jesus!" he said in a low voice once Maxwell was out of earshot. "If that ain't the purtiest damned devil I ever did see. Those eyes of his'd put most gals to shame."

"Don't let those baby blues fool you," Aaron warned as they dismounted. "Even Apaches hightail it when they see Maxwell coming. And his oldest boy is every bit as mean."

A small boy, bare feet scuffing up dust and tangled black hair hanging over his eyes, ran up and offered to take their horses. Aaron flipped him a coin as he handed over the reins.

"You mean that devil's got a family?" Simon asked.

"Yeah. Maxwell came west with his two older boys back when this territory wasn't anything but rattlesnakes and Apaches. Got hitched up with a rich heiress down near Mexico City. Turned out her daddy didn't take to being Maxwell's father-in-law. They had to hightail it before the marriage ended with a shoot-out. Or so Maxwell once told me. He dragged his wife along when he turned to raiding. She gave him twins—a girl and a boy, born in this very hellhole. Died birthing 'em, poor lady."

"If that don't beat all! I cain't imagine Harrison Maxwell as a daddy."

"Don't figure he is much of a daddy, at that," Aaron commented.

They made sure the boy stabled their horses, then ambled toward the cave to join their new comrades. The *cerveza* and mescal served at the bar—a fancy wooden piece carted from Tucson by wagon—was far from being cold, but the cave walls at least provided shelter from the early evening heat.

The saloon was better populated than the sunbaked amphitheater. At least a dozen of the rough tables were occupied, and a score of men leaned against the bar. Liquor was being served up by a man whose girth almost filled the space between the bar and the bottle racks that lined the rock wall behind him. Several women strolled from table to table, some serving drinks, some hawking tortillas, frijoles, and *chile verde,* and others peddling themselves.

Aaron and Simon took a table and seated themselves with their backs against the wall. Suspicious eyes turned their way until Maxwell himself gave them a half-mocking salute. At their leader's sign of acceptance the others went back to their card games, liquor, and whores.

"Can I get you something, señor?" A tired-looking girl with lank black hair and a greasy complexion sidled up to their table. She was dressed in the simple cotton skirt and blouse of the typical Mexican woman, but the blouse was cut so low that it scarcely covered her large nipples. With every movement it gaped to reveal large, dusky breasts swinging pendulously from her chest.

"*Cerveza,*" Aaron told her. "And a couple of tortillas and frijoles."

Simon ordered the same.

"Anything else?" she asked. A certain brightness had come into her dark eyes as they roamed over Aaron's face, shoulders, chest, and came to rest appreciatively between his legs. She leaned suggestively closer.

Aaron spared only a brief glance at the breasts that almost brushed his face. He gave the girl a half smile. "Not right now. *Gracias.*"

Her lower lip, full and wet, came out in a practiced pout. "If you change your mind . . ." Her blouse slipped farther down one shoulder as she walked away. Simon squirmed in his chair and whistled low under his breath.

Aaron tilted his chair back against the wall and looked around him. Somehow the cave seemed smaller, smokier, mustier than he remembered, the whores greasier, the customers dirtier. The bartender wasn't the same, but then the bartender Aaron had known here—José had been his name—had gotten himself shot by a disgruntled customer two days before Aaron left for that last ill-fated robbery.

Their drinks and food were served by a different señorita, this one plump and pert and smelling of a cheap, musky perfume. She also tried her luck. Aaron politely but firmly declined her favors.

"You'd better watch your step," Simon warned with a

lopsided grin. "These ladies are gonna think you're un-friendly. Wasn't you sayin' we had to fit in here?"

Aaron bit into a tortilla that he'd piled high with a sloppy mixture of beans and chili. "You go play with the ladies," he said between bites. "I prefer to wrestle cows on the range, not in bed."

Simon shook his head. "I sure ain't never met a man so picky. That fancy eastern gal of yours spoiled you for real women, son. Out here a woman's a woman, and there ain't so many of 'em that a man can get choosy about them lookin' like cows, or smellin' like cows."

Aaron's scowl didn't drive the mischief from Simon's eyes.

"Besides, there's a gal over there that don't noways look like a cow. And she's been giving you the eye ever since we walked into this palace o' pleasure."

Aaron glanced in the direction of Simon's gaze. "You sure that's a girl?"

"Ain't no heifer."

"Couldn't be more'n thirteen years old."

"No thirteen-year-old's got tits like that."

Aaron stared for a moment, then agreed. "You're right. It's a girl."

"Don't look right you sittin' here like some sort of a monk," Simon said solemnly. "Bad fella like you is supposed to enjoy his womanflesh."

"Dry up, Simon."

"Already have. That's why the ladies are swingin' their hips at you, not me."

Simon was right about one thing, Aaron decided. The little whore had been staring at him as if he'd grown horns and sprouted a tail, though when he returned her stare she broke off her gaze abruptly. He saw a slow flush crawl up her neck and stain her cheeks. Imagine! A whore who could blush!

Simon was right about something else as well. This whore didn't resemble a cow in any way. She was small—almost childlike—and if she had any curves at all they were well hidden beneath baggy trousers and an overlarge shirt. The breasts that Simon had found so alluring were only a hint of swelling flesh where the vee neckline of her shirt gaped away from her body. Her face was almost elfin—pointed chin, dark sloe eyes, gracefully arched brows, and a slightly upturned nose. A tinge of sunburn on her nose and cheeks attested to the fairness of her skin, as did the crop of freckles that sprouted in the same area. Jet-black hair was pulled into two fat braids that hung to her waist, but tightly as her hair was pulled back, it still crinkled in frustrated curls. Most surprising of all, even at a distance Aaron could detect the startling clear blue of her eyes.

"I guess it wouldn't hurt to give it a try," Aaron conceded, sacrificing himself with a grin. The little slut did have a certain appeal, he decided.

Aaron was halfway across the room before he realized that he'd seen the girl somewhere before. In the cathouse in Motherlode, perhaps, though Mother Moses didn't usually take her girls so young. Could be this one was longer in the tooth than she looked from a distance.

The girl glanced his way again as Aaron closed the distance between them. Those sky-blue eyes narrowed as she regarded his advance toward her, and for a moment Aaron was ridiculously aware of the sticky sweat dried on his skin, the tangled disarray of his hair, and the dust that clung to his clothes. Suddenly his limp, a memento of the war that he'd long ago learned to ignore, seemed more conspicuous than ever.

Then he remembered where he was and what she was. He'd never known a Stronghold whore to be choosy. They didn't care how dirty a man was as long as his pockets were lined with either gold or silver.

"Howdy, ma'am." Aaron opened with the standard line. "You look mighty lonely sitting over here all by yourself."

The girl looked at the group of men and their women who crowded that end of the bar. Aaron could have sworn that her lip twitched in a sneer. Playing hard to get, was she?

"What're you drinkin'?" He dug a coin from his pocket and flipped it onto the bar. Was it his imagination or had the bustle and buzz of the cave saloon quieted? Were eyes turning his way? Harrison Maxwell gave him an amused look, one of the whores muffled a snicker, and the bartender shook his head, a distinct gleam of sympathy in his eye.

"Come on, love. Order yourself a drink and we can go someplace more private." He glanced toward the back of the cave where the girls conducted their business. Partitions of worn blankets divided off cubicles furnished with lice-ridden straw pallets. Back when Aaron had been a denizen of this vipers' nest, he had used those pallets often with an eighteen-year-old's eagerness to prove his manhood.

The little whore stared at him long and hard, as though waiting for him to say something else.

He nodded toward his coin on the bar. "Don't be shy. There's more where that came from."

Her eyes flared; she smiled. Straight white teeth gleamed behind sweetly curved lips, and Aaron began to feel the first stirrings of real hunger in his groin.

He'd started this act as a show—after all, Simon was right. He did have to fit into his role. But suddenly, as those clear blue eyes met his, desire became genuine. He reached out and encircled the whore's waist with his hands to gently detach her from the bar. Her waist was amazingly narrow, and the feel of womanflesh beneath his hands so bemused Aaron that the girl's reaction caught him completely unprepared. The lightning blow of her knee in his groin effectively wiped all thoughts of pleasure from his mind.

"You son of a bitch asshole!" she hissed.

Aaron staggered back, doubled over, and cradled the injured area. He straightened, only to realize that he didn't have time to dodge the blow that was heading for his stomach.

Aaron scarcely managed to keep his feet when the child-size fist slammed into his solar plexus. The air whooshed out of his lungs in a rush; black spots swam before his eyes. He was still bent over in agony as his attacker dusted her hands together in satisfaction, turned, and strutted proudly out of the cave.

The saloon erupted in laughter as soon as the girl-size whirlwind disappeared. Hunter staggered against the bar and gasped, trying to draw air into his lungs. That brought more laughter—deep hoots from the men and titters from the women. The only voice raised in sympathy belonged to the huge bartender, who clapped Aaron's shoulder in rough comradeship.

"Pay no mind, hombre. These braying jackasses—they've all gotten a taste of the same at some time or another. And they are so stupid they keep trying!" He joined the others' laughter.

Aaron's next gasp came out with a question mark. The bartender grinned.

"Thought she was one of my *putas*? Eh? Well, you'll know better next time, señor. She is no *puta*, that one. That"—he gestured grandly in the direction in which the little she-wolf had strutted off—"that is Harrison Maxwell's youngest. We call her Cactus Maxie."

"He didn't even recognize me!" Maxie snarled. "The bastard didn't even recognize me!"

Hilda, sitting cross-legged on the dirt floor of the ocotillo lean-to she shared with Maxie, merely shrugged and continued sewing together a corset that had been ripped by an overenthusiastic customer. She was accustomed to her friend's outbursts of temper. "So what? It's been a few years, hasn't it?"

"I saved his goddamned life!" Maxie continued in the same indignant tone. "I saved the son of a bitch's life and he doesn't even know who I am! He thought I was a fancy lady!"

Hilda snorted. "He musta' been funnin' ya, sweets. Most

gents wouldn't mistake ya fer a female, much less a whore—even if ya was stripped bare." She ignored Maxie's glare and continued. "He probably don't remember the skinny kid who once pulled him outta trouble. Men don't got memories for those kinda things."

"I recognized him!" Maxie insisted, thrusting out a pointed, pugnacious chin.

"Honey, any female would remember that man. And sometimes you do come close to bein' a female, whether ya like it or not."

Maxie grimaced. She had to admit that for a few minutes she hadn't believed the newcomer was Aaron Hunter. Eight years ago his shoulders hadn't been so broad, nor had he walked with the slight limp that marked his gait now. The lanky, curly-headed boy with the loud mouth and the angry eyes was gone. He'd grown taller, broader, more muscled—almost not the same man.

But he was the same man. His hair was the same—rich brown and curling around his neck in uncombed disarray. His face was the same, though it had filled out some, just like the rest of him, and a tiny scar that she didn't remember marred one brow. But the eyes—the eyes were different. Just as dark, just as deep, just as angry as she remembered, they glittered with a new quality—something hard and dangerous. Maxie didn't quite know what it was. She wasn't sure she wanted to know.

"If ya ask me, sweets, that Hunter fella is about the best-lookin' gent that's drifted this way. Saw him ride in this afternoon, and I said to myself—Hilda, honey, now there's one hombre I wouldn't mind gettin' on my back for. Leastways he looks like he washes his clothes ever' now and then. More 'n I can say about most of the boys around here."

"He shoulda recognized me," Maxie muttered.

"Get off. You're just pissed 'cause you was too chicken to take up his offer. Even a gal who don't make her livin' on her back would be glad ta have that one on top of her. It'd do ya good, little Maxie. Believe me."

"That's a load of shit!" Maxie snapped. "I swear! All you ever think about is spreadin' your legs!" She headed toward the door with an indignant huff.

Hilda shrugged as Maxie stomped out of the lean-to. "I like my work!" She called after her roommate. "So what?"

"So what!" Maxie muttered as she stalked into the sweltering night. So what if she had cried her stupid eyes out that day when Aaron Hunter hadn't come back? She'd thought him dead. Everyone had. For eight long years she'd thought him dead and dreamed foolish dreams about what might have happened had he lived—how he might have been so grateful for her help that he'd let her be a special friend, and how she would ride out with him on all the raids, and he would teach her to shoot straighter and ride better than anyone else in Stronghold. And then one day he would realize she was grown up. They would live together in a real house that he would build especially for her, and they would spend the rest of their days as partners raiding the mines and the mail coaches.

Her boots scuffing dejectedly in the dust, Maxie headed toward the path that led up the cliff to the entrance lookout. She wanted to be alone to sulk. Hilda was right. She was pissed. But not about being chicken. Cactus Maxie wasn't chicken about anything! But here she was, all grown up, and Aaron Hunter wasn't dead. Not only wasn't he dead, but he didn't give a damn about her, didn't remember her. The son of a bitch probably didn't even recall that someone had saved his miserable skin on that day long ago.

Maxie saw a dark form loom up in front of her. She reached for the pistol she carried at her hip, thumbing back the hammer as she pulled it from its holster.

"What're you doing out here?" she demanded. Dark as it was, she recognized the form as Hunter's. Something about the set of those broad shoulders . . .

He turned, and Maxie could imagine an indifferent lift of his scarred brow. "Kicking and punching weren't enough?"

he answered, a hint of laughter in his deep voice. "Now you're going to shoot me?"

She lowered the pistol and slipped it back home. "I could," she asserted.

"No doubt." He fell into step beside her as she walked on. Again she noticed the slight hesitation in his gait, but it didn't prevent him from keeping up as she lengthened her stride. "Out for a breath of air?" he inquired.

"Go stick your head in the privy."

"Nice night, isn't it?"

"No. Don't you have somewhere else to go?"

He put a hand on her shoulder and halted their progress. "Look, Maxie. I'm sorry I didn't know who you were back there. You've grown some."

Not according to Hilda. Hilda said she couldn't attract a man's notice if she stripped bare naked. Maxie glared at Hunter in silence, trying not to appreciate the fact that he had grown some himself.

"Where've you been, anyway?" she asked, her voice sharp with hostility. "I . . . we all thought you were dead when you didn't come back."

"Did it matter?"

"It mattered to me." Maxie was glad that it was dark, because she felt a flush heat her face. "You had my horse, remember? It was a good horse."

"Yeah. That's right. It was a good horse."

They walked on, passing the path that led up to the lookout, but Maxie had forgotten her desire to be alone.

"Where'd you go if you wasn't dead?"

"Decided I'd had enough of Stronghold," he replied. "Holed up with the Pima Indians for a while until I healed, then I headed up to Gila City to dig for gold."

Maxie's interest was piqued. "Find any?"

"Not a nugget," he said with a smile. "Ended up joining the Confederate Army. They sent me back East for a while to fight the war."

"Why'd you come back now?" They seated themselves on a low ledge that stuck out at chair level from the cliff.

He was silent a moment before he answered. "Nothing better to do."

"You pissed at my brothers Blackjack and Tom?"

"What?"

"For leaving you that day at the mine. You come back to get even?"

He chuckled bitterly. "Blackjack and Tom? Naw. I've got nothing special against them. Might as well hate a mule for kicking as hate a man for looking out for himself. Besides, their kid sister stayed and saved my life that day."

The air suddenly seemed to grow thick between them. Maxie was glad Hunter couldn't see her face. She figured it showed a damned sight too many of the foolish things she was feeling.

"I haven't forgotten that, Maxie. I owe you. And I'm a man who always pays his debts."

"Awww . . . It wasn't no trouble. Fact is, it was a real kick." She laughed awkwardly and stared at her feet. Suddenly it seemed very right to be sitting in the dark with Hunter. "Besides, I couldn't leave you there. I thought . . . well . . . back then I sorta thought you were some kind of a hero."

He didn't say anything, and the silence seemed to swell around her. Somehow he seemed very close, and very big, and the feel of him sitting there beside her did things to her nerves that shouldn't be done to anyone's nerves.

Maybe it was those abused nerves that gave Maxie the idea. If Aaron Hunter had been sitting beneath a starry sky with a real female, he wouldn't be lounging like a lizard on a rock, Maxie figured; he'd probably be doing some kissing. He was being nice to her, thanking her politely for being brave enough to save him. And here she had just admitted that she'd fancied him when she was a kid. The situation did seem to call for something special.

Not that Maxie knew a thing about kissing. But it couldn't

be that hard, because the girls who worked in the cave did it all the time, and they were useless at doing anything that required brains or guts. All she had to do was lean over, take aim, and plant one on Hunter's lips. And then let Hilda call her chicken!

Very quickly, before she could lose her nerve, Maxie leaned, aimed, and managed to hit her target. As her lips touched Hunter's, his whole body jerked like a fish snagged on a hook, then froze.

Why the hell did everyone get so excited? Maxie wondered. It was no big thing to kiss a man.

Only a few seconds passed before she learned differently.

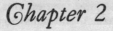

Chapter 2

$\mathcal{A}$aron sat immobile as a stone, and just as cold-blooded, for the first few seconds after Maxie's lips touched his. He hadn't expected this from a half-grown kid with braids and freckles. Her mouth was so childish, and yet the soft, tentative touch, the innocent assertiveness, held a sensual promise that reminded him that he'd been without a woman since Julia. Sweet Julia.

Then desire rose in his body like a spring flood, tearing icicles from where they'd grown around passions too long unused. Cold stone turned to molten steel as his hands came up to grasp Maxie's arms in a hurting grip, and his mouth welcomed her shy caress with one much more bold. With a startled gasp, Maxie froze. Her hands pushed against him with surprising strength; her mouth twisted under his, trying to escape. But he only deepened his kiss, probing her sweet mouth with his tongue. One of his hands moved to tangle in her hair, loosening the braids; the other slipped slowly down over her breast to finally light at her narrow waist.

Maxie's struggles slowed, then ceased. Her mouth parted

in hesitant acceptance of his possession. Her hands left off their pushing and trailed over his ribs, skimmed the wide breadth of his shoulders, and finally clasped around his neck in a grip that was both hesitant and desperate.

Aaron pulled her across his lap. An animal growl rattled in his throat as she flowed against him like warm liquid honey. As though some mysterious tether inside him had snapped, his passion surged forward, engulfing reason and conscience both. With every second that passed he was growing harder, swelling with male need. He wanted nothing more than to tumble them both to the ground, strip off those ridiculous baggy trousers of hers, and show her the ultimate goal of what she had so unwisely started.

With a startling jolt his roving hand lit upon the cold steel of the pistol Maxie carried at her hip. His senses snapped back into focus, reminding him that he held a child—a mere smudge-faced urchin in pigtails, a half-grown gun-toting brat who didn't even know how to kiss, much less take a man between her legs and bring him into paradise. And Aaron Hunter wasn't going to be the man to show her. Cactus Maxie might be the Devil's own spawn—and a veritable imp of hell in her own right—but Aaron owed her more than casual seduction. He wasn't a man to forget his debts.

He pushed her away as gently as he could, considering that she was wound around him like a Mexican boa. For a moment Maxie looked dazed. Her hands untangled themselves from around his neck and fluttered in confusion, finally pressing to her swollen lips and then fussing with her shirt, which somehow had come unbuttoned almost to her waist. She closed her eyes, swayed slightly, then opened them again. They widened as though she was surprised to find him still sitting there in front of her. The look she gave him—disbelief mingled with horror—made him feel kin to a snake.

"What the hell did you do that for?" he demanded, guilt

prodding anger. "Do you go around kissing every man you talk to?"

Those eyes, brilliant blue even in the shadows of night, grew wider as she started to shrink away. She stopped herself. Her brows drew together and she straightened. He could almost see her pulling her scattered composure back into order.

"No reason," she said, her little chin thrusting forward. "I just wondered how it would feel. You didn't have to turn a little kiss into some sort of wrestling match."

He glared. "You have a lot to learn about men."

"I figure there's not a lot worth learning."

"Well, you're going to learn more than you think if you keep behaving like some sort of . . . of . . . God! You're just a kid." Instead of cooling, his anger grew. Maxwell's daughter had always grated on his nerves, and eight years hadn't changed her knack for getting under his skin.

"What're you still doing in this place, anyway? I'd think your father would've had enough sense to send you away by now."

Maxie shrugged. "Why should he send me away? Where would I go? My family's here—Pa and Blackjack and Tom and Dirty Jim. A body's got to have family, ya know."

A body had to have family. Aaron thought of the family he might have right now if his Julia hadn't been prey to scum like the devils who lived at Stronghold. Perhaps the very men who had killed her had stood next to him in the cave or were the men Cactus Maxie called family. He should recall why he was here risking his life—not to diddle some tempting hoyden, but to get rid of the rats that infested this canyon. Partly for the law, partly for his murdered Julia, partly for himself.

"Get going, Maxie, before I forget what a baby you are."

"I'm not a baby!"

Hands on hips, Maxie glared. All trace of any embarrassment was gone, Aaron noted. She probably didn't even know how close she had come to getting tumbled like a whore.

"All right. You're not a baby. I just don't want you hanging around."

"You can't give me orders." Her mouth slanted into a sassy smile. "Only Pa gives me orders."

Her expression reminded Aaron of the cheeky ten-year-old who had put him on her horse and sent him galloping away from a felon's death. His heart softened a small measure. She couldn't help what she was, or what she was bound to become.

"I'm not giving you orders. I'm just telling you I'd like to be alone—as a friend. All right?"

Maxie shrugged. "All right. Have it your way." She turned, walked a few steps, then turned back. "I'm sorry I kissed you, Hunter. You're right. It was stupid." One brow lifted in a cocky arch. "And not very interesting."

Aaron watched her walk away into the dark, noting as he watched that even in the loose trousers, the lilt of her gait was anything but childlike.

"Well now, son," came a voice out of the darkness. "Seems as if that particular little heifer ain't quite ready to eat outta your hand. Not like most of 'em."

Aaron sighed and gave a rueful shake of his head. "How long you been out there, Simon?"

"Long enough. I was scoutin' around. Thought you was, too, till I saw you snuggle up to that there female hornet. Looks like she was fixin' to change her mind about you. Leastways I didn't see her throwin' any more gut-punches."

"And of course," Aaron said with a chuckle, "you were figuring to stay and watch."

"Old coot my age has to get his entertainment somehow. Why'd ya stop?"

Aaron frowned in the direction that Maxie had disappeared. "She's just a kid. Bold as brass but doesn't half know what she's doing. Besides, I've got more important things on my mind. So do you."

He might get to those important things if he could get the sweet taste of Maxie's mouth off his lips, the feel and smell of her out of his senses. Damn, but the itch for a woman could turn a man's brain to mush! Hunter snorted in disgust.

"Beg pardon?" There was a hint of laughter in Simon's voice.

"Nothing!" Aaron willed the irritating imp from his mind. "How long do you suppose we'll have to stay in this rathole before we get this over with?"

"Thought you was lookin' forward to this, son. Wasn't you the one so hell-bent to clean out this snakes' nest?"

"Clean it out, not live in it for any length of time. This place is enough to set anyone on edge."

Simon grinned. "The place, or the women?"

"Compadre, you're ridin' mighty close to the edge." Aaron scowled for a moment, then shook his head. His mouth twitched upward in a grin as he threw one final glance after Maxie. "I'll feel a whole heap easier when I've put both the place and the women behind us."

"You ain't the only one, son. But from what I'm hearin', it'll be another two, three days before most of Maxwell's men return from that raid over by Cananea."

"Guess we can survive that long."

Simon grinned. "Figger we can. Give us time to scout out the place, win a few hands of poker, entertain some of the ladies . . ."

"Just remember why you're here, compadre."

"Ain't likely to forget."

Aaron was silent as they walked back toward the cave. Except for a few raucous voices drifting from the saloon, the night was silent. The swath of stars that showed above the surrounding cliff walls glittered serenely through the clear desert air, and the faint plashing of the spring at the foot of the cliff only emphasized the night's quiet. Stronghold—rathole home of the frontier's worst trash—knew an ironic peace. Tucson was rowdier. So were Tubac, Motherlode, Cananea, and any of the scattered settlements that dotted this unholy desert. The border bandits stirred up trouble wherever else they rode, but their own refuge they left in peace. A few even had families here. Maxwell himself had his children, and the two youngest had been born and raised in this hellhole.

Maxwell's damned children—two hell-bent sons brought west with him and twins—a son and a daughter—sired on the poor lady he'd dragged up from Mexico. Troublemaker that he was, Maxwell just had to sire a daughter. *Dammit! What does one do with Satan's own imp if that imp is a girl?*

"Simon." Aaron slowed to a stop. "I want a favor from you."

"Yeah?" Simon didn't sound surprised.

"When the ruckus starts around here, I want you to get Maxie out of the way."

The older man snorted in amusement. "Figgered you might."

"It's not what you think."

"That right? Funny. Even in the dark I thought I saw a gleam in those eyes o' yours while she was walkin' away."

"She's Maxwell's daughter, Simon. She did me a big favor eight years ago. I don't owe her a noose in return."

"Folks in Motherlode ain't gonna hang no gal."

Aaron chuckled sourly. "If they were smart, they'd hang this one."

"And what do you think you're gonna do with her?"

"Damned if I know. You just get her out of the way of any stray bullets. I'll think of something."

Maxie lay on her pallet listening to Hilda's snores. The woman hadn't come in until the night was almost gone; her evening must have been a profitable one.

Under the edge of the ragged canvas that covered the ocotillo walls of the lean-to, Maxie could see that the night was fading. Dawn was on its way, and she still hadn't slept. It had been the same for the last three nights, ever since her run-in with Hunter.

If Hilda's snores weren't so damned loud, she might sleep now, Maxie thought irritably. She was tired enough. That was for sure. But sometimes sleeping in the same space with Hilda was like trying to sleep through a volley of gunfire.

Maxie turned over, punched the saddle pad that served as her pillow, and pulled the blanket up over her head. But the blanket blocked neither the snores coming from the other pallet nor the thoughts that kept her mind from peace.

Damn Aaron Hunter anyway! Dead, he'd been a harmless daydream, an idol built from a child's fantasies. Whenever she was bored she pulled him from the back rooms of her mind, dusted him off, and spent a few hours speculating on the good times they would have had together if only he had survived.

But alive, Hunter was a nuisance. He upset the balance of her mind, inspired silly gut churnings and thought wanderings, and was nothing like the fantasy she had concocted from the youthful Aaron Hunter—the hero she had imagined chased down by angry miners and killed in an exciting, tragic blaze of violence. The Hunter who had survived had an irritating hint of laughter in his eyes—not nice laughter, but a cynical mirth all mixed in with chilling anger. When he looked at her—and she caught him looking quite a lot—those fine dark eyes of his went blank. The son of a bitch had a friendly word for everyone at Stronghold except her. For Cactus Maxie, the girl who had saved his worthless life, he had only surly scowls and blank stares.

Maxie flopped over and punched her pillow again. That was the trouble with a fantasy coming alive. A body could make a dream do whatever she pleased; a living breathing man was a bit harder to make behave.

Not that her own behavior the last few days was anything to brag about. She was glad she had punched the bastard, but that little kiss hadn't been a good idea at all.

At first it seemed he hadn't noticed when her lips plunked down on top of his. He'd been unmoving as granite, cold as steel. She was wondering what all the hoo-ha was about when he grabbed her and started acting like he was going to eat her alive.

That had started her guts to churning. No doubt about it. The sheer power of him had sent her into a panic. His grip hurt her arms, and the fierce and frighteningly intimate things he did to her mouth horrified her—and then fascinated her. Never had she felt so helpless, never in her whole life. At that moment she knew how the mouse felt as it struggled in the hawk's talons, or the antelope as it stared into the eyes of a hungry puma.

But Hunter's strength and surprising ferocity were not what haunted Maxie's nights and kept her from sleep. What gnawed at her mind was her yen to give in to that ferocity. Some weak-kneed, pissant, female part of her had wanted to surrender. And she had surrendered, goddamn it. It made her wonder if she knew herself as well as she thought. She would have let Hunter do whatever he'd wanted with her. In fact, she'd practically begged him to, crawling all over him like one of Hernando's *putas,* making a fool out of herself. And what had Hunter done? He'd pushed her away! That's what the bastard had done!

Maxie groaned out loud, as she had the other hundred times she'd thought about that humiliating moment. She should have left this woman stuff to the women—like Hilda. Hunter wouldn't have pushed Hilda away.

Damn the man anyway! If the coward would ever come close enough, she'd spit in his eye. But he'd kept a safe distance, and now, before she could think of a fitting revenge, he was gone. He'd ridden out alone yesterday afternoon. The old man who was his sidekick had stayed behind, but he wouldn't tell her where Hunter had gone. Not that she cared. If he never came back she'd be perfectly happy about it. From now on Cactus Maxie was going to stick to the things she knew. She'd leave diddling the men to Hilda and the other girls in the cave.

Maxie was just beginning to doze when an explosive snore from Hilda shook her from sleep. It took her a few moments to realize that no one, not even Hilda, snored that loudly.

She recognized the second burst of gunfire for what it was. It brought her out of bed with a quick jump. A slowly growing chorus of shouts and curses told her the gunfire was no early morning quarrel between hung over Strongholders. Someone running by hit the lean-to. A warning? Shit! What was going on?

"Whazzat?" Hilda was awake now, peering blearily through the lean-to's gray gloom. "What's all the goddamn noise?"

"Don't know." With the clumsiness of haste Maxie yanked on her trousers, shirt, and boots. "Whatever it is, it sounds like trouble."

"Well, whatever it is, you tell it to shut up, huh?"

"I'll do that." Maxie headed for the door, but before she could get there, Dirty Jim burst through the canvas flap.

"Shit!" he gasped as they collided. "Maxie! It's a raid. Get to the corral, girl, and grab a horse. We're going out the back door."

He didn't stay to elaborate, but ran out before Maxie could open her mouth to ask a question.

"What's he mean, a raid?" Maxie stuck her head out the flap, and just as quickly pulled it back in. "Lordy! It's a raid, all right," she breathed in amazement. "God knows who or how." She turned back to her pallet and strapped on the single-holster gunbelt that lay at its head. Nudging Hilda with her toe, she warned, "You better drag it outta bed, Hilda, and get to the cave. Or that soft hide of yours is going to end up full of holes. We got visitors, and they ain't friendly."

Maxie didn't linger to listen to Hilda's curses. She stepped out of the lean-to and into chaos. Strongholders ran to and fro, shouting, cursing, screaming, but doing little to repel the mounted men who were fanning out from the narrow entrance. How the invaders had gotten past the entrance guards was anybody's guess. But they had, and that spelled disaster.

The gunfire was a steady barrage by now. The bandits sent wild shots in the direction of the attackers, but few were firing to any effect. Everyone was so intent on saving his own hide that an organized counterattack was impossible.

The invaders must have counted on that, Maxie decided as she crouched beside the lean-to wall for shelter. The early morning hours were not the best for bandit brains woozy from sleep or hung over from a night's drinking. Not that the Stronghold crew—with the exception of her father and brothers—had brains at any other hour of the day. As Maxie watched, a naked bandit stumbled from his tent, aimed his pistol at the nearest raider, and fired. Nothing happened. Maxie snorted in disgust. The fool had forgotten to load his gun.

"Maxie! Holy Mary! Maxie girl! There you are!"

Maxie spun around, pistol in hand. But it was only Simon Curtis coming from behind the corner of her lean-to. "Come on, girl." He motioned to her frantically. "I know a place where you'll be safe."

She stood and motioned him to be on his way. "Thanks, but no. I got my own plans."

Simon grabbed her arm as she started in the direction of the corral. "This ain't no time to be stubborn," he insisted. "Come with . . ."

As if to punctuate his urgency, a bullet plowed up the dust at their feet, then another hit the ground behind them.

"Let me go, Curtis!" If she didn't get to the corral soon, her pa and brothers would get caught in this trap while waiting for her. They'd all hang, and it would be her fault. "I told you I got my own plans!"

"And I got my—"

Maxie didn't let him finish before she landed a well-placed blow to the center of his chest. He released her as

the air whooshed out of his lungs and his knees slowly buck-
led under him.

Before he hit the ground, Maxie was on her way. She'd
hated to hit the oldster, but it was his own damned fault. He
hadn't believed her words, so she'd used her fist instead.
Just in time, too. The day was practically lost already.
Stronghold men and women were being rounded up like
cattle and herded into groups under the guns of the invaders. Only a few were still free, and they were fighting a
hopeless battle.

Maxie ducked behind a tall stone fireplace that in calmer
times was used to cook tortillas and roast *chile verde.* Now it
served as a shield against the wild gunfire that was ricochet-
ing around the canyon enclosure. She was spying out the
safest route to the corral when a mounted figure came into
her view. It was the first close look she had gotten at the
man who seemed to be leading the invaders. She could
scarcely believe her eyes.

Aaron Hunter! He wasn't riding the horse he'd left on, or
wearing the same clothes. But she couldn't mistake the set
of his broad shoulders, or the way he sat his horse, or any of
the other countless things Maxie had memorized about him
in the short two days he had stayed in Stronghold. No mistake. Aaron Hunter was leading the raiders. Aaron Hunter
—bastard, sidewinder, low-down worm of a turncoat.

Without really being aware of how it got there, Maxie
found her pistol in her hand. She checked the loading.
Empty. Goddamn it! She was as brainless as the rest of the
Stronghold idiots! She clenched her teeth and ground them
in frustration. Empty or not, the pistol provided some satisfaction as she raised it and aimed at the face that had
marched right out of her dreams and into her nightmares.
Again and again she pulled the trigger, cursing with every
futile click of the hammer. Furious, she tossed the gun away
and ran toward the corral, not caring at the moment if a
bullet found her along the way.

Thirty breathless seconds later she dashed past the ocotillo corral and into the big adobe shed that sheltered tack and grain. She called softly into the gloom.

"Pa. Blackjack. I'm here."

No answer.

"Dirty Jim? Tom?"

Her eyes adjusted to the relative darkness, and she could see the shed was empty except for a horse standing placidly with its head in the grain bin.

Empty!

Where were they? Her father and brothers wouldn't have left without her.

Maxie looked at the horse. The horse looked back. Its face sported a blaze that ended in peculiar white freckles on the nose. Maxie recognized it as the gelding that Tom had brought back from his last raid. Pa and the boys had left it for her. Why else would it be standing in the tack shed instead of the corral? Her family had left without her after all.

"Shit!" Maxie aimed a vicious kick at a handy saddle rack. Damn them! Maxie had always known that trusting anyone except family was pure foolishness, and now family had failed her also. Damn them! She snatched a halter off a peg and started forward. Wait till she caught up to that family of hers! She'd give their ears a blistering they'd not soon forget.

The horse pricked its ears, and Maxie felt a tingle of danger along her spine. Someone had come into the shed behind her.

Hunter kneed his horse in a circle so he could survey all the action around him. His pistol was in his hand, pointed toward the sky, and its hammer was thumbed back and ready. But there was no need to fire. Everything was going just as planned—better than planned, really. Simon had done his job and taken care of the entrance lookouts in the early hour before dawn, and Hunter's posse from Motherlode had ridden into Stronghold unchallenged. The outlaws

were caught unaware, undressed, unarmed, woozy from
sleep, and hung over from drink. Those who had managed
to grab pistols and rifles were doing more running than
firing, and the attackers were quickly herding them into
groups that were helpless under the posse's guns. The
messy job of cleaning out the snake hole known as Stronghold was over almost before it was begun.

A flicker of movement in the direction of the corral
caught Hunter's eye. He whirled his horse, pistol ready.
Nothing was there—nothing that he could see, at least. But
he could feel the weight of someone's eyes as surely as he
could feel the sweat running down his back. His horse did a
little dance in response to its rider's taut nerves. Hunter let
it go, let it rear and turn and seem to divert his attention.
Then quickly he looked back—to catch sight of black braids
and a faded red shirt. None other than little Cactus Maxie
crouched behind a stone fireplace. Her pistol was leveled,
held steady in both hands, and her finger was already tightening on the trigger. Hunter instinctively ducked, but he
knew that he was a dead man.

A split second passed before he realized that his skull had
not shattered, neither had his chest felt the fire of ripping
lead. He looked up. Maxie fired again, and again, apparently
not caring that her pistol was empty. The look on her face
was almost as likely to kill as a bullet.

Hunter was about to spur his horse toward the little devil
when two of his posse rode up, blocking his view of Maxie
and demanding his attention.

"We've got 'em!" one reported. "Most of the yellerbel-
lies gave in without even puttin' up a fight. What do
you . . . ?"

Hunter brushed the question aside. "Later. I've got one
more little outlaw to chase down, dammit."

Maxie had disappeared by the time he looked back. He
cursed; then he saw a small figure dash from the cover of the
corral into the tack shed. Without waiting to explain,
Hunter set spurs to his mount. Moments later, his feet

touched the ground before the horse slid to a stop in front of the shed.

She was there, all right, halter in hand and heading for a horse standing near the back of the shed. She didn't turn when Hunter stepped into the shed. But she did stop and stand rock still—like a statue carved from pure tension.

"Going somewhere?" he asked in a casual voice.

She turned. The devil's own fire was in her eyes. "Think you can stop me?"

"Figure I can."

"Figger one of us will be dead if you try."

Hunter shook his head and smiled. "You always did talk big for such a little britches, Maxie."

For a moment she regarded him thoughtfully, as if assessing his strength and quickness. Her eyes narrowed. "You owe me, bastard. Remember."

"I remember." He smiled a not very pleasant smile. "And I'm a man who pays his debts."

"Then let me pass."

"Sorry, Maxie. You're going out of here with me."

"Like hell!" She lunged forward and swung the halter toward his face. He caught it on his upraised arm, but was unprepared when she launched herself at him, fingers curled into claws. The horse stomped nervously as they crashed to the packed dirt floor, Maxie on top. Her nails raked his face, aiming for his eyes, and when he managed to brush them away, she balled her hands into fists and pummeled away at his solar plexus.

"Goddamn! Shit! You little wildcat!" He grunted as she nearly knocked the breath from his lungs, then heaved up in frustrated fury and threw her off.

Maxie crashed to the floor with a painful thud. Hunter was on top of her before she could catch her breath. He captured her flailing fists and pinned them to the dirt.

"Bastard!" she gasped. "Traitor! Turncoat! Snake! We take you in as a friend, and you do this!"

"There's no such thing as friendship among thieves and

murderers, or honor either. Haven't you learned that yet, Maxie?"

She heaved up under him, but his weight pressed her down into the dirt. All she could manage was·a futile squirming that scraped the skin from her back. "You pile of cow shit! Let me up!"

"Not quite yet." Grabbing both her wrists in one large hand, he pulled off his neckerchief with the other. "This is a good a place as any for you to stay until things calm down a bit, and this ought to shut that dirty mouth of yours."

"I'll . . . !" Her threat was smothered as he tied the gag over her mouth, but she made use of her freed fists to land a hearty blow to his head. He hardly noticed it. Her sharp little teeth, gag and all, bit into his arm.

"Yeow!" His roar, born more of fury than pain, seemed to shake the adobe walls. "You little mongrel bitch! And here I'm trying to do you a favor!" With relentless efficiency he caught her wrists and tied them with the halter rope. When she continued to pound on him with her bound hands, he tossed the rope around the horn of a nearby saddle and pulled her arms over her head. The free end of the rope he looped around her ankles. "That ought to fix you!"

But Maxie wasn't one to acknowledge defeat. With a painful heave she managed to lift her shoulders from the ground and twist her hips, almost toppling Hunter from his perch astride her body. He regained his balance by reaching out and grabbing a handful of her shirt. Once he had righted himself, he slammed her back down to the dirt, driving the breath from her lungs.

"You little . . . !" The insults he was about to heap on her never came out of his mouth, for in their struggle Maxie's shirt had suffered fatal damage. The buttons down the front had ripped free when Hunter grabbed it, and now the rough cotton gaped to reveal one plump, round, and very female breast.

Hunter stared and froze. As the morning air caressed her bare skin, Maxie froze as well. For an endless-seeming span of time, the world itself seemed to hang suspended. Hunter's eyes lifted and met Maxie's. For a moment a glimmer of fear flashed in the crystal blue—fear and a certain proud defiance. But as he watched, the clear blue hardened to a dark glitter of fury. Behind her gag she managed an outraged screech followed by a muffled gibberish that Hunter had no trouble interpreting as a string of curses.

Hastily he yanked the shirt across her exposed flesh. "Don't worry, kid. I'm hardly going to lose control and ravish a draggletailed little ragamuffin like you."

This statement brought another screech of outrage.

"Aaron!" Simon's lanky figure was silhouetted in the entrance. He gave Maxie the same cautious look he might give a scorpion. "I see you found the little lady. Holy Mary, but does she pack a vicious right undercut!"

"You don't have to tell me!" Hunter rose, breathing more easily now that Maxie's hips were not between his legs. She kicked at his groin as he got off her. He saved himself only by an acrobatic leap out of harm's way.

Simon grinned. "Full o' piss, ain't she?"

"I'd rather try to hog-tie a rattler." He turned his back on Maxie's furious glare. "What's up?"

"Got most of the stragglers rounded up. Maxwell and two of his boys got away. The youngest Maxwell boy we got, though. He's every bit as nasty as his sister."

Hunter felt Maxie's eyes burn a hole in his back. "They're twins," he supplied. "Like father like son—and daughter."

"Well, amigo, some of the boys'd like to string up the prisoners right here, with their women watchin'. You want to take any of these bandidos back to Motherlode alive, you'd better get over there."

"I'm coming." He turned a warning frown on Maxie, but said nothing before he strode away.

Simon grinned at her lying helpless on the shed floor. "Don't worry, little gal. Hunter's got something special in mind for you."

* * *

Maxie ground her teeth as she watched Hunter walk away. She hoped that limp of his meant he was in tortured pain with every step. She hoped the Apaches took him and stuck burning splinters under his nails, then flayed every inch of skin from his body until he begged for death. She hoped . . .

Closing her eyes, Maxie reined in her thoughts. What she really hoped was that she could get out of this mess before Hunter returned. There wasn't a rope made that could hold her for long, nor a man who could tie a knot she couldn't escape. But how long did she have?

She squirmed, twisted, and slid. Just what did Curtis mean by something special? Lordy, she didn't want to find out! There was something in Hunter's eyes that made her quiver inside—with fear or what else she didn't know. But she did know that she couldn't face him again. He shattered her confidence like glass, shook the very core of her until she didn't feel like Cactus Maxie anymore—didn't know herself, or trust herself. Goddamn! She had to get away!

Hunter had looped one end of the rope around a saddle horn. With much twisting and struggling Maxie managed to get to her knees and lurch to the saddle, only to find that her fingers were too numb to do anything but fumble uselessly with the loop. So she applied her teeth to the task of unlooping the rope—a process made tedious by the gag that covered her mouth. Finally the rope dropped free. With the tension removed from the simple knot that Hunter had tied at her ankles, she was able to free her feet and rip off the gag in only a few moments. The knot at her wrists still defied her efforts, but at least some feeling flowed back into her hands.

So what if her hands were still tied? No matter. Such a small thing would never stop Cactus Maxie. All she needed to do was bridle the horse, climb on the animal's back, and ride like hell for the back door. The back way out of Stronghold was so treacherous that anyone who followed her and didn't know the trail would soon find himself in deep trouble.

Maxie grabbed a bridle with her bound hands and stopped to consider a saddle. Should she try to saddle the horse as well? She shook her head. With her hands tied, the task would take too long.

"Easy, big boy." Maxie lifted the bridle over the horse's head and jiggled the bit against its teeth, hoping the beast would be cooperative. Lordy! What she would give for the use of both hands!

The horse jerked its head up, pricked its ears, and fastened its eyes, not on her, but over her shoulder. Maxie froze.

"Maxie, darlin', I always knew you were a brat."

She turned.

Leaning against the doorway, Aaron Hunter watched her with a wry grimace on his face. "But this time, kid, you've pushed my patience a little too far."

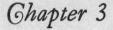

Chapter 3

$\mathcal{M}$axie's backside hurt as it rocked against her saddle. Her head throbbed, her back ached, and one arm sported a bruise where that ham-handed, snake-kissing, dog turd Aaron Hunter had grabbed her. The rope that bound her wrists to the saddle horn chafed painfully. Sweat trickled into her eyes and down her neck, and she hadn't a free hand to wipe it away.

But physical discomforts were nothing compared to the smarting of Maxie's pride. Her face was still hot from her final humiliation in the shed. The bastard had sauntered in —smiling that half smile of his that wasn't a smile—grabbed her bound hands, dragged her over his lap, yanked down her britches, and spanked her. Spanked her! As if she weren't good enough to shoot, or even beat the way a man beats a woman. No! Hunter had spanked her as though she were a bratty child! When she'd tried to wriggle free, he'd just spanked all the harder, until her poor backside felt as if a thousand bees were stinging it. The brute wasn't satisfied until there were tears in her eyes and she was cursing a blue streak with every breath.

When Hunter finally set her on her feet he'd looked at her with a stiff-faced broody expression that made her hope he'd broken his hand, or at least a finger. But when she spit at him, he laughed—then threatened another spanking if she misbehaved again.

As if Maxie could misbehave, tied to the saddle of Tom's freckled-nosed gelding, which patiently trundled down the canyon along behind Hunter's roan stallion. Even if she could jerk the lead rope free, the long-legged stallion looked as though it would have very little trouble running her down. She'd been staring at that broad roan rump for hours now, and she knew power when she saw it—power, too, in the back and shoulders of the man who rode the roan. Maxie had no desire to feel that power again in the form of his big hand whacking against her backside.

Hunter twisted in his saddle and glanced back at her. "How're you doin', kid?"

She gave him a murderous glare.

"Still givin' me the silent treatment, eh?"

Maxie would give him a good deal more than the silent treatment if she could only get her hands free from their bonds.

"Just wait, kid. You'll thank me some day. Besides, anything's better than hanging—or prison. Right?"

She'd thank him all right, Maxie fumed as Hunter turned back around. She'd thank him with a fist into one of those devil-black eyes of his. That would wipe the smile from his face!

They plodded on, reached the mouth of the canyon, and turned north toward the border. The June sun climbed steadily in the sky, burning down upon a land painted in muted browns and greens. The spring grass was not yet stiff and dry from the summer heat, and it softened the rugged valley floor with a haze of green. Here and there mesquite, yucca, and sotol added a darker splotch of color. In a few weeks the land would turn brown, withered by the blazing sun. Even now the furnacelike heat made the air shimmer.

Birds were silent. Lizards and snakes had already sought
shelter in cool underground nests or in the shade of a rock.

The two horses, their necks and rumps glistening with
sweat, seemed to be the only creatures that moved in the
vast rugged landscape. Their plodding grew slower and
slower as the temperature climbed, and Maxie allowed herself to be lulled by her mount's rocking motion. Her
thoughts progressed from vengeance to the misery of her
own fate.

Hunter was taking her to the Agua Linda Ranch. She
would be safe there, he said, and the ranch had work
enough to keep her busy earning her keep. Maxie snorted as
she thought back upon his words. Earn her keep, indeed!
That black-hearted piece of buzzard bait was in for a surprise if he expected Cactus Maxie to lift a finger washing
floors or tending cows.

Not that she didn't have an itch to see the Agua Linda.
The ranch was a legend in the border country. Six miles
north of the Mexican border, it lay directly on an Apache
plunder trail. When the Apaches had driven every other
rancher and miner out of Arizona Territory during the war
years, Pete Kelley and his Agua Linda had stubbornly survived. Maxie had heard stories aplenty. The redskins had
tried to level the place, burn it, kill its livestock, murder its
people—the same as they'd done to every other white settlement, ranch, or mine when the federal troops had left to
fight the war back East. But Pete Kelley—"Iron Pete," he
was called—had turned his ranch into a fortress. He'd killed
two Apaches for every drover who was murdered, every
hog, bull, or heifer that was felled. Maxie wondered which
Kelley considered a greater loss—his men or his prize hogs,
both of which the Indians habitually stuck full of arrows.

Under different circumstances Maxie might have enjoyed
making the acquaintance of a tough varmint like Kelley,
but no man this side of hell was going to keep Cactus Maxie
penned up. If Kelley was in league with Hunter, she would

just have to show Iron Pete what iron felt like when it was being stuffed up his . . .

"We'll stop here for a bit."

Hunter's voice broke abruptly into Maxie's reverie, and her horse lurched to a halt as its lead rope went slack. In front of them rippled the Santa Cruz River, a cool green artery of life flowing placidly on its northward journey to meet the Gila. Its grassy banks were shaded by cottonwood, and the water gurgled an invitation to sit awhile and rest.

"The horses could use a break," Hunter continued, dismounting, "and I could use a bite. How about you?"

The look Maxie sent his way could have put frost on the grass, even under the blazing June sun.

"Still sulking, eh?"

He led the roan stallion into the shade, then returned. A spark of impossible hope ignited Maxie's soul as Hunter began to untie the rope that fastened her wrists to the saddlehorn.

"I wouldn't try it if I were you," Hunter warned, as though he could read her mind. "I'm bigger than you are, faster than you are—even with this gimp leg—and if I have to chase you down in this god-awful heat, I'm likely to lose patience entirely." He looked up at her with the half grin that Maxie had learned was dangerous as well as irritating. "I'll beat your little butt so hard you'll think that last spanking was just a love pat. You behave yourself, kid. Otherwise you're gonna be so sore you won't sit down for a week."

Her hands were finally loose. Maxie rubbed her wrists and scowled. The ropes hadn't really been too tight, but it wouldn't hurt if Hunter thought they were. Next time he might not tie them so securely.

"Climb down. Take the horses over to the water, and I'll get out the jerky."

Hunter turned his back, walked to his horse, and lifted a set of saddlebags from the stallion's back. For a moment Maxie considered kicking the freckle-nosed gelding into a gallop and making a run for it. But the consequences of failure made her reconsider. She was willing to risk hot lead in her back, but not Hunter's hand against her bare buttocks. She'd already had one spanking too many this day.

"What are you waiting for?" Hunter threw the saddlebags into the shade. One brow slanted upward as he awaited her answer.

Maxie lifted her chin higher. "Water the horses yourself, you son of a bitch. I ain't lifting a finger for you."

His brow inched higher. "You don't say."

"I ain't eatin' your jerky, I ain't followin' your orders, I ain't walkin' where you point me, or sittin' where you put me. In fact, I ain't movin' from this here very spot."

Hunter seemed to consider, lifting his hat from his head and running his fingers through the riot of brown waves that fell over his brow. The tiny scar over his eye puckered ominously. "Well, now," he said calmly, "I don't much mind you starvin' yourself, kid. But that horse of yours could use some water—and a rest from having your butt resting on his back."

Maxie folded her arms across her chest and settled more firmly into the saddle. "Stuff it, buzzard bait."

Hunter shook his head. "Always knew you were a stubborn little brat."

In two long strides he was beside the gelding. So quickly did he reach up and jerk her from the saddle, Maxie had no opportunity to resist. She tumbled to the ground in an ungraceful heap.

"You'll get down when I tell you, you'll eat when I tell you, you'll walk, sit, run, jump, squat, or stay still when I tell you! Or you'll wish you had, you little imp of the Devil!"

"Go eat cow shit!"

Hunter grasped her arms, pinned them against her sides, and lifted her until her eyes were on a level with his. Nose to nose, he growled, "One of the first things you'll do is clean up that filthy mouth of yours. The people I'm taking you to don't take to cussing in females, or spitting, or running around in britches, for that matter."

"They can just . . . !"

Hunter gave her a shake. "Don't push your luck, kid." He dropped her abruptly. "Go down to the stream and wash. You smell like you haven't seen soap for a week. There's a bar in my saddlebags.

"I ain't takin' no bath!"

"Goddamn it! You little . . . !"

"And you could stand to clean up your own mouth some!"

She hopped away from his first angry grab, but the second one caught her off-balance. His hand grasped her upper arm in a steel vise, and no amount of struggling availed to set her free.

"Leggo of me, you miserable shit-assed son of a dirty sow!"

"I warned you about that mouth of yours."

Maxie dug her heels into the dirt as Hunter dragged her first toward the saddlebags, where he dug out a bar of soap, then toward the river. Her boots plowed two angry welts into their campsite.

The Santa Cruz River was swift-flowing and shallow, rippling over smooth stones and foaming around moss-covered boulders. But along one cutbank under a scraggly mesquite tree, the water quieted into a smooth-surfaced pool.

Hunter deposited Maxie in an indignant heap at the base of the mesquite. He held the bar of soap in front of her face.

"Take a bath, Maxie. You stink."

"Stick it up your—"

Her colorful suggestion ended in a squeak as he grabbed the front of her shirt and yanked her to her feet. He shook the soap in front of her nose. "Your choice, kid. Easy or hard."

Maxie gave him a smile that was almost sweet, then her knee jerked up toward his groin. But this time Hunter was too fast for her. He sidestepped, curled one long leg around hers, and sent her crashing to the ground. While she was still trying to catch her breath, he grabbed one ankle and tugged the boot from her foot. Dodging a vicious kick from her bare foot, he pulled off her other boot, then threw them both up the bank.

"Just don't give up, do you," he said as she threw a handful of dirt in his face. "We'll see if we can't cool off that temper of yours a bit."

Before Maxie could grab another fistful of dirt, Hunter picked her up by the collar of her shirt and the seat of her britches. With a mighty heave he launched her into the air. Her shriek ended with a stinging splat as she landed face first into the river. The pool that seconds before had been so calm erupted into churning chaos as Maxie flailed for a foothold on the sandy bottom. She broke the surface sputtering and coughing. Her braids had come loose, and hair straggled over her face in wet corkscrews.

Maxie's jaw clenched so tightly she could hear her teeth grind. The water was cold—goddamn it!—and it tasted like fish turds. She couldn't swim, and she'd nearly messed her britches in fear before her feet found the bottom of the pool, while that blackhearted Hunter sat there on the bank grinning like a mad coyote.

Hunter held up the soap again. "Are you going to be a good girl, Maxie? Or am I going to have to do the honors?"

"Go screw a porcupine, shithead."

Hunter sighed, put down the soap, and pulled off his boots. "Have it your way, then."

Maxie moved back as Hunter stepped into the stream. But the farther back she moved, the deeper the pool became. Already the water swirled around her waist, and she pictured herself dropping into a green abyss with one more step backward. Hunter no doubt would bray like a jackass while she drowned.

"I ain't takin' no bath." Maxie held out a hand to fend him off. "It ain't healthy, or decent!"

Hunter grabbed the outthrust arm and pulled her forward. "What the hell do you know about decent?" He grabbed her hair, pushed her under the murky green, and pulled her back up gasping and spitting.

"You . . . !"

Hunter shoved a handful of soap into her mouth. "That's for cussing like a mule skinner." He pushed her under again, then up. "Spit," he advised as she started to choke.

Maxie spit in his face, then choked again.

"Shoulda let you go with your pa," Hunter mumbled, trying to control her squirming with one hand and lather soap into her hair with the other. "Bastard wouldn't cause near as much trouble if he had you on his hands."

Maxie shrieked as soap ran into her eyes, and Hunter dunked her again, then turned her around and stripped her shirt down around her arms to stop her flailing. He rid her of her britches while she struggled to untangle her arms from the shirt.

Drowning was preferable, Maxie decided, if she could only take Hunter to the bottom with her. She kicked out behind her, trying to trip him, or better still, smash his face with her foot. But the slippery bastard sidestepped her. Trousers around her ankles, Maxie lost her footing and plunged into the deepest part of the pool, only to be tugged back into the shallows by her tormentor.

"You rotten piece of mule shit!" she sputtered. "You piss-yellow son of a . . . !"

"Need more soap in your mouth?" Hunter grabbed her shoulder and turned her to face him. "I've never met such a dirty-mouthed, grimy little . . . Holy shit!"

Maxie kicked free of her britches, pulled her arms out of the tangling shirt, and stood up. The foaming stream hid her feet and ankles—nothing else. Water flowed from the black chaotic curls of her hair, ran in rivers through the valley between outthrust breasts, pooled briefly in her navel, then cascaded in a minor waterfall toward the lush dark vee at the juncture of her thighs. From there it dripped in tantalizing paths down the smooth columns of her legs until it rejoined the Santa Cruz swirling around her calves.

"Holy shit!" Hunter repeated. That seemed to be the limit of his vocabulary. Color crawled from his neck to his face, deepening his sunbrowned bronze. "I . . . I . . . shit! And I've been callin' you a kid." Abruptly, he turned around. "Take the soap and wash yourself!"

Maxie saw her chance. The only thing on her mind was escape, and with Hunter's broad back turned, the butt of his pistol was temptingly within reach of her hand. She lunged, grabbed, and danced away before he could react.

"I'm going to kill you, buzzard bait."

Hunter whirled when Maxie grabbed his pistol, but he wasn't fast enough to catch her as she leaped out of his way with the buoyant grace of a naked wood sprite. He took two steps in pursuit, then halted as he came nose to muzzle with his own loaded gun.

"I'm going to kill you," Maxie repeated, savoring the sound of her own power. "Because you're a stinking traitor, because you turned your own friends over to the law, because my brother Dirty Jim might be hanging at the end of a stinkin' rope right now."

Slowly, cautiously, Hunter raised his hands and put them on top of his head. "I didn't turn my friends over to the law, Maxie. I am the law."

"Another good reason to kill you."

Maxie gripped the pistol in both hands, which for some reason were starting to shake. The trigger felt like fire against her finger, and she could feel sweat start to run from under her arms. All she had to do was pull the damned trigger. Hunter was helpless, his broad chest a perfect target. He had destroyed her life, destroyed her home, killed her friends . . . perhaps even her brother. What kind of yellow-bellied, pissant coward was she that she just stood there quaking?

"You'd better shoot, Maxie." Hunter's eyes—those devil-black eyes that had made her quiver even when she was ten years old—shifted between her face, the pistol, and other items that he seemed to find of interest. "If you're going to stand there bare-assed naked, you'd better shoot, or else get dressed. Elsewise I'm going to do something that you won't like, even if I have to walk through a spray of lead to do it."

His eyes dropped in a deliberate fashion to fasten on her breasts, then the juncture of her thighs. Suddenly Maxie was very aware of something that hadn't bothered her before. She was naked—stark, jaybird naked—and Hunter was looking at her as a lustful man looks at a woman. The pistol wavered as she instinctively glanced down at her exposed body.

Hunter lunged. He grabbed Maxie's right hand, and the pistol fired at the sky as they both tumbled back into the stream. The struggle was brief, and Hunter ended up on top, pinning Maxie to the streambed while she fought to keep her head above the water.

"That's enough of that." He wrested the pistol from her grip and threw it onto the bank. "You damned well look like a grown woman," he gritted out as he lifted her to her feet and raked her form with appreciative male eyes. "Let's see if you can act like one." Pushing her toward the pool, he flung the soap after her. "Now wash, dammit!"

They arrived at Pete Kelley's Agua Linda Ranch just as the stars were beginning to pop out in the darkening sky. Maxie was as clean as she had ever been in her life, for Hunter had allowed her to leave no patch of skin unscrubbed, no lock of hair that wasn't so clean it squeaked. She had to be fit to meet civilized people, he'd said, as though Maxie were a savage straight from an Apache rancheria.

Maxie had hated the way he'd watched her as she washed. Sitting on the riverbank while she splashed reluctantly in the pool, fingering the butt of his pistol, smirking with that silly half grin, he'd looked as though he were enjoying her humiliation. She'd hated him more every minute, and once they were on their way she had spent the hours in the saddle alternately kicking herself for not killing him when she had the chance and planning the painful way he would die next time she had him in her gunsights.

When they finally arrived at the Kelley ranch, just enough evening light remained to reveal planted fields, a small orchard bordering the Santa Cruz River, a barn, a large bunkhouse, and storage sheds. Several sturdy-looking pens held fat, grunting hogs, and a remuda of horses stood placidly in an ocotillo corral.

The ranchhouse itself was more a fortress than a dwelling. A thick adobe wall enclosed an area roughly a quarter the size of Stronghold, Maxie estimated. A single gate was the only entrance she could see, and that was mounted on real metal hinges and closed tight against intruders. Three guards atop the wall were silhouetted against the fading sky. They held their rifles ready as she and Hunter approached. Maxie understood now why her pa and brothers —and most other border bandits as well—avoided raiding this place.

"Just me, Duffy," Hunter called out. "I've got a guest for La Doña."

" 'Lo there, Hunter," one of the guards replied as he lowered his rifle. "Didn't expect to see you tonight."

"Didn't expect to be here tonight," Hunter agreed. "Boss lady around?"

"She's around somewheres. So's Pete." He turned and shouted to a comrade. "Don't just stand there like dead stump, get that gate open. And you, Ramon! Go tell Doña Medina that Marshal Hunter's here."

Once through the gate, Maxie could see that the perimeter wall was not quite finished. On the opposite side of the enclosure it ended in a ragged stairstep of adobe bricks, and a twenty-foot gap stood open to attack.

Within the incomplete circle of the wall's protecting arms stood a one-story adobe dwelling that boasted four real glass windows set on either side of a carved wooden door. Off to one side of the house a brick walkway led to a detached kitchen building and, a few steps away, an outdoor stone oven. The smell in the air—mesquite smoke, frying tortillas, and dust—reminded Maxie of Stronghold. So familiar, and yet not quite the same. Her stomach twisted in a painful spasm of homesickness.

Two people met them in front of the house. Iron Pete looked every bit as formidable as his reputation made him —tall, lean, brown, and tough-looking as well-used leather. His hair was long enough to hang in lank strands over his ears. Deep lines creased his face from nose to jowls, giving him a permanent scowl. He looked the part of the toughest, most savvy rancher in the border country, but the image was ruined by the arm he draped in casual affection around the shoulders of a small woman who stood next to him, and the look in his eyes when she smiled up at him. Anyone who truly deserved the name "Iron Pete" shouldn't go soft-eyed because of a woman. Certainly the men Maxie knew wouldn't.

The woman stood comfortably under Kelley's arm. She was an interesting contrast to his leathery lankiness. Small, dark-haired, gentle-faced, she reminded Maxie of a picture drawing of the Madonna that was in the front of her mother's old Bible.

"Evenin', Hunter." Kelley's eyes, which seemed to gleam with unnatural brightness in the torchlight, shifted from Hunter to Maxie, then back to Hunter again. "What brings you out this way?"

"Pete." Hunter tipped his hat toward the small, dark woman standing beside Kelley. "Medina. I . . . uh . . . have a favor to ask."

Maxie detected a note of unease in Hunter's voice and delighted in thinking that perhaps his plans were not as well laid as he thought. She cheered even more when Medina's eyes flicked to Maxie, paused for a moment on her bound hands, traveled over her clothing, which was much the worse for the little tussle in the river, and then returned to Hunter in a questioning look that was almost a glare.

"Aaron, why do you have this child tied to her saddle?"

"I . . ." He scowled as he groped for an acceptable explanation. "It's a long story, Medina."

The little woman, who seemed to wield an authority all out of proportion to her size, stepped over to Maxie's horse and peered up into her face. "Gracious, girl, look at that bruise on your cheek. And your . . ." She trailed off as she examined Maxie's face more carefully. "Aaron! Who is this child?"

Pete scowled as his gaze shifted from his wife to Maxie to Hunter. "Maybe we'd better all go inside. No sense letting the mosquitoes eat us alive."

Maxie had never seen a house quite as grand as the Kelleys', though to tell the truth the number of actual honest-to-God houses that she had been inside could be counted on one hand. The front door led into a small, brick-floored entrance that was brightly lighted by a chandelier made from iron horseshoes. Medina led them into a chamber to the left of the entrance—a glorious room that overlooked a courtyard. Maxie guessed that the house was built in the fashion of one other house she had seen down in Mexico— with adobe rooms set in a protective rectangle around a central open area. A window provided a view of several trees, and the aroma of flowers lightly scented the air.

The room was furnished with a woven wool rug, a velveteen sofa, three comfortable-looking wood-and-leather chairs, two small, roughhewn tables, and a real piano—of all things. Maxie remembered an almost identical instrument in a Tucson bar, the only other piano she'd ever seen.

"Let's all sit down," Medina invited in a somewhat sharp voice, "and hear this tale of Aaron's."

Hunter guided Maxie toward a chair. He'd had to untie her to let her dismount her horse, but he kept a firm grip on her arm, and the set of his mouth warned her that any misbehavior would be unwise. He insisted that she behave in this "civilized company," but apparently he wouldn't hesitate to give her an uncivilized thump if he thought a thump was called for, the two-faced snake.

"What's up, Aaron?" Pete asked, settling beside his wife on the sofa. "What happened to your lip?"

Hunter touched a finger to the left side of his mouth, which was swollen where it had come into violent contact with Maxie's fist. "Well," he began with a lopsided, swollen grin, "it's this way . . ."

Maxie was forced to sit and listen to the lies Hunter concocted about her life. Some of it was true. He did tell the Kelleys that she was Harrison Maxwell's daughter, but their reaction was not what Maxie expected. No doubt they weren't suitably impressed because Hunter made her sound like some kind of weak-kneed, know-nothing girl who sat around thinking law-abiding thoughts while her father and brothers had all the fun. He also didn't tell them about the time she had saved his life. Old Iron Pete might be surprised to learn that his friend the big hoo-ha lawman was as much a horse-thieving, cattle-rustling, mine-robbing adventurer as the rest of the free spirits the posse had rounded up for the hangman's noose—or at least he'd once been. Now he was a self-righteous, holier-than-thou stick-in-the-mud preaching up prissy manners and "civilization."

Medina Kelley's eyes never left Maxie's face during Hunter's recitation. When he concluded his short tale with a request that Maxie be sheltered at Agua Linda and given some menial position to earn her keep, Medina smiled.

"I should have known," she said. "She is Maria Theresa's very image."

"Pardon?" Hunter frowned.

"I knew Maxie's mother, Aaron. We were children together."

Maxie's eyes flashed to Medina's face, and for a brief moment lit up with unguarded curiosity.

"There were so few people in northern Sonora—even now there are so few—that the families who ran cattle there knew each other well, even though we saw each other quite seldom. Maria Theresa and I went to school together in Mexico City, and we were good friends until the time she married Harrison Maxwell and left." She looked over at Maxie, who promptly shifted her gaze back to the floor in a sullen denial of interest. "She's all Maria Theresa, Aaron. There's not a drop of Harrison Maxwell in her."

Hunter snorted. "There's more than a drop of Maxwell in her. Trust me on that score."

Medina ignored Hunter's acid tone. "You're welcome to stay at Agua Linda for as long as you like . . . Maxie? That can't be your real name, dear. Is it?"

Maxie was stubbornly silent. She felt like a horse on an auction block, poked and prodded and discussed as if she were a dumb animal. Her name was her own business. These "civilized" idiots could call her whatever they liked. She didn't plan to be around long enough for it to matter.

Medina raised her brows at the glare Maxie gave her, but her tone remained polite. "Whatever you wish, dear." She smiled and added, "For now. Will you stay the night, Aaron?"

Aaron stood, looking relieved to hand his responsibilities to someone else. "No, thank you, Medina. I've got a heap of work—and prisoners—back in town. I'll be heading out."

"Well, then, we'll leave you to say your good-byes." She raised a brow at her husband, who shrugged and followed her out of the room.

Maxie turned a murderous scowl on Hunter. "I'll just bet these law-abiding civilized friends of yours would like to hear about what you were doing some years ago. They might not let you in their fancy parlors if they knew you were no more civilized than the poor men you're plannin' to hang."

"Go ahead and tell them, Maxie." Hunter smiled in a way that Maxie didn't like. "See what it gets you."

"I know what it'd get you! I'll make you sorry for doing this to me, Hunter, you just see if I don't. You're going to be goddamned sorry."

Hunter slapped his hat on his head and walked toward the door. He turned and gave her one last look, a thoughtful expression on his face. "Could be I'm sorry already, kid. Just could be."

Chapter 4

"It is not fancy, girl." Elsa Herrmann, whom Medina had introduced as Agua Linda's cook and chief housekeeper, ushered Maxie into a closet of a room that shared an outbuilding with the kitchen. "But it is cool. We used to store vegetables in here, but since the cellar was dug the vegetables are kept underground, and this room has been vacant. Doña Medina had the cot carried out here so Mr. Hunter would have a place to sleep when he came visiting."

The plump German woman almost filled the room by herself when she walked in. She glanced around, pursed her mouth when she spied a cobweb clinging to one corner of the wall and ceiling, fluffed the skimpy pillow that lay on the cot, then opened the shutter of the room's one unglassed window.

"I'll have Justin and Duffy carry out a trunk for your clothes and mount some pegs in the walls tomorrow. You can ask Maria or Catalina for a broom and scrub brush and pail. You'll want to clean the walls and floor before you sleep here."

Why would she want to clean? Maxie wondered. The

little room was already cleaner than any place she had ever laid her head. At Stronghold she had slept in a dirt-floored ocotillo lean-to. This little room had whitewashed walls, a brick floor, and a window to let in the cool night air. The cot boasted an iron bedstead and a fine straw-ticked mattress. Maxie almost pushed her finger into the mattress to see if it was really as soft as it looked, but she reminded herself that she wouldn't be sticking around long enough to enjoy all this soft living.

Appearing satisfied that she had everything in order, the German cook clucked to herself—rather like a hen laying an egg, Maxie thought—and set the bundle she had been carrying on the cot.

"The house girls—Maria and Catalina—asked me to give you these." Out of the bundle Frau Herrmann shook two plain white cotton bodices and two ankle-length skirts of a colorful print material. She cast a disapproving eye over Maxie's shirt and britches. "They noticed you have no decent clothing. Also—Doña Medina sent a brush, comb, and soap."

Maxie gave the items a sour look. She'd had enough soap for one day, thanks to that jackass Hunter, and she wasn't about to don those fancy women's duds while her sturdy hand-me-downs from Dirty Jim were still wearable, despite a few missing buttons and a rip here and there. If that prim-faced Doña Medina and her cook thought that Cactus Maxie was going to prance about in those stupid clothes, wash her hands and face every time she turned around, cook, clean, fetch, and carry for this ranch full of lackwit horse's asses, then they would very soon learn differently.

"You seem tired, girl. Is that why you are so silent?"

"I ain't tired," Maxie snapped, more to be contrary than anything else.

Frau Herrmann glowered. "Perhaps we should forget the cleaning tonight. You go to bed. Sleep. Perhaps you will awaken in a more congenial state of mind. We get up before the sun to start the bread rising. Mr. Kelley always insists on good yeast bread along with his tortillas. Do you know how to bake bread, girl?"

"No." No, she didn't know how to bake bread, and she wasn't going to learn. To hell with congenial.

"You will learn tomorrow. Now go to sleep. There is a cistern in back of the kitchen for drinking, and the horse trough for washing. Now I will leave you to have a good night."

Did these fools think of nothing besides washing? Lordy! How clean could a body get?

Maxie sank wearily down on the cot. She was tired—bone tired. But she couldn't rest now, not surrounded by enemies who thought they could keep her penned up like one of their pigs. She had to stay awake, stay alert while the rest of the ranch settled into slumber. The fools had neither locked her door nor barred her window. By morning she could be halfway to . . . to where?

Where indeed? Stronghold was destroyed, her family gone, her friends in jail or scattered. Maxie was as trapped and helpless as a chicken on a chopping block. Sighing, she held up a soft white bodice, wadded the material in her hand, and wished that the crushed ball of cloth was Aaron Hunter's head.

Many times during the days that followed Maxie had occasion to curse Aaron Hunter and the hellish place he'd stuck her in. Fine thanks for saving his worthless life! Prison would have been more pleasant. Even hanging would have been better than Agua Linda, Maxie decided after a few days. At least if a body got hanged, the neck stretching lasted only a few minutes. But torture at Iron Pete's ranch seemed to never end. Maxie figured she'd never done anything rotten enough in her short life to deserve the punishment she was getting.

She worked from sunup until well past sundown under the exacting eye of Elsa Herrmann, who was worse than any Apache, as far as Maxie was concerned, in devising tortures for her victims. Maxie's frustration grew with every task she was assigned. She had never before worked at feminine chores and had always thought herself above turning her hand to "women's work." She had never butchered a hog, scrubbed a floor, weeded a garden patch, mended a shirt, milked a cow, tanned a hide, made soap or candles, or beat the dirt from a rug. Neither had she made a pie, seasoned a stew, fried tortillas, churned butter, or kneaded bread. Furthermore, she had absolutely no desire to learn. Neither did she cotton to her daily sessions with La Doña, studying reading and writing out of a silly child's primer. Medina told Maxie the primer once belonged to her young son, who'd been killed in an Apache raid on Agua Linda seven years ago. Maxie softened momentarily toward the Spanish woman when La Doña told the story of her boy, but it hardened again at the next simple word she stumbled over. Who needed to read or write, anyway! And who needed the constant admonitions about manners that Medina scattered throughout the lesson!

Maxie might have put up with the humiliation of working at such menial and useless tasks had she shown any aptitude. But at everything Frau Herrmann and La Doña expected her to do, she had two left hands and ten thumbs. Days ago she had failed at the first womanly task she had tried—kissing Aaron Hunter. Now she was failing miserably at everything else that was expected of a woman.

Cactus Maxie was not a person accustomed to failure. She was good at everything important. An accomplished liar, a natural-born sneak, she could ride like the wind and shoot like the very devil. Her fist, though small, could knock a grown man off his feet. In drinking, cussing, fighting, poker cheating, and lie swapping, Cactus Maxie could match any man. But at cooking, scrubbing, sewing—and kissing, she was a simpleton, it seemed.

The humiliation of constant failure did not make Maxie's imprisonment any easier to bear. She scowled and sulked her way through the days and cried through the dark hours of the night. More than once when the ranch was fast asleep she stood at the window of her little room and stared out into the night, her entire being aching to escape, to run out into the desert and forget all about Aaron Hunter, Agua Linda, cooking, scrubbing, sewing, laundry, washing behind her ears and under her fingernails (Lordy, but everyone at the cursed ranch was crazy about clean!). As she stared out her window into the darkness, she could picture herself slipping from her room and tiptoeing silently into the shadows of the wall. The wall guards would be drowsy and inattentive, having nothing to do but watch the stars wheel silently overhead and keep an eye out for Indians and bandidos. They would be none the wiser as Maxie stole through the gate right beneath their noses, so stealthily that God Himself wouldn't know she was there.

Once outside the compound she would cleverly melt into the cover provided by the outbuildings—first the hog shed, then the corral with its drowsing horses, and then, farthest out, the waddies' bunkhouse. The desert would welcome her like a lost and beloved child. It would shelter her from her enemies, confound and confuse any who tried to follow her. Finally, Aaron Hunter, Iron Pete and Medina, the sour German housekeeper—all of them would have to admit they'd been outsmarted and outmanuevered by Cactus Maxie. They'd be lucky if she didn't tell her father and brothers to ride over and give all of them a lesson in how to treat a Maxwell!

But Maxie had the sense to realize that her dream of escape into the desert was impractical. She could slip away easily enough. That was no problem—not for Cactus Maxie, the natural-born sneak. She could steal a beer from under a bandit's nose, walk over a path of clinky cobbles so quietly that not even an Apache could hear her, blend into shadows better than a rabbit. The guard would need owl's eyes to detect her stealthy escape through the night.

The problem was surviving after she left. In spite of Maxie's fantasies, the desert was no friend, and she knew it. Without a horse and a weapon, she wouldn't stand a chance.

The sun would wring her out and fry her crisp—if the Apaches didn't get her first. She had no one to help her, no one to run to. The desert was a more effective jail than a lock on her door or bars on her window. So, until her father and brothers rescued her, Maxie would simply have to endure.

Maliciously, she hoped Aaron Hunter was at Agua Linda the day her pa rode in and demanded his mistreated daughter. Then that slimy snake's ass would be sorry he'd messed with a Maxwell! Just see if he wasn't! And her pa would come. The whole U.S. Army and all the Apaches in Arizona Territory couldn't keep Harrison Maxwell from coming to the rescue of his own!

But the miserable days passed with no sign of father or brothers, and with each day Maxie grew less confident and more surly. She refused to wear the skirts and bodices that she'd been given, refused to smile, even to speak beyond the necessities. The little housemaids, Maria and Catalina, took to avoiding her altogether. Elsa Herrmann mumbled unpleasant-sounding German and eyed Maxie with Teutonic distaste. Even Doña Medina's patience wore thin and then finally frayed through on a morning that Maxie's did the same.

Five days after Hunter delivered Maxie to Agua Linda, her fuse—always short and ready to flare—burned down to nothing. She had labored all morning in the hot kitchen. Under Elsa's watchful and—Maxie thought—disapproving eye, she had painstakingly measured flour, salt, yeast, and milk for a batch of the bread Pete Kelley so favored. She had kneaded until her arms ached, formed each rubbery lump of dough into a perfect loaf, and set the loaves aside to rise.

As always, her efforts ended in disaster. Two hours later the loaves were still heavy, rubbery lumps that weren't fit for pigs, much less Pete Kelley. Elsa shook her head and lectured Maxie about the milk being too warm and the kneading too vigorous. Her recalcitrant pupil answered with a hot glare, kicked the table, and stalked out of the room.

Maxie's hot-tempered exit sent her bumbling into Catalina, who was just about to walk through the kitchen door. The clean linen in the maid's arms tumbled to the ground and lay scattered in a thick layer of dust.

"Estúpida!" the maid cried. *"Idiota!* Look what you have . . . !" Catalina trailed off, indignation shriveled by the look of cold ferocity that Maxie sent her way. "I . . . I'm sorry . . ." she offered in a tentative voice.

Maxie pushed past her without apology. She had little use for the housemaids. They were always giggling together like useless girls, and Maxie was sure that the giggling was mostly at her expense. Catalina would have to rewash the linen, but doubtless she would have a fine time laughing with Maria about Maxie's clumsiness while she scrubbed.

Maxie headed toward the break in the perimeter wall, intending to circle around to the barn and find a cool stall where she could hide for a few hours. Out of the corner of her eye she saw Elsa emerge from the kitchen and march toward the main house. No doubt the German woman was on her way to inform Doña Medina of Maxie's latest sins. Maxie didn't care. She was here by Aaron Hunter's choice, not hers. Let them all shake their heads and growl at her. They'd change their tune fast enough when Harrison Maxwell himself rode up to demand her release.

"Well look'ee here, Sam! Ain't that a sight?"

Maxie slowed her steps. Five waddies lounged against the barn wall. Maxie had seen most of the men who worked at the ranch. She'd helped serve their meals at the plank table that filled one end of the bunkhouse, endured their laughter about her britches and their silly attempts to make her smile. These faces, though, were unfamiliar. Covered with dust, they looked as though they'd just ridden in from the range.

"Never did see the like," another drover replied with a grin. "Suppose that's a female?"

"Don't look much like one," the first waddie drawled. "Don't fill those britches out near like a female should. Shirt neither." He chuckled.

A third joined in the conversation. "Too puny t'be a lad."

The group of men, all grinning, moved to block her way into the barn. She stopped and regarded them with eyes narrowed, hands balled into hard little fists on her hips.

"Mebbe it's a Mex boy. They grow 'em puny."

"Naw. Mex's ain't got braids. Injuns got braids."

"Kelley ain't gonna let no Injun on his place. It's a little Mex gal."

"What'sa matter, little gal? Ain't got no money fer a dress?"

"I'd buy you a dress, honey, if'n you was ta be nice. How 'bout it, gal? You any good?"

"I'm good," Maxie replied, a tight little smile stretching her mouth and a gleam appearing in her eye. "I'll show you what I'm good at."

She strode up to the closest man and, before he realized what she was doing, grabbed the knife from the scabbard on his belt. For the first time in days Maxie felt right at home. Here at last was something she could handle.

"What're you—"

The knife sliced down and across, almost singing through the air. The waddie's belt parted, his trousers slid down around his knees, and his shirt gaped open where the buttons had been neatly cut from the cloth. Once again the knife flicked, and the man's red long underwear joined his trousers.

The victim's eyes grew wide. He turned his stricken gaze downward, seemingly fascinated by the sight of his rather paunchy belly. Maxie's eyes followed his, then dropped lower. She laughed at the sight.

The waddies broke into uproarious guffaws as their comrade's face grew red. Maxie casually flipped the knife in the air, feeling much better than she had in days. With a final double flip, she lofted the blade into a neat arc that stuck it into the ground at her victim's feet.

The laughter grew rowdier, then abruptly ceased as if Maxie's knife had cut the sound from the air.

"Aleta Maria Maxwell!"

Doña Medina had wrung the name from Maxie just the day before. Maxie cringed whenever she heard it, even when the tone of voice speaking it was not enough to frighten a starved coyote from a fresh kill, as the tone was now.

"Dios! What is going on here? Sam, Abraham, Tyler?"

The drovers lowered their eyes as their comrade hastily pulled up his trousers.

"Ramon? Leo?"

Sam cleared his throat. "Ah . . . well, ma'am, we was . . ."

"Never mind," Medina told him. She looked at Maxie and sighed. "I can guess. You!" The little mistress of the Agua Linda was no taller than Maxie herself, but somehow she managed to look down her nose to meet Maxie's eyes. "Come with me."

Maxie lifted her chin higher and set her lips in a tight, defiant line.

"Now!" Medina reached for Maxie's ear, twisted, and pulled.

"Ow! Ouch! Shit! Damn! Stop!"

"I said now!"

"Goddamn it to hell! You can't . . . ouch!" Maxie struck out as Medina twisted harder on her ear, but La Doña neatly avoided the blow, stepping back and seizing Maxie's arm with an iron grip. The little lady was faster than she looked—stronger too. Maxie was forced to follow or lose an arm.

Medina dragged a cussing Maxie through the break in the perimeter wall and backed her up against the rough adobe bricks. "You and I will now reach an understanding, young woman."

"Stuff it up—"

"Hold your tongue and listen! I have had enough of your childish temper, your foul mouth, and your silly pouting. It's time to grow up and show some respect for the people around you—and for yourself."

"You cain't—"

"Silence!"

Maxie's eyes grew wide at the roar that came from Medina's dainty mouth.

"I certainly can tell you what to do. You are in my employ, living in my home. For the sake of your mother's memory and my friendship with Aaron Hunter, I took you in. But I will not put up with your outrageous behavior a moment longer. Do you understand?"

Maxie snorted contemptuously.

"From now on, you will wear feminine attire, use decent language, and be courteous to those around you. Elsa tells me that Maria and Catalina both gave you some of their own clothing. If their clothing doesn't fit"—she swept Maxie's shirt and britches with disdainful eyes—"then we can find something from my wardrobe that you can use until suitable clothing can be made."

"I don't wear no women's prissy dresses." Maxie spit—one of her natural talents—and just missed the toe of Medina's polished boot.

Medina sighed. "I can see that grammar lessons are in order, also." She regarded Maxie for a long moment, her eyes sad. "Aleta Maria, your mother was a gentle soul and a true lady. You are the very image of her on the outside, and I can't help but believe that somewhere inside of you a part of her still lives. How she would grieve to see her daughter dressed like a saddle tramp, spitting, and cussing."

Medina had hit a tender spot in Maxie's soul. That her mother hadn't been one of the Stronghold whores was a point of great pride to Maxie. Doña Theresa had been a real lady from a fancy hacienda with servants, fine furniture, soft beds, real china plates, and crystal glasses. She had sacrificed her comforts out of love of Harrison Maxwell, and of course she looked down from heaven each day to watch her daughter with great love and pride. So Maxie had imagined during her childhood, and to hear someone state otherwise stung like a scorpion's tail.

"You don't know what my ma would think! I don't care if you did know her! You're lyin' to say I'd grieve her!"

Medina shook her head. "I could tell you much about your mother if you would listen, Aleta. So many things. Wouldn't you like to hear what kind of a fine lady she was?"

Maxie doused her curiosity with anger, but the task was difficult. The only people who'd been able to tell her about Maria Theresa Delgado Maxwell were her pa and half brothers Blackjack and Tom. Their descriptions, concerned mostly with the Delgado family wealth, left a lot to be desired.

"No!" she flung back, face stubbornly stony. "I know all about my ma! She wouldn't have made me wear those silly girls' clothes, and I ain't wearin' 'em. I'm good as any man. I can shoot straighter, ride harder, and I ain't wearin' no stupid skirt!"

"What has your father done to you?" Medina asked softly. "Do you think that riding and shooting make you something special, Aleta? Let me show you something."

Dragging Maxie with her, Doña Medina crossed to the back of the house and picked up a rifle that was propped against the wall. At Agua Linda, a weapon was always within reach of everyone's hand. She pumped the rifle once, strode back to the break in the wall, raised the weapon to her shoulder, and fired. Fifty yards away on the bank of the river, a small branch exploded from a cottonwood tree.

Maxie blinked. The woman couldn't have been aiming at that tiny thing!

"Throw a rock into the air," Medina commanded.

Maxie complied. She chose a round pebble about three inches in diameter and tossed it high into the air. Medina fired. The rock shattered. The Spanish woman fired again, and a fragment that had flown off the original shattered. Only dust was left to swirl lazily in the hot air.

"Any idiot can learn to shoot," Medina told Maxie. "Or learn to ride. If you're really special, Aleta, someday you might learn to be a lady with half the grace of your mother. Right now you are nothing more than a troublesome, self-willed child, and if you don't grow up soon, I'm going to take a stick to your hide. That I promise!"

Maxie was spared having to reply, for at that moment gunfire erupted on the other side of the wall. A horse screamed, a wall sentry shouted an unintelligible warning, and the thunder of guns filled the air.

La Doña sucked in a sharp breath. "Apaches! Damn!"

So the straitlaced little doña *could* cuss, Maxie thought as the two of them hastened to take cover behind the ragged edge of the wall. Maybe the woman wasn't so bad after all.

"They'll be out front having their sport with our poor hogs, the devils. Keep down!" Medina grabbed one of Maxie's braids and yanked her behind the sheltering adobe.

"I just wanted to look over the low part of the wall." Maxie's hands itched for a gun. "Will they come back here?"

"Not if we're lucky. Come on. We'll make a run for the house."

They ran, just as a buckskin pony careened around the edge of the wall, a near-naked Apache crouched low over its neck. "Eeeeiiiiiy-yiyiyiyi!" The savage screamed and raised his rifle. Medina turned and fired. Her rifle ball plowed through the brave's chest before he could get off a shot.

"That's one down." The mistress of Agua Linda calmly cocked her rifle. Maxie regarded her with wide eyes.

"Get to the house," Medina urged Maxie.

"But—"

"I'm right behind you."

Maxie made it to the rear door just as another brave

galloped through the gap in the wall. She grasped the latch and pulled. The door was barred. She pounded. Out of the corner of her eye she saw Medina raise her rifle and draw a bead on the Apache. The click of the empty chamber seemed to echo around the enclosure. Charging straight toward La Doña, the warrior grinned a death's-head grin. He raised his stone war club for a fatal blow.

"Oh shit!" Maxie whispered to herself.

Chapter 5

$\mathcal{T}$he scene seemed to slow—the charging Apache pony, the temporarily helpless Medina, who had turned to flee, the naked savage—they all floated through a nightmare in which all motion decelerated to a crawl. Maxie was scarcely aware of bending down, picking up a rock half the size of her fist, and hurling it toward the Indian.

By a quirk of good luck the stone hit its target. The Apache tumbled to the ground; the pony galloped on, riderless. Maxie sprinted toward the fallen warrior, but as soon as he hit the ground he regained his feet. Swaying slightly, he shook his head, then turned toward Medina, who was reloading her rifle in desperate haste. Once again he raised his war club and grinned.

From a slow crawl the nightmare accelerated again to a frightening pace. Everything happened too fast, with no time to think—just to react.

Maxie launched herself at the Apache and landed on his back. He grunted as she pummeled his head with her fists, then began a hopping, jerking dance that rivaled any unruly bucking horse that Maxie had ever ridden. She went flying, hit the dust hard with her backside, and bounced to her feet. The Apache swung around, murder on his face. He yipped in glee and swung his war club. Maxie ducked under the blow and used her head as a battering ram. She hit him squarely below the breastbone. The warrior staggered, recovered, and met Maxie's fist full in his face. He brushed her aside with a furious swipe, then laughed as she danced around him like an angry hornet.

"See how you like this, Cochise!"

She aimed a foot at his groin. He sidestepped, still laughing. Behind Maxie, a rifle exploded. The Apache's laughter stopped. His mouth still stretched across his face in a silly grin, but his forehead had shattered into crimson splinters. Without a scream or even a groan he slipped down onto the dust.

"Go!" Medina nudged Maxie, whose feet seemed suddenly frozen to the ground. "Are you waiting for more of them?"

This time Catalina responded to their pounding on the door and admitted them to the back dining room. "I'm sorry, señora. We were at the front of the house. The doors are all barred. El señor Pete is on the wall with the men."

"It's all right, Catalina," Medina said soothingly. "We're fine. Don't look so worried, child. The devils will soon be driven away."

"Sí, La Doña."

Maxie was still panting. Sweat trickled down the side of her face. How could Medina look so cool, so calm? As if she shot Apaches every day and thought nothing of it.

"The courtyard should be safe enough if you want a drink," Medina suggested.

"Right," Maxie croaked.

Gesturing to Maxie to follow, Medina turned into the inner sanctuary of fruit trees, flowers, and stone benches that was surrounded on all sides by the rectangle of the house. Here, in the most protected refuge of the ranch, was their most precious asset—the well. Medina smiled when

Maxie offered her the dipper for the first drink. She sipped a small amount, then handed the dipper back.

"I'll credit you with courage, Aleta Maxwell. You're as good as any man in a fight." Medina's mouth lifted in a smile that made her face look impossibly young. "But I'm going to make you as good as any woman, my little friend. Just see if I don't! It's the least I can do for a girl who just saved my life."

Maxie's stomach sank, and for the first time in her life, she knew that she was about to be bested.

"I goddamn it to hell want that goddamned silver back, goddamn it. And I want those goddamn dirty sons of bitches hanging from a tree before the sun goes down!" The madder John Hamblin got the less original his cussing became. His fury grew with every stride as he stormed back and forth in front of the little Santa Rita mine shack, cussing and sweating and turning the very air purple with his rage. "Those goddamned bastards took at least five thousand in silver, blast their goddamn hides, and I goddamn it to hell want it back!"

Hunter tipped his hat back on his head and looked around. Hamblin's laborers stood in a sullen group off to one side listening to the boss man rant. Behind them, a mule plodded the circle of the arrastra, patiently towing the revolving boulder around the rock-lined pit to crush the silver ore. The mine site looked as though nothing had happened other than the usual work of the day. The bodies of the two laborers shot down in the robbery had been buried. Most of the day shift was back at work in the mine—Hamblin was not one to let his men shirk their labor, not even when two of them had been shot down trying to protect his property.

"How many men was it?" Hunter asked the Santa Rita's owner.

"Three. Maybe four. Goddamned bastards are worse than Apaches. Rode in after the day shift had gone down into the tunnel." He gave his men a scowl. "Four men were still in the crew shack. Yellow-bellied bastards just stood there and let the sons of bitches take whatever they wanted."

Except for the two who had resisted and earned themselves lead slugs in their gut, Hunter noted silently.

Hamblin squinted his way. "Nail those bastards, Hunter, and you'll be two hundred goddamned dollars richer—I promise you that."

Hunter gave him a flat, black look. He didn't like Hamblin, and he didn't much care about the reward the man was offering. But this war with the border bandits was a personal thing with him, and the whole territory knew it. Everyone knew Hunter's fiancée from back East had been murdered by bandits, practically on her way to her own wedding. So when a mine was robbed, a ranch was rustled, or a freight wagon was held up, the victims hunted up Hunter. They figured they were doing him a favor, giving him a chance to turn another bandit or two into a notch on his gun or an inmate of the territorial pen. For a man who had come back from the war hoping for peace he'd certainly been putting his trigger finger through a lot of exercise. He'd hunted bandits and murderers from one end of the border country to the other, bringing in some, killing some, missing others. Then he'd taken the battle to the ruffians' own filthy den—Stronghold.

Putting every bandit in the territory out of business wouldn't bring back Julia, wouldn't give Hunter the family and the peaceful life he'd longed for when he'd asked Julia to marry him after the war. But the vendetta eased his heart just a bit. He hadn't been able to save Julia, but at least he could avenge her.

"I'll have to round up a posse," Hunter finally said. "There'll be enough men willing to ride for the kind of money you're offering, but it'll take a few hours."

Hamblin gestured to the night crew. "You don't need no posse from town. Every one of these sons of bitches will ride with you." The men shuffled their feet and looked at the ground. "They'll ride with you"—Hamblin raised his voice to a bellow—"or I'll kick their goddamn-it-to-hell brown asses back over the border. *Comprende*?"

As Hunter expected, when he left the mine, none of the miners rode at his back. After all, the stolen silver wasn't theirs, and Hamblin wasn't a man who inspired self-sacrificing loyalty, or even friendship. Probably not a man in the territory would lift a finger to help him if it weren't for the reward he offered.

Aaron was certain that the Maxwells were the bandidos who'd paid an early morning call on the Santa Rita. He'd ridden in enough Maxwell heists to know their stamp—a daylight raid while most of the miners were underground, the casual killing, the hit-and-run tactics. If Hunter could bring in the Maxwell clan, vicious hell-raisers that they were, the territory thereabouts would become a good deal quieter.

If he could bring them in. The Maxwells were as sly as weasels when it came to slinking off to hide. Clever as weasels too. Of the whole stinking family only Maxie hadn't been shrewd enough to escape Aaron's well-laid trap. Dirty Jim, netted with the rest of the Stronghold scum, had managed to give Simon Curtis the slip somewhere between the Mexican border and Motherlode. No doubt the kid was back riding with his older brothers. The only Maxwell Hunter had bagged and managed to keep bagged was little Maxie.

Aaron grimaced at the thought. Maxie. Damn her hide. Why did she keep creeping into his mind like that? That Maxwell he'd just as soon not tangle with again. She was cut from the same cloth as the rest of her family. And being a woman made her twice as dangerous.

Hunter had resisted the temptation to visit Agua Linda over the last few weeks. Part of him wanted to see her, wanted to discover if the crystal blue of her eyes and the impish allure of her face—visible even through her scowls —was just a product of his imagination. He wondered how she was faring in her new life and if she had forgiven him for dragging her out of her father's pesthole hideout. Unlikely, he mused. She'd walk into a nest of rattlers before admitting that he'd done her a favor by taking her out of there.

Not that the little she-wolf needed his concern. She was aptly named—tough as a cactus and just as prickly. One day alone with Cactus Maxie had been enough—more than enough. The farther away from Agua Linda he stayed, Hunter advised himself, the better off he would be.

He continued toward town, trying to think of the day's demands. But Maxie stubbornly stayed in his thoughts. Maxie—grubby little ragamuffin who could turn into a woman at the flick of an eye. She had dogged his days ever since he'd left her behind. Thoughts of her lurked around every corner of his mind, and even Julia's sweet features didn't burn in his memory with half the clarity of Cactus Maxie's dirty little face. Of course, Julia had been a lady. She didn't whip up a man's mind with sass and spit. Not like Maxie. Maxie was poison. One small drop of her spread through a man's brain like fungus. That was why her hoydenish little face seemed to overprint Julia's sweet features in Aaron's memory, why he had awakened more than once in a sweat, dreams of Maxie—a naked, sensual nymph rising from the river—still flaming in his mind and his loins.

Hunter had ridden four miles from the mine when a certain uneasiness niggled its way into his thoughts and made him realize that something was not quite right. Similar instincts had enabled him to live through two years of lawless border raiding, four long bloody years of war, and the violent years since. Maxie's image retreated to the back rooms of his consciousness.

He reined his roan stallion to a halt. The horse's ears pricked forward; its neck arched in interest at something ahead. Fifty yards farther along, the track narrowed to squeeze through an arroyo whose brushy sides rose steeply on either side. Hunter could see nothing wrong, nothing out of place, but a tightening in his gut served as warning.

When a lead slug whined past his ear, it was almost too late to concede that his gut had been right. Hunter vaulted from his horse, rifle in one hand, pistol in the other. Before another shot could come his way, he zigzagged to cover, finding a niche between a boulder and a large piñon pine. His horse whinnied fearfully and bolted away as two more shots zinged off the boulder that served as Aaron's shelter.

"You fool!" Hidden behind the lip of the little canyon, Blackjack Maxwell turned to his brother Tom and slapped the rifle from his hands in fury. Tom's weapon clattered against the rocks that rimmed the arroyo. "You shit-faced fool! I told you to wait until he was closer!"

"He stopped!" Tom shouted back. All need for quiet was now gone. "He wasn't gonna come no further, dammit!"

"Shit!" Blackjack continued. "You've gone and done it now, you rockhead. The one thing we don't wanna do is let that bastard get outta here alive. He's got too long a memory." He raised his Winchester and fired two shots toward Hunter's refuge. Both slugs ricocheted off the boulder and whined away into the distance. The answer from Hunter was quick and efficient. One shot hit close enough to send rock shards needling into Blackjack's face, and another plowed into a tree two inches from Tom's head. Dirty Jim, who had held his tongue as well as his fire during the last few minutes, ducked behind a boulder.

"Damn, he's good!" Jim said with a grin. "I figger you didn't come near that close to him, Jack."

"Shut up," Blackjack growled. "We'll see how good he is with one of my slugs in his stinkin' heart."

Jim snickered. "You're not likely to put lead in 'im now he knows we're here. And from what I learned about Hunter from that bean pole deputy of his, we're likely to get our asses kicked unless we back off."

"Back off? After what he done to us? What kinda shit talk is that?" Blackjack glared, narrow-eyed. "Stronghold was the best damned operation we had goin' until he come back and screwed it up."

"Ain't the first time we got screwed. Pa wasn't too proud to hightail it down south."

"Pa's gettin' to be an old man." Blackjack spat. "I ain't gettin' run out of the territory by some buzzard-shit lawman—'specially a snake who turns on his own kind. No son of a bitch crosses Blackjack Maxwell and gets away with it." He skewered Jim with eyes like knives. "Understand?"

Jim's face flushed. His mouth jerked in a nervous twitch.

"Understand?" Blackjack insisted.

"Whatever you say, Jack."

"Yeah. Whatever I say." Blackjack drew his pistol and spun the cylinder. "And I say this: Tom, listen up."

Tom had been listening uneasily to the exchange between his brothers. "What?"

"Circle around Hunter and get his attention on you so Jim and I can come up from the other side."

"Hell, no! Not me, Jack. Hunter's too good. He's gonna plug me before you two ever get him!"

"Then you better keep your wits about you so he don't!" Jack told him. "This is your goddamned fault. If you hadn't fired so soon the bastard would be dead now. So git!" He shoved Tom away from the mesquite thicket where they'd waited all morning in ambush. "And take your pistol with you, shithead."

Tom did as Blackjack told him, a habit he'd acquired at a very early age, even before he and Jack and their pa had stolen their way west from St. Louis on an emigrant train, then drifted down to Mexico. Blackjack wasn't bigger, but he was a heap smarter. Their arrangement was usually a good one: Blackjack did the thinking for the both of them and Tom did whatever Jack told him to do.

But this time Tom was doing a bit of thinking on his own, and rusty though his thinking parts were, they were telling him that on this occasion Jack had gotten them all into one hell of a fix.

They'd deliberately raided the Santa Rita that morning to draw Hunter out. Tom understood that much. Between the Santa Rita mine and the town of Motherlode there was only one road that wasn't hell on a horse and rider, and Hunter was bound to travel down it. He understood that, too. The plan was supposed to be easy as pie. Hunter would be dead and the Maxwell boys could stop worrying about him.

So if Blackjack's plan had been so great, what was Tom doing sneaking around behind a man with a fast gun and a temper that was probably even faster? Sure as hell was hot he was going to get himself nailed.

After a tortuous climb down and around the ravine, Tom finally sighted his prey. He crept as close as he could—much closer than he found comfortable, even though Hunter's eyes were turned toward the lip of the canyon where Blackjack and Jim still waited. His gut twisted with tension. To hell with drawing Hunter's attention and giving Jack the glory of shooting the bastard, Tom decided. Back shooting was one thing that Tom was good at. He'd do the killing himself.

Tom lifted his pistol and fired. The hammer fell on an empty chamber—he never had been able to keep track of how many shots he had left. But the empty click drew Hunter's head around—along with his gun. Tom ducked behind a boulder as Hunter fired, then thundered forward like an angry bull. Both men hit the ground in a flailing heap, Tom on top. Hunter's rifle and pistol both flew up into the air and hit ground well out of either man's reach.

In a mere moment they were on their feet, fists doubled, circling each other warily like two wolves with a taste for blood. Remembering a bit late that he had one weapon left, Tom drew the knife from his belt. He struck out with the blade, but Hunter ducked, then in one lithe movement stepped forward and trapped Tom's wrist in a grip of steel. In a silent, almost unmoving battle of muscle power they fought for control of Tom's hand—and the knife in it. Sweat poured off them both, running in streams down corded necks and soaking their shirts.

The contest ended abruptly when the muzzle of a Colt Navy pistol touched cold steel to Hunter's temple.

"Bang," Blackjack said, a smirk in his voice. "You're dead, Hunter."

Tom relaxed—a mistake. Hunter, in a quicksilver movement, grabbed the knife, grabbed Tom's neck, and brought the two together in a threat of bloody death.

"Ever see a man jerk when a bullet goes through his brain, Blackjack?" Hunter asked in a cold, steady voice. "My arm's going to jerk and pull this knife right across your brother's throat. He's going to be as dead as I am when you pull that trigger."

Blackjack hesitated. Hunter was sweat-drenched and bloody, but he looked cooler than any man had a right to look when he had a pistol pointing at his head. The hand holding the knife at Tom's neck was rock steady, and Tom's struggling didn't make the marshal turn a hair. The black eyes that were unwaveringly fixed on Blackjack's face were cold as steel—contemptuous, not fearful. Blackjack was the man holding the gun, but suddenly he was afraid.

He eased the pistol back, but kept it aimed steadily at Hunter. "Let him go."

"Back off," Hunter ordered. "You too." His eyes shifted to Dirty Jim, who stood beside Blackjack, gun in hand. "You might get me, but your brother's going to hell right along with me."

Slowly the two Maxwells retreated, pistols still steady in Hunter's direction.

"It's a standoff." Blackjack's eyes narrowed. "Let Tom go and we'll call it a draw. I'll kill you another day."

"I'm a hard man to kill, Maxwell."

"I've had a lot of practice killing men who are hard to kill," Jack answered with a sneer.

"I'll just bet you have."

"Next time," Blackjack concluded.

Hunter dragged Tom with him as he picked up his pistol. He laid it against Tom's temple and shoved the knife in his belt. "There won't be a next time, Blackjack. You boys throw your guns down. I'm taking you in for the robbery of the Santa Rita."

"Like hell!"

Tom grunted when Hunter thumbed the hammer of his pistol.

"You're mighty casual about your brother's life."

"I figger Tom would rather be dead than in jail. Ain't that right, Tom?"

Tom's voice shook. "Hell, Jack . . . !"

His protest was drowned out by the thunder of Blackjack's gunfire. Hunter dived for cover as Tom jerked out of his grasp and ran toward his brothers. Blackjack, yipping wildly, fired off another series of shots to cover their retreat. As they disappeared up the ravine, Blackjack still yipped like a triumphant Apache.

"Shit!" Hunter emerged from behind his boulder and watched the brothers climb up to where they'd left their horses. He looked at his pistol—an old-style percussion Colt .36 that he'd carried since the beginning of the war—and hefted it fondly in his hand, wondering what the brothers would have done if they'd known that the pistol was empty —all six chambers.

Hunter shook his head, then slowly smiled. He was a fool. No doubt about it. Like a green boy he let his attention meander and allowed these snakes to get the drop on him. Cactus Maxie—little urchin witch—had tangled up his mind while her treacherous family circled around for the ambush. The girl was going to get him killed yet.

Poor Maxie. Her brothers hadn't even asked what had become of her, the bastards.

"What do you think of this?" Maxie set needle and thread on the table beside her parlor chair and held up a dark blue linen skirt. Proudly she shook it out. "Ain't a stitch out of place. Least not where you'd notice."

Jake the dog, who lay on the rug at Maxie's feet, twitched an eye in her direction. His tail thumped lazily on the floor.

Maxie stood and held the skirt up to her waist. "I guess it ain't exactly even, is it? But it's good enough. I already done it over three times. Medina says I'm getting better."

Jake looked approval from his dark brown eyes. His tail thumped again. Maxie gave him a smile.

"That's what I like about you, Jake. You don't say much, and you don't care what a body says or how they says it, long as somebody talks to you. You got better sense than most people I know."

Frau Herrmann's voice preceded the cook into the room. "Is that mangy black wolf in the parlor again? Maxie! I have warned you—"

"He ain't a wolf!"

"Isn't a wolf."

"Right. He ain't a wolf. And La Doña said I could have him."

"Not in the parlor!"

"He ain't . . . isn't hurtin' the goddamned parlor!"

Elsa threw up her hands in despair. "Out with you both! You, Maxie, go cut the vegetables for the stew. Here! Give me the skirt. I will give it to Maria to wash. And keep that . . . that dog out of the kitchen!"

Maxie almost tripped over her skirt on the way out of the house. The garment belonged to Catalina, who was several inches taller than Maxie. Walking in skirts was difficult enough without the hem dragging the ground, but La Doña insisted that Maxie alter the clothes herself—a good lesson in practical stitchery, she had declared. Maxie had objected hotly, but Medina was firm, giving Maxie a gentle smile at the same time she insisted that Maxie follow her instructions. Maxie had come to recognize the smile as affection. It made her feel strange, that smile. No one had ever cared about her enough to insist she learn anything she didn't want to learn.

But as a result only two of her hand-me-down skirts had been hemmed to a proper length.

Medina's affection wasn't the only aspect of Agua Linda

that made Maxie feel strange. Watching La Doña and her husband upset all her ideas of men and women together. Pete Kelley talked to his wife. He didn't just tell her to do this, do that, fetch this, sew that; he actually talked to her. And Medina talked back—sometimes even gave her husband a bit of lip. Pete was one tough varmint, Maxie admitted. He wasn't afraid of Apaches or bandidos. Yet he didn't hit his wife—unless he did it in private where Maxie couldn't see—and he talked to her. That made Maxie wonder what kind of a topsy-turvy world she'd been dragged into.

Jake followed Maxie across the dusty courtyard and into the kitchen, where onions, parsnips, and potatoes lay washed and ready on the worktable. He wagged an expectant tail as she started chopping the vegetables and tossing pieces into the stewpot.

"Dogs ain't—damn it!—aren't supposed to like greens," Maxie commented as she tossed a piece of potato in the dog's direction and he neatly snapped it out of midair.

"*Sí!*" Maria stepped through the door and gave Jake an amused look. "And if la señora Elsa sees you give our good food to that animal, next week's stewpot will be simmering with dog meat."

Maxie shrugged and grinned. She had reached a precarious truce with the two Mexican house girls. In fact, Maria had helped her stitch the new linen skirt Maxie was so proud of—when Doña Medina wasn't looking, of course. And Catalina hadn't uttered a word of rebuke yesterday when Maxie tripped over a pail of soapy water and flooded the just-scrubbed dining room floor. In return for the girl's tolerance, Maxie had felt obligated to help her clean up the mess, and lending that helping hand had given her a strange satisfaction. When Elsa saw Maxie on her knees scrubbing the floor with Catalina, she'd cocked a brow and given them both a smile. Maxie hadn't known that the woman knew how to smile.

"Elsa comes near my dog, she'll find herself cooking over a slow fire."

Maria giggled. "I didn't mean it."

"I did." Maxie threw the dog another morsel. "Jake works hard. He deserves a treat now and then."

"Jake used to work hard," Maria corrected. "Now all he does is follow you around."

"Well, it's about time he retired, old fart that he is."

Maria gasped with delighted horror, then giggled again.

Jake had been a resident of the Agua Linda stables until Maxie elevated his status. She'd found him there one hot afternoon when the corner of a vacant stall provided her with a private refuge for a good cry. His stare penetrated her misery, and she lifted her face from tear-drenched hands to find herself confronted by a dog that looked to be a combination of wolf and mastiff. The beast's shoulder stood as high as Maxie's hip when she shot up in alarm. He was black and shaggy with pricked-up pointed ears and a long feathery tail that crooked curiously down at midlength. The pointed muzzle was flecked with gray. One shoulder bore a hairless, leathery scar—legacy, Maxie learned later, of a flaming Apache arrow.

Maxie had little experience with pets. Most dogs at Stronghold had suffered the fate Maria had threatened for Jake, and the few that didn't were mangy, half-wild scavengers. But after her first alarm had passed, Maxie realized there was no threat in the black dog's eyes. His tongue lolled in a friendly manner, and his tail waved back and forth in greeting.

"What're you smiling at?" she had flung at him. "There ain't nuthin' here to be smilin' at! I just burned a whole batch of bread, that German witch stole away my britches and won't give 'em back, and I been puttin' holes in my fingers all morning tryin' to sew a straight seam."

The dog sat down and seemed to eye her with sympathy. Mollified, Maxie squatted Indian-style a few feet away.

"I bet you ain't burned when a body uses perfectly natural cuss words."

The dog flapped his tongue around his lips a few times, then once again gave her a doggy grin.

"Yeah," Maxie confirmed. "You ain't."

From that moment on they were friends. Jake was a good listener. He never corrected Maxie's grammar, never criticized her behavior, and always seemed to agree with her point of view. As if sensing in her a kindred spirit, the big dog followed at her heels like an adoring puppy, letting her out of his sight only when forced to do so. After three days of pleading—or at least as near pleading as her pride would allow—Maxie persuaded Doña Medina to allow Jake into the house. The drovers seldom used him as a herd dog anymore since age and old injuries had slowed him down, and the loyal beast didn't deserve such a lonely fate as being exiled to the stables to wither away in uselessness.

Medina had actually given Maxie a brief peck on the cheek after she'd listened to her pleas for Jake.

"You have a tender heart, dear, and you're a much sweeter person than you know."

Surprised, Maxie hadn't known what to say. Approval was a rare experience in her young life. Strange how it made a person glow inside.

"Are there any biscuits left from this morning?" Maria asked. "Or did you give all those to the dog too?"

"They're in the bread box," Maxie answered. She couldn't suppress a smile. This morning was the first time her biscuits—made by her own hands with no help at all from anyone—had turned out neither burned nor the texture of dried mud. Even Frau Herrmann had approved and given her another one of her rare smiles, which were surprisingly warm for a woman so fierce. The small success had made her proud as a hen with her first egg, ridiculous when she thought about it. After all, why should she care if the ranch hands approved her attempts at cooking, or if Pete himself had gobbled down three of her biscuits? Cooking was still just a dumb woman's chore, wasn't it?

"Oh, yes," Maria mentioned casually. "La Doña wants to see you in the house, when you have a moment. I will finish the vegetables if you like. Just give me a chance to eat this biscuit."

Maxie's little bubble of pride about the morning's success burst. What had she done wrong now? She searched over the last few days' fumbles to remember what task might have been so badly performed to merit Doña Medina's attention. With a grimace she rephrased her own question. What hadn't she done wrong?

"What have you done wrong this time?" Medina asked with a slight smile. "Such a belligerent tone, Aleta, is not suitable for a lady."

Maxie grimaced. "Aleta" rasped across her nerves like a cholla cactus across bare skin. The name sounded as though it should be pinned on some pasty-skinned, flounce-be-decked female, and La Doña seemed to pronounce the silly name with such relish.

"I ain't . . ." Maxie paused, aware that she was risking a lecture on grammar as well as on belligerence. "I am not a lady. I don't want to be a lady."

Medina's smile didn't waver. "Not yet, perhaps. But you have made some strides in that direction, dear. That's why I asked to talk to you—not because you've done something that deserves a scolding."

"Oh?"

"I merely thought to offer you the chance to accompany me to town, as I must make a trip for groceries and some yard goods. We might stay over and go to church Sunday morning, and Sunday evening there's a social in the schoolhouse. But if you would rather stay here—"

"No! No! I want to go!"

"You do deserve a reward, Aleta. I know you've been trying your best over the past days. You've been working well with the girls, and even Elsa has complimented your work. I can tell that you've also tried to patch up your differences with some of the hands."

Indeed she had! Maxie didn't tell Medina that she'd snuck out two nights and played poker with the waddies in the bunkhouse. She'd hauled in a stash—even without cheating. Those boys didn't know anything about poker!

"I think you deserve a bit of an outing," Medina said with a smile. "Don't you?"

"Yes, ma'am!"

To get away from the cooking and sewing and scrubbing floors and washing dishes! She danced an unladylike jig of joy that ended in her tripping over her skirt.

Medina shook her head and laughed. "Most certainly you can't wear that to town. Where is the new skirt I was helping you hem yesterday afternoon?"

"Maria's washing it," Maxie told her in dismay. Would La Doña make her stay home just because she had nothing proper to wear?

"I suppose we can fit you into my clothes for the trip to town. We are about of a size, I think. Let's see if we can't find something suitable."

Maxie followed eagerly at Medina's heels as the little Spanish matron led the way toward the master bedroom. For a jaunt into town she would do anything—even wear a dress and pretend to be a lady. Her eyes sparkled, and her stride regained the characteristic lilt that had been sadly lacking these last few weeks. She could see all kinds of opportunities just around the corner.

Chapter 6

$\mathcal{T}$he town of Motherlode had once been described by a traveler as a pimple on Arizona's backside. It rose from the face of the desert like a drab blemish—ramshackle, impermanent, an amorphous collection of frame and adobe buildings that had been erected in haste and would disintegrate with equal speed once the nearby silver deposits were played out and the town was abandoned.

But as the Agua Linda buckboard rattled along Motherlode's dusty main street, Maxie gazed at the town through eyes that were wide with wonder. The rest of the Agua Linda party—Medina, Elsa, and the hands who had accompanied them (Pete never let La Doña off the ranch without a sizable troop of guards, even if the ranch was shorthanded; the man was mighty considerate for such a tough bird, to Maxie's amazement)—to them the town was just a town; to Maxie it was a wonderland. Seven years ago she had visited Tucson, and twice in her life she had actually stayed overnight in Tubac. In her eyes, Motherlode was a jewel of civilization.

"Is that the dry goods store?" she asked Medina eagerly as

they passed an impressive frame house. Painted bright yellow, the house had a second-story balcony and first-floor veranda that lent it a touch of genteel luxury.

"No, Aleta. The dry goods store is over there." Medina nodded toward a squat adobe building down the street.

"That's too bad." Maxie ran admiring eyes over the fancy gingerbread trim that decorated the house's eaves. "If I had a dry goods store, I would want it to look just like that. Does somebody live there?"

"Yes, dear," Medina said with equanimity. "Someone does."

Elsa gave a snort of laughter, and one of the drovers who had accompanied them winked at Maxie and mouthed the word "whorehouse" in her direction.

"Oh!" Maxie mouthed back, then gave the man a mischievous grin of thanks. Wouldn't Hernando's fancy ladies— wherever they were now—just love a place like that? With a real house and soft beds, whoring would hardly be any work at all.

The local whorehouse was one of the few frame buildings in Motherlode, the steepled church and several prosperous-looking residences, set well back from the dusty street, being the others. The rest of the town was adobe, built from the same gray-brown dirt that surrounded it. Each place of business sported a sign with both words and symbols. Maxie could identify a bank, four saloons and gambling halls, a blacksmith shop and livery, a harness shop, and a jail. One building whose sign she could not understand Medina explained was a theater. It was vacant all but about three months of the year, she said. But the winter before they had been treated to a troupe of players from New York. Another building that Maxie had assumed was a residence Medina told her was a small hotel with an eating establishment attached.

"We will have to start you on reading lessons as well, I see," Medina commented. "What a shame your mother didn't live to see to your education. She could read five languages and speak three fluently." Medina sighed. "The only education Maria Theresa lacked was wisdom in love."

"She married my father!" Maxie reminded her indignantly.

Medina was meaningfully silent.

In the days since the Apache raid Maxie had subtly pried quite a bit of information about her mother from Medina without sacrificing her pride by actually asking questions. Maria Theresa's hair had been as black as Maxie's, she'd learned, and her stature as small. She'd come from a rich family, just as Maxie's father had told her—a lady with fine manners and silk clothes. Medina said she was sweet and giving, and also not very wise. The day dimmed a bit as Maxie suddenly wondered if her mother had regretted sacrificing her fine life for Harrison Maxwell. If she'd survived her first childbearing, would she have stayed with him? Would the woman Medina described to Maxie be happy at Stronghold? Maxie suspected not—an uncomfortable suspicion that had been growing since she first began to understand that Agua Linda represented a whole way of life that she'd never imagined.

Medina guided the team of mules to the side of the street and stopped them in front of a sprawling adobe building whose sign displayed a carving of a needle and thread and a flour sack. Maxie climbed down from the buckboard seat and looked around. The sights were a welcome distraction. She'd never seen so many people in one place before. The plank walk that bordered the street seemed a veritable thoroughfare of humanity.

Two Mexican matrons walked casually by with *ollas* balanced gracefully upon their heads and rebozos half-draped over their faces, just as if they were walking down a street in Mexico and didn't have to thread their way through the gringos who littered the walkways. Several passing men paid the señoras no heed but tipped their hats respectfully to the Agua Linda women. Maxie glanced at Medina, uncertain how to acknowledge such a greeting from these properly civilized gents. Before this moment, every masculine hat tipped in her direction had been intended to swat her behind or some other part of her anatomy. Unaccustomed to being the object of respect, she wondered if she should curtsy—not that she knew how—or smile, or touch the brim of her bonnet in return. Medina and Elsa simply returned the men's courtesies with a smile. So Maxie did the same. Smiling was the only ladylike talent she had completely mastered.

While Medina secured the mule team and assigned errands to the ranch hands who had accompanied them into town, Maxie peered down the street, where a scruffier breed of men drifted in and out of the saloons. Even though the sun was still high, these busy establishments were already leaking sounds of music and rowdiness onto the street.

Maxie felt a stab of homesickness. There, just fifty feet away, was her world—hard-drinking, hard-fighting men who lived by their own rules and damned anyone who didn't like it. Those fellows would fit right in at Stronghold, and maybe they had drifted through there a time or two. Likewise, her brothers would have certainly felt at home with the little group of men emerging from the closest gambling hall, swaying on their feet and singing a raucous ditty. Of course, Blackjack was handsomer than any of those hombres—probably a better shot, too. And Tom could beat any three of those toughs to a pulp with just one hand.

"Are you coming?"

"What?"

Medina's voice was like a dash of cold water in Maxie's face. For a moment it had seemed as though Stronghold wasn't empty and she and her family were still living the good life—free and wild. . . .

"Into the store, Aleta," Medina said with a touch of impatience. "Elsa has gone ahead to the hotel, but I'd like to get some shopping out of the way."

"I'm coming." With a final wistful glance at the rowdier

side of town, Maxie allowed herself to be propelled through the doorway.

She was immediately assaulted by smells—coffee, tobacco, even the sugary sweet odor of candy sticks in a barrel by the long counter that ran nearly the length of the store. Behind the counter stood a round, harmless-looking man whose one claim to individuality was the most spectacular brushy moustache Maxie had ever seen. Behind the man, displayed on shelves that covered the wall from floor to ceiling, were bottles of every shape and size filled with liquids of green, dazzling blue, red, and black.

The proprietor noticed Maxie's interest.

"Best supply of tonics west of St. Louis, miss. Cures for fluxes, stomach cramps, toothaches, loss of hair, and delicate nerves. Can I be of help?"

Medina answered for Maxie. "We just need some yard goods today, Mr. Pruitt. And some flour, salt, sugar, tobacco . . ." She handed him a list. "Could you fill this while we look at the materials, please?"

"Certainly, Mrs. Kelley. Certainly. Take your time."

Maxie followed Medina to the back wall of the store, where the dress goods were displayed. How the little Spanish woman could fasten her attention on cloth and ribbons and lace when the store held so many fascinating items was beyond Maxie's understanding. The store was truly a treasure house—a collection of everything a body could want or need. A glassed-in display case with real glass held an array of pistols that would make Blackjack's mouth water. Some of them were the new-style cartridge pistols that didn't require loading with powder and a lead ball, just a sleek, self-contained, efficient bullet. Opposite the gun case, one whole wall was filled with racks of saddles, bridles, harnesses, halters, and bits. Shelves along another wall were stacked with jars and cans of delicacies that Maxie could only guess at. Elsewhere there were barrels of crackers, sweet cookies, pickles—such a wealth of delicious and interesting things.

And all Medina wanted to look at was dress goods!

"I think this red wool would look good on you for this winter, Aleta. And the blue cotton is something we could make up right away—perhaps with this lace as trim. The selection isn't very large, but . . ."

The selection was certainly larger than what Maxie cared to inspect. She cast a longing eye on a stack of neatly folded ready-made britches. She'd never had a new pair in her life.

"Well, these will have to do." Medina had set aside four bolts of cloth and two spools of ribbon. "Carry these up to Mr. Pruitt, Aleta. But wait. Perhaps we should look at bonnets as well."

"Elsa gave me one of her bonnets," Maxie objected. Bonnets! Trust women to wear such a senseless piece of apparel. A good hat sheltered a body from the sun, kept off the rain, and served as a handy water bucket if need be. But women's bonnets were filled with useless lace and ribbon and shut out the whole world except a tiny portion right in front of a body's eyes.

"You must certainly have more than one bonnet, Aleta!" Maxie sighed. The afternoon was going to be a long one.

By the time Medina and Maxie emerged from Pruitt's Dry Goods, Mr. Pruitt was richer by the price of two bonnets, four dress-lengths of wool and cotton, a variety of ribbon and lace, a pair of boys' sturdy boots (Maxie had gotten her way on that purchase), and a small pair of ladies' slippers in addition to the Kelleys' usual purchase of food staples. Maxie looked on in chagrin as the ranch hands loaded the purchases into the wagon. At her wages—and come to think of it, she didn't even know for certain that she was getting any wages—Maxie would be old and wrinkled before she could pay the Kelleys back for the dress goods and other fripperies. Not that paying her own way had ever been a priority with her before. Life at Agua Linda was putting some strange ideas into her head!

"Shall we go to the hotel to see if Elsa has gotten us rooms?" Medina suggested. "I was going to suggest that you might like to stroll around town, but the sun is very hot this afternoon. Perhaps a glass of lemonade in the hotel would be wiser."

"Um," Maxie replied without interest. She squinted against the glare at a man and woman walking toward them along the plank walkway. The man looked very much like . . . damn! It was! Aaron Hunter!

If Maxie had had more time to think before Medina and Elsa hurried her along on this trip, she would have realized that they were bound to encounter the villain. After all, he was the law in Motherlode. Wasn't that what he'd told her? Being friends with the toad, Medina would want to say hello to him.

Hunter had never been far from Maxie's mind during the last few weeks. A hundred times she had fantasized the ways in which she would make him sorry for spoiling her life and imagined him pleading for her forgiveness and absolution. But she was unprepared for the sight of a flesh-and-blood Aaron Hunter walking toward her, the sun at his back lending him a spectacular halo he certainly didn't deserve, his stride supple and sure and easy—despite the slight limp—as though he had every right to be walking around free while the men he had betrayed were penned somewhere behind bars—or, worse still, rotting with stretched necks in their graves.

Maxie stood rooted to the spot, unable to tear her eyes away from this man who had knocked the foundations from her world. The beard stubble that had shadowed his jaw was gone, making the dimple in his cheek—she could see it even at this distance—show to great advantage. And his hair was more neatly trimmed than when she'd seen him last. It ruffled playfully in the breeze, for he didn't wear a hat. No one said a thing if a man went out without a hat on his head, but if a lady—like the lady walking with Hunter . . .

The first thing Maxie noticed about the woman was her bonnet, a contrast to Hunter's sunlit bare head. The bonnet was possibly the most frivolous, stupid piece of apparel Maxie had ever seen, and it shadowed an insipid face that was pasty white. Her slender hands, encased in lacy gloves, no doubt did nothing but delicate stitchery all day long—when she wasn't out strolling with Motherlode's high-and-mighty marshal. Her dress, covered with silly bows and lace, certainly didn't hide the bitch's curves in spite of covering her from neck to toe. Not an ounce of muscle on the girl's whole body, Maxie decided. She was all plump, useless padding.

"Medina. Maxie."

Maxie jumped at Hunter's polite greeting. She'd been so busy in her critique that she hadn't realized the pair had drawn close. She opened her mouth to answer, then snapped it shut. Everything she had to say to him she'd already said. If she gave voice to what she truly felt, Medina would no doubt scrub her mouth with soap.

Medina sighed as Aaron and his lady friend disappeared into the doorway of the dry goods store. "I see we must work some more on the social graces, Aleta."

"Who was that?"

Medina gave her a strange look. "I certainly think you would recognize him—"

"No. Not Hunter. Who's the girl?"

"Cynthia Pruitt. Her father owns the store."

Maxie stared into the store's dark interior.

"She's lovely, isn't she?" Medina continued. "And most accomplished. It's almost a shame to see such a beautiful girl waste her youth in a place such as this."

"Don't look to me like she's wasting it," Maxie replied quietly. It would serve Hunter right to get stuck with a piece of sugary fluff like the most accomplished Cynthia Pruitt, Maxie decided promptly. She hoped the woman made him miserable someday.

"Doesn't look like . . . ," Medina corrected her. "Now come along. That lemonade is going to taste good."

Maxie climbed aboard the wagon. Her homesickness had

just tripled, and uppermost in her mind was a renewed anger at the man who had so arrogantly swept away her home, her family, and her life.

"Hunter's limp looks worse," she commented with satisfaction.

Medina slanted her an enigmatic glance. "Pete told me that a few days ago Aaron was ambushed by some border scum who'd just raided the Santa Rita. He outgunned them, but ended up walking home. About fifteen miles." She smiled. "I guess his horse left without him."

Served him right for being on the wrong side of the law, Maxie smirked to herself. She turned to Medina with a grin. "A lemonade does sound good." She'd be a good girl and play the demure miss with La Doña, Maxie decided. Then it would be time to make some use of this jaunt to town. Aaron Hunter had more trouble coming. He was going to be sorry he'd ever tangled with Cactus Maxie Maxwell.

Two hours later Maxie stood in front of the jailhouse door. She scowled at the barrier as if it were the threshold to hell. This would certainly be the very first time a Maxwell had entered a jailhouse willingly. But the door wasn't going to slam shut behind her, locking her inside, Maxie reminded herself. She was free as a bird, not like poor Dirty Jim and the rest of the Stronghold crew.

The afternoon's brief encounter with Hunter had fanned the embers of her anger. Maxie was ashamed that in the rush of her own troubles she had almost forgotten she was far luckier than her comrades. Thanks to Aaron Hunter, they were rotting in jail—or worse—while she had only to worry about scrubbing floors and wearing skirts. Agua Linda's isolation had narrowed her attention down to herself, and she'd even started to get used to these silly civilized ways. But the sight of her enemy's face had jolted her awareness. The Maxwells were on one side in this world; the Kelleys, the upstanding citizens of Motherlode, and Aaron Hunter—especially Aaron Hunter—were on the other.

The time had come for Hunter to stop getting his boots

licked and his backside kissed by people like that simpering Pruitt woman. He needed his butt kicked, not kissed, and Maxie figured she was just the person to do it. Lips compressed to a grim line of determination, she pushed the door open.

The jailhouse was dim and cool. One desk, several scattered chairs, and a potbellied stove comprised the only furniture. The walls were decorated with a few wanted posters, a pencil sketch of the nearby Cerro Colorado Mountains, and a gunrack. Three cells were set off in a separate room whose door right now hung open. Maxie could see past the iron bars to the dubious accommodations. Each cell had two cots with thin mattresses, and one held a sprawled, snoring occupant who exuded an odor of liquor that Maxie could smell clear across the room. No chains, no manacles, no mob of miserable prisoners from Stronghold —the hoosegow wasn't exactly what she had expected.

Simon Curtis looked up in polite inquiry as she closed the door behind her. His face froze for a mere second, then stretched into a grin.

"Holy Mary herself! Look'ee what we've got here! An' wearin' a dress, no less!"

"Where's Hunter?" Maxie demanded.

"Not here," Simon supplied. "He'll sure be tickled he missed ya."

Maxie grinned boldly. "Still sore I hit ya, huh, Curtis?"

"Nah," Simon replied. "I been hit plenty harder, girl. Jest not by someone I was goin' outta my way to help. Next time I'll know better."

"If there's a next time, maybe I'll hit harder," she shot back. "When's Hunter comin' back?"

"Marshal Hunter is out on business. I don't think he has time for palaverin' with the likes o' you."

"Business, my butt!"

The door squeaked as it opened and then closed again. "I thought Medina would've made a silk purse out of a sow's ear by now," Hunter commented. "I can see she hasn't."

Maxie whirled. Her pulse leaped. Shit! Every time she saw Hunter he hit her eyes like that.

"Your lady friend let you off the leash?" she inquired, her voice an irritated meow.

"Yes, she did," Hunter replied mildly. He regarded her with a strange intensity. "Too bad Medina let you off yours."

Simon looked from one to the other of them as the air seemed to thicken. "Think I'll go up to the hotel for coffee. Ya mind, Aaron?"

Hunter started, as if he hadn't been aware Simon was in the room. He grinned. "Coward!"

"Jest smart," Simon replied.

As the door closed behind the deputy and the jail's one prisoner continued to snore, Hunter combed a restless hand through his hair. "What the devil are you doing here? I would've thought Medina had more sense than to turn you loose in a town like this."

"Medina knows I can take care of myself," Maxie declared.

"No argument there. But who's going to protect the town from you?"

Maxie gave him a venomous look as he crossed to the desk and sat down. "Where's my brother?" Maxie asked in a sudden shift of subject.

"How the hell do I know where your damned brother is? He's probably out shooting up some innocent mining camp."

"My family doesn't shoot anyone unless it's in self-defense!" she declared. "I heard Curtis tell you he rounded Jim up with the others at Stronghold. Don't deny it."

"Proud to admit it," Hunter acknowledged. "That boy belongs in a cage, just like the rest of his family."

"If you've hurt him . . ."

"Unfortunately"—Hunter grimaced his regret—"he escaped before he even got here."

"He escaped?"

"He escaped."

"Dirty Jim escaped!" Maxie exclaimed joyfully. She'd known all along he would, of course. There wasn't a jail stout enough or a lawman clever enough to corral a Maxwell. "And the rest?"

"Most of them we shipped down to the territorial prison at Yuma." Hunter told her. "All but three. Pete and Tyler Jackson and Manuel Garcia got the rope. Two months ago they shot up a ranch a few miles east of here—just for the fun of it, I guess. Killed a little boy. Folks around here weren't too happy about that. Figured they'd save the prison the trouble of feeding those three."

"Dirty Jim escaped," Maxie whispered to herself. She couldn't get upset about Garcia and the Jacksons. They'd been slime. Not at all like her father and brothers. "Guess that'll show you that Maxwells ain't as easy to beat as you thought."

Hunter sent her a needling half smile. "I know at least one that is."

Maxie's face grew red. "You're gonna be sorry some day when a Maxwell pulls you off that high horse of yours."

He leaned back in his chair, propped his dusty boots up on the desk, and shook his head. "Your family's going to be the ones pulled down, Maxie. Just you behave yourself out at the Agua Linda so you don't get pulled down with them."

Maxie turned her back on him, strode to the window, and nearly stumbled over her own skirt. But she didn't let that slight loss of dignity shake her sour mood.

"Who do you think you are, anyway, Hunter? Do you think you're God or something, sittin' up there on an almighty throne makin' judgments on everybody? You used to know what fun is. Now you're just a stick-in-the-mud who has to think about manners and laws for ten minutes before every step he takes."

He was silent.

"Why cain't you just mind your own business and let everybody else mind theirs? You talk like Maxwells are some sorta disease! You know they're just wild and free.

Maxwell men can't be bottled up in a town or"—she glanced around the office contemptuously—"in a dingy hole like this. They've gotta blow off steam every once in a while."

"You call robbing hardworking people, killing people, blowing off steam?"

"Maxwells aren't killers!" she insisted loudly. "My brothers have never shot anyone except in self-defense!"

"And just how many of their jobs have you ridden on, Maxie girl?"

"Lots!" she lied. The actual count was three, including the mine robbery where she'd rescued Hunter. Even when her brothers had let her tag along—both times when they'd been drunk—she'd been stuck holding horses well away from any action. But Hunter didn't have to know that.

Hunter shook his head. His expression looked suspiciously like pity. "I have reasons for what I'm doing, Maxie."

"Yeah. I just bet. You told me you wasn't mad at my brothers for leaving you down there in that ravine. That what's got your hackles up?"

"This is something else, kid—something real personal. You just stay out of it."

Maxie turned to face him, her eyes glinting. "You touch my family, you dirty belly-slitherin' snake, and I'll get real personal. I'll tell everyone with ears that Motherlode's damned hero of a marshal is a murderin', thievin', gunfightin', cattle-rustlin', stage-robbin', low-down bucket o' slime. Since they think bandidos are such scum, they oughta know you fit right in with the rest of us!"

Hunter took a step toward her, and in spite of herself Maxie backed away. But if his size and a certain hardness of eye signaled danger, his words were calm, matter-of-fact, and confident.

"Don't push your luck with me, Maxie. You can't win."

"Don't push your luck with me, buzzard bait. The Maxwells go to prison, you'll be marchin' right alongside 'em."

Hunter lifted a brow. "How do you think *you* would like

Yuma Territorial? I hear their facilities for women are pretty limited. Of course, once the good citizens of Motherlode understand what an essential part of the Maxwell gang you are, they'll probably just hang you and be done with it. Might be a mercy that way."

Maxie refused to back up one more step. She clenched her jaw and stood her ground, ignoring the sudden claustrophobia, and a twinge of something else, that gripped her as he came closer.

"Don't push me, Maxie. I had a debt to you and I paid it. I've got another debt—a bloodier one—to every son of a bitch border bandit who rides this territory, and I'm going to pay that, too."

"I ain't afraid of you, Hunter," she declared, and suddenly knew that she lied.

"Well, maybe you ought to be, kid." He turned, walked a few steps toward his desk, then turned back. Whatever threat hung in the room suddenly seemed to dissolve as he slanted a self-mocking smile in her direction. "Sometimes I'm afraid of myself, I'm such a blackhearted scoundrel. You'd better watch out for me, Maxie girl."

The look he gave her, though Maxie couldn't define quite what it meant, made her even more afraid than his threats. Somewhere in those devil-black eyes lurked a challenge she wasn't prepared to meet—yet. It had nothing to do with his threat to drag her with him to prison, or worse.

"You just listen to your own warnings, Hunter," she cautioned, trying to hide her confusion in the sharpness of her voice.

"I really should," he said softly as she turned and strode out the door. "If I had a brain in my fool head, I would."

Maxie stormed down the street, kicking her skirts out of the way in disgust. Lordy! How could a body take a decent stride with all that material swirling around her legs? Women had to be out of their minds to wear such things. Maxie had to be out of her mind! What was she doing walking down the street in a damned skirt and bonnet? Why was she talking to Hunter instead of laying her fist across his chops as he deserved? She was Harrison Maxwell's daughter, and a true Maxwell didn't get pushed around without pushing back—hard!

She slowed as she neared the hotel. Medina and Elsa would no doubt still be sitting in the eatery sipping their lemonade. Maxie had pleaded a headache and excused herself from their company in polite language that had pleased Medina immensely. A headache, she had discovered, was a legitimate excuse to get a female out of just about anything. She had climbed the stairs to her room, then lowered herself from the window and dropped the ten or so feet to the street. Her landing had smarted a bit, but Maxie had endured much worse. One passing matron and her Mexican maidservant had given her startled glances, but otherwise her escape was a complete success. Now she wondered how she was to get back into her room.

The thought suddenly struck her that perhaps she didn't want back in. As Hunter had scathingly noted, Medina had let her off the leash. Maxie would be a fool not to take advantage of it. Scrubbing floors, baking biscuits, and wearing skirts had addled her mind. She was free for the first time in weeks—and just about to walk back into her prison willingly. What a shitbrain she was!

Maxie stopped, for a moment indecisive. An unexpected lump formed in her throat at the thought of not returning to Agua Linda. Jake the dog would miss her. Medina would be disappointed, and Pete might miss her biscuits—he had praised them so. She had started to make friends with some of the hands, in spite of beating them at poker, and even sourpuss Elsa was beginning to seem not quite so bad. But her family was more important than anything else. Family was all she had in this world. Agua Linda be damned! The ranch wasn't her home, and its people weren't her family.

Decision made, Maxie turned away from the hotel and didn't allow herself even a glance back. Her mind whirled with plans, first how to get out of Motherlode with no one

the wiser, then how to find her family, who—rot their hides
—didn't seem to be in any great hurry to find her!

Putting her talent for inventive mischief to good use,
Maxie went to work. Her first stop was at the dry goods
store, where she gave Mr. Pruitt her most innocent smile.

"Doña Medina forgot when we were here earlier—she'd
like a pair of trousers and a work shirt for . . . for one of
the hands' little boys."

"Ah!" Mr. Pruitt nodded. "That Mrs. Kelley is kindness
itself. She treats those Mexes like they was her own kids.
They don't deserve it."

Maxie stiffened, every inch of her suddenly very proud of
her Mexican heritage. Did the fool think because Maxie had
blue eyes and light skin that she was different from any
other "Mex"? Was Doña Medina made from finer cloth simply because she had married an American? But her smile
never wavered. Acting, after all, was akin to lying. And
lying was something she had always done well.

"Those duds . . . uh . . . britches over there would be
fine."

Mr. Pruitt came from behind the counter and joined her
as she sifted through the ready-made britches and sturdy
denim shirts. "What size would the boy be, miss?"

"My size . . . that is, about my size. These look like they
will do."

"Does he need boots?"

How fortunate that she had put on her new boots before
escaping the hotel. "Just the shirt and trousers. And this hat.
That's all."

The storekeeper folded the clothes with meticulous care
and wrapped the bundle in coarse brown paper. "I'll put
this on the Kelleys' account, miss. Tell Mrs. Kelley I always
appreciate her business."

"I certainly will."

Feeling very clever, Maxie sauntered out onto the street.
The next step was to find a place to change out of these
ridiculous female duds, and then find a horse. She couldn't

hope to escape on foot, but if she could steal a mount—
Lordy! even a mule would do—she could ride to Cañon
d'Or, another bandit hideaway south of the Mexican border. Her family could well be there, and if not, someone
there might know where the Maxwells were.

Motherlode had fewer alleys than it had buildings, but
Maxie managed to find a secluded corner tucked between
the back of a gambling house and a storage shed. She
shucked her feminine clothing and quickly pulled on the
new britches and denim shirt. Not a perfect fit, but they
would do. She was beginning to feel like Cactus Maxie again
—and about time!

With a wicked, satisfied smile Maxie wadded up the discarded dress and started to stuff it behind a bin full of empty
bottles. Then she paused and sighed, the smile becoming a
grimace. She unwadded the dress, carefully smoothed out
the wrinkles, and folded it into the brown wrapping paper
that Mr. Pruitt had used for her shirt and trousers. The dress
was Medina's, she told herself sheepishly. She would keep it
as a remembrance of the lady who, in her own way, had
seemed to care about her. If it had been one of Maxie's own,
she would surely have chucked it without a thought of regret.

The bonnet, though, she discarded with great joy. When
she wound her braids on top of her head and hid them
under her new low-crowned, flat-brimmed hat, pulling it
low over her eyes, Maxie decided that Medina herself
wouldn't recognize her if they passed walking down the
street. Aleta Maria was gone. Maxie was back. At last.

Maxie tucked Medina's dress under her arm, sauntered
out onto the street, and headed for the livery stable, which
was at the opposite end of town. The hotel was behind her,
and Maxie thanked her guardian angel—or guardian imp,
whichever it was she rated—that she didn't have to walk
past the building where Medina and Elsa were no doubt
gazing out a window. It was bad enough thinking every
hombre on the street was one of Agua Linda's ranch hands.

Two of the gambling houses were now behind her, as well as Pruitt's dry goods store, the jailhouse, Herrera's harness shop, and the theater. Maxie wondered perversely why Hunter didn't recognize her when she walked past the open door to his office. No doubt he had his mind off in dreamland thinking about his pasty-faced lady friend. She hoped she had a front row seat when that man got his comeuppance!

Maxie was almost there. Her mind whirled with plans of snitching a horse from under the blacksmith's nose. She had learned horse thieving from the best in the business, and now was the time to put her expertise to the test.

The situation was a risky one, Maxie decided as she stopped to size up the task in front of her. The corral, the milling horses, and the barn were all in clear view of the attached smithy, where the proprietor was banging away at his anvil. The job called for a true sneak thief. But after all, Maxie reminded herself, she was a Maxwell. This game should be child's play for her.

Then, as though they had a will of their own, her eyes drifted to the last building that stood between her and the livery. It was the eye-catching house that she'd noticed when they first arrived in town, the place that the drover named Sam had told her was a whorehouse.

The house had piqued Maxie's interest when she first saw it. Now, in spite of the gravity of her task, she couldn't resist the chance for a closer look. With studied nonchalance she strolled from the street onto the house's porch and peeked through a curtained window. All was quiet. The house itself seemed to sleep in the afternoon sun. Maxie peered more intently, but all she could discern was a hint of the room beyond the lace curtain. The furniture—what she could see of it—looked too fancy to sit on. And the curtain itself—delicate lace whiter than sun-bleached bone! What the ladies at Stronghold would've given to have a palace like this for their business. Fancy chairs and lace, and probably featherbeds as well. If she ever saw Hilda again, Maxie would have to tell her how the real fancy ladies worked. Hilda would croak with envy, and so would every other whore who had worked her tail off on one of Hernando's flea-bitten pallets.

"Well, what have we here?" A deep voice behind her said. "A lad sneakin' a peek? You look a tad young for hangin' around this establishment, boy."

Chapter 7

$\mathcal{M}$axie jumped with a guilty start and turned to face a woman who was certainly the finest-looking whore she'd ever seen. That the lady was a whore Maxie didn't doubt for a moment. She had a whore's gaze, a whore's stance. Maxie had rubbed elbows with whores all her young life, and she recognized one of the breed when she met one.

But what a splendid one! Her face was painted with the subtle skill of an artist; her hair, a brilliant red, framed the artistic face in carefully sculpted curls. The green silk and lace of her gown accented rather than hid a figure whose curves were indeed something to behold. Even if those curves did push the boundary between voluptuous and pudgy, Maxie was sure most men would be panting to give the lady business. Men were like that.

The redhead's blue eyes twinkled at Maxie in amused tolerance. Her voice was husky and almost as deep as a man's. "Come back in a couple a' years, lad, and we'll give you a treat. But until then, scat! You'll be givin' my place a bad name."

"I'm not a lad!" Maxie huffed.

The whore arched a penciled brow. "Not a lad?"

"Ain't you got eyes? I'm a woman! Same as you!" Well, perhaps not quite the same as such an impressive female, Maxie admitted to herself, but a woman nonetheless. A few months ago she would have enjoyed being taken for a boy. But today, for some reason, it rankled.

The redhead looked her up and down. "What d'ya know?" she finally said. "You're right. What're you doin' peekin' in my window, honey?"

Maxie shrugged. "Just lookin'. I ain't never seen such a fancied-up whorehouse before. It's a right nice place."

"Yeah? Well, it's nice all right. And I worked my butt off to get it."

"This is your place?"

"You bet it is. I'm Mosalleria Cartwright. Most folks just call me Mother Moses."

"You don't look like no one's mother to me," Maxie commented.

"Damn right I don't." She threw Maxie a suspicious look. "You ain't huntin' a job, are you?"

"A job? Here?" Maxie laughed. Her a whore! What an idea. She couldn't even kiss a man without him losing his pucker. She'd starve to death trying to make a living as a whore. "Nah! I ain't after a job. Got no talent for whorin'."

"You ain't got the build for it neither, honey. Not unless you got something under that shirt and britches that I ain't seein'."

"I got other talents," Maxie assured her a bit defensively.

"Sure you do. We all got our talents. You want to see the house?" Mother Moses asked, her tone friendlier now that she knew Maxie wasn't going to hit her up for employment.

"Really? Could I?"

"Well, I don't usually invite just anybody in. But since you're the sort who appreciates quality when you see it . . . This is a class house, you know. I don't hire but the best to service my gents."

Maxie followed the redhead through the door, admiring

the way the feathery plumes on the whore's bonnet bounced with every step. She would stay only long enough to glance around, Maxie promised herself—just to brag to Hilda someday that she, Cactus Maxie herself, had once been inside such a marvelous place. Her escape could wait a few moments more.

"We receive our gentlemen callers in here." Mother Moses gestured proudly to a lush parlor that opened out from the entrance hall. The room was beautiful, with heavy brocade draperies, ornately carved tables, velveteen-upholstered chairs, and a piano. Another piano! Arizona Territory was getting downright civilized.

"Across the hall we have a small dance floor, and a bar, of course. But we don't allow our gentlemen to get drunk, you understand. This is a class joint, not a saloon."

"Lordy! What Hilda would give to plunk her behind down on a sofa like that one," Maxie commented, taking off her hat and holding it to her chest in reverence.

"Hilda?" Mother Moses gave an assessing look to the thick, lustrous braids that, released from the confines of Maxie's hat, fell down to the middle of her back. "Who is Hilda?"

"Friend of mine who's in the same business as you. Only she never had it so good. Look at those fancy pillows! And that carpet!"

"The carpet's imported," Mother Moses said proudly.

"The ladies who work here must be really somethin'!"

"Yeah! We are."

The voice, high-pitched and nasal, came from a willowy wisp of a girl with light blond hair and the palest skin Maxie had ever seen.

"Who's this, Ma?" The girl yawned, revealing a less than complete set of teeth. Her flimsy peignoir left no doubt that all other parts of her were quite complete. "New girl?"

"Call me 'Ma' again and you'll be out a night's pay, Sophie."

"Yeah?" Sophie sounded unconcerned.

"Yeah. And watch your manners. Say hello to . . . I didn't get your name, honey."

"Maxie."

"Maxie?" Sophie giggled. "What kind of a name is Maxie? You gonna take Carlotta's place?"

"Maxie's just a visitor," Mother Moses explained. "She's admirin' our establishment."

Two more of the residents were wandering down the stairway, their attire, or lack of it, similar to Sophie's.

"How many times have I told you girls to get dressed before you come downstairs? This ain't a common ordinary cathouse, it's . . ."

"Yes, ma'am," one of the girls said sheepishly. She was also a redhead—the color must be popular, Maxie decided.

The other one said with a grimace, "Who's this?"

Within a few minutes all ten of Mother Moses' girls were downstairs, sprawled on the couches, sitting cross-legged on the floor, or draped over the piano. Maxie was the center of attention as she regaled them with the story—only half a fabrication—of how she had once won fifty dollars' worth of silver off of Billy Joe Carter at seven-card stud. She didn't include the detail that she'd outcheated Billy Joe rather than outplayed him. The whores were impressed. Billy Joe had made quite a name for himself a couple of years back, both as a gambler and as a mean-tempered gunman.

Maxie felt more at home than she had in weeks. Whores were familiar companions and a welcome change from the civilized company she'd been keeping for the last few weeks. They didn't correct her grammar, or tell her to stand up straight, or look at her britches in horror, or glare if a cuss word slipped out. These girls were her kind of people, Maxie decided.

"Billy Joe used to come in here a lot," one of the girls said, referring to Maxie's story. "You remember him, Carmen? You were here then, too. Hell, he was so handsome I woulda' paid him almost. He liked it rough and fast, but he always left me a little something extra when we was done."

"*Sí,*" Carmen replied. "Like a split lip. That's all I ever got off of that hombre."

"Well, you're doin' better now, honey, so I wouldn't complain," Sophie chimed in petulantly. "If Aaron Hunter was hot to get in my pants, I tell ya, I wouldn't take no other customers."

Maxie's ears perked up.

"Aaron is sweet, *sí.*" Carmen shrugged and smiled. "But I still must make a living. And he has not been here for a long time now. Over three weeks."

"I can tell you why," Sophie said with malicious satisfaction. "He's been sauntering all over town with Miss Lily-White Prissy Pruitt, that's why."

Carmen gave Sophie a murderous glare. "That means nothing. One like that cannot give my Aaron what he needs. He has the balls of a stallion, that man." She cupped her hand in illustration. "It takes a real woman to . . ."

"Watch your mouth, Carmen," Mother Moses chided, glancing at Maxie.

"Oh, I know all about Mr. Aaron Hunter," Maxie said with a sniff. "As far as I'm concerned he's a pig, not a stallion." All this unexpected talk of Hunter had reminded Maxie that she had lingered far longer than she should have. "I gotta go, Mother Moses. Thanks for showin' me your place. It's been nice meetin' all of you ladies."

"You should stay and take Carlotta's room," a girl named Jacqueline said. "You could make a bundle here, ya know."

Maxie and Mother Moses protested at the same time.

"I'm surprised at you, Ma," Jacqueline said. "You cain't see a jewel when it's put right into your hand." She got up, pulled the tie from one of Maxie's braids, and spread the black, riotous waves like a lustrous blanket over Maxie's shoulder. "Look at this"—she touched a finger to the high, clean line of Maxie's cheekbone—"and this. I could fix her up to be a real stunner."

"Yeah," Sophie scoffed. "More like you want an amateur

in Carlotta's place so her customers will start comin' to you."

Jacqueline made an obscene gesture in Sophie's direction. "You think everyone is as low as you are." Taking Maxie's hand, she pulled her toward the stairs. "Come with me! I'll show you!"

"I gotta go!" Maxie protested. But she was surrounded by enthusiastic whores who were suddenly taken with the idea of making her every bit as beautiful as they were. She might just as well have tried to escape from a band of bloodthirsty Apaches.

"Let's put her in that gown that Sophie wore last night," one girl suggested as they swept Maxie up the stairs to Jacqueline's room. "It would do wonders for her coloring!"

"Why don't you offer the twit one of *your* gowns?" Sophie countered.

"Because one of my gowns would fit two of her, you bitch! She's no bigger'n half a minute."

"She's got what it takes, though," Carmen commented as she tugged at Maxie's shirt. "Look here."

Maxie pulled away, her face flaming.

"Don't know why you want to dress like a boy, honey," Jacqueline chimed in. "Not when you have tits like those."

"Now you've embarrassed the kid," Mother Moses chided. "Leave her clothes alone."

"Well, her face could use some attention," Carmen insisted.

The paints and powders sitting on Jacqueline's dressing table were surely enough to dress up every whore from Tucson to San Francisco, Maxie thought with despair. And every one of the girls had her own suggestions about where to place this dab of paint and where to put that one. Maxie was sure she was starting to look like the painted lady over Garcia's Saloon in Tucson before many minutes had passed.

"That's . . . nice," she lied when she finally was allowed to look in a mirror. She tried to smile, but her face threatened to crack.

"Told you she was a stunner!" Jacqueline said triumphantly.

"Stunner" was not exactly what Maxie would have called herself. Different, yes. Her eyes looked bluer than ever, and the heavy fringe of her lashes was darker and longer than she had imagined possible. The shadowing of rouge under her cheekbones made her face look almost ascetically thin, and her freckles—a trademark ever since she could remember—were completely covered over. She looked, Maxie decided, like a perfectly acceptable fledgling whore. Jacqueline was right, she might be able to make a living at this business—if only it didn't involve . . . well, what it involved.

"This is nice. It really is. But I really gotta go now," Maxie reminded them. "I guess I'd better wash this stuff off."

"Why don't you offer the kid a job, Ma?" Carmen suggested. "Look how pretty she turned out."

"I don't use amateurs," Mother Moses declared, not unkindly. "Rebecca, go get the girl a washcloth for her face. She can't go out painted up for business."

Rebecca left the group that was huddled around Maxie and made for the door. Halfway there she stopped and gasped in surprise.

"Afternoon, ladies."

The whores turned en masse at the sound of a masculine voice. Carmen gave a little squeal of delight, and Jacqueline giggled.

"Aaron Hunter!" Mother Moses chided in a fond voice. "Came up here quiet as an Injun, didn't you? You know that gentlemen ain't allowed upstairs before six o'clock."

"Just on a friendly visit, Ma. Not business. Thought I might find a . . . friend here." His eyes shifted to Maxie with an intensity that almost knocked the breath from her lungs. "Interesting-looking newcomer to your stable, Ma. Lowering your standards a bit, though, aren't you?"

* * *

"Here she is," Aaron told Medina as he set a furious Maxie on her feet in the middle of the hotel room. "I see it didn't take her long to sink back to her natural level."

"Aaron!" Medina chided, but her gentle reprimand was drowned out by the volume of Maxie's fury.

"You slime-eating, belly-slithering, son of a bitch bastard!" Maxie almost hissed, she was so mad. "Who the hell do you think you are, anyway—tiltin' me ass-up over your shoulder in front of my friends."

"Aleta!" Medina said sternly. "Watch your language, young woman!"

"Aleta?" Aaron chortled. He made the name sound worse to Maxie's ears than even she thought it was. "Aleta?"

"Yes! My name is Aleta, you worm! Want to make something of it?" She doubled her fists at her sides.

The smile he gave her was worse than his chortling.

"Now, Aaron, behave yourself!" Medina insisted. "Aleta, settle down! You're both acting like five-year-olds. What in Jesu's name have you done to your face? And clothes!"

"I hesitate to tell you where I found this baggage, Medina," Aaron started.

"That ain't true!" Maxie shot at him. "You're gonna love every word of tellin' her where I was, Mr. High and Mighty!"

"Shut up, you little imp of the Devil! You're just lucky it was me who found you up there instead of one of Ma's customers who likes his whores young and feisty. I don't think you would like the profession you were about to try, Maxie."

"I wasn't . . . !"

"You found her at Mother Moses' house?" Medina asked with admirable calm. But her face paled under her olive complexion.

"As God is my witness! I'm sorry I saddled you with the little hellion, Medina. I should've known better than to think that someone like her could . . ."

"Now, Aaron!"

"I wasn't gonna be a whore!" Maxie interjected. "I was just admirin' the house, and Mother Moses invited me in. She asked if I was lookin' for work and I said no."

"You were . . . admiring the house?" Medina asked, as if admiring a whorehouse was something entirely extraordinary.

"Yeah. The ladies was just bein' friendly."

"Were being friendly," Medina corrected. "Not was."

"They was . . . were fixin' me up, trying to make me look good, when this . . . this loco lawman"—she spit out the word as if it were poison—"shoves his way in and hauls me out like a sack of flour. By the way, Hunter," she added in a sugary voice, "Carmen misses you. She had some nice things to say about your . . ."

"That's enough from you!" Aaron gritted out as Medina gave him a peculiar look. "What were you doing in those clothes? When you came to town you were dressed up like a decent female."

Maxie stuck out her small, pugnacious chin. "I was leavin' —goin' to find my family and tell them that a half-brained, blockheaded, tin badge is still on their trail."

"They already know," Aaron said, then grimaced as Medina smothered a chuckle.

"I think there might be more than one half-brained blockhead in the room at the moment," Medina said, recovering her composure and looking sternly at Maxie. "Aaron, thank you for finding her, and please don't feel you've 'saddled' me with her. A woman needs a challenge every now and then to keep her young."

Maxie glared at both of them.

"Perhaps it would be best if you left Aleta and me to talk this out woman to woman."

"More like woman to scorpion."

"Aaron . . ."

"All right. I'm leaving. If you get tired of her, Medina, bring her back to me. I'll find a way to keep her out of trouble."

* * *

Aaron eased the door shut behind him, trying not to give in to his irritation. First the little hellion came to his office and scolded like an angry chipmunk, and then she ran off and ended up in a whorehouse. He ought to be angry as hell, but his irritation was more with himself than with Maxie, and that irritated him even more.

He descended the stairway into the hotel lobby, his frowning absorption so complete that he didn't see the clerk greet him from behind the desk. Once on the street, he didn't notice the early evening heat, or the rowdy singing coming from the Silver Saddle Saloon, or the passersby who cast dubious glances toward his scowl.

If he had any sense at all he would dismiss the girl as a lost cause, but she stuck to his mind like a burr to a blanket. Somewhere inside prickly little Cactus Maxie was a tender bud that he'd only glimpsed. Guarded by thorns, it hid deep in the heart of her—fascinating, compelling. Perhaps in taking her to Agua Linda Aaron had hoped that Medina could make that bud blossom, but he was beginning to think that no one could perform that miracle.

Why couldn't he be sensible and forget the girl? She was a complication his life didn't need. Aaron shook his head, smiling grimly. When in his life had he ever been sensible?

Maxie glared at the door that shut quietly behind Aaron's back. "Buzzard shit!" she said under her breath.

"Aleta!"

Damn! Medina had the ears of an owl.

Medina sighed and gave Maxie a look that made her feel lower than a bug under a rock. La Doña had a knack of yelling at people with her eyes. "Why were you running away, Aleta? I thought you were beginning to settle in at the ranch. I was hoping even that you were happy with us."

Maxie scowled. How could she be happy while her family was enjoying adventures and dangers and she was scrubbing pots and stumbling around in stupid skirts? "Seeing Hunter reminded me where I come from. Where I belong."

"It doesn't matter where you come from, Aleta. It's where you're going that counts."

Maxie studied the floor.

"This wouldn't have anything to do with Miss Pruitt, would it?" Medina gave her a look that was all too penetrating.

"Hell, no! What do I care who Hunter keeps company with? He can go dive into the nearest outhouse as far as I'm concerned."

The little Spanish woman gave Maxie a long look, then shook her head as though she had reached a conclusion that didn't please her. "Aleta, dear . . . There are many things you don't know about Marshal Hunter. He's not a man to mess with."

Maxie snorted. "I know a lot about Aaron Hunter. A lot more than you do."

"If you think that Pete and I don't know of Aaron's past, you're mistaken." She smiled as Maxie's head whipped up in surprise. "As I said before, it's not where you come from, it's where you're going that counts. And you still don't know everything about the man, Aleta. Leave him alone."

"Tell him to leave me alone. And leave my pa and brothers alone, too." Maxie plopped herself down on the edge of the bed, suddenly feeling very tired. "Hunter acts like they're scorpions that need squashing!"

Medina came to sit beside her, putting a motherly arm around her shoulders. "Did you know your pa and brothers robbed the Santa Rita mine? They were the men who ambushed Aaron and tried to kill him."

"Shi—shoot! My family aren't killers! They wouldn't try to kill Hunter. They were just trying to warn him off. That's all. If they'd tried to kill him, he wouldn't be here!"

"Aaron Hunter's a hard man to kill, Aleta. He managed to turn the tables on them. But they were out to fill him full of holes. There's no doubt about it."

Maxie's heart gave a thump. Her family weren't cold-blooded killers, she assured herself. But a vision of Hunter's deep, dark eyes staring sightlessly at the sky, the broad, muscular chest torn open by a lead slug intruded into her mind. Her pa and brothers wouldn't do that! Damn Hunter anyway!

"They're my family," Maxie asserted, as much to herself as Medina. "I belong with them."

Medina touched Maxie's chin and turned her face toward hers. Reluctantly, Maxie met the older woman's gaze.

"Your family knows exactly where you are, Aleta. They've been drinking in the bars in Tucson and Tubac. Everyone there knows that Aleta Maria Maxwell is living at Agua Linda. If they wanted you with them, don't you think they would have come to fetch you?"

They knew where she was. Why hadn't they come for her? Maxwells were supposed to stick together.

"Think about it, dear."

Maxie thought about it, and thought—until she wished she could get the thought out of her mind.

The next morning Medina announced that she and Elsa were going to church, and that Maxie was going with them.

"Church?" Maxie squeaked. She'd never been to a church in her unholy life, and she had no desire to be introduced to the institution.

"It will do your soul good," Elsa pontificated.

"I can't go to church." Maxie thought fast. "I . . . I'm Catholic." She doubted that the little steepled frame church she had seen yesterday was Catholic. If Catholics went to any other kind of church they were bound for hell, weren't they?

"That's all right, dear," Medina assured her. "People of all faiths attend here. There's no Catholic priest closer than Tucson right now, so we make do with the Reverend Cahill."

"I have a headache." The old feminine standby.

"From the imps running around in your head, no doubt," Elsa suggested smugly. "Church will do you good."

Church did Maxie anything but good. In another dress borrowed from Medina—the first she had left at Mother Moses' place when she had been dragged so abruptly from the whorehouse—she sat, or rather squirmed, for two full hours on an uncomfortable wooden pew that made spending all day in a saddle seem a lark in comparison. The whole world, it seemed, was staring at her. Or at least everyone in that stuffy little steepled church was certainly staring at her. Hunter and Maxie hadn't been inconspicuous in leaving Mother Moses' house the afternoon before, and from the looks she was getting, Maxie guessed that the whole town of Motherlode knew that she had been carried out of the local whorehouse ass-up over the town marshal's shoulder.

The only churchgoer who did not stare at her was the town marshal himself, who was sitting in the front pew with his lily-white, prissy-faced girl friend. He'd given Maxie one look when she came through the door with Medina and Elsa, then turned his face away and had not looked back, almost as if the sight of her bothered him. He was worse even than the rest of Motherlode's self-righteous snobs, Maxie decided. He would sing hymns in church that morning and let the storekeeper's daughter drool all over him for the afternoon—in a most proper way, of course. Then when night fell he'd no doubt be romping in bed with Carmen and have her cooing over the size of his . . .

Maxie reined in her thoughts, not at all liking the path they were taking.

"The wages of sin are fire, fire eternal, fire so hot that our earthly fires are nothing in comparison," the preacher intoned. Was he talking to her? Maxie wondered. He was certainly looking straight at her.

"The Bible tells us that to even think of sin is as damning as the sin itself. Those of us who would follow the path to heaven must be constantly repentent, and alert for the evil that awaits us at every turn—for the ones who show us the face of innocence but would lure us into corruption and degradation by their . . ."

The road to heaven didn't sound very interesting to Maxie. Not if the Reverend Cahill and his congregation were examples of travelers along that path. Looking at Hunter's broad back was more interesting. Did he really believe the shit that hombre was shoveling out to the congregation? Was that why he had turned from a sensible lawbreaker into a straitlaced lawman?

The service finally came to an end. The congregation rose, sang a shaky rendition of a hymn, and then milled— like a herd of cattle, Maxie thought—toward the door, where the Reverend Cahill waited in ambush to rain additional tidbits of holiness upon the departing faithful. A few of the congregation said a word of greeting to Medina and Elsa. Some sent looks of sympathy their way. No one had a single word to say to Maxie. She got plenty of looks—dagger-eyed glances from the matrons and curious interest from the men. The whole crowd was acting as though she had rolled in cow manure before walking into the church— the stiff-backed, narrow-minded, holier-than-thou horses' asses.

By the time she reached the door, Maxie was feeling drunk with anger. She saw that Medina's color was high, whether from anger or embarrassment Maxie didn't know, and the fact that the little Spanish woman, who in her own way had been kind since the day Maxie had been dumped on her doorstep, was also the target of these people's cruelty made her twice as angry. Even Elsa looked uncomfortable, and Maxie had thought her impervious to anything short of dynamite.

"Good morning, Mrs. Fairchild," the reverend was saying to a plump woman in front of Maxie. "So glad you enjoyed the sermon. Yes, I too thought it was very timely."

"Your wife did a lovely job on the piano this morning," the woman said. Her smile was so angelic that the saints themselves must have swooned with envy. "I vow she made even our singing sound wonderful."

"She will be pleased to hear you enjoyed her playing," the reverend replied.

Maxie had listened to enough of this painfully polite chit-chat. She had a thing or two she herself wanted to say to His Holiness. With an angelic smile of her own pasted across her face, she gave the plump matron a tiny nudge.

The woman turned her head, saw who had touched her, and froze. Her smile fell into a harsh bow of displeasure as she quickly moved on.

"Hi, Reverend." Maxie grinned at the preacher, offering her hand for a friendly shake.

Without actually backing up a step, Reverend Cahill shrank back as though she had offered him a live rattle-snake. A gleeful spark in her eyes, Maxie grabbed his hand and shook it vigorously.

"About your speech up there . . ." She smiled impishly. "All I got to say is, same to you, Your Reverence." She hoped her touch gave him blood poisoning!

Medina, whose expression vacillated between horror and amusement, quickly pulled Maxie away from the amazed preacher and into the churchyard. "Aleta Maxwell, what do you think you're . . . ?" Her voice trailed off and ended with a sigh. Maxie grinned. What could Medina scold her about? All she had done was offer a friendly greeting to the preacher man. Medina tried again. "Aleta, sometimes you are just . . . just . . ."

Medina was still struggling to find the right phrase when Maxie felt the heavy weight of someone's eyes. The whole congregation had stared at her off and on during the church service, but all of their attention had not struck her with as great a force.

She turned, knowing before she did whose eyes she would find. Aaron Hunter stood a little distance away with his proper lady friend, his eyes resting directly and squarely on Maxie. When she met his gaze, he tried to discipline his face into a disapproving frown. But he couldn't do it. An amused and somewhat rueful grin won out. He chuckled, shook his head, looked away, and made a comment to his frilly companion. She cocked her head toward him and laughed softly.

Laugh at her, would they? Maxie gritted her teeth and marched over to where they stood. She looked Cynthia Pruitt up and down with narrowed eyes. "Something funny?"

Miss Pruitt was startled out of her laughter, and Hunter gave Maxie a warning frown.

"Oh!" Miss Pruitt fluttered. "Miss . . ."

"Maxwell," Hunter supplied in a strained voice.

"Miss Maxwell. I vow that was delightful." She lowered her voice, and her perfect green eyes sparkled with humor. "It's about time someone pricked at the good reverend and let some of the hot air out. You really did a splendid job!"

Maxie blinked. "I . . . you think so?"

"Oh, definitely. I never would have had the nerve. But I'm glad somebody did."

Feeling like a stick of lit dynamite suddenly doused in a bucket of water, Maxie thought fast. How did one score a victory over someone who pretended to be on your side? She shot Aaron a resentful glance. He merely smiled.

"Well, I'm glad you were . . . entertained."

"I saw you by the store with the Kelley party yesterday. Will you be in town long?"

"I . . ."

"You are staying for the social tonight, aren't you? It would be such a pleasure to have someone new to talk to." She smiled up at Aaron—a disgustingly sweet, insipid smile, Maxie thought. "Not that Marshal Hunter isn't always entertaining."

If the prissy miss wanted to know just how entertaining Hunter could be, Maxie sniped silently, she should talk to Carmen.

"I don't think we'll be here for any social," Maxie told her.

"Of course we will." Medina came up to stand by Maxie's side. "We're not coming all the way into town and missing the social, Cynthia. We'll be looking forward to seeing you there."

Maxie sighed. A party with all these cordial people. Wonderful!

As far as Maxie was concerned, Motherlode's church social was rivaled only by the evening she filched a bottle of Hernando's rum, drank half of it down, and stumbled into a patch of jumping cactus. Pleading a headache, a stomachache, and every other ailment she knew hadn't moved Medina to let her stay at the hotel—even under guard. Someone—a Kelley ranch hand, Medina, Elsa, or all of them—had kept a watchful eye on her since she had climbed out of bed that morning. She'd probably been watched as she slept, as well, Maxie mused. Not that she blamed them. Medina was too smart to give Maxie a second chance at escape.

Medina and Elsa had ganged up on her, lacing her into one of Medina's dresses and cooing over how the red gown with its prissy white lace brought out her coloring. They unbraided her hair, brushed it until her scalp hurt, then refused to let her braid it again. Maxie felt silly with only a ribbon tying her riotous curls back from her face.

"Miss Maxwell. Are you having a good time?" Cynthia Pruitt glided up, her skirts swishing gracefully.

"Sure," Maxie lied. She wondered how the girl managed to walk so smoothly, almost as though she had little wheels under her skirt instead of feet. Such a thing had to take years of practice, Maxie decided.

Cynthia gave her a look of understanding, seeming to know from the tone of her reply that Maxie would rather be anyplace at that moment than in the churchyard clutching a mug of tasteless punch and watching the whole town of Motherlode dance by and turn up their noses at her. The same sour-faced matrons who had snubbed her in church were repeating their performance at the social, and fully half of the gentlemen present were eyeing her as though she were a juicy piece of meat they'd like to spit on their own personal skewers.

"I hope you'll give the good citizens of Motherlode a little more time," Cynthia said. "They're really not as boorish as they appear. It's just that . . . well, we're so far from civilization out here, sometimes we grab at straws to convince ourselves that we haven't been corrupted by the savagery and wildness of this land."

Maxie finished the last swallow of her punch. "I don't care that they don't talk to me. And I don't care what they think of me. I'd rather be friends with Mother Moses' whores." That would send the prissy miss flying off in a dither, Maxie told herself.

But Cynthia merely smiled. "Aaron told me that you were an original. Now I see what he meant. At this moment I can't say that I blame you for feeling that way. Considering how the upstanding citizens of this town have acted today, I wouldn't give you a cent for the lot of them."

An awkward silence followed. Cynthia was obviously trying not to stare at Maxie in curiosity. Maxie had no such polite qualms. She looked her fill at the girl and decided that maybe she had been too quick to think Cynthia was a useless piece of fluff. The girl was being friendly, after all—probably to her own detriment, judging by the old biddies who even now were eyeing them both with disdain.

"Miss Pruitt?"

"Oh, please call me Cynthia."

"Yeah. Cynthia. I just want to say that when I first saw you I thought you were . . . one of those twittery female sorts. But I guess I was wrong. I appreciate your acting like I was a normal person."

Cynthia looked taken aback by such frankness. Then she smiled. "I think you're quite an extraordinary person, Miss Maxwell."

"You can call me Maxie," Maxie offered, feeling generous.

"I hope we're going to be friends."

"Sure thing." Maybe Hunter didn't have such bad taste in women after all.

"Are you ladies too occupied to dance?"

Maxie jumped at the sound of Aaron Hunter's voice. She whirled and looked up at him. Damn him for being so tall. His size—both his height and the broad span of his chest— always made her feel smaller than she was.

"Hello, Aaron," Cynthia said easily. She didn't seem intimidated at all by the overwhelming mass of male. "We were just indulging in girl talk. I don't think we're too busy to dance if the right gentleman should ask."

Maxie was surprised that Hunter had the nerve to get this close to her after yesterday afternoon. She would just as soon spit at him as look at him, and she would have had they not been in polite company. He had to have a serious yen for Cynthia to risk getting in range of Cactus Maxie's ire.

"That's a nice tune they're playing," Cynthia hinted. Maxie thought the girl's head inclined slightly in Maxie's direction, and a shadow of a frown clouded Hunter's face.

"Come on, Maxie," he said. "Let's dance."

Maxie blinked in surprise. "I don't know how."

"I'll teach you. Come on." His hand grasped her elbow, giving her no choice. Before she could tell him she would rather take lessons from a polecat, they were out on the dance floor.

Chapter 8

Like a wolf scenting prey, Aaron's senses had all come alert the minute Maxie walked into the churchyard. The social was crowded, but his eyes had picked her out of the mob. She was unique. Her free-moving stride, her open gestures, the flash in her eyes all bespoke a creature who belonged under the wide sky of the desert plains and canyons, not in a yard filled with chattering people. Even tiptoeing around the yard on her painfully best behavior, dressed in a fetching red gown with her hair, for once, combed and fastened with a ribbon like a proper lady's, she radiated a quality of desert-bred wildness that seemed to send ripples through the crowd of "civilized" men and women. Perhaps that was why the instant she made her appearance a momentary hush fell over the chattering women, and the men's eyes turned toward her as though they were all drawn by invisible strings.

The good people of Motherlode were afraid of little Cactus Maxie, Aaron decided. She personified everything they hated about this desert wilderness. He was afraid of her, too, he finally admitted to himself. But he feared her for a different reason. He feared the tightening in his groin every time he saw her; he feared the way he couldn't stop thinking about her, couldn't keep from staring at her when she was within sight. He didn't want to desire her, but his heart and body didn't pay attention to what he wanted.

Aaron had watched as Medina led Maxie to the refreshment table, shoved a mug of punch into her hand, and frowned out a few words. Probably she was telling the little hoyden to behave herself—a pointless waste of words. Aaron doubted that Maxie knew how to behave herself. But flanked by Medina and Elsa like a dangerous criminal escorted by guards, Maxie wouldn't get much opportunity to create her usual mayhem.

Standing beside him and lightly holding his arm, Cynthia also watched Maxie with interest. "My goodness, Aaron. Your little friend certainly looks stunning in that red dress. Her hair is beautiful without the braids."

"My little friend?" he snorted.

"Well, she is your friend, isn't she?"

"I'd hardly call Maxie and me friends, Cyn. We're more like . . . well, picture a rattler and a mouse."

Cynthia raised a brow. "She doesn't look like the mouse type to me."

Aaron grinned. "I had her in mind for the rattler."

"Aaron Hunter"—Cynthia arched a skeptical brow—"I do believe you're blind. I'm going over to say hello to the poor girl, since it seems that no one else will unbend their stiff spines and talk to her."

Aaron wasn't blind. The dress Maxie wore—he recognized it as one of Medina's—left no doubt that Maxie was a woman grown. After he had seen her emerge from the river spectacularly naked, all illusions that she was a child had vanished. He had tried to forget, or at least to push that image to the back of his mind—unsuccessfully.

Even from a distance Aaron had seen the suspicion on Maxie's face as Cynthia approached her. But Cynthia was persistent. He watched for a moment as they talked. Feature by feature he took Maxie's face apart and tried to decide why it haunted him. What was so special? The tilted-up nose, freckle spattered and sunburnt? The cobalt-blue eyes? The girlish smile?

The answer eluded him. Perhaps it wasn't her face at all, but her spirit that drew him—her refusal to be cowed, her artlessness, her innocent if misguided belief in her family's worth. Were those the things about her that was wrapping him in knots?

With a sigh and a shake of his head, he ignored his better judgment and ambled toward the object of his conjecture. Cynthia greeted him with a knowing look and a few polite words about the music.

"Come on, Maxie," Aaron said, feeling as though he were surrendering a long and hopeless battle. "Let's dance."

For once she seemed more surprised than hostile. "I don't know how."

"I'll teach you. Come on."

Without waiting for a refusal, he whirled her into the crowd of dancers, for whom two fiddlers were playing a lively tune. Aaron discovered in the first few steps that Maxie had told the truth for a change. She didn't know how to dance, and his feet would probably never be the same. But the feel of her swaying in his arms, her lithe little body so close to his, was worth the sacrifice of his feet. She was warm, supple, and more tempting than any woman had a right to be.

"You don't have to dance with me just because Cynthia told you to."

"Cyn didn't tell me to do anything."

"Bull. I saw her eyes talking to you."

Aaron grinned. "That's not what her eyes were saying. Besides, someone has to teach you to dance."

His body was longing to teach her a dance much more intimate than this chaste waltz. Sweat began to bead his brow. He never should have gotten this close to the little witch!

Maxie tripped over Aaron's feet again. She snorted contemptuously. "I don't want to learn how to dance."

"Cactus Maxie admitting she can't do something?" he asked in mock amazement, one brow arched toward the night sky.

"I didn't say I couldn't do it. I said I didn't want to do it. There's a difference."

"Um-hum."

"Well! There is!"

Aaron suspected the greater part of her treading on his feet was intention rather than clumsiness. Maxie never quit spelling out her contempt for him, yet still the little she-cat drew him the way gold drew a prospector. Damned if he didn't admire her nerve, her independence—and the feel of those very unchildlike curves moving against him in rhythm to the dance. Half Mexican aristocrat, half dirty Maxwell, and poisonous as a rattler—that was Cactus Maxie. Her poison could creep into a man's heart and do him in if he didn't watch himself.

"Ouch!" Aaron winced. His big toe had been trodden upon one too many times. The limp he'd had since the war wouldn't be anything compared to the limp he was going to have tomorrow.

Maxie merely gave him an innocent smile. "Sorry."

"Maybe that's enough dancing for just now. Let's go over to where it's not so crowded. I have a couple of things I want to say to you."

He saw wary alertness tighten her features. To everyone else she showed a face of devil-may-care defiance. Facing him, she looked almost afraid. Did she think him such a monster? She stiffened when he led her out of the yard to a secluded nook at the back of the church house.

"Maxie," he started hesitantly, sensing her uneasiness. "Not afraid to be alone with me, are you?"

"Of course not!" she lied.

"Good. Because I'm sure as hell not going to apologize where anyone else can hear me!"

"Apologize?" She blinked in surprise.

"Yes. Apologize. I'm sorry I said those things to you last night. I know damn well you're not a whore, and . . . well, if you weren't exactly acting like a lady, I wasn't on my best behavior either."

She looked like a child who expected a blow but got a pat on the head instead.

He shifted his gaze to the dirt. Looking at Maxie, with her hair loose and curling across her shoulders, her face flushed from the dance, and her eyes suddenly vulnerable, was too distracting—and tempting. "Maybe I was a bit high-handed about turning your life upside down. But I only wanted to keep you out of danger. You did save my hide once, and I couldn't see putting your life at risk by what I did at Stronghold."

Maxie frowned, then turned her back. When she finally spoke, her voice sounded confused. "Why are you saying this?"

"Because I'm sorry for causing you pain. I admire the effort you're making. Medina told me that you're doing a fine job at the ranch, and everybody likes you."

"Medina said . . . that I was fine?" Her voice caught.

"She likes you, Maxie. She says you've got a lot of your mother in you."

Maxie was silent. Aaron took her by the shoulders and gently turned her around to face him. Her expression was unexpectedly somber.

"Don't run away again, Maxie. I know you miss your family. I know you do. But—goddamn it!—why would you want to live in fear of getting shot, getting scalped, or getting strung up by the law when you could be living a good life at Agua Linda?"

Maxie snorted. "Maxwells stick together, Hunter." The words sounded like a litany, oft repeated and losing meaning.

"Then why hasn't your pa and brothers come to fetch you?" he asked.

The question dropped like a stone tossed into a deep well. Maxie was silent; the silence stretched tight, waiting for the stone to reach bottom and shatter.

Aaron sensed the weak point in her confidence. "Let me make you a deal, Maxie."

"What deal?" Her voice was quiet, angry.

"So happens I'm the only judge around here as well as being town marshal."

"You've come quite a ways from being the green boy my father took under his wing, haven't you."

Aaron smiled without malice. "They're not too picky about who runs the court. There's not exactly a line for the job."

"So what?"

"Stay here, Maxie—with Pete and Medina. Do what Medina tells you and learn what she's trying to teach you. If you do, I promise if your pa and brothers ever come to trial, they won't hang. Not that they don't deserve it, but I'll see they don't hang."

"You'll never bring 'em in, Hunter."

Aaron looked grim. "I wouldn't count on it, kid." Maxie met his gaze for an instant only, then frowned and dropped her eyes.

"Why do you even care if I stay? You did your good deed for the year—saved poor little Cactus Maxie from a life of crime. Why should you care what I do?"

Aaron stared at her. Why should he care? Because Maxie's face haunted him, her body tempted him, her nerve and independence challenged him, her vulnerability—though she would deny it existed—reached out to him? He didn't want these feelings. She was exactly what he *didn't* need.

"I'm a goddamned idiot," he said softly, more to himself than to her.

He reached out and gently pulled her to him. Startled, she scarcely resisted as he brought her into his arms and lowered his mouth to hers. The kiss was a gentle searching for answers to his dilemma. Her warmth and startled pliancy flooded him with longing. He wanted to make her feel what he was feeling, and knew the task was hopeless. She didn't respond, but her sweet mouth salved his aching confusion. Part of him had hoped that in the reality of a kiss, Maxie would prove no more tempting than any other woman. He'd been wrong. Passion flooded his groin in hurtful force, and insanity—it had to be insanity—seared his brain and burned its way through his heart.

Maxie stiffened, then stood frozen under Hunter's caress. She had closed her eyes under the assault, knowing she ought to struggle, to pull away and land one across Hunter's chops that would spin his head right off his neck. She couldn't do anything so sensible, though. All she could do was stand there with Hunter's arms around her, letting his mouth conquer hers, feeling strange and woozy as warmth softened her innards and her knees grew idiotically weak. The masculine smell of him—leather and a faint whiff of smoke—the gentleness of his seeking lips, the hard strength of his arms all combined to disable her good sense, while a newborn spark deep inside her grew into a flame, then a blaze that charred her anger and left confusion in its place.

The heat grew as Hunter's kiss became more intense. For a moment only he surfaced for breath. Maxie heard her name softly on his lips, and then he kissed her again. He slipped his hands down her back to her buttocks and pressed her close to his hips. The heat of his arousal pressed into her stomach, adding to the heat of her own fire.

Suddenly, he set her free. Gasping for breath, Hunter tore himself away from Maxie and retreated a step. "Shit and damnation!" he growled, then turned and, without another word, strode back to the safety of light, laughter, and fiddle music.

Wide-eyed, scarcely breathing, Maxie touched her fingers to her tingling mouth and watched him go.

By the time the Agua Linda wagon pulled out of town the next morning the day was oven hot. By nine o'clock the flies that usually buzzed around horses and humans alike had already sought shelter from the sun. The sky burned like a furnace, and dust churned from beneath the horses' plodding hooves and swirled around the wagon in a private little storm. What little breeze stirred the air was a breath straight from hell.

Maxie noticed none of the discomforts of the day. She paid no mind to Elsa's complaints, or to the curious glances Medina sent her way. Her mind was locked in a wrestling match with itself, and the struggle left no attention to spare for minor distractions.

"Put on your bonnet, Aleta," Medina finally instructed her. "Your nose is looking redder than last night's sunset."

"What?" Maxie jerked as if just coming awake.

"Put your bonnet on."

"Yes, ma'am." She flipped up the bonnet from where it was hanging from her wrist, pulled it down upon her head, and tied the ribbons under her chin. Her dutiful compliance earned a look of mild surprise from both of the other women in the wagon, but Maxie didn't notice.

The night before, Maxie's world had been lifted from its foundations, then dropped down with a cockeyed slant that set her head to spinning. It wasn't as though she'd never been kissed before. Sam McConnell had once caught her alone in Stronghold's tack shed and had kissed her a good one, but the only world that had moved then had been his—when she plowed her fist into his gut. Of course, she herself had planted a kiss on Hunter that night he first returned to the outlaw hideaway. And though that kiss had tilted the world a bit, the world had righted itself quickly enough.

But last night—last night the hinges of her mind had torn completely loose. Aaron Hunter had gone out of his way to kiss her. After all the nasty things he'd said to her in the past, and all the terrible things she'd said to him, still he'd pulled her out into the darkness and kissed her—hard and hot and heavy, as though she was really a woman who could rouse a passion in a man. Her blood had boiled; her stomach had danced a jig. Aaron Hunter—for a moment he had melted into the very core of her, and when he fled, part of him had stayed behind. Even now he was still singing in her pulse, burning a path through every nerve in her body.

She touched a shaking hand to her mouth. All things considered, perhaps there was something to be said for living the straight life. Medina had told Aaron that Maxie was fine, that people actually liked her, and now Aaron . . . She smiled wistfully, then frowned.

Unless, of course, Cynthia had put Hunter up to the whole thing. . . .

The thought struck Maxie like a ton of bricks. Could it be that Miss Perfect felt sorry for the desert scum that her lover had unearthed from under a rock and dragged into the light of day? The blond piece of fluff had her hooks so securely into Aaron that she didn't mind giving poor little Maxie a thrill. Such charity probably made her feel holier than singing all those hymns in Reverend Cahill's church.

On the other hand . . .

Maxie smiled again. Hunter's kiss, his seeking lips and hands, the heat of his desire—all that hadn't seemed like mere charity, or cruel mockery either.

"Shit!" Just what was she supposed to think, anyway?

Maxie didn't realize that she'd spoken aloud until every head in their little party swiveled her way. But for once Medina looked concerned instead of angry.

"Aleta? Are you all right?"

"I'm fine!" Maxie declared hastily. But she wasn't fine. She was confused. Her world was awry and she couldn't get her balance. Damn Aaron Hunter anyway! How could he give her such a kiss, knowing she wasn't any good at that woman stuff! He had to be making fun of her—just to see her squirm. How like him!

Medina gave her a strange look, then shrugged her dainty shoulders in seeming dismissal. "Start getting out our dinner, then, will you please, Aleta? I put it under those bolts of cloth so it wouldn't be in the direct sunlight. There's a canyon coming up with a nice little stream where we can rest and have a bite to eat. If that seems all right with you, Leo."

The Agua Linda waddie who'd been serving as their lookout touched his hat in respect as La Doña addressed him. "I'll just ride ahead and check things out a bit, ma'am. Things around here seem real quiet right now, but you can't be too careful."

Maxie gave one envious glance to Leo as he galloped ahead, wishing as she always did for the freedom of a strong horse between her legs instead of hard wagon planks beneath her backside. She gave one small sigh as he disappeared behind his own wake of dust, then climbed into the back of the wagon to seek out their lunch basket.

By the time the wagon rattled into the ravine, Maxie had unearthed the lunch basket from beneath a mountainous pile of cloth and was searching the back of the wagon for a blanket to spread on the ground. The wagon bumped to a stop before she had found what she was looking for, but when she glanced up she didn't see the grassy-banked stream and shade trees that Medina had promised.

"Leo should have come back by now," Medina said. "I don't like this."

Maxie stood up in the back of the wagon and took a sharp look around. They had scarcely entered the little canyon, but the rock walls rose at least thirty feet on either side of the trail. Farther up the canyon the cliffs were even higher. The trail ahead disappeared into shadow. None of the usual birdsong or small animal rustlings disturbed the stillness. Even the insects seemed reluctant to buzz. The whole canyon appeared to be holding its breath—watching, waiting. . . .

"Leo's just takin' his time," Sam suggested. His voice held more hope than conviction.

Maxie frowned. The trail was too narrow to turn the wagon around easily, but a shivering along her spine told her that was the thing to do, and fast. Then a quiet scraping

of ironshod hooves along the rocky wagon track announced
the return of their scout.

"Here he comes now," Sam announced. "That lollygag-
gin' ol' . . . Shit!"

Medina didn't reprimand her employee's slip of the
tongue. They all gazed in mute horror at the figure riding
slowly toward them. Leo sat straight in the saddle—much
too straight. He was held erect by a four-foot-long sharp-
ened stake that had been rammed through the center of his
body like an unnatural spine. The closer he came, the more
painfully clear were the details of his horrible death.

Sam was the first to recover. "Get this wagon turned
around!" he yelled, then reached down and grabbed at the
lead mule's headstall. Medina came out of her trance and
tugged at the lines, signaling the team to turn.

But the track was too narrow, the walls too close. They'd
been neatly trapped. The Apaches had made sure of that
before they sent their gory calling card ambling down the
road. Sam shouted and cursed at the mules as he attempted
to drive them around. They milled in confusion, then panicked. A joyous, almost inhuman war cry from the cliffs
above added to the beasts' terror. Two arrows thudded into
the wagon planks at Maxie's feet, and the air was suddenly
filled with rifle fire.

"Go! Dammit!"

Somewhere in the back of Maxie's mind she found time to
note that even ladies occasionally cussed. Medina had finally given up the idea of turning the wagon and urged the
team ahead, straight toward the yipping Apaches who were
descending the canyon walls. The Agua Linda men fanned
out, trying to defend the wagon. More of the savages thundered toward them on horseback. The mules plunged forward in panic, jerking the wagon forward and toppling
Maxie to the floorboards.

Maxie sobbed out every cuss word in her considerable
vocabulary as she attempted to hang on. The wagon track
was rutted and rocky, and she bounced like a rubber ball,

grabbing at the sides, the cargo, anything that came within reach of her hands. The lunch basket was the first to fly out, followed by several bolts of cloth. As the Apache screams rose in volume, part of her mused that she wouldn't be needing any dresses from that cloth—not even to be gussied up for a coffin. The Apaches wouldn't leave enough of any of them to be buried.

The team was in full flight now, and Maxie saw that the lines had been wrenched from Medina's hands. One of the guards had fallen with an arrow in his neck. Another was shouting at the team and whipping at their hindquarters, urging them to still greater speed, firing at the Apaches at the same time. Incredibly, she saw that the canyon was opening up. They had broken through the first line of Apaches, and only those on horseback could keep up with their careening flight. Maybe, just maybe they were going to make it. If only they could reach the open, flatter ground where they could turn and fight.

With horror she saw the rock. It couldn't be avoided; they were going to bounce right over that nasty protrusion of granite, and only by a miracle could the wagon stay in one piece. Maxie grabbed the side of the wagon with one hand and wrapped her other arm around a heavy sack of flour. She heard Elsa scream, Medina utter a string of Spanish that didn't sound at all ladylike, and then both Maxie and the wagon were sailing through the air.

They didn't come down together. The wagon landed on the far side of the rock, still in one piece. Maxie and the sack of flour both landed in the bushes at the side of the track. The flour sack split open, powdering the bushes, the ground, and Maxie with white. Maxie fared better than the sack, suffering only a host of scratches and a good-size bruise on her backside.

Maxie lost no time getting to her feet. The Apaches on horseback were still pursuing the wagon, but several of the foot warriors who had been on the canyon walls were rushing her way with bloodthirsty screams. She didn't allow herself to think, she merely reacted. Snatching a rifle from the ground beside a dead Apache, she clambered up the steep wall behind her and wedged herself behind a jutting rock that afforded at least an illusion of shelter.

Strangely calm, she fired into the advancing Indians, efficiently sending two of them to the land of spirits. They scattered, then stopped and gobbled among themselves like turkeys. Maxie figured she must be a sight, covered with flour and streaked with blood from her cuts and scratches. For one wild moment she fancied that she looked enough like one of their evil spirits to scare them off, but that hope was dashed when they came at her again. The mounted warriors were returning, apparently preferring the easy prey back in the canyon to facing the guards' rifle fire on the open plain. And here she was with no ammunition.

Maxie had never figured she would die like this. She thought she might hang, or get shot, or even—if she was careless and a mite stupid—get bitten by a snake; but getting clobbered by a pack of screaming Apaches had never presented itself as a possibility. Plenty of folks out in these parts met their end that way, but she never thought to be one of them.

Time seemed to slow down, and her pa, Blackjack, Tom, Dirty Jim, Hilda, Elsa, Medina, and even Jake the dog all marched through her mind as if to say good-bye. The faces flashed by, but the one that stayed in that final moment belonged to Aaron Hunter. He looked at her through inscrutable black eyes, a half smile curving his mouth—that beautiful mouth that Maxie could almost feel upon hers again. . . .

Samson Hendricks leaned over and grabbed the headstall of the lead mule, jerking its head to one side to throw it off-balance. The beast stumbled, recovered, slowed to a trot, then to a walk. It wheezed and blew a great rattling breath from its flared nostrils as Medina scrambled down from the wagon seat to recover the lines.

"Don't need to worry no more about the team, ma'am," Hendricks told her. "They're tuckered."

"We've got to turn them around," Medina declared. "Aleta's back there. Oh sweet Jesu, Aleta!"

"No, ma'am! You cain't be headin' back that way! Ain't nuthin' we can do for that little gal, and those devils'll be after our hides again if we give 'em a chance. We've already lost Leo, Ed, and little Maxie. No sense in losin' any more."

The other men nodded. Their horses, as well as the mules, were flecked with foam and blowing hard.

"Well I'm certainly not going to leave Aleta in there without any attempt to rescue her!" Medina looked toward Elsa for support, but Elsa sat stony faced and withdrawn, her eyes unfocused and expressionless.

"La Doña," Hendricks said gently. "She's dead by now, God rest her poor little soul. It's over for her."

"You don't know that!" Medina almost screamed. "They might be . . . might be . . ."

"I'll ride back and see what I can do," he conceded. "You and Miz Herrmann git, now. Ramon"—he turned to the man beside him—"you and the boys take Miz Kelley home."

Hendricks watched to make sure that Medina turned the team toward Agua Linda, then reined his horse around to gallop back toward the canyon. Rifle ready, he hid in the deep shadow of the canyon wall as he came within sight of the Apaches. Damn their hides! They were still there, and from their midst flashed the bright red of Maxie's dress. She was on the ground, limp as a rag doll, and he decided with relief that the girl was dead, out of whatever misery they had put her through.

The braves were mounting their horses, and those afoot were wandering back toward where they had left theirs tethered. One still stood above Maxie, looking down at her.

Abruptly he scooped her up, and Hendricks saw her fist rise
and fall in an attempt to fend him off.

Damn! She was still alive. His stomach wrenched at the
thought of what those devils would do to her. With grim
determination he raised his rifle, thinking that a quick
death would be a mercy. The Apache might give chase, but
the risk was worth saving the girl from torture. Just as Hendricks's finger tightened on the trigger the warrior swung
Maxie aboard his horse and turned. Momentarily she was
out of the line of sight, and before the drover could draw
another bead, the Apache and his prize disappeared around
the canyon bend.

The Apache rancheria was situated far back in a canyon
that made Maxie think of the entrance to hell. Her senses
had returned only moments before her captors made their
triumphant entrance, their ponies galloping, the warriors
screaming to announce their victory. She bounced along on
the back of her captor's horse, her exhausted body held
erect by a brown, muscular arm curled around her waist.

Maxie's mind was a confused jumble, and the jolting of
her poor brain at the pony's every bounce did nothing to
help her memory. She did remember dimly that the
Apaches had been surprised at her ferocity. Hunter would
have been proud of the way she fought. She recalled trying
to stab at least one warrior with his own knife, then turning
the weapon on herself. Obviously her attempt at a quick,
clean death hadn't worked, because here she was.

The war party came to a sliding halt that sent clouds of
dust and sand from beneath the ponies' hooves. While
women, children, old men, and barking dogs hailed the
returning victors, Maxie wondered if she could reach back
and pull the knife from her captor's belt. But before she
could act he swung abruptly from the horse's back and
pulled her with him. Maxie was immediately surrounded by
women who looked every bit as fierce as their men.

One of the older women gobbled something at the brave

who still held tightly to her waist. Maxie could speak some Apache—legacy from the half-breed, Injun John, who had lived at Stronghold several years back—but these people were speaking much too fast for her to understand. Only a word here and there let her know that the woman certainly meant her no good. Her captor grunted what sounded like a command, and after spitting a few final words in Maxie's direction, the woman gathered her Apache sisters around her and stalked away.

"They want to torture you, white woman." Maxie jumped in surprise as her captor addressed her in guttural English. "Little Bird's brother was killed five moons ago while he rode against Thunderface's hacienda. She would like to take her revenge."

The local Apache bands had christened Pete Kelley Thunderface, Maxie knew. Just her luck to be taken by a band that had a personal grudge against the Kelleys. She tried not to flinch as the brave released her waist and turned her around. His eyes examined her head to toe, and she wondered from the look on his face if he was gauging how much entertainment she might provide under torture.

He reached out and squeezed her arm, then nodded.

"Keep your dirty hands off me, you dog-eatin' Apache."

The Apache laughed, then grasped both her shoulders and kneaded, as if to judge the meat on her bones. "You are a strong woman," he said, still laughing. "Small, but strong. I think you will be more use as a slave than under Little Bird's knife."

A slave. Lordy! She knew what happened to women who were Indian slaves! She'd heard the pitiful stories. He meant to rape her for certain! "I won't be one of your women, you stinkin' savage! You lay a hand on me—or anything else—and I'll find a way to cut it off! I swear I will! I'm not some—"

His derisive snort cut her off. "Why would I want a *pindah*—a white—for a woman? I have too many women already." He grunted at the sudden relief on Maxie's face.

"A man does not force a woman to spread her legs, or he will lose his luck. Better that you serve my wives as a slave. Maybe then they will not complain to me so much."

For the next three days Maxie learned the ins and outs of Apache slavery. She'd thought Elsa and Medina were harsh taskmasters, but they couldn't hold a candle to the two wives of her captor, whose name she learned was Noches.

The younger wife was tolerable. Her name was Running Woman, and she was still young enough to be given to fits of giggling. With a baby at her breast and a toddler hanging on to her skirts, she had little time for petty maliciousness against the new slave.

But the elder wife had time to spare to make Maxie's life miserable. She was called Cut-Nose Woman. Maxie knew the mutilation that made Cut-Nose so ugly was the Apache punishment for adultery. What the woman's real name was, Maxie didn't know. Whatever it was, though, it had to mean vicious.

Maxie's first night at the rancheria Cut-Nose Woman beat her with a mesquite switch for not being able to start a fire with the fire drill. While Noches and his family ate a meal of pronghorn antelope, roasted yucca, and sumac berries in honey, she ate nothing. She was tied to a post in the brush ramada that stood adjacent to the wickiup, there to spend a chilly night with nothing but the ground for a bed and her own arm for a pillow.

The second day Maxie learned from Running Woman how to repair the wickiup, which was nothing more than brush and skins laid over a dome-shaped frame of bent saplings. She successfully started a fire—Cut-Nose Woman's switch was a great inspiration to quick learning—made a stew of boiled wood rats, squirrel, and wild onions, skinned five rabbits, helped Running Woman grind parched piñon nuts into flour, and carried enough water to drown the entire camp, so it seemed. She ate a sparse meal of wood rat stew and mescal hearts, then collapsed in the cold ramada, tied to her post. She no longer cared that the ground was hard.

The third day Maxie determined to escape. If she waited any longer, she would be exhausted, starved, and—if Cut-Nose had her way—beaten to a useless, bloody pulp. Noches's senior wife slapped, pummeled, or switched her at the least offense. Maxie feared that if she didn't escape soon, she was going to lose her temper—and her sanity—and give the old witch a dose of her own abuse. No wonder Apaches were such mean devils if they had to ride home to wives like Cut-Nose.

At the end of the third day's labor—hauling wood and water, skinning a deer, chasing after Running Woman's toddler—Maxie was so exhausted she felt sick to her stomach. She didn't have the energy left to spit, much less make a run for freedom.

She waited until the moon had sunk from view and only faint starlight illuminated the night. The little clump of Apache wickiups was scarcely visible against the dark canyon wall. The only sound was the occasional stomping and whuffing of the ponies, which were hobbled to graze upon the sparse desert grass. Even the dogs were asleep, and the lookouts were posted too far down the canyon to see an insignificant slip of a slave sneak out of the village.

Getting loose from her bonds was no trouble. Her bed had sharp rocks aplenty, which Cut-Nose apparently thought Maxie too dull witted to use for cutting the rope. She stole past the wickiup on silent feet, debating if she should take a pony and call attention to herself, or brave the desert on foot. She had no supplies except a small skin of water and a few strips of jerky she had hidden under her skirt—not much if she couldn't find help within a couple of days. She wouldn't die of thirst; she knew the Apache trick of chewing the inner pulp of a barrel cactus for moisture. But she could well starve. Not a pleasant prospect, but, all things considered, starving was probably a better fate than staying with the Apaches.

Maxie hesitated for a moment, then decided that her only chance to escape undetected was to leave on foot. She bore to the right, out of the circle of wickiups and toward a clump of piñon pine that made a dark blotch against the canyon wall. She almost couldn't believe how easy the task had been. Once she reached the canyon wall she would follow it out onto the plain, and by sunup she should be well past the Apache lookouts. Old Cut-Nose would have to find someone else to abuse from now on.

"Where are you going, slave of Noches?"

Maxie nearly jumped out of her skin. The deep masculine voice was a disembodied whisper in the dark.

"Wha-what?"

As though he had materialized from the black nothingness of the night, a man appeared beside her. He was young, broad shouldered, and nearly naked. His only clothing was a breechclout that hung to his knees in front and nearly to his ankles in back. Deerhide boots covered his calves and were snugged just below the knee. Coarse black hair reached well past his shoulders and framed a face with hawkish features and black eyes that glittered even in the faint starlight.

Maxie had no trouble recognizing him. Choto, Running Woman had said his name was. He'd been staring at her for the past three days, even to the point where Noches's younger wife had remarked upon it.

A faint smile played around his thin-lipped mouth. Maxie hadn't known Apaches knew how to smile, but this was definitely a smile, even though it had an ominous tilt to it. "I think you are not supposed to be here, slave of Noches." He spoke slowly in his guttural tongue, pausing to make sure she understood.

"I . . . I came out to take a pee." Damn! Now she was in for it! Couldn't she think of a better lie than that? "Can't a body have any privacy around here?"

Choto reached for her wrist, which still wore the sawed loop of rope that had tied her to the ramada post. His face was close enough to Maxie's for her to see the upward tilt of a disbelieving brow.

"Uh . . ." She groped for an explanation, but her tongue wasn't nearly as facile in Apache as in English.

His hand closed more tightly around her wrist as he drew her toward him. "You should not try to escape, little slave. Soon you will be a slave no longer."

Maxie tried to draw away, but he pulled her closer still. His blatant arousal pressed insistently into her stomach. What had Noches told her? Forcing a female captive would make an Apache warrior lose his luck? Maybe Choto didn't care about his damned luck!

"Do not make noise, little slave, or Noches will know you are gone." His teeth—surprisingly strong and white—flashed in the darkness as he grinned. His hand groped between their bodies and curled into her crotch. She struggled, but she dared not struggle too fiercely for fear of waking the entire rancheria.

"Get your hand off me, you filthy low-down son of a snake."

Choto merely gave a low, good-natured chuckle. "No, little slave. I like it where my hand can feel your woman's parts. Soon I will buy you from Noches and make you my wife, and then I will mount you like the stallion mounts the mare. Feel my great rod, little slave. It is big like the rod of a stallion, and you will cry from joy when I spear you upon it. You will be glad you didn't escape."

"Horseshit!" Maxie whispered furiously. Forgetting the risk, she brought her knee up sharply toward that organ that gave him such pride.

He deflected the blow off his muscular thigh, then laughed and set her back from him. "You are not like other white women. It is good. You are strong. Your eyes flash with spirit."

"I'm not a damn white woman!" Maxie corrected. "I'm Mexican!"

"You have the eyes of the sky, and skin like pale honey.

You are a white woman, but brave and tough like Apache. You are a woman who is a fit mate for an Apache warrior." He grinned at her expression. She'd never seen an Apache so damned happy. "You growl and snap now, woman, but soon, when you are mine and I have you beneath me, you will howl and whine and pant like a bitch in heat. We will have good times. Now come. Noches must not discover you tried to escape or he will let his wife beat you until you die. Then you will be of no use to me."

"Let me go!" she demanded as he grasped her arm.

"Soon you will learn obedience," he said in a tolerant tone.

Choto fetched a rope from his own wickiup to retie her in Noches's ramada. She was back where she started, exhausted, discouraged, still a prisoner, and having missed a night's sleep in the bargain. Dammit! Where was Aaron Hunter when she needed him? He was the one who was so good at destroying people's homes. Why didn't he ride in, wreak havoc, and carry her off, as he'd done once before? Damn him!

By the time Choto left, reminding her once more of the merry romps they would have once she was his wife, the sky was paling in anticipation of dawn. Soon Running Woman would be out to awaken her to the drudgery and pain of another day. Maxie realized that Hunter didn't have a chance of finding her, even if he was trying, which she doubted. He'd probably said good riddance when he heard of her capture.

Her heart wrenched at the thought, and she scolded herself. She had enough troubles without thinking like some weak-kneed, pissant female and expecting a hero to come to her rescue. Hunter wasn't a hero. Even if he cared about her—which he didn't—no man was stupid enough to take on the Apaches for the sake of a woman. Even if he thought of her as a woman—which he also didn't.

She could do without Hunter. Cactus Maxie could manage fine on her own. These Apaches had bitten off more than they could chew when they'd taken her. She would show them that Harrison Maxwell's daughter was tougher, smarter, and just plain meaner than any Indian ever born.

Maxie lay down on the ground and hugged her knees to her chest. Tough, mean, and smart as she was, she couldn't prevent a little-girl-scared tear from dribbling down her cheek.

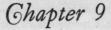

Chapter 9

"The girl's got grit," Pete Kelley admitted. "I'll give 'er that. Only female with as much grit is Medina, only Dina's a mite quieter about it."

Aaron looked up from where he squatted on the ground examining a track in the sand. "Takes more'n grit to survive the Apaches," he said darkly. "A lot more'n grit."

"Yep." Pete scratched the back of his neck, grimacing, then batted at the flies that buzzed around his horse's ears. "Takes a heap o' luck, an' the saints all bein' on your side. But if they rode off with her still alive, like Sam said, it figgers they'll either make 'er a slave or at least wait until some big celebration to kill her. Could be she's still alive."

"Could be." Aaron rose wearily and dusted his hands on his jeans. "The track's from an Indian pony, all right. Unshod. But it's the first track we've seen in half a mile, and there's enough Apaches with unshod ponies ridin' this country that it could be from any of 'em. Or if it is from the band that took Maxie, they could've gone up any one of these damned canyons."

His despairing glance swept the surrounding countryside

—jumbled mountains that hid a thousand canyons, rocky ground that an army could march across and leave no trace. Damn the Apaches! Why did they have to be so smart?

"We're not going to find her today, boy," Pete said. "It's time to turn back."

Pete's voice held a hint of sympathy. Just a hint, but enough to let Aaron know that Pete thought Maxie was dead. Everyone thought she was dead—or hoped she was, for Maxie's sake. Medina would grieve for a little while, and even tough old Pete might feel a pang or two, but for the most part those who had known the little imp would take the tragedy in stride. In Arizona Territory one expected to lose the people and things one loved to the Apaches, heat, snakes, and the god-awful killing desert. Pete knew that better than anyone. He'd been in the territory since before '48, when the United States had won the land from Mexico. Over the years he'd lost two ranches and a son to the Apaches and his first wife to the overpowering summer heat. Aaron himself had lost all he had—all he had ever dreamed of having—to the Apaches and to bandits. By now he should be accustomed to the bitter truth that this country, given half a chance, would take everything a man held dear.

But Maxie! Dear God! Why did it have to be her? The thought of little Maxie in the hands of the Apaches made him want to moan aloud. The different facets of her being kept flashing through his mind. A curly-headed ten-year old —or had she been nine?—who had a habit of falling into trouble like a pig falling into slop. A blue-eyed, hot-tempered outlaw lass whose fist had made mincemeat of his gut, not to mention the havoc her knee had wrought in other, more personal areas. An indignant Venus rising from the shallows of the Santa Cruz River. A confused and oddly vulnerable target for the malicious tongues of Motherlode's clacking hens. God! How sweet her warm lips had tasted. How right that little body had felt nestled close to his. And now . . . ?

"She's a tough little gal," Pete said, interrupting his thoughts. "If she's alive today, she'll likely be alive tomorrow, or next week. If not . . . I don't blame you for being sweet on 'er, boy, but don't let it carry away your reason."

Aaron glared as he swung up into the saddle. "I'm not sweet on her. You of all people know I don't need some gun-toting, draggletailed female from the other side of the law in my life, reminding me of my own past. Maxie is just a responsibility. I owe her."

But Aaron's voice cracked as he said Maxie's name, and he knew that he didn't for one minute fool Pete, who simply responded with a sympathetic nod.

As they turned their horses back toward Agua Linda, sunset was turning the western sky the color of blood.

Maxie set down her burden and paused a moment to gaze at the same vivid red sunset. Not that she was overly appreciative of the spectacular sight—she had long ago passed the point where she had the energy to appreciate anything other than sleep, but her arms felt as though they had been pulled right out of their sockets, and she needed an excuse to rest. If she had to haul many more skins of water from the stream, her knuckles were truly going to drag the ground.

Her partner in labor trudged up and followed Maxie's lead in letting her waterskins drop to the ground. A young girl with a pinched, angular face, she gave Maxie a tired smile.

"Tough day, huh?" Maxie asked. She knew she would get no answer. Loco never spoke to anyone. Not a word. Maxie had tried both Apache and English. Neither language roused the girl to give any response other than a nod or a smile.

"I hope these folks don't do this too often," she continued to her silent companion. "I don't think I could survive another one."

The rancheria had moved that day. Maxie had been roused from her dirt bed long before dawn to help with the packing. She had dismantled wickiups, bundled up food-stuffs and personal belongings for her two mistresses, helped obliterate the last traces of the camp from the old site, then hauled a pack of skins and wickiup poles to the new site, a ten-hour march away.

When they had arrived Noches's wives had given her no rest. She had helped erect a new wickiup, tying the bent saplings together with thongs of deerhide, then scouring the area for brush suitable to weave between the poles. Now she and Loco had to haul water for cooking, washing, and drinking—and the puny little spring that was the only source of water was a hundred yards down the canyon.

"I suppose we'd better get a move on," she sighed, "or ol' Cut-Nose'll take a switch to our hides—or my hide, at least."

Loco had worked beside Maxie all day long, and Maxie felt sorrier for the youngster than she felt for herself. The kid couldn't have been more than eleven or twelve years old, but she worked harder than any grown woman in the whole band. She was always assigned the most unpleasant of the women's tasks, which frequently paired her up with Maxie. The reason for the girl's treatment was no mystery, for the mass of hair bundled at her thin neck was dirty brown instead of black, clearly marking her as a white child. She didn't seem to be a prisoner, yet neither was she treated as a full-fledged member of the band. Maxie guessed the child had been formally adopted into the tribe, yet her light hair and speechlessness set her apart.

They dumped their waterskins into a large woven grass jug caulked inside and outside with pine gum, then trudged back to the stream for more. Maxie began to think that the damned jug was bottomless. She and Loco had made four trips already, and if the jug wasn't full after this one, then she was of a mind to take her waterskin and shove it down around Cut-Nose's ears. It would be an improvement to the woman's face.

A trickle of water flowed out of the cliff wall and carved a mossy path through the rocks. Maxie squatted beside it, sighing with weariness. The waterskin filled slowly—too slowly for Maxie's cramped and aching legs. It was less than half full when a voice took her by surprise.

"You come!" Running Woman seemed to have materialized from the air, the way only an Apache could. "Soon it is dark. Cut-Nose not want you away from wickiup when dark."

"And I suppose Cut-Nose is going to haul the rest of the water?" Maxie snorted.

Running Woman scowled, but Maxie paid no heed. For an Apache, Noches's younger wife was a real pussycat—which meant that when vexed she was more likely to give her hapless slave a whipping with words than with a mesquite switch. Maxie's command of the Apache language had improved to the point where she understood every word of the woman's vitriol.

"Close your flapping mouth, slave, or I will have my husband sharpen his knife on your bones. You do as I say."

Only one waterskin was full. The jug at camp would be shy several skinfuls. No water for washing tonight.

As Maxie tied the top flaps of the waterskin and hefted it over her shoulder, Running Woman gave her a sly smile. "Choto came to the wickiup of Noches this afternoon."

Maxie pretended unconcern, giving no reply. Choto was the young buck who had foiled her escape. Was he now reporting her misbehavior to Noches?

"He offered two good ponies for you," Running Woman continued. "He wants you for his second wife."

"He what?" Maxie gasped in alarm.

Running Woman smiled in satisfaction at Maxie's reaction. "Choto's first wife died from the white-man's-pox sickness. So he took her sister, as a good man should. But she is lazy, and ugly besides. Choto wants another wife to warm his bed at night. He wants you." She paused, smiling maliciously. "But my husband refused."

If Running Woman had hoped that Noches's refusal

would crush Maxie, she was sorely disappointed, for Maxie kept her face blank. But inside, panic was growing.

Who would've thought the horny redskin had been serious about marriage? She'd thought all that talk about her womanly virtues had simply been drivel to get her to romp with him. But if he really meant to make her some kind of squaw, she was really in a fix.

"You don't think Noches will give in, do you?" she asked Running Woman in an anxious voice.

Running Woman gave her a sideways, haughty look. "Noches will not allow you to become wife to Choto. He won you in battle and gave you to us, Cut-Nose and me. We will not let you go."

Maxie's sigh of relief drew a puzzled frown from both Loco and Running Woman. Noches wouldn't let her go. Good for ol' Noches. Good for Cut-Nose. Good for Running Woman.

When they arrived back at Noches's wickiup, the cookfire was already lit, tended by a sour-looking Cut-Nose. As Maxie walked by, Cut-Nose swatted at her with the glowing branch she was using to poke at the fire.

"Go get firewood," Noches's older wife ordered. Firewood had been gathered earlier for the whole rancheria and lay in a pile on the other side of the camp, 150 feet away. "Bring enough for the night," she added.

Maxie sighed. That would be five or six trips at least. Lordy, but she was tired.

Without being asked, Loco went with her.

"You don't have to help," Maxie told her. "You go back to your own wickiup and eat your dinner."

Loco merely smiled and shook her head. They walked together to the stash of wood, then started to pile a load on their arms. All the while Loco regarded Maxie with frank curiosity. Maxie knew exactly what she was thinking.

"What?" she asked sharply. "You think I should be jumpin' for joy because that big buck tried to buy me?" Maxie snorted. "I tell you, Loco, you and your redskin friends around here may think Choto is every girl's dream come true, but I don't fancy living out my life in some wickiup in the middle of the desert. I've got better things to do with my life."

Loco shook her head in disbelief as they carried the first load back to Cut-Nose's fire. Maxie barely avoided a poke with a hot stick as Cut-Nose urged greater speed.

"All right," Maxie continued as they walked back to the woodpile. "He may be a good-lookin' hombre—for an Apache. And I suppose he's a decent sort. He could've gotten me in a heap of trouble by tellin' Noches about my little stroll in the dark. But to tell the truth, kid, I've been staked out by another man, and I ain't allowin' no claim jumpin'."

She rambled on, telling her silent companion about Hunter—how she had saved his life when she was only ten, and how he had dragged her from her home eight years later. She paused in her story every time their wood hauling task brought them in range of Cut-Nose's sharp ears, then resumed as they once again walked toward the woodpile. The tale grew in the telling.

"He only meant to help me," Maxie explained to Loco. "Hunter's crazy about me. Even if I hadn't helped him shoot his way out of that mine robbery when I was just a kid, he'd still be crazy for me."

Maxie didn't think glorifying her role would hurt anything. Loco seemed mightily entertained.

"Last time I saw him was at a social—you know, a dance." Her voice lowered to a confidential whisper as they both loaded their arms with wood. "He kissed me like kissin' was goin' outta style—told me how much he loves me and how every other woman looks like a wilted flower compared to me. He uses fancy language like that."

Encouraged by Loco's smile, Maxie continued. "Hunter's got shoulders much broader than Choto's," she claimed happily. "He's much handsomer, and he's so fast with a gun that he's become a real important war chief."

Maxie didn't know if small-town marshal was equivalent

to a war chief, but she decided the title would have to do. Loco looked impressed, at least.

"We're gonna get married. Hunter's gonna build me a house near the river, where we can graze cattle and raise hogs—just like Iron Pete . . . uh . . . Thunderface. Hunter won't let anything happen to me. Those Apaches will be lucky if he doesn't ride in here and corral every one of 'em, just like he did at Stronghold."

She paused, frowning. "Actually, Hunter can be a real arrogant stick-in-the-mud at times, but I can put up with that. Leading the straight life is worth it if I'm living with him."

As they struggled back toward the fire with their loads of wood, Maxie realized just what it was she had said. With a feeling that the world was somehow sinking beneath her feet, she realized that she wasn't entirely spinning a tall tale. Contained in her ridiculous yarn were hopes that had suddenly become crystal clear. Dreams that she hadn't even admitted to herself resolved into sharp focus. As Maxie told Loco that the straight life was worth living if having Hunter was the reward, she found herself believing that the words were true. Though such a thing was impossible, of course.

The discovery of such foolish dreams deep inside of her was upsetting, and just a little frightening. It also renewed her determination to escape from the Apaches, just so she could strut back into Motherlode and show Aaron Hunter how much she didn't care that he hadn't tried to rescue her.

The pile of wood at Noches's wickiup had grown to at least two nights' worth of dry mesquite when Running Woman stopped them. "Go to bed," she commanded. "You talk more than you work. Maybe when the sun is in the sky you will work more and not chatter like a squirrel." She put a dried piece of unleavened bread—made from the flour of piñon nuts—into Maxie's hand. The tasteless bread was to be her only dinner, Maxie assumed. Damned if these people weren't determined to starve her. Soon she would be so skinny that Cut-Nose wouldn't be able to find her with that switch of hers.

The brush ramada that was to be built beside the wickiup —Maxie's usual sleeping quarters—was not yet erected, so Maxie was allowed to sleep in the wickiup itself—hardly an improvement over the ramada. After fifteen minutes of fidgeting Maxie abandoned hope of finding a position that was comfortable. The ground was every bit as hard here as it had been at the old campsite, and in addition she had to listen to the rustlings of three other bodies who were also trying to get comfortable. At least they had piñon branches, skins, and furs to soften their beds. Maxie felt as though she were resting on hard-baked brick.

She tossed for a few minutes, waiting for exhaustion to claim her. But sleep wouldn't come, and her mind busied itself with thoughts that could exist only in that hazy area between slumber and wakefulness.

So Choto really wanted her for a wife. What a strange feeling that notion gave her. Not that the idea didn't properly horrify her. It did. But no man had ever really wanted her before. The men at Stronghold had tried to corral her every now and then—until they'd found out that she could outgun and outfight them when she got riled, but those scum bags would jump atop a dead sow if they thought it might still be alive. And Hunter—had he really wanted her when he kissed her? With his abrupt shift of moods and all that cussing, he'd seemed as confused as she when he left. Maxie couldn't guess what Hunter really wanted of her, if he wanted anything at all, and thinking on the subject just muddled her mind even more.

But Choto wasn't at all confused, or confusing. Among the Apache women he was considered a good catch. He was young, strong, good-looking, and, by Apache standards, an honorable, well-thought-of warrior. He thought she was attractive. He didn't think she was a draggletailed kid who was too skinny, or too freckled, or too homely to crawl into bed with—not as a lark, but night after night after night.

Choto saw her as a woman. The thought was encouraging. Or at least it would have been had Maxie not been rotting away in a filthy Apache rancheria. Maybe, just maybe, Hunter had seen her as a woman as well.

Maxie's half-conscious meanderings were cut off by a rustling on the other side of the wickiup where Running Woman had made her bed. Then came a deep-voiced command followed by Running Woman's giggle. The titter had to come from Running Woman. Cut-Nose could never make such a lighthearted, frivolous, downright seductive sound. Soon came a thrashing, a loud sucking sound, and the thud of something—perhaps an elbow or knee or foot—hitting the wall of the wickiup, all accompanied by Cut-Nose's snores rising and falling in discordant harmony.

Maxie lay silently and listened. Fascinated, she couldn't help herself. The flounderings and giggles were soon followed by a rhythmic rustling punctuated by occasional feminine moans and masculine grunts—the sounds of desire, Maxie realized. Noches was mounting his younger wife. And she was apparently enjoying every moment of the chore. The rhythmic rattling of the branches under Running Woman's bed accelerated suddenly. A series of sharp grunts from Noches ended in a fierce growl. Running Woman moaned—a long, low whisper of sound that reminded Maxie of someone sighing in relief after having squatted behind a bush.

Disgusting. The whole thing was disgusting, Maxie tried to convince herself. A man and woman rutting were reduced to the level of animals—moaning and grunting, sucking at each other, panting and gurgling as they flopped around like two fish stranded on dry land. She didn't want to try it, Maxie decided—not ever, no matter how much fun Hilda had said it was. And she certainly wasn't going to marry some Apache buck and let him grunt over her like a boar slobbering over a sow. She'd rather be a slave to ol' Cut-Nose than wife to Choto, no matter how handsome he was or how many muscles rippled under that copper skin whenever he moved. Better still, she'd rather escape.

Sooner or later her captors would grow overconfident. The moment would come when no one had an eye turned her way, and then she would take her chance. Giving up was not in Maxie's nature. She would escape. Once back with her family the weals on her skin would heal, her stomach would forget about starvation, and Cut-Nose, Noches, Running Woman, and Choto would fade from her memory. And Aaron Hunter? Maxie wrinkled her nose. If she were smart, she would forget Aaron Hunter completely.

With that thought giving her some comfort, Maxie finally drifted off to sleep. But the sounds of mating from across the wickiup had burned a path in her mind, and erotic images marched through her dreams. She saw Choto claiming her as his wife, carrying her to a wickiup on the banks of the Santa Cruz River. But when he laid her on their marriage bed and crouched over her, suddenly the man was no longer Choto. Aaron Hunter stood in his place and looked down upon her as though he were gazing at a feast laid out for his pleasure.

The dream changed in a flash. Maxie was naked, rising from the rippling waters of the Santa Cruz. Hunter strode toward her, his face intent with purpose. He stopped in front of her, and in her dream Maxie could feel her breathing quicken, her heart pound. He reached out and traced the path of a rivulet of water that ran from her sodden hair, down her shoulder, between her breasts, arrow-straight toward her navel . . . and farther still. Like a wanton she arched toward him. She could see his smile, see the fire in his eyes.

Suddenly they were in the wickiup again. She lay waiting for him, feeling as though she would die if he didn't touch her. Hunter took off his gun belt, unfastened his belt, reached for the buttons of his trousers . . .

And then she woke; the dream slipped from her grasp like fog melting in the morning sun. For a moment Maxie lay breathless, wondering at the feelings that were still washing through her. Hunter's image was so clear in her mind, she could still feel the hot trail of the finger that had burned a path over her skin. Hard to believe it had all been a dream . . . a dream of Aaron Hunter, who was probably sniffing around Cynthia Pruitt while Cactus Maxie rotted away in an Apache wickiup, who had probably not lifted a finger to find her, who had probably even laughed when he learned of her fate. She could almost hear his words: "Little draggletailed hell-raiser landed right where she belongs."

The uncomfortable, frustrating, absolutely fascinating feelings inspired by the dream faded as Maxie's anger grew. In a few moments she could scarcely remember what she had dreamed about, except that Hunter and she had been involved in a clench that would have made Hilda blush. Stupid, weak-kneed, pissant dream! What kind of a fool was she to let herself dream about such trash? And right after deciding Aaron Hunter was a memory that was going to fade right down to nothing! She didn't sleep the rest of the night. Her fear of more dreams was stronger than her exhaustion.

Before Noches and his wives awoke, a woozy and sour-tempered Maxie stumbled out of the wickiup to build the cookfire. The morning was still just a pale streak of light behind the mountains to the east, but unless the fire was burning well before Cut-Nose arose, an unlucky slave was likely to get a stick across her back.

Moving automatically, she used the fire drill to catch a spark to dry tinder—someone had forgotten to bank the fire the night before. When the fire was burning steadily, she checked the supply of firewood—plenty left after her many treks to and from the community pile last night. But the water jug was low. Without Loco's help, the jug would take at least three trips to fill. Maxie had spied some soapweed growing by the spring. If Cut-Nose wasn't out and about by the time the jug was filled, perhaps she could take a few minutes to bathe and wash her hair. Washing was a luxury she had come to appreciate.

Maxie did not get a chance to take her bath. She made three trips back and forth to the stream with the waterskins, and when she returned from the last trip Cut-Nose was bustling around the fire making a great show of preparing the morning meal, giving Running Woman the edge of her tongue every few moments, and once even swatting at little Crip-Chee—Running Woman's daughter—when the awkward toddler got in her way. The swat, of course, brought on an attack of maternal wrath from Running Woman that threatened to escalate into physical blows.

As usual, Noches sat in the sparse shade of a bush repairing a war club and ignoring the bickering. He had a long-suffering look on his face that made Maxie suspect the middle-aged warrior would rather face the massed strength of the U.S. Cavalry than try to break up the mayhem between his wives.

Neither did he turn an eyelash when his older wife rounded on Maxie as she walked up to the wickiup with the full waterskins. Cut-Nose spit out a question in guttural Apache. When Maxie only looked belligerent, the Apache woman eyed her with angry contempt. She repeated the question with more force.

"Where have you been, daughter of laziness? Why am I forced to do your work, troublesome *pindah* slut?"

Maxie's lips tightened. What a load of trash. After Maxie's first attempt at cooking Apache style, Noches's older wife had forbidden her to touch any food but her own, no doubt convinced that her new slave was determined to poison them all. Now she was looking for an excuse to take out her temper on someone who couldn't fight back. Maxie was in no mood to put up with the Apache woman's viciousness this morning.

"You do not allow me to prepare the food. I was merely fetching water." Her tone was not as reasonable as her

words. She, also, was spoiling for a fight. Cactus Maxie had
reached the end of her stretched-thin patience.

Cut-Nose advanced, brandishing the stick that had lately
been prodding wood rats roasting over the fire. "Do not
give me your excuses, troublesome snake of a slave! You will
have no food on this day for your words, and if you do not do
as I say, I will tie you out for the sun to bake and the ants to
eat." Her voice rose to a screech that earned even her
husband's attention. Running Woman grabbed her little
daughter and sought shelter in the wickiup. "Go and dig the
holes for the frame of Running Woman's wickiup!" Cut-
Nose shouted. "Now!"

Maxie threw her tormentor a resentful glance and slowly
went to where the sapling poles for the second wickiup had
been piled. She had had no supper the night before after a
whole day's walking, and now she was to be denied breakfast as well. Cut-Nose was determined to kill her by slow
starvation.

"Go now, daughter of trouble! Not tomorrow!" Cut-Nose,
not satisfied with the speed of Maxie's obedience, gave her a
hefty push followed by a kick.

Maxie could almost hear her patience snap, like a string
pulled too tightly. She turned with a snarl. "Daughter of
trouble, you call me? Lady, you haven't seen trouble yet!"
She lunged, fingers curled into claws.

Taken by surprise, Cut-Nose stepped back and stumbled
to the ground. In the blink of an eye Maxie was atop her,
pounding her head against the hard-packed dirt. The
Apache woman let loose a howl of fury and pain, heaved up,
and managed to topple Maxie from her perch. She began to
use her stick to good advantage, aiming at any part of Maxie
that was within her reach.

"I'll show you trouble, you old witch!" Maxie promised,
springing to her feet and dancing out of the stick's reach.
Then with lightning swiftness, fighting like the scrappy ten-
year-old ruffian she had never quite outgrown, she dodged
under the flailing weapon and plowed her head into Cut-

Nose's none-too-firm middle. With a loud "Oof!" the Indian woman landed once again on her ample backside. Maxie dived upon her, and the two of them tumbled around in the dirt, kicking, scratching, pulling hair, biting. Other members of the band drifted over to watch the entertainment. They nodded approval, shouted encouragement, and once or twice had to hop out of the way as the flailing dust devil tumbled in their direction.

Noches sat calmly where he was, his war club set aside for the moment as he watched with casual interest. The spark in his black eyes showed more amused approval than anger. He seemed perfectly content to let his wife and her slave settle the matter between themselves—until Running Woman emerged from the wickiup and skewered him with a disapproving stare. Reluctantly he picked up the repaired war club, hefted it in his hand, unfolded himself from his seat on the ground, and strolled over to where the women were locked in a shrieking ball of arms, legs, and dirt. He considered a moment, then raised the war club above his head. But before the club could descend with deadly force, a masculine voice called out.

"Noches! Do not! Five ponies I will give you for the slave."

Five ponies was a handsome price. Noches lowered the club slowly to his side and looked around at Choto. He pointed to the women, who had slowed to occasional blows and hostile scowls.

"Neither one of them is worth five good ponies. But if the ponies are tied to that bush tomorrow morning, then you may have the slave." Noches shook his head and chuckled. "For five good ponies you may have them both."

Cut-Nose shrieked the Apache version of a cussword. Maxie sank down into the dirt, panting, her head drooping so low it almost touched the ground.

Then a new voice spoke, in English.

"Mornin', Noches," the voice said in a very un-Apache drawl. "I think we can give you a more interestin' bid."

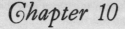

Chapter 10

"You want me to do what?" Maxie cried.

"Come on, Max. It ain't that much."

Maxie leaned forward and let her head rest on her horse's mane. She was so very tired. "You're all crazier than horses grazing on locoweed. Aaron Hunter doesn't give a rat's-ass damn about me."

The words hurt, but she figured they were true. At first, when she'd heard the white man's voice interrupt Noches and Choto, she'd imagined wildly that Hunter had come to rescue her, that he'd somehow bluffed his way into Noches's rancheria, that she had her hero after all.

But her hero had turned out to be her brothers—all three of them. Her sharp disappointment had been due to exhaustion, she'd convinced herself. She truly was happy that her brothers had ridden into that camp instead of Hunter. Truly she was. Though she was still a bit confused about how they'd done it. Blackjack had mumbled some explanation about doing business with Noches before, though what possible dealings her brothers might have with the Apaches Maxie couldn't imagine. She was too tired to think about it.

"Is that why you got me outta there?" Maxie demanded. "Because you think Aaron Hunter's sweet on me and I can lead him into a damned trap?"

"Hell no, Max! You're our sister." Blackjack's look of brotherly concern was not entirely convincing. "I handed over ten good ponies to get you outta that place, and two more for her."

Maxie felt Loco's arms tighten spasmodically around her waist. The girl seemed scared to death of Blackjack for some reason, and the tone of that comment didn't help. Maxie had persuaded Blackjack to take Loco with them, but he hadn't been real happy about it.

"Shit!" he continued in the same tone. "I thought you'd jump at the chance. After what he done to us—and to you."

What had Hunter done to her to make her feel this way about her brothers? She didn't remember them being this loud, or this coarse. Had Dirty Jim's face always had that sullen look, as though he were mad at the entire world?

"It's a stupid plan," she insisted. "Hunter ain't sweet on me. He thinks I'm a draggletailed ragamuffin. That's what he said."

"For a man who thinks you're a draggletail, he's sure been goin' to a lot of trouble to find ya," Blackjack told her, his eyes on her face.

Maxie's heart skipped a beat. "He what?"

"He's been ridin' out near every day, and it ain't no secret that he's lookin' for you. Folks around here are beginnin' to think he's touched in the head."

Hunter had been looking for her? Unaccountably, one of the clouds that darkened her mood lifted. "How would you know?" She raised a skeptical brow.

"We got our ways," Jim bragged. " 'Course, if he'd a' found you, Noches and his buddies woulda lifted his scalp."

"Cain't say that woulda broke my heart," Tom said with a chuckle.

"Only reason I know for a man to act so damned foolish is that he's sweet on some woman," Blackjack told her.

"Well, Hunter's not sweet on me. He's sweet on Cynthia Pruitt, the storekeeper's daughter."

"Old man Pruitt's girl? Don't blame him much for that. Her daddy's got a load of cash hidden away in his safe. Wish I knew of some way to break into that store of his."

The idea of Pruitt's being robbed by her brothers didn't sit well on Maxie's fledgling conscience. Mr. Pruitt had been right nice to her when she was in Motherlode. And even Cynthia wasn't as snooty as Maxie had first believed.

"Anyway, Hunter feels about me the same way I feel about him. He's a dirty stinkin' skunk."

Blackjack chuckled—not a particularly pleasant sound. "Don't think so, little sis. Cynthia or no Cynthia, I think our friend Hunter's got a case of the hots for the littlest Maxwell."

Maxie didn't care for the way her brother had phrased that statement, nor for the way Tom laughed and Dirty Jim just looked disgusted.

"Yeah!" Tom enthusiastically agreed. "Just how 'bout that! Motherlode's hotshot marshal's pinin' after our little sis!"

"Oh, just shut up!" Maxie snapped.

Blackjack spat into the sand. "I can see you been with these posy-pickin' do-gooders too long, sis. You gotta learn not to be so squeamish, 'specially seein' that the family needs your help."

"What're you talkin' about?"

"I'm talkin' about Hunter, Max. He's been givin' us a load of trouble. It's gettin' so a hardworkin' bandit cain't make a livin' anymore without Hunter hangin' on his trail like some damned cocklebur."

Maxie snorted. "One single man can't be so much of a bother." Though she did remember Medina's story about the ambush where Hunter had bested all three of them. But that story had to be an exaggeration. Hunter might have gotten away in one piece, but nobody bested her brothers. "He got lucky at Stronghold," she insisted. "Most of the lazy slobs there wouldn't have been caught if they'd kept half an eye out and used their brains."

Blackjack shook his head. "Hunter's good. He's too damned good. The man needs takin' down a peg or two . . ."

Maxie wondered uncomfortably how far down a "peg or two" was.

". . . and now I think I know just the way we can do it."

As he looked over at her, Maxie felt her stomach tie itself into a painful knot.

Four hours later as they rode out of the hills above the old mission at Tumacacori, the knot was still there. Her brothers' plan was about as underhanded as anything she had ever heard. They wanted her to make eyes at Hunter, and then leave the rest of the work to them. They would set the trap. Maxie would be the bait.

Not that before this very moment she'd had any objections to being underhanded. Whatever it took to get a job done—her pa always said, and Maxie had grown up thinking that underhandedness was right up there with a fast gun and a glib tongue as a necessity for survival in this world.

Of course, Hunter wouldn't fall for such a stupid scheme. He would sooner snuggle up to a scorpion than to Cactus Maxie Maxwell. And he certainly wasn't stupid enough to walk into some trap while sniffing after a woman—especially her.

But for every one of her objections to their scheme her brothers had pulled out the old "Maxwells always stick together" line—as if the horses' asses had stuck by her at Stronghold! How was warming up to Hunter going to hurt her? Blackjack had cajoled. Hunter was slime, sure, and he understood her reluctance, but there were a lot of dirty jobs a body had to do to get ahead in this world. The Maxwells couldn't rest easy until Hunter was persuaded to leave them alone, and Maxie had just the tools they needed to maneuver the snake into a trap where he could be taught a lesson.

"What's Pa think about all this?" Maxie asked sullenly.

Her brothers exchanged uneasy glances. "Pa don't think nothin' about it," Blackjack finally said. "He hightailed it down south right after Stronghold got busted. But he'd want you to help, Max. You know how he feels about everyone pullin' their share."

"Sure he would," she said with a grimace.

The sun was sinking behind the hills to the west when they spotted a lone figure on horseback riding toward the ruins at Tumacacori.

"That's him!" Dirty Jim declared. "I know that roan stud horse he rides! That's Hunter!"

Maxie's heart jumped into her throat. She too had recognized Hunter's mount—and more than that. The easy way he rode the saddle, the way he seemed to flow with the horse—all that was unmistakably Hunter.

"So it is." Blackjack motioned them to stop. "A piece of luck."

"Let's get 'im," Tom growled.

Blackjack held up a restraining hand. "We'll never hit 'im at this distance, and he'll likely outrun us on that damned fast horse of his. We can wait until the odds are a little more in our favor." He turned to Maxie. "Here's your chance, little sis. He can't see us here in the hill shadows. Why don't you just ride out and let our friend there think he's rescued you."

"What am I supposed to tell him?"

"You'll think of something. Wasn't you always saying that you're the best damned liar west of St. Louis?"

One more try. Lordy, but she didn't want to do this. "Blackjack, he's not sweet on me. Honest. This isn't going to work."

"You gotta lot to learn about men, Max. If he's not sweet on you now, girl, it should be easy enough to make him that way. You got the equipment, even if you don't know how to use it yet. Climb into bed with him a few times and he'll be eatin' outta your hand just like that mean stud horse you broke when you was a kid. Ain't no harder than that."

Climb into bed with him? Is that what Blackjack meant by making eyes at a man?

"I can't do that, Jack! Really I can't. This ain't gonna work!"

"You just do your part, honey, and we'll do ours. You're a Maxwell just like the rest of us. And we all gotta pull a part of the load."

Maxie closed her eyes. Was this a nightmare? Were these the same brothers she had grown up with? Had they changed, or had she?

"Get down there, Max."

Blackjack's voice sounded implacable. Without a word of good-bye, Maxie kneed her horse into a walk, then a jog trot, Loco clinging on behind. She rode out into the fading sunlight, then looked back. Blackjack was right. Her brothers were well hidden in the hill shadows. But Hunter had spotted her and was galloping her way.

If her brothers thought Cactus Maxie was going to be bait for a trap—like some kind of whore—then they were stupider than she'd thought.

Damn it all, but life was a pit! Maxie wondered if she could ever go back to riding with her brothers. She wondered if she wanted to.

"Maxie! My God! Maxie!" Hunter grabbed Maxie by the upper arms—gingerly, as though he half expected the girl before him to be a hallucination. "You're here! Alive! In one piece!"

Maxie's smile wavered. While riding toward him, something had built up inside her—a tightness in her chest, a shortness of breath, a strange fluttering of her heart. When she slid from her horse, her knees had scarcely held her. But Hunter had grabbed her and kept her from falling. Now, held in his strong grip, looking at the dark swell of feeling in his eyes, Maxie began to shiver. Her eyes burned from the pressure of unshed tears.

"Hunter." The word was a hoarse whisper. She couldn't force any other sound through her tightening throat.

"Maxie. God, Maxie."

As her features twisted in the prelude to tears, he pulled her close against him. Willingly she buried her face in his broad chest and let the tears flow. The constant fear, the starvation, the beatings, the exhaustion, her father's desertion, her brothers' callousness—it all came together in choking, weeping, blubbering misery.

Hunter released the death grip he had on her shoulders and gently encircled her trembling body with his arms. For some reason that simple gesture inspired a new round of hysterical weeping. Ridiculously, she felt safe with his strong arms around her, protected, as if he were shutting out all the cruelties, all the doubts, all the fear that assaulted her world. Ridiculous, childish, foolish feeling. But she couldn't help herself.

Hunter's mouth moved against her hair, and his warm breath sent a peculiar chill crawling down her spine. "Maxie. I thought I'd never find you, and here you are riding out of the hills as if you were out for an afternoon jaunt."

Her weeping slowed to intermittent sobs and sniffles as Hunter gently pried her away from his now saturated shirt front. "Maxie girl, how did you escape?"

"I . . . I don't want to talk about it." A new gush of tears poured down her cheeks. "I c-c-can't."

"Okay. Okay. Easy now." He eased her back within the circle of his arms as a fit of weeping once again shook her all-too-thin body. "Are the Apaches following you?"

She shook her head and felt some of the coiled-spring tension go out of his body. What a fool she was making of herself! But she couldn't seem to stop. Forever wouldn't be too long to stay here plastered up against him, his heartbeat drumming in her ear, the hard swell of his chest like bands of warm steel beneath her hands. The contrast between Aaron Hunter and her brothers was . . .

No! She wouldn't think that way. She couldn't! Her brothers were family, all the family she had left. Dirty Jim was her twin, for Chrissakes—the other half of her! How could she even for a split second compare them to the enemy and find them wanting? She was a traitor. She didn't deserve to be a Maxwell.

But still, she didn't pull away.

"Could you maybe introduce . . . uh . . . your friend, Maxie?"

Her friend? She'd forgotten all about poor Loco! Reluctantly she extricated herself from Hunter's embrace and wiped her eyes on the sleeve of her deerskin shirt, which was a hand-me-down from Running Woman. The gesture only smeared more dirt across her cheeks. Loco, still perched behind the empty saddle on Maxie's mount, gripped the saddle cantle with white-knuckled fingers and stared at them through huge eyes only half-visible behind a veil of dirty, tangled hair. The poor kid was terrified, and here Maxie had been blubbering away thinking only of her own misery.

"This is Loco. She came with me."

"So I see."

Now that Hunter's gaze was turned upon her, Loco cringed. She looked undecided whether to slip backward off the horse's rump and hide or to stay where she was and shrivel into a little ball of terror.

"It's okay, Loco," Maxie said in a gentle tone, then turned to Hunter to explain. "She was living with the Apache band —adopted, I guess, 'cause she ain't . . . isn't . . . Apache." Peculiar how sounding like a civilized lady suddenly seemed important. "Those Apaches were mean to her, Hunter. She wanted to come with me, and I couldn't leave her behind."

"I'm sure Medina will be glad to take her under a wing. Maybe we can find her family, if she has one."

Medina. Agua Linda. Of course he would take her back. What had she expected?

She felt his eyes upon her, eyes that were entirely too penetrating. "Pete and Medina are going to be awfully glad to see you alive, kid."

Almost as if he could read her mind, damn him! She looked down, embarrassed. "I'll be glad to see them, too." The words were true, she realized. She would be glad to see Medina and Iron Pete, and Elsa, Maria, Catalina, Sam, Duffy, and Ramon as well. Not to mention Jake the dog. But not tonight. The sun had already sunk below the horizon, and traveling in the desert at night was for lizards and snakes, not for people and horses.

They made the night's camp at the old Spanish mission at Tumacacori. Maxie had explored the ruins several times before, as the abandoned mission was one of her family's favorite places to hide rustled cattle temporarily. Behind the big church was an adobe-walled courtyard that had plenty of room for ten or twenty cattle to be hidden in perfect safety, and the church itself was still tight enough to afford good shelter not only from the elements but also from marauding Indians. Sitting on the open valley floor, the mission was safe from sneak attack by even the wiliest of marauders.

But Indians and whites seldom intruded on the mission's privacy these days. It had once been a thriving community built by the Spanish priests for the mostly peaceful Pima Indians. But both Indians and missionaries had abandoned it years ago because of the Apache terror. Now the church, the courtyards, the long, low barrackslike adobe buildings that had been the priests' offices and dormitory were falling into disrepair. The orchards that had been lovingly planted still bore fruit, but more and more as the years passed the neat rows of cultivated trees were taken over by wild grasses and scrubby mesquite.

By the time Hunter, Maxie, and Loco arrived at the ruins and made camp in the sheltered courtyard behind the

church, night had fallen. Not enough light remained to
scavenge the orchards for fruit, as Maxie and her brothers
had frequently done, or to bring down a rabbit or ground
squirrel for fresh meat. But Maxie and Loco both chewed
with great enthusiasm on the jerky and hard, dry biscuits
that Aaron had brought with him in his saddlebags.

Aaron squatted by the fire and stared across the flames to
where Maxie sat on a block of adobe that had crumbled
from the courtyard wall. No wonder she ate with such relish, he thought. Her cheeks were hollow, and her collar-
bone was a stark bony ridge that ran from one too sharp
shoulder to the other. The damned savages must have
starved her. Were the shadows on her face and arms hollows
brought on by lack of food, or were they bruises?

Of course, she was damned lucky that she was alive and in
one piece. By Apache standards, she had probably been
treated well. All the time Maxie had been gone Aaron had
been haunted by visions of her subjected to Apache torture
—stuck full of arrows, all carefully placed in nonlethal spots
to prolong the sport, stripped of her skin piece by piece,
burned and gouged and flayed, then left for the insects and
scavengers to finish off. The visions had driven him to ride
out day after day, even after hope was gone. Simon had
tended the marshal's duties in Motherlode as Aaron had all
but deserted his post. The folks thereabouts had thought
him sunstruck, Aaron suspected. But he hadn't cared. He'd
cared only about getting Maxie away from the Apaches—or
confirming that she was dead and beyond earthly pain, so
his mind could be at peace.

Aaron had seen enough death and experienced enough
loss since returning to Arizona after the war. That war—the
killing, the brutality, the senseless, seemingly endless blood-
letting—had wiped the wild streak right out of him. All he'd
wanted when he returned was to live and let live—in peace.
He bought land for a ranch. He dreamed of Julia, whom
he'd met back East—the angel who'd consented to marry
him. He had his entire future neatly mapped out.

Hunter thought he should be used to loss by now. His ranch had been burned by the Apaches. Then Julia had been murdered by bandits. Poor, sweet Julia. She had braved the difficult journey by ship from New York to San Francisco, then boarded another ship that sailed down the western coast of Baja California and up the Gulf of California. Finally she endured the hot and miserable steamboat passage up the Colorado River to Yuma, and there had bought passage on a train of freight wagons leaving for Tucson, where they would have been married. All that, Julia had endured for him. Because she loved him. And he had loved her. But he hadn't been able to save her when bandits riding up from Mexico robbed the freight train, taking her along with every other item of value on the train. He hadn't been able to save her, or to find and punish her murderers.

After long months, the agony of losing Julia had faded into a gnawing ache in the back of his mind. Aaron had figured the heart had been burned right out of him. He never expected to care so much about anything ever again —until Pete Kelley told him that Maxie had been taken alive by the Apaches.

Now, watching her sitting in the glow of the fire, stuffing herself with his jerky and encouraging her little scruff bag friend to do the same, Aaron almost felt giddy with relief. Who would have thought that losing her would shake him so, and finding her would lift a ton of weight from his shoulders?

His eyes followed Maxie as she got up and helped herself to one of the blankets tied to the back of his saddle—not for herself, but to wrap around Loco as she settled the frightened little refugee in a tree-guarded corner of the courtyard away from the light of the fire. When Maxie bent over the child, the firelight highlighted her trim little buttocks, which were displayed all too well by the too small rawhide skirt she wore. Those Indian garments of hers were going to have to go, Aaron mused. When she was in the saddle, the skirt rode up her legs, and whenever she moved, some interesting part of her anatomy was displayed to catch his eye. God knew the girl had gotten thin and bony, but she sure hadn't lost her female shape, more's the pity. If she had, maybe he wouldn't have been squirming in his pants during the entire ride to Tumacacori.

Maxie came back and sat across the fire from him. Her eyes skittered away from his when their gazes met. Damn! Was the need for her that plain—that frightening? Embarrassed, and annoyed at being embarrassed, he stared down into his coffee, swirling the dark liquid in his tin cup as though it held a particular fascination for him.

He was an idiot, and he'd been acting like an idiot ever since he'd dragged the girl kicking and screaming out of that rathole she'd called home. Since then she'd preyed on his mind, her image tagging along on the back of his every thought like some powerful curse set on him by an Apache *di-yin*. Somehow he had to bring himself to his senses. Maxie wasn't for him. He shouldn't want her, and certainly didn't need her complicating his life, in spite of his wayward lust. Pure and simple, lust was what plagued him, what was making him burn right now. Lust.

"I'm going to sleep," Maxie said.

Aaron looked up. Maxie was looking at him with a peculiar expression on her face. What was she thinking? "Take the other blanket," was all he said.

"I don't need it."

"Take it. You don't have enough meat on your bones to keep out the cold."

She looked offended. "Don't need it." Without another word, she turned and walked from the firelight.

Aaron listened to the rustling of her settling down next to the courtyard wall. Damned stubborn girl. Didn't have a lick of sense, or femininity, either. Women were supposed to accept help and comfort from a man. She hadn't hesitated to appropriate one of his blankets for her little tag-along, but she was too damned proud to accept help for herself.

The good, healthy anger that he was managing to build was snuffed instantly when he detected the sound of sobbing. She was at it again, weeping her heart out, poor kid. What kind of nightmare had her life been these past days?

Without even thinking he untied the second blanket from his saddle and went to comfort her. He knew it was a mistake, knew he was asking for more trouble than he could handle. But where Cactus Maxie was concerned, he admitted to himself, he didn't have the sense God gave a chipmunk.

Chapter 11

"Maxie. Don't cry, girl. You're safe now. Safe."

She seemed startled by his voice. When she turned to look at him, the distant glow from the fire glistened on wet tracks of tears that streaked her cheeks.

"Are you afraid of Apaches, kid? You oughta know they don't go ridin' around at night. At least not without a better reason than tracking down one puny little prisoner. Besides, this place is so wide open we could hear someone coming for miles. No one's going to jump us here."

She looked embarrassed, almost vulnerable. Perhaps little Cactus Maxie was not quite as tough as she wanted everyone to think. With awkward gentleness, he shook out the blanket and covered her. She was shivering, even though the night was warm.

"Come here, Maxie." Aaron pulled her with him against the wall and gathered her in his arms. "There's nobody here to see, and you don't need to put on your hard-as-nails act for me. We know each other too well for that, girl."

Maxie burrowed against him like a small forlorn kitten seeking warmth. His body reacted in a predictable fashion.

A jolt traveled from his groin clear up to his heart. Aaron ignored it, telling himself that as always, he was under control.

"You'll be back at Agua Linda before dinnertime—hell, before the sun's well up if that's what you want." What did a man say to a young girl who'd just spent two weeks as an Apache prisoner? What had those devils done to turn his cocky, know-it-all Cactus Maxie into this sad little teary-eyed creature? He remembered the one other occasion he'd seen her cry—many years ago when that son of a bitch Maxwell had laughed at her being thrown from a horse she was trying to break—a feisty unbroke colt her brothers had stolen from one of the wealthy Mexican rancheros near Cananea. Maxwell had taken the horse away and given it to her brother Jim, rubbing salt into the wound by telling her the colt was too strong and too fast for a girl to ride. Funny how he remembered the incident. She'd really been taken with that colt.

"Go to sleep, Maxie. No sense in cryin', now. Everything's over."

His hand slipped down her arm in a comforting caress. How it managed to brush over her breast he didn't know. But she didn't seem to object. In fact, after a second's hesitation, she shifted position in his arms—an invitation to take more liberties?

He couldn't resist. Maxie no longer seemed thin and angular; she was soft and warm and yielding, and she gazed up at him with a half-scared, half-willing look on her face that would melt a stone. When he moved his hand to cup her breast, she closed her eyes, as if savoring the sensation. Beneath the firm round globe that filled his hand he could feel her heart flutter like a panicked, trapped little bird.

"Maxie?"

"Aaron?"

Never before had she called him by his given name. The sound of it on her lips seemed an invitation. Slowly, almost

against his will, he unlaced her rawhide tunic. "If you want
me to stop, Maxie girl, you've got to tell me now."

She only sighed as he slipped the tunic off her shoulders
and let his eyes drink in the sight of her pale, perfectly
formed breasts glowing in the dim firelight. Her skin was
like fine satin, and her small rosy nipples puckered in anticipation of his touch.

"Maxie," he whispered. "You're beautiful. You know that?
You're goddamned beautiful." He could feel the last vestige
of his control dissolve. His whole body ached with wanting
her. She was willing enough, it seemed. Her cobalt eyes
flickered with a hint of nervousness, but they also were
growing dark with desire.

In urgent haste he shed his shirt. He wanted to feel her
naked breasts against his chest. More than anything he
wanted her naked as the day she was born, lying beneath
him with the two of them wrapped around each other so
that nothing could pry them apart. "God, Maxie. I've
wanted you since I first saw you sitting in the cave at Stronghold. You're the damnedest woman I ever did run across,
and you stick in a man's mind like a burr on a blanket."

He fumbled with the fastenings to his trousers, suddenly
clumsy, for some reason feeling like a thirteen-year-old kid
who'd never been between a woman's legs. When he finally
threw the trousers impatiently aside, the touch of the night
air did nothing to cool the heat in his loins. He was hard and
eager to the point of pain, and the feel of Maxie's eyes
surveying his nakedness made him harder still. She lifted
one brow, as if in cynical assessment—a gesture so like her
old cocky self that Aaron almost had to laugh.

"Come here, girl." She didn't resist as he stretched out
beside her and gathered her in his arms. A few deft maneu-
vers and the crude Apache tunic disappeared. They lay skin
to skin, hers marked by scratches and weals that bore witness to her ordeal. His heart cried for her. He wove his
fingers through her hair, loosening her braids, tenderly covering her face, her neck, her beautiful soft breasts with

kisses. His mouth and tongue blazed a trail over her ribs, around her delicate little navel, down her thighs, over each of her tiny toes, back up her calf, and then over the satiny skin of her inner thigh. He could feel her pulse jump and race beneath his seeking hands.

She never made a move—not so much as a maidenly cringe or flinch. Neither did she try to touch him. For the first time a hint of worry momentarily dimmed the hot blaze of his desire. This docility wasn't like the Cactus Maxie he knew. Maxie was a fighter. If she wanted to do something, she did it with vigor. If she didn't want to do something, she would set hell itself ablaze before she would move an inch.

But his doubt was short-lived, buried under the urgency of his need and soothed by her acceptance of his passion.

"Maxie, are you okay, sweet girl?" He covered her yielding body with his own, and the contrast between them suddenly made him feel his muscled bulk as he never had before. "Are you with me, sweetheart?"

Her answering smile was a bit tremulous, but showed no hesitation. In her eyes was a need as deep as his own.

Gently he nestled his hand between her legs. She was warm and wet and silken—enough of a woman to drive a man to desperation, if he weren't already there. When he slipped a finger inside her, she jerked in surprise, then, after a moment's tense hesitation, let her legs ease apart.

"You're beautiful, Maxie," he whispered in a hoarse voice. He was going to explode with need if he didn't end this soon. But she was so small, so tight. He couldn't rush, he couldn't take advantage of this strange un-Maxielike vulnerability that seemed to hold her in its grip.

Then he remembered just why she was so small and tight. She was a virgin, goddamn it! How could he have forgotten her reputation at Stronghold of kicking the balls off any man who came at her? Including Aaron Hunter.

Aaron's body screamed in protest as he withdrew his hand, moved aside, and reluctantly covered Maxie's naked body with the blanket. He gritted his teeth and told himself to behave. He wasn't a man to take advantage of a girl who was apparently still in shock, who any other time would have carved the heart right out of his chest for what he was doing.

As if Maxie hadn't already carved up his heart and had it for a snack. He had lost his good sense when it came to the little she-wolf. If he weren't such a sunstruck idiot he would be relieving himself right now in the welcoming warmth of her body. But no. His damned calf-eyed conscience kept needling him. Maxie deserved better than to lose her virginity when she didn't know what she was doing, all for a little comfort from nighttime terrors.

Aaron sat up, sighed and ran his fingers through his hair. All things considered, he would probably live longer this way. Goddamn him for a stupid noble fool.

Maxie looked up at him with those impossibly blue eyes. The confusion there almost broke his resolve.

"What is it?" she asked. "Is something wrong?"

He brushed her cheek with one gentle finger. "Nothing's wrong, sweetheart. But I figure maybe we've gone about as far as we ought to go."

"Hunter . . . Aaron . . ."

"I'm sorry, Maxie girl. I didn't mean to take advantage of you this way." He pulled up the blanket and tucked it firmly around her, as much to keep his hands away from her tempting little body than anything else. "You go to sleep. I think I'll sit up and keep watch."

Before she could reply he left, still fastening his trousers as he walked away. If he hadn't put some space between them he would have ended up crawling under that blanket with her, and he didn't have the strength to pull away from her a second time.

Maxie gritted her teeth as she watched Hunter leave. Her body ached with frustration and her mind was black with confusion and anger. The unspeakable, unbelievable things

Hunter had done had her still awash in sensations she never knew existed. His abrupt departure left her feeling hollow, empty, wracked with need. And she knew exactly what it was her body needed. She had lived with whores and ruffians all her life, and no detail of the physical joining of man and woman was unfamiliar to her. The only unexpected surprise was that Maxie had actually wanted him to do the very thing she had always believed the most ridiculous, offensive act possible. No, want was too mild a word. She was wild for him to take her. Unbelievable, but true.

And he'd left! Just as Maxie had thought her brothers might have been right about Hunter being sweet on her, he had spurned her offer of herself! What had she done wrong? She'd been so uncertain that she'd scarcely moved a muscle, convinced that if she let her instincts guide her she'd make a fool of herself. Hadn't she always fumbled before when trying to act the woman? Had he thought her awkward, clumsy, disgusting? What had gone wrong?

And how could he possibly still call her a girl after the things he'd done to her? Didn't he know yet that she was a woman? Damn him!

Maxie ground her teeth. She felt like biting the blanket in her rage, or better still, biting some sensitive and essential part of Hunter's anatomy. Some day! she promised herself. Some day she was going to be feminine and desirable, and Aaron Hunter was going to drool all over himself trying to get to her. He was going to kneel down, grovel, beg, and plead for her favors; and she was going to turn up her nose and tell him to go screw a snake hole. She'd heard Tom fling that particular insult one day, and she'd stored it away in her mental catalog of useful phrases. The suggestion fit Aaron Hunter quite nicely, she decided. "Go screw a snake hole, Hunter." That's what she would tell him. He'd be sorry he had ever messed with her, sorry that he'd touched her with those wonderful hands of his and then walked off, leaving her to stew in her own juices. He would be damned sorry he'd ever gotten tangled up with Cactus Maxie!

She growled to herself, ground her teeth, and prepared to spend a sleepless night.

Morning was Elsa Herrmann's favorite time of day—when the just-risen sun turned the hills to burnished copper and the river to molten gold. The air was cool, the animals in the yard quiet—not scuffing up swirls of dust as they did as the day grew older.

The morning chores—feeding the chickens, collecting eggs, throwing scraps to the hogs—were more pleasure than drudgery for Elsa. They got her out of the hot kitchen building and into the freshness of a new day. This morning, like every other morning, the first sliver of the rising sun found her leaning her sturdy frame against the sides of the hogpens, throwing vegetable leavings to the eager porkers and filling their ears with comments and observations—all in German—about the people and events at Agua Linda.

But on this morning her one-sided conversation was interrupted by the sight of a pair of riders coming up the south river trail. Elsa reached down for the shotgun that she always carried when she went outside the wall. She held the gun ready as she squinted into the distance, then put it down again. A smile spread across her broad face. The rider was Hunter, and with him was their little Maxie. She had told La Doña that the marshal would find her. She had known from the look in his eye that he wouldn't give up until he did find her. He should have been a German, that man. When he started a job, he didn't stop until he finished it.

Elsa hallooed to the guards on the wall, and they waved back. They, too, recognized the pair riding in. She dumped the rest of the scraps on the hogs, eager to be back at the house to greet Maxie. The day was going to be a happy one for Agua Linda—and also for Elsa Herrmann, she admitted somewhat ruefully.

The German cook prided herself on being a closed-minded woman. Open minds, she often said, were for people who didn't know what they thought. But she had to admit she had been wrong about the little Maxwell girl. When Hunter had first brought her around, Elsa concluded after just a few moments in the girl's company that the little ragamuffin was a tramp, a troublemaker, and a self-centered brat.

But as days had stretched into weeks, Elsa was forced to revise her opinion—something she rarely did. She remembered the evening that she had discovered Maxie and Catalina scrubbing the dining room floor together. Maxie had looked almost shamefaced to be caught helping out. Elsa had been so surprised she'd forgotten to scold about Jake following after them with his dirty paws. A few days later the girl had been so proud of her first successful biscuits— mercy knew she'd had enough unsuccessful batches! She had stood by and watched everyone eat the lot of them, looking like a hen who'd laid her first egg. With every compliment her face had glowed even brighter.

The girl was a troublemaker, all right—a spoiled, brattish little hoyden when she first came to the ranch. But she had come around, day by day, and in Elsa's closely guarded heart, there lurked a growing fondness for the little scamp that she was almost ashamed to admit.

And now—now she shared a bond with Maxie that she shared with no one else, for Maxie had survived the same trial that Elsa herself had managed to survive some five years past—capture and escape from the Apaches.

Elsa did not often allow herself to think back on that nightmare time of her life when she had seen her husband Frederick tortured and killed and her twin sons callously murdered by having their little heads bashed against a rock. Nor could she bear thinking about the days that followed while she was a prisoner of the Apaches, or of the three tortured days she spent walking out of the desert after she had miraculously escaped.

Agua Linda had become Elsa's refuge. She did her job efficiently and expected very little of life other than raw

survival. Day by day she preserved her sanity by building a
wall around the horrors of the past. The memories could not
be banished, but they could be caged. In that cage also
dwelt what was left of her heart.

As Hunter and his dirty refugees rode into the compound
and slid from their mounts, Elsa joined the crowd that
greeted them. Medina ran forward, embraced Maxie, and
cried. Maxie wept also, though she appeared to try valiantly
to stifle her sobs. When her scraggly dog shoved its nose into
her hand, Maxie lost the battle altogether and surrendered
to a flood of tears. Elsa felt her throat close with emotion.

Poor Maxie. And the poor child she had brought back
with her! They both had the smell of Apache on them, and
the look that Elsa remembered from seeing her own face in
a mirror right after she had returned. It was the same look
of starvation, abuse, terror, and hopelessness that had remained with Elsa for weeks after she had come back to
safety.

The sight of them was enough to open a crack in Elsa's
wall of self-containment. She shoved through the crowd of
ranch hands that had gathered in greeting and snatched the
refugees almost from Medina's arms. Before either girl
could protest, the cook herded them into the kitchen, filled
a tub with warm water, stripped the filthy clothing from
their bodies, and plunked them willy-nilly into the water.
Medina followed, and promptly hurried off to fetch salve for
the wounds that striped most of Maxie's skin.

"There now, girls. Once you get that dirt off you'll feel a
good bit better. Don't you scratch at those welts!" She
slapped at Maxie's hands. "Medina is bringing some salve
that will take the sting from them." She shook her head
sadly. "Someone has beaten you, little Maxie. Many times, I
see. Poor child."

Her stream of admonitions and sympathy drowned out
the two girls' silence. Maxie had a hurt and angry look about
her—a legacy, Elsa shrewdly guessed, not so much from her
Apache captors as from something between the girl and

that devil Aaron Hunter. She had noted the awkward good-bye the two of them had said, Maxie with her nose up in the air and her eyes spitting fire at the poor fellow, Hunter a bit chagrined and not a little confused. Maxie's brooding silence didn't bother Elsa. Better that the girl have her mind on a man than whatever those Apache devils had done to her.

But the child—the child was greater concern. Elsa was certain a few weeks of her cooking would put some much-needed flesh on that puny frame, but the little one was as skittish as a rabbit in a pack of coyotes. She didn't speak, Maxie had said. Not a word. And who knew how much the youngster understood? But her eyes spoke volumes. They cringed at everything she saw. By rights she should be laughing and singing like a soul just released from hell, but here she was acting as if the good people of Agua Linda were more frightening than the Apaches.

Poor child. She was starving for love. For the first time in several years Elsa regretted that she had no love left to give.

Within a few days, Agua Linda settled down into its usual routine. Maxie was more subdued than the ranch had ever seen her, and almost everyone was unabashedly grateful. The uproar that always before had followed in her footsteps was missing. She went about her daily tasks in brooding silence, and more than once she was caught with a task half done and forgotten, a faraway look in her eyes and a flush on her face.

But if Maxie was broody, she was also harder working than before her abduction. Cooking she treated as a special joy, enthusiastically kneading bread, peeling vegetables, and baking pies. Even the cleaning tasks she tackled willingly—both cleaning house and cleaning herself. Elsa and Medina agreed that some of the changes in Maxie were definitely for the better. Therefore they didn't question her moods and even tolerated the unmannerly and uncalled for cusswords that sprang out of her mouth at odd times. Maxie was tough, everyone figured. She would heal.

Loco, on the other hand, was a worry. She detached herself from Maxie and started tagging along at Elsa's skirts with the same devotion that Jake showed Maxie. Elsa alternately fussed at her and tolerated her. The German woman gave her a good Christian name—Mary. No one should be called such an insulting thing as "Loco," the cook insisted. She made sure the child stayed clean and fed and busy with chores that were suited to her puny frame. But when the little one's eyes seemed to beg for something more, Elsa managed to turn away. She had nothing in her heart to help a lonely child. Best that the little girl turn to someone who still had love to give.

Then one day two weeks after Maxie's return to the ranch, Mary did not spend the morning in the kitchen as was her habit.

"Loco? I mean . . . uh . . . Mary?" Maxie frowned when Elsa inquired of the girl's whereabouts. "I haven't seen her. Thought she was with you. Do you want these pies taken out to cool?"

"You put them under cover of the well shed, eh? And keep your hands off them, hear? They are for dinner!"

"Yes'm." Maxie grimaced. Her hunger must have shone through her eyes. "And if I see Mary, I'll tell her you're looking for her."

"Thank you."

Two hours later Mary had still not been found. When Sam Hendricks reported that a horse was missing from the stable, Elsa grew frantic, and Maxie was pricked by a guilty fear that she had not lived up to her responsibility to Loco. Immersed in her own anger and confusion over Hunter, she had all but ignored the child.

Maxie was the first to report to the corral to ride in the search party, with or without Pete and Medina's permission. But before anyone could throw a saddle on a horse a hail from the wall halted the preparations.

"Rider comin' in! Looks like Simon Curtis, and he's got the kid with 'im."

Maxie gusted out a sigh of relief. Elsa should have left the girl's name Loco. Why would the brat do such a stupid thing? Life at Agua Linda wasn't a free ride—that was for sure. But it was a damned sight better than being with the Apaches. The ungrateful little snakelet deserved a thrashing for causing her to worry so! And for worrying Elsa too!

She unfastened the cinch on her saddle as Simon Curtis rode in. Elsa, standing just inside the wall gate, looked every bit as apprehensive as she did relieved, Maxie noted curiously. As Simon dismounted, lifted Mary from her saddle, and towed her toward the waiting German woman, the brusque cook had the oddest tinge of pallor to her face. Maxie grinned. The old sourpuss actually looked shy! And Mary had a sullen rebellious look on her face that reminded Maxie strangely of herself.

Maxie strained to pick up a bit of the conversation between Elsa and Simon—if such could be called conversation. Elsa was looking stolidly at the ground, and Simon was turning red as a cabbage.

". . . found her trottin' along the road to Tubac. Looked like she has ever'thin' she owns in that there little bundle, so I figgered she wasn't plannin' to come back on 'er own."

Elsa dragged her eyes away from the ground. "We're beholden to you, Mr. Curtis. I don't know what got into the child."

"Figger she's just a mite scared, Miz Herrmann."

The old man might just have a point there, Maxie thought. She'd been a bit scared herself when she first came to Agua Linda, and how much more strange must the place and the people seem to little Loco-Mary. Hell, they'd even taken the little squirt's name away from her.

She started to move toward the trio, thinking to add her two bits to the conversation, when the sight of the three of them together started the wheels turning in her mind. Mary was hanging onto Simon's hand as though they were glued together, and Simon and Mary were both looking at

Elsa with an expression that reminded Maxie of Jake looking at a fat ham. Could be, she mused, that those three were
just odd enough to deserve each other. The possibilities
were downright entertaining.

Chapter 12

The first week in September the Kelleys hosted a barbecue and dance at the Agua Linda Ranch. The party welcomed the cooler, more comfortable weather that was just around the corner. It was also a homecoming celebration for Maxie.

Hunter, however, leaning against the perimeter wall and watching the festivities, wasn't in a mood for celebration. His Sunday clothes itched; too many of Motherlode's straitlaced matrons were around for a man to have a really good time; and, perhaps most bothersome of all, this shindig was bound to bring him face to face with Maxie.

A week had passed since he'd brought her back from the desert—a week since he had nearly lost control of himself and taken her in the dirt of a ruined mission courtyard. God knew that he had nearly been ruined by that night, having spent most of it in acute and unrelieved discomfort while Maxie tossed and turned—entirely too close at hand—in her blanket.

The days since then hadn't been much better. Blood running alternately hot and cold, he wished Maxie gone, gone anywhere where he would not have to hear her voice or see her impish smile. And then in the next moment he wanted to throw wisdom to the hot desert wind and pursue her in earnest like a wolf after a bitch in heat.

The long days searching for that Devil's imp in the Arizona sun had fried his brain, Hunter decided. Never had he been this at odds with himself. Often during his misspent youth he hadn't liked himself, had felt like the slime on top of a stock pond; but even then he had known who he was and what he wanted. Now he had his doubts.

Maxie, bless her contrary little soul, had lighted a fire inside him that was tempering the steel of a single-minded desire. He wanted her. He wanted her smile, her sky-blue eyes dark with anger or sparkling with indignation. He wanted her corkscrew curls, her freckles, her courage, her odd vulnerability, even her sassy mouth. And her body. Oh yes, he definitely wanted her body.

And at the same time, in a duality that made his mind reel, Hunter didn't want her. Or perhaps he didn't want what she represented—all that had been foolish and just downright evil in his life. He was afraid of her, dammit. Aaron Hunter, who'd fought a war, ridden with killers, bandits, and been counted one of the Devil's own, was afraid of a slip of a girl. He was afraid to be in love with her, afraid of his own foolishness. She'd made him a man of mush.

"There you are!"

He was trapped. Medina had found his hiding place in the shadow of the wall and was attacking with a smile.

"The fiddlers are about to begin playing, Aaron. Since this is Maxie's party, why don't you ask her to lead off the dancing. She's right over there by the barbecue pit."

Twice in the last week he'd had to come to Agua Linda, and both times he'd managed to avoid Maxie. He'd hoped that time away from the girl might bring him to his senses. But now the game was up.

"Medina," he replied with a grimace. "You have an odd

idea of a good time." Under La Doña's watchful eye he headed toward Maxie.

Maxie looked no happier to see Aaron than he was to see her. Her face a bright red, she placed her hand in his as if she were offering her fingers as a meal to a gila monster.

"Remember the steps I showed you?" he asked in a civil voice.

Her glare told him she remembered a good deal more. Little Maxie was still not pleased with him, it seemed. He didn't blame her. There was no excuse for his behavior at Tumacacori, especially after he had lectured her on behaving like a lady. If he had any guts at all, he would tell her how he felt and hope she had a glimmer of the same feelings herself. Was that what he hoped? He didn't know anymore. He had the courage to face down bandits and ride out where the Apaches roamed, but he didn't have the guts to confront Maxie. Not yet, anyway.

Hump MacIntosh played a lively tune on the fiddle, and Sam Hendricks was blowing right along on his harmonica. Hunter and Maxie moved together to the music, eyeing each other like two scorpions whose tails were quivering to strike. Maxie didn't even step on his toes, Hunter noted. She didn't want to get that close to him.

"Maxie, I apologize for what happened at the mission. I'm usually not that much of an ass."

Her eyes widened slightly. "How much of an ass are you usually?"

She lowered her gaze, managing to look embarrassed and grim at the same time. Her hair was disheveled, piled on top of her head in a haphazard crown of braids. Her dress, a Mexican-style gathered bodice and skirt, was somewhat askew, and her freckles grew brighter as her face grew hotter with embarrassment. Probably no one, Hunter realized, not Medina, not him, not anyone, was ever going to make a civilized lady out of Cactus Maxie. And it was just as well. As she was she could burrow into a man's unsuspecting heart so deeply that dynamite couldn't blast her loose.

"I'm sorry, Maxie. I wish it hadn't happened. I wish we could forget about it."

Her chin came up and thrust out. "Oh, I've forgotten about it already. It isn't important."

The area roped off for dancing was becoming crowded. "Do you suppose we've done our part to start the party?" Maxie pulled out of Hunter's light embrace and was gone before he could answer.

Maxie sat herself down on one of the rough plank benches that had been set up around the walled ranch yard; she didn't feel in a celebrating mood, especially after a dance with Hunter, who had the nerve to say he was sorry he'd diddled with her that night in the mission ruins. Sorry indeed! If so many people weren't crowded in the yard she'd teach him the true meaning of sorry, the snake. He'd made her want him—kissing her at the church social, treating her as though she meant something to him, and then subjecting her to that sweet torment at the mission. He wanted her, too. Maxie could feel his longing vibrate the air between them when they talked, when they danced, even when they sniped at each other. His longing struck a familiar chord, harmonizing with her own. Dammit! If she was going to make a fool of herself panting over the likes of Hunter, he could make a fool of himself as well! If he were any kind of a man, he'd admit it!

Indignant, Maxie sat on her bench and let the party pass her by. Jake had snuck into the festivities to sit by her side, and she let her hand rest upon his shaggy head, telling herself she'd rather sit with the dog than be out dancing.

Almost fifty people ate the Kelleys' fine barbecued ham and pork, drank their wine and *cerveza*, danced on the hard-packed dirt of the yard, or talked among themselves about everything from the latest Apache threat and the current price of silver and gold to the quality of the latest cloth and tinware being sold by Mr. Pruitt and his competitor in Motherlode, George Strassel.

Mr. Pruitt and Mr. Strassel were both in attendance,

along with their families. In fact, everybody who was anybody in southern Arizona Territory was there in Agua
Linda's walled ranch yard—including two prominent of-
ficers of the Arizona Mining Corporation, the young captain
of the federal troops stationed at Tubac, several bureau-
cratic officials visiting from the territorial governor's office
in Tucson, a smattering of prosperous mine owners, and a
fair number of ranchers.

Maxie had never seen quite so many people together at
the same time. Arizona Territory was becoming downright
crowded. Someday, she thought morosely, the army would
find a way to hog-tie the Apaches, and then no doubt a
whole herd of easterners would stampede into the Territory, bringing their upright law-abiding ideas and spoiling
everybody's fun. Right at this moment she figured she'd
rather put up with the Apaches than more stiff-backed souls
like Mrs. Whitney and Mrs. Selbeck, wives of the two gov-
ernment gentlemen who were visiting from Tucson.

Not in a charitable mood with anyone, Maxie sat on her
bench and watched the dancing couples weave through the
flickering light given off by torches set around the yard. She
felt like an absolute frump. Her dress—a do-it-yourself cre-
ation sewn by Maxie's own less than skilled hands—pinched
where it shouldn't and gapped in the most awkward places.
She'd had plenty of offers to help make it, but Maxie had
been working diligently on her sewing skills and had insisted she could make the dress herself—a bit of overconfi-
dence, she discovered. Last-minute tucks and adjustments
by a sympathetic Medina had helped, but the bodice still
gapped and the skirt gathers were uneven. Sewing, Maxie
admitted, was another feminine skill that she hopelessly
botched.

And as if the ill-fitting dress weren't bad enough, Maria
had urged Maxie to arrange her heavy braids in a more
sophisticated style for the party—a coronet atop her head.
And then the house girl had been called off to help with
preparations. Without Maria's help, Maxie's fumbling fin-

gers had braided and stuffed and wound and pinned—to a near-disastrous result. To say the coronet looked haphazard was being generous.

Maxie felt as ugly as one of the Kelleys' old sows. Worse still, she felt a fool. His duty to Maxie finished, Aaron Hunter do-si-doed around the yard with Cynthia Pruitt. Cynthia's blond curls were in place—every single gilt ringlet—and her fresh, ivory-skinned face glowed with rosy color. Her eyes sparkled up at Hunter as he laughed at something she said. All in all, Cynthia looked like a prime example of healthy, beautiful, sickeningly wholesome womanhood. Hunter looked as though he appreciated every feminine inch of her.

Maxie squirmed uncomfortably. Why the hell *should* Hunter look at her when Cynthia was blinding him with her dazzle? Could Hunter want Cynthia and still have some wanting left over for Maxie? Probably, Maxie reflected sourly. She'd never know a man—except maybe Pete Kelley—who didn't have an eye on almost every female in sight. No doubt Hunter had a heap more longing for Cynthia than he had for Maxie. What man wouldn't?

Maxie got up and wandered disconsolately over to the big spits where the barbecued pork and hams were turning, Jake padding hopefully behind her. She helped herself to a beer from the barrel of *cerveza* that the Kelleys provided for their guests.

"Aleta, a lady drinks wine. Not beer," Medina said from behind.

Maxie turned. "I like beer. I guess I'm not cut out to be a lady."

Medina nodded her approval at the correct grammar. "Yes, you are, dear. It's in your blood."

Maxie sighed. "Was my mother truly beautiful?"

"She was lovely," Medina assured her. "You are every bit as lovely as she was, you know. Especially when you smile." Medina took Maxie's hand and patted it.

Maxie shook her head silently. She swept her arm in a gesture that included both dress and hair.

Medina smiled. "Next party we'll get Maria to make you a special dress. Don't be too hard on yourself, dear. Your reading and writing is coming along nicely, and Elsa tells me you've become a real help in the kitchen. You've been trying very hard this past week, but you can't expect yourself to be good at everything."

Maxie felt a rush of affection for Medina. "I wish I'd known my mother," she admitted. "Especially if she was like you. I've never had anyone care enough about me to scold me."

Medina looked surprised. She squeezed Maxie's hand. "Aleta, dear. Sometimes you just can't help but be sweet, in spite of yourself." She leaned forward and kissed Maxie lightly on the cheek. "Now, why aren't you dancing? This is your party. You should be having fun."

"I'm having loads of fun," Maxie lied.

The fiddler started sawing away at his fiddle again, and Pete came over to claim Medina, whisking her off for a dance. Maxie sighed, watching the two of them together. Suddenly the longing to have a man care about her the way Pete cared about Medina overwhelmed her. Trying to ignore such an impossible desire, she picked up a basting brush, and slapped some more of Elsa's barbecue sauce on the ham.

"Howdy, Maxie. Glad to see you're back in one piece." Simon Curtis was leaning up against a nearby torch pole, his spare frame scarcely distinguishable from the pole. "Figgered you were a mite too tough for those Cherrycows to chew up and spit out."

"Right. I was just too tough." She smiled at him. If Curtis could forgive her for punching him in the stomach, then she could forgive him for being a lawman. Maybe.

Simon didn't note her attempt at friendliness, though, because his eyes were following the approach of Elsa Herrmann.

"Are you watching the meat, Maxie?"

"Yes, ma'am."

"You shouldn't be doing the cooking duties, girl. This is your party, after all. Where is Catalina?"

"Cat's dancing. That's okay. I don't mind."

"Well, if you want to take your turn at the dancing, come get me or one of the girls. Oh," she said, her tone suddenly uneasy. "Good evening, Mr. Curtis. I didn't see you standing there."

"Howdy, Miz Herrmann."

Elsa hurried off as if she'd been bitten by a horse fly. Maxie watched her curiously, then looked back at Simon. His eyes hadn't left the German woman for a moment.

"Why don't you ask her to dance?"

"Huh? Me?"

"Sure. Don't you know how to dance?"

Simon shrugged. "I can get out and jump around a bit. I guess that's dancin'."

"I bet she'd be pleased as a pig."

"To dance with me? Naw. She wouldn't want to dance with an old fart like me."

He was wrong, Maxie guessed. Elsa would like very much to dance with Simon Curtis. Even if the stubborn old sourpuss German wouldn't admit it to anyone. Maxie had seen the blush on her cheeks the day Simon brought Mary back.

Maxie shook her head sadly. "I tell you what, Simon Curtis. After seeing you in action, I sure did never think to see you run scared from some . . . some female."

Simon gave her a sour look. "I ain't scared. I was off fightin' the Mexicans before you wasn't even a sparkle in your daddy's eye, girl. And while you were still wettin' your nappies I was a U.S. of A. marshal huntin' down the worst lawbreakin' scum between here and St. Louie. Scared of a woman? Hell!"

"I can see where Elsa could be a mite scarier than Mexicans or bandits. She sure is to me," Maxie admitted with a grin.

Simon shifted his weight from one foot to the other, then back again. He looked up at the torch, then at the spitted meat turning over the fire, then back at Maxie. Slowly, a wry grin twisted his face. "You really think she wants to dance?"

"Ask her and find out. She might snap your head off, but she'll blush and coo while she does it."

"How do you know so much about women, anyway?" Simon asked innocently.

Maxie growled. "I had a relative who was a woman."

Simon chuckled. "Just joshin', kid. Could be you know what you're talkin' about." He stuffed his hands in his trouser pockets and scuffed the dirt with his boot heel. "Maybe I'll just stroll on over and see which way the wind blows." Hitching his trousers up higher on his lean hips and clenching his jaw, Simon strode forward to meet the challenge.

Maxie smiled as she watched him go. At least somebody was going to have fun at this party.

"Do you think she'll say yes?"

The unexpected feminine voice made Maxie jump. She turned to see an unwelcome vision of blond loveliness smiling at her. Cynthia.

"Dunno." Her mood had lifted while talking to Simon. Now it plunged.

"That was a nice thing you did."

"What?"

"Talk Mr. Curtis into asking Elsa to dance. You have a way with people, don't you?"

"Not so's I'd noticed."

"Don't be modest," Cynthia chided. "Mr. Curtis scarcely ever says more than two words to anyone except Aaron. But you made him comfortable, it seems."

They both watched as Simon caught up to Elsa. His hemming and hawing was visible, if not audible. Elsa looked distressed and confused. She blushed, her lips twitched in agitation, and she started to shake her head no. Then in the middle of a headshake the no became a yes. Maxie couldn't tell who was more surprised—Simon or Elsa.

"You're a miracle worker," Cynthia told her.

"Nah. He would've asked her anyway."

"And I suppose that little girl trailing after Elsa—Mary? Is that her name?—I suppose she would have gotten away from the Apaches without you as well. Aaron told me how you rescued her."

"I didn't exactly rescue her." The great Cactus Maxie hadn't even been able to rescue herself, Maxie thought in disgust.

Cynthia would have none of Maxie's honesty. "You know, Maxie. I don't think you give yourself half-enough credit for the extraordinary person you are."

"Extra . . . ?"

"Extraordinary. I think you're one of the most refreshing, remarkable people I've ever met."

Maxie was nonplussed. She was doing her best to dislike Cynthia—both for her beauty and for the way she had Hunter trailing after her like a dog after a juicy bone. But disliking someone who insisted on being gracious and complimentary was a hard thing to do, especially since Cynthia didn't seem to have a bit of guile in her. Her lovely face was as open and honest as a child's, and her words had the ring of sincerity.

"I ain't . . . uh . . . haven't ever had someone tell me I was remarkable before. Mostly folks just tell me I'm a . . . a"—what was the term Hunter had used?—"draggletailed ragamuffin."

"A what?"

"A draggle—"

"Yes. I guess I did hear you correctly. Who ever called you that?"

"Hunter." Maxie's eyes narrowed with suspicion. "He put you up to all this? Or Medina?"

"Put me up to what?" Cynthia asked with a little frown.

"Sayin' that I'm . . . all that good stuff."

"Certainly not! Aaron Hunter called you a . . . a . . . ? Mercy me!" Cynthia's eyes rolled in Hunter's direction. He, Maxie noticed, was watching them with a studied blank expression on his features. "How unlike him," Cynthia said, her mouth twitching in a mischievous smile. "I wonder if our brave marshal might just be defending himself."

"Defending himself?" Maxie asked, confused.

When Cynthia looked back at Maxie, her face was alight. "I think we should launch a frontal attack. Dear Maxie, you must come spend a week or two with me in town. I'm sure Medina will give permission, and we would have a wonderful time together."

Maxie frowned suspiciously. Why would a lady like Cynthia Pruitt want Cactus Maxie, the social outcast of Motherlode, for a house guest? "Why should I come visit you?" she asked.

Cynthia was only momentarily taken aback by the question. Then she smiled and answered with an honesty that matched Maxie's. "For two reasons, dear. First, I would truly enjoy your company. Believe me, the ladies of Motherlode leave something to be desired in intelligent conversation. And second, you are a challenge I simply cannot resist—a nugget of pure gold in a shell of dull, ordinary rock. With a little work, if you are willing, we will have the true you shining forth so that no one will ever call you a draggletailed ragamuffin again."

Maxie was hesitant. She wasn't sure that she didn't like being a ragamuffin. "Medina's already giving me lessons on how to become . . . civilized."

"Oh, my dear," Cynthia crooned. "You are going to become much, much more than merely civilized."

The Pruitts lived in one of the finest houses in Motherlode. Their home was surpassed in grandeur only by the dwelling of Shady Sam Guenther, who owned the gambling parlor across the street from Pruitt's Dry Goods, and by the house of the brothers Johnston, two well-to-do lawyers who specialized in mining litigation. The house was more spectacular even than Mother Moses' place at the opposite end of town, but when Maxie remarked upon that fact, Georgia Pruitt, Cynthia's mother, looked as though she might faint dead away. Cynthia, on the other hand, thanked Maxie for the compliment and merely smiled at her mother's vapors.

Cynthia didn't let Maxie catch her breath before she got down to work. Bolts of material from her father's store were each examined for color against Maxie's skin. Many were discarded, but the pile that met with Cynthia's approval grew to an alarming size.

"Cynthia, I don't have any money to pay your pa for this cloth," Maxie told her.

"Pay Daddy? Don't be silly."

Cynthia's father, the round-faced, spectacularly mustachioed man who had been so kind to Maxie in the general store, shrugged agreement. Where his daughter was concerned, Maxie guessed, the man was helpless.

She tried one more time to speak with the voice of reason. "I couldn't possibly wear all these dresses you're planning."

"Shame on you!" Cynthia chided gaily. "There is no limit to the clothes a lady can use. You will see."

"But I ain't . . . uh . . . I'm just a servant out at the Kelley ranch."

"Oh, pooh! You're much more important than that! You're going to be a lady. And ladies don't wear"—she regarded, with a jaundiced eye, Maxie's skirt and blouse, donations from Maria that Maxie had laboriously taken in and shortened—"garments like that."

"Yeah. You're right. I'd rather be wearing britches."

For a moment Cynthia looked at her in dismay. Then they both laughed.

"Let's go upstairs and take your measurements," Cynthia directed. She loaded her arms full of material and made for the stairs like a trooper charging a hill. Casting an apologetic glance at Cynthia's father, who was smiling benignly, Maxie followed suit.

Cynthia's bedroom was like nothing Maxie had ever seen. While Cynthia stacked the cloth and dug a measuring tape out of her chest, Maxie admired the flounced bed canopy and matching window curtains, the real glass mirror above the dressing table, the luxurious rug that cushioned their feet. Who would have thought, she wondered, that an honest merchant could make enough money to have such things! Raiding and pillaging were the only way to get rich —that was the Maxwell family motto.

"Take your clothes off," Cynthia ordered.

"Huh?"

"You don't expect me to measure you over those baggy things, do you?"

"They're not so baggy. I took them in myself."

"I can tell. Just take them off, dear."

Maxie stripped down to her shift, and Cynthia went to work with her tape.

"Goodness, you're small! All those lovely curves in such a tiny package. What I would give for those breasts!"

Maxie blinked in surprise. "Your breasts look fine to me."

"That's because you don't have to wear them. I would much rather be small and nicely shaped. Like you."

Maxie was willing to wager that the male population of Motherlode wouldn't agree. Especially Aaron Hunter.

"You're going to look wonderful in what we sew up. And . . . let me see . . ." She took Maxie's chin and turned her head to one side and then the other. "What shall we do with all that hair? Such a lovely little face you have. Cute pointed chin, dainty little nose . . . And those eyes! When I'm done with you, you'll knock the breath from anything that's male." A smile that was almost sly curved her mouth. "One in particular, I think."

"Are you and Hunter getting hitched?" Maxie didn't know quite why or how the question had escaped her mouth. But there it was.

"Me marry Aaron?" Cynthia chortled. "Oh, no. Not me. Turn around. I need to take the length from neck to waist."

"What do you mean, you're not going to marry Hunter?" Did the woman think Hunter wasn't good enough for her? "I thought when a decent woman walks with a man and dances with him and sashays everywhere around town with him, that means she's going to marry him!"

"Maybe back East that's the way it is, but not out here. Aaron and I are just friends. He's one of the few men in Motherlode that I would give you two cents for, but I wouldn't think of marrying him."

Maxie pushed the measuring tape aside, angry for reasons she didn't quite understand. "Why? Isn't he good enough?"

Cynthia's delicate brows puckered in irritation. "Of course he's good enough! Aaron's a fine man—honest, hardworking, handsome, intelligent, gentlemanly . . ."

Hunter gentlemanly? Maxie thought. That was a new one.

"I'm not in love with him. That's all. He can be so intense, and down inside him is a . . . a violent streak that scares me. I've never really seen him act anything but a gentleman, but a demon lurks somewhere behind that facade of his." Cynthia sighed, her momentary irritation gone. "I need someone who would be content to sit by a fire with children on his knee. A man of business who will be able to take over Daddy's store—maybe expand, get into local politics, live a quiet life where I will always know he'll come home to me in the evening. Aaron's more interested in working himself to death on his ranch. Not to mention that every miner and rancher in this part of the territory expects him to go chasing after bandidos and Apaches, even though he has jurisdiction only for things that happen in Motherlode."

"Hunter has a ranch?"

"Yes. His pride and joy. It's on river bottom land near . . ." She broke off and leveled a suddenly knowing stare at Maxie. "You're jealous, aren't you, Maxie? That's why all the questions about me and Aaron. You're in love with him!"

"The hell I am!" came Maxie's thunderous response. She stalked over to the window, then back, looking as if she were about to spit nails. "I don't even like your goddamned Aaron Hunter, much less love him. And he's not," she continued in a superior tone, "the goddamn gentleman you think he is!"

Cynthia shook her head, crossed her arms, and gave Maxie a look that was half amused, half sympathetic. "So that's the way it is, is it? Oh, mercy! I do adore love stories!"

The woman was deaf! She hadn't heard a single word. Maxie drew herself up to deliver another blast.

"I can see the path now," Cynthia continued before Maxie could spit out more invectives. "We have some work to do before we can reach the 'happily ever after,' don't we? For the first thing, dear: Ladies do not even think words like 'hell' and 'damn' much less use them. If you must express strong feelings in verbal form, choose an acceptable expression that is suitable for the more delicate gender. Such as . . ."

"Such as 'pooh'?" Maxie offered with a mischievous grin, her ire dissolved by the very insanity of what Cynthia was thinking.

" 'Pooh' will serve very nicely," Cynthia acknowledged with a grin. "Perhaps I do overuse it a bit, but we ladies are rather limited in our choice of vocabulary."

"I really don't like Hunter, Cynthia. I'll admit he has a sort of animal appeal, but I don't love him at all!"

"No dear, of course you don't." Cynthia's eyes gleamed with knowing merriment. "But if you did, we could have him fairly groveling at your feet once you have graduated from Cynthia Pruitt's private—very private"—she said with a grin—"school for devastating young ladies. You are quite a natural beauty, you know, and on top of that, you have a refreshing charm that comes from just being you."

A natural beauty? Her? Maxie turned and regarded her-

self in the mirror. Her corkscrew hair would not be restrained even by a tight braid, for soft wisps and tendrils had
escaped and curled around her face in a midnight halo. The
face looked like a twelve-year-old boy's, Maxie noted—a
fact that had always pleased her until the last few weeks.
The little pointed chin, pert nose, and freckles could never
belong to a "devastating young lady."

Another person had once told her she was pretty, now
that Maxie thought about it. Blackjack had brought a sweetheart to Stronghold a year or so back—well, not really a
sweetheart. Her brother had kidnapped the girl and
courted her much against her will. (Blackjack did have a
nasty habit of taking what he wanted and damn the consequences.) Julia had been at Stronghold for six months before
a bout with heatstroke had killed her. She and Maxie had
become friends of a sort. The poor little greenhorn had
been a real lady from back East, and she'd had a queer way
of talking sometimes. But she also had thought that Maxie
could be something other than a draggletail. Julia had said
that Maxie would be a beauty if she would let her real self
escape from the—how had Julia said it?—the tarnished
shell.

"Do you really think Hunter would notice me? As a
woman, I mean?"

"I think he's noticed you already."

Damned if he'd admit it, Maxie told herself sourly. But
getting Hunter to acknowledge such a thing might be a
worthy challenge. Cynthia's promise of Hunter groveling at
Maxie's feet held an appeal that was almost impossible to
resist. Lord knew the man deserved to be embarrassed
once in a while. It would do his character good.

But she didn't love him, Maxie assured herself. She didn't
love him one little bit. All those silly gut churnings and
longings would pass in time. The only reason she might go
along with Cynthia's plan was to see Aaron Hunter get his
comeuppance.

The next week was hell for Maxie and not much better for

a determined Cynthia. Maxie practiced how to sit, how to stand, how to walk and talk, and many other things that she had known how to do—she thought—from the time she shed diapers. The reading, sewing, and cooking lessons that Medina had begun at Agua Linda were continued. Her hair was pulled back, pinned up, tortured into curls and rolls that made both Maxie and Cynthia choke with laughter, and finally trimmed and allowed to fall down her back after being tied up with a simple ribbon.

At the end of the exhausting week Medina paid a call. She put her stamp of approval on the new Maxie and gave permission for Maxie to extend her visit another week. "You look positively civilized, Aleta," was her comment. "Jake won't recognize you." She laughed. "You've spoiled that hound unspeakably, you know. He spends all day lying around the kitchen, getting under Elsa's feet, begging for tidbits, and every twenty seconds or so looking longingly at the door to discover if you're home yet."

"Oh! Don't let Elsa swat him with her wooden spoon handle! She gets so mad when Jake gets in her way."

"Don't worry about it, dear. Elsa has been surprisingly cheerful this past week. In her present mood I don't think she'd take after the dog if he climbed up on the table and ate everything on it."

Maxie and Cynthia smiled at each other, both wondering if Simon Curtis and his encounter with Elsa at the party had anything to do with the cook's strange behavior.

"Well, tell Jake I haven't forgotten him and that I'll be home soon."

The next week Maxie attacked her "lady lessons" with renewed fervor. She was actually seeing results. The young woman who stared back at her from the mirror over Cynthia's dresser was almost a stranger. Her hair still curled around her face, but now it looked feminine instead of merely messy. Cynthia's creams and ointments had taken the dryness from her skin, and eye patches of cucumbers worn for half an hour each night had washed away the redness that the Arizona sun had put into her eyes.

At the end of that second week, Maxie felt ready to take on anyone and anything. She hadn't cussed all week. Her new clothes—flattering but simple designs, as Cynthia thought would best suit her—were finished. With long skirts gracefully swishing around her ankles and lace decorating her wrists and neckband, Maxie was inspired to stand up straight instead of slouch. The urge to take the stairs two at a time and walk in strides that were—as Cynthia told her— twice as long as proper ladylike steps was easy to resist in garments that made her feel beautiful. There was no other way to describe how she felt as she stood in front of Cynthia's dresser mirror and allowed her friend to wrap the newly trimmed ends of her hair around a heated curling iron. She felt impossibly beautiful.

"I need to go to the bank for Daddy," Cynthia told her. "Would you like to walk with me?" Cynthia's eyes twinkled naughtily. "I heard that Aaron is back in town. Perhaps we can stop by his office and say hello."

A hard boot of nervousness kicked Maxie in the stomach. Suddenly her new confidence fled. Hunter had been out with Pete Kelley chasing down rustlers who'd made off with some of Agua Linda's longhorns, so he hadn't been in town to witness her transformation. She was terribly anxious to see how he would react to her now that she was all gussied up, and at the same time she was scared to death. They hadn't talked since they'd said an awkward goodnight at the Kelleys' party, and then he'd been . . . God only knew what he had been. Silent. Stony faced. Even his mocking little half smile had been gone. He'd looked at her with such strange intensity that Maxie had almost been frightened.

Now she had to face him again.

"Of course I'll walk with you," she said, reminding herself sternly that Maxwells were not cowards.

Cynthia finished her task and tied Maxie's hair back with a bright blue ribbon—one that matched both Maxie's eyes and the new dress she wore. Maxie smoothed her skirts and flicked at an imaginary speck of dirt on her nose. Lordy, what she would give to get rid of those unladylike freckles!

As it turned out, there was no need to stop by the jail to give Hunter his hello. They met him walking down the street. He looked tired—plumb worn out, Maxie noticed. His limp was more noticeable than usual, and the tiny scar that marred one brow seemed to be just one crease in a near-permanent scowl. Deep in his black eyes lurked the devil Cynthia thought so frightening.

"Good morning, Aaron!" Cynthia chimed, heedless of his mood. "I'm glad to see you're back and safe. Did you bring in the rustlers?"

"Two of them," he growled. "Three slipped through our hands." He glanced briefly at Maxie. "Relatives of yours." Then he looked at her a second time. His eyes widened.

"I think I'll just toddle on to the bank, now," Cynthia said. "I'll meet you at the store, Maxie."

Maxie desperately wanted Cynthia to stay, but she couldn't open her mouth to voice the request as her friend swished happily away. She was frozen in place, her heart bucking in her chest like an unbroke horse.

"Good God! What happened to you?"

Maxie managed a ladylike smile and tried to ignore the very unencouraging look on Hunter's face. His eyes were cold enough to freeze the fangs off a snake. Dammit! How was she ever going to get anywhere with this man if her idiot brothers kept making him mad at Maxwells? Shit! There she went again. And she hadn't cussed all week! Well, at least she hadn't said it out loud.

"I've been visiting Cynthia," she said politely.

"What have you done to yourself?" His mouth tightened, and Maxie knew right away that this hadn't been the time to pry a compliment from him. Her brothers must have really given him a hell of a time. And their escaping, of course, was bound to make him a bit testy. "You look like

. . . like . . . a kid playing dress-up. What are you trying
to do, anyway? Make everyone forget you're a Maxwell?"

That did it! A number of unladylike responses flashed into
Maxie's mind, but for Cynthia's sake she didn't give any of
them voice. "You . . . you . . ." She couldn't find a word
that was strong enough but still polite. So she raised a disdainful brow, gave him a scathing look, and tried Cynthia's
word on for size. "Oh, pooh!"

"Pooh?" For a moment he was nonplussed. Then he
chuckled, and then he laughed aloud. "POOH?"

Maxie had had enough. She had tried so hard! "I'm not
ashamed to be a Maxwell, you toad-eating, yellow-livered
piece of mule shit! I think you're the one who's running
away ashamed of his past!"

"You're a philosopher now, too?" His voice was like ice,
contempt in every frozen crystal.

She would have liked to give him a kick, but kicking was
even more unladylike than cussing. "Go to hell, Hunter!"

Maxie turned and fled. When she finally slowed to catch
her breath, she was nearing the other end of town and
people were giving her curious looks. As if by a miraculous
decree she had run heedlessly toward the one place she
might patch up her tattered self esteem. Mother Moses'
house loomed ahead. Her friends the whores would properly appreciate her painfully acquired ladylike airs, even if
no one else did!

Hunter stood in the street, following Maxie's fleeing form
with hot eyes. He was beset by Maxwells. Which was worse
—chasing after the Maxwell brothers, who'd made off with
Pete's longhorns, or coming back to see the Maxwell sister
all decked out as a feast for male eyes? As if the little tempt-
ress hadn't already nailed his heart to the barn door and
used it for target practice. The whole damned clan was
conspiring to make his life difficult!

Chapter 13

"*T*he trouble with men is," Sophie advised Maxie, "they all got their brains in their pants. And if you wanna get anything out of 'em, you gotta appeal to the part of 'em that thinks."

Mother Moses' girls lounged around the whorehouse parlor in various states of undress, Maxie the center of their attention. She had barged in, head held high, ready to spit nails, then suddenly dissolved into tears. The lounging ladies had fluttered around her like half-dressed butterflies, pulled her over to the velveteen settee, and listened raptly as she sobbed out her complaints of the thickheaded stupidity of all men in general and one in particular.

Heads bobbed in agreement to Sophie's observation.

"That's right," Andalusia said. "A man thinks he is the most important creature in the world." Andalusia, a buxom, sable-haired seductress with deceptively sleepy-looking eyes, had been introduced to Maxie as Carlotta's successor. Maxie remembered that not too long ago the girls had tried to persuade her to step into Carlotta's place. She should have taken them up on the offer, Maxie reflected bitterly.

At least then she would have gotten some appreciation for her efforts to be feminine.

"There is only one reason a man pays attention to a woman," Andalusia continued, "and that is when he is hungry for what no one else can give him."

"Perhaps the kind of men you're acquainted with," Carmen sniped. "My customers are looking for something more than a fast ride between someone's legs. They're looking for someone they can talk to, someone compassionate, understanding."

"Well, it's a good thing they're not looking for brains," Jacqueline chimed in. "Maxie, honey, don't listen to those two. They couldn't hold a man longer than it takes to do a night's business. You want a man for something more."

"I don't want a man at all! For anything!"

"Then what are you all upset about? Tell me that. Now don't start the waterfall again. Sweet Jesus, I hate women who cry."

"I don't ever cry!" Maxie sobbed. "Well, hardly ever!"

"Then you're making up for it now. Pull yourself together, girl. So what if Aaron Hunter's being a jackass. All you've got to do is learn to manage him a bit. A man's a lot like a mule. Sometimes a carrot in front of the nose gets the job done, sometimes it takes a yank on the bit."

"Every gal I seen try to ride Hunter got herself throwed," said Sophie.

"That's not what I hear!" Andalusia sighed. "I hear that some high-nosed lady from back East had him all tamed down and ready to go."

"Shit!" Sophie replied. "That wouldn't of lasted."

"What lady from back East?" Maxie demanded.

"Some gal he was gonna marry. She got kilt comin' out on a freight wagon."

"Speakin' of ladies," Jacqueline said. "Take a look at our little Maxie here. Darlin', I don't know what you done to yourself, but you look pretty as a little cactus blossom. You've got the material there to put any man away for life, but I figure you might need a lesson or two on how to use it."

"I've been learning everything under the sun about being a lady," Maxie complained. "How to walk, how to talk, how to eat, how to dress, how to . . ."

"Sweetie," Jacqueline said. "Ain't nobody said nothin' about learnin' to be a lady."

In the half hour that followed these frontier flowers of the oldest profession regaled Maxie with advice so explicit that Hilda and the rest of Hernando's whores suddenly seemed tame. Maxie didn't believe half their advice was possible, and the other half, if perhaps possible, surely was not commonly put into practice by normal men and women.

Maxie's ears were beginning to burn when the lesson was mercifully interrupted by Mother Moses' entrance. "Well, look what we have here. Little Maxie, ain't it?"

"Yes, ma'am."

"It's nice to see you in one piece, girl. Our friend Hunter let you outta his sight again?" Her wink was as lewd a suggestion as a wink could be.

"Oh, no, ma'am! I mean . . . Hunter didn't . . . it isn't . . ." The very idea left her speechless. Did Moses really believe that Hunter had carried her out of the house that night with the intention of taking her to bed?

Mother Moses raised a curious brow, then looked at her girls. "And what are we all doin' down here? 'Becca, did you clean up that mess in your room? And Carmen—I thought you were gonna help me choose new curtains for your window."

"We were just giving Maxie the benefit of our experience," Sophie told her.

"Yeah, I overheard some of that advice while I was upstairs. Don't listen to 'em, honey. You want a man, just do what's natural. You're not in the business to sell it, like we are, and the only time to give it away is when it feels right."

The sound of gunshots ripped through Maxie's cynical reply.

"Christ and hell!" Carmen huffed. "What's going on?"

A bevy of startled butterflies, the whores flocked to the window and pushed aside the lace curtains. "It's a holdup!" Rebecca said happily. "Someone's robbing the bank!"

"Let me see!" Jacqueline pushed the others aside. "Look! There's Hunter runnin' down the street! He'll give 'em hell!" More gunshots. "Come on, marshal! Fill the bastards full o' lead!"

Maxie hopped up and down, hoping to see over the heads of the taller women who crowded the window. But when she heard Hunter's name, she gave up and headed straight for the front door. Mother Moses—the only one besides Maxie who was fully dressed—joined her as she ran out onto the porch.

"Lord have mercy!" Moses said. "Where do you think you're going!" She grabbed Maxie's arm as the excited girl bolted out into the street.

This was just like the old days. For years she'd listened in envy as Blackjack and Tom told tales of their larcenous capers. As she watched gunsmoke drift from the open door of the bank and saw three masked men emerge with guns drawn, she felt the Maxwell blood stir in her veins.

"Those bastards!" Moses groaned. "This is awful!"

Maxie didn't think it was awful at all. It was exciting! She admired the practiced timing of the gang of four bandits. One had stood outside the bank with the horses while the other three went inside and pulled off a quick, neat, efficient robbery. As Maxie and Mother Moses stood watching, the three burst out of the bank door and swung aboard their horses. All four of the bandits spurred their mounts into a gallop down the street. The smooth, rehearsed precision of their getaway was a thing of beauty.

But of course Hunter had to try to spoil the fun! He and Simon Curtis were sprinting toward the bank, pistols drawn.

"Come on!" Maxie urged her bandit heroes. "Get a move on!"

She knew a second of alarm as one bandit turned and fired at Hunter. A lead slug plowed up the dust less than a foot from the marshal's boots—too close for comfort. Maxie wouldn't have minded landing a few hard punches on Hunter's arrogant face; the bastard deserved them. But she didn't really want to see him shot full of lead either.

Still, she didn't think it fair when Hunter returned the bandit's fire with obvious lethal intent. The man clutched at his shoulder, shouted an obscenity, and toppled from his horse. His friends didn't stop to help him. They were off in a cloud of dust.

Hunter left the wounded man to Simon's not too gentle attentions while he grabbed men to form a posse.

"Marshal Hunter!" A man shouted from the bank door and waved his arms in a panicky appeal. "Come quickly!"

Hunter dashed through the crowd, and it parted to let him through. Maxie could almost hear the townfolk take a collective breath and hold it, though she couldn't guess what could interest them now. The robbery was over.

"Come on!" She tugged Mother Moses toward the bank. "Let's go see!"

"Not me, honey!" Moses responded. "I've learned to mind my own business in this town. Besides, you don't need to be seen in my company. You got troubles enough as it is. Go on."

Maxie hurried to the bank at a most unladylike pace. As she pushed through the barrier of people in front of the door, a queer fluttery forboding quivered in her stomach, though she didn't know why. A holdup was a lark, nothing more. If people didn't want to be robbed, they shouldn't put their money in a bank. They should keep it home where it was safe.

"Is someone hurt?" she asked.

No one answered her. No one even paid her any mind. The crowd was too busy buzzing in speculation about what was happening inside the bank.

Suddenly, Maxie remembered that Cynthia had been

heading for the bank. The flutter of forboding in her stomach swelled into panic. She elbowed her way to the door and went in.

Cynthia lay in front of one of the teller's windows. Both Hunter and Doc Carter knelt beside her still form, partially hiding her from view, but Maxie could see that her side was crimson with blood. Maxie's stomach rose into her throat.

"Cynthia?"

Hunter turned to look at her. His face was expressionless —frighteningly so. Maxie would have been less alarmed if his features had been twisted in anger.

He stood, wiped blood-smeared hands on his pants, and regarded her with glacial eyes. "Are you satisfied?" he said softly.

"Is she . . . is she . . . ?"

He pushed past her, ignoring her question. "Let's ride!" she heard him shout to the posse gathered outside.

"She's alive," Doc Carter said.

"Oh, God. Thank you!" Maxie dropped to her knees beside her friend. She could see that Cynthia was breathing with steady but shallow breaths.

"The ball lodged between her ribs. We'll have to get her to my surgery. Will you help, miss?"

"Of course I'll help," Maxie cried, her voice a mere sob. "Of course. Of course. Just tell me what to do." She glanced at the other body that was lying prone on the bank floor at the other end of the teller's counter. "What about . . . what about him?" She recognized the small frame, the wire-rimmed glasses, and the sparse fringe of graying hair as belonging to John Tuttle, a kind little man who was a bank teller. She had met him at the church social, and when almost all of Motherlode was turning their noses up at her, he had still given her a friendly word.

"He's dead," Doc Carter told her.

"Dead?" A timid little bank teller and a harmless girl. How could that be? "Why would . . . why would they shoot at . . . ?"

"At these two?" Doc asked, a cynical ring to his voice. "They weren't shooting at these two, miss. Those bastards were just shooting, just firing off those pistols of theirs to show how tough they are. What do they care if a girl and a harmless old man get in the way of their damned lead? 'Scuse me, miss, for cussing in front of a lady. But some things just naturally make a man cuss."

The next few hours seemed endless. Cynthia's parents joined Maxie in the small anteroom of Doc Carter's surgery. All three of them sat, paced, wrung their hands, prayed, and waited for Carter to emerge from behind the closed door that led to the treatment room. The longer they waited, the more Maxie feared that Cynthia was worse off than Doc had first believed. What else could be taking so long? Poor Cynthia. Poor, sweet, innocent Cynthia. And poor Cynthia's parents. Maxie felt she had suddenly been catapulted into a nightmare from which she couldn't awaken.

How had this happened? What had Hunter meant when he asked her if she was satisfied? Did he think this was her fault? Did he think those bandits were her brothers? Well, she could tell him for certain they were not. She would have recognized her brothers, masks and all. Her brothers never would have thrown lead around in such a heedless fashion. Her brothers never would have hurt an innocent like Cynthia and killed a sweet old man like John Tuttle.

Would they?

An uncomfortable memory came to mind. Blackjack's kidnapped sweetheart had been an innocent. She'd been coming out west to get married, Julia had told Maxie. She had seemed so forlorn when she'd said it. Since being taken by the Apaches Maxie had a new appreciation for the miseries of abduction. Poor Julia had probably felt about Blackjack the way Maxie had felt about Choto. That summer Julia had died of heatstroke. If her brothers had left well enough alone, Julia would be alive and happy, living with a husband who loved her.

Damn, but life was getting complicated! Maxie had never

been on the losing end of a robbery before. The experience certainly wasn't a pleasant one, and it gave her second thoughts about the Maxwell family occupation. She looked at the Pruitts' anxious faces, felt the pain in her own heart. Did every caper her family pulled hurt people this much? The question was one that had never occurred to her before.

The door to the surgery opened and Doc Carter walked out. "I think she's going to be all right—if the wound doesn't putrefy, that is. Her rib stopped the ball before it could puncture her lung. All in all, the wound is pretty superficial. A couple of weeks in bed should see her right again."

Georgia Pruitt, who had fretted in silence all the time they waited, burst into tears. Mr. Pruitt harrumphed and wiped surreptitiously at his eyes.

"I hope Hunter catches up to those bastards," Doc continued. "And I hope he brings 'em back to town alive, so all of us can enjoy seeing 'em hang."

Maxie's visit to the Pruitts was extended once again, this time to nurse Cynthia. Her help freed Mrs. Pruitt to work in the store, as was her habit, and at the same time assuaged some of the inexplicable guilt she felt for what had happened. Nineteen was a bit late in life for a body to grow a conscience, Maxie tried to tell herself, but damned if a brand spanking new one hadn't been delivered to her doorstep. And it was working overtime to make up for all those lost years. The Maxwells had nothing to do with Mr. Tuttle's death and Cynthia's injury, but just the same she felt as though she herself had fired the lead slug that had torn into her friend's side.

But the life of freewheeling lawlessness was where she belonged.

Wasn't it?

Hunter visited every day, the first time to tell Cynthia that the bandits had been caught and soon would stand trial. Since Aaron himself was judge as well as town marshal, Maxie had little doubt what the sentence would be.

After the first official visit Hunter found one excuse after another to drop by. His visits were short, usually consisting of a terse greeting to Maxie, a few minutes of trivial conversation with Cynthia, and a certain amount of awkward hat twiddling and throat clearing before he took his leave. He came every day, sometimes twice a day, until Maxie wondered if Cynthia realized how fond of her the marshal was. Perhaps Cynthia didn't see marriage in their future, but what did Hunter see?

"He certainly didn't treat me with such solicitous care when I was well," Cynthia remarked one day after Hunter had left. She looked at Maxie thoughtfully. "I think perhaps it's not me he's coming to see."

Maxie stopped straightening the counterpane of Cynthia's bed when she caught sight of her friend's meaningfully upraised brow.

"Don't be silly."

"Well, Aaron's never wanted to see this much of me. He's always treated me like a sister—before now, that is. And there's certainly no reason for these daily visits. I'm not at death's door, after all. Heavens! If you'd only let me get out of bed I'd be bouncing with energy."

"Stay in bed," Maxie ordered for the tenth time that day.

"What about a nice easy outing? I vow the stale air in this house could kill a stronger woman than I. Suppose I get Aaron to take us out in the buggy for a little ride? All I would have to do is lounge on the seat and enjoy the healthful fresh air."

"Hunter wouldn't have time. And I don't know how to drive a fancy buggy. I'm better at riding horseback."

"Ladies are driven. They don't ride horseback like a drover."

The woman never gave up, Maxie thought wryly. Almost the moment she'd been strong enough to talk their "lady lessons" had resumed.

"Besides," Cynthia continued. "He will too have time. You just wait and see."

Hunter point-blank refused to take Cynthia on an outing when the question was put to him the very next day. She belonged in bed, he insisted, for once agreeing with Maxie. Besides, he had better things to do than dally away the day with a couple of women.

Maxie refrained from pointing out that he dallied away a significant amount of time each day visiting with Cynthia at her bedside. If he had better things to do then why wasn't he doing them?

When Hunter next came to visit, however, Cynthia was dressed and sitting in the parlor. Boredom, she complained, was more likely to do her in than her rapidly healing wound. Maxie watched as she played on Hunter's affection, loyalty, and guilt with the expertise of long practice. Lady-like little Cynthia Pruitt, Maxie decided, could probably teach Mother Moses' girls a bit about how to handle a man, even though she never allowed more from any man than a chaste kiss. Predictably, Hunter crumbled. The outing was set for the following morning.

Cynthia's complaints of a headache a half hour before Hunter was due to pick them up were also predictable, Maxie thought. She should have known that the whole outing idea was a plot to get her and Hunter together. Part of her—an unruly, giddy part of her that had been growing by leaps and bounds—was eager. Another part of her rebelled.

"I am not riding in a buggy anywhere with that worm! The only reason I was going in the first place was to keep you company."

"I never thought I would see the day you'd turn chicken!" Cynthia threw back.

"I am not chicken!" For a brief moment their words reminded Maxie of a similar argument she'd had one day many years ago with her twin. "Chicken" had been Dirty Jim's favorite insult, sure to rile her to the point of flailing fists. But on that day her twin had been the chicken. He had run, and Maxie had rescued Aaron Hunter from a mob of angry miners. How long ago that had been!

"All right. I'm chicken. Besides, I don't want Hunter's attentions. We're natural-born enemies, like cats and dogs."

"My mother's cat gets along just fine with every dog in town."

Maxie wondered how the stupid cat would like to come face to face with a hungry desert coyote. That was what Hunter reminded her of at times. Strong, single-minded, smart, and driven. A coyote was driven by his empty stomach. Maxie wasn't sure what drove Hunter. Pure orneriness, maybe.

"Miss Cynthia!" Inez, a Mexican-Indian girl who helped with the cleaning, called up the stairway. "Mr. Hunter's here, Miss Cynthia."

"I really don't want to go," Maxie claimed.

Cynthia raised a brow. They both knew she was lying.

"Oh, all right!" She huffed toward the door.

"Take your bonnet, Maxie," Cynthia called after her, a smile in her voice. "Ladies don't go out with their heads uncovered."

Hunter stood in the Pruitt parlor, turning his hat in restless circles, when Mrs. Pruitt glided into the room.

"Good day, Aaron," she greeted him. "I suppose you've come to take the girls on their outing."

"Yes, ma'am."

From Mrs. Pruitt's enigmatic smile, Aaron guessed that something was up, and he suspected what it was. Cynthia wasn't exactly subtle in her little plots. She'd been talking up Maxie's virtues ever since the two girls had first met.

"Did Inez go up to fetch the girls?" Mrs. Pruitt asked.

"Yes, ma'am. I expect they'll be down any minute."

Mrs. Pruitt settled herself gracefully on the settee and sighed. "I do hope Cynthia is feeling better than she did this morning. She had a dreadful headache. All this has been such a shock to her system, poor dear."

Aaron could see it coming. Mrs. Pruitt was part of the plot, and she lied no better than her daughter. Only yesterday Cyn had been practically bouncing out of her bed, held there only by Maxie's threats of retribution if she got up. Any headache Cynthia had was from thinking up ways to get him alone with Maxie.

Not that he hadn't asked for it. Cyn knew damned well he hadn't been coming every day to see her, good friends as they were. He just couldn't stay away from Maxie. Like a tongue worrying a bad tooth, he couldn't leave her be.

Every time the Maxwells pulled a job, Hunter managed to work up an anger that included Maxie along with her brothers. He'd worked up a damn good mad the day Cyn had been shot. His fury at Cynthia's attackers had spilled over to anyone who'd once followed the outlaw trail—including himself.

The incident at the bank had been a grim reminder of just where Maxie had come from, and where she still longed to be. His anger had added fuel to his determination to stay away from her—until he heard she was staying with the Pruitts to nurse Cynthia. The thought of her there, so close, pulled at him like a tightening noose. He'd given in to temptation, made excuses to come every day, and every day had noticed something more about Maxie that was irresistible, until he wondered if he could ever escape his own foolish passion. He was at war with himself and had been ever since Maxie had first kissed him at Stronghold. At this point in the battle, he conceded, the besotted fool in him was winning.

"What's taking the girls so long?" Mrs. Pruitt wondered aloud. "By the way, Aaron, I had our cook pack you young people a basket lunch, so be sure to go by the kitchen on your way out."

"That was kind of you," Aaron replied. "I'm sure . . ."

His voice died away. Maxie came down the stairs, a beribboned bonnet swinging from one hand, a blue dress heightening the color of her eyes. Its gracefully full skirt and tightly fitted bodice did everything possible to announce tastefully that Maxie was a mature, desirable woman.

Hunter felt an unreasoning flood of anger. Cactus Maxie Maxwell had no right to look that good. His good sense didn't have a chance with her using such high-caliber ammunition.

"Oh, dear!" Mrs. Pruitt lamented, right on cue, no doubt. "Is Cynthia not coming down?"

Maxie looked reluctant—almost innocent of this plot. She had an uncertain air that made her even more desirable.

"I'm afraid not," she replied.

Damn it to hell! He ought to make his apologies to Mrs. Pruitt and walk out the door, turn his back on the vision on the stairway and put her from his mind. But he couldn't. Too much of him wanted to drive out of town with Maxie sitting beside him.

Maxie gave him a doubtful glance. He met her eyes and knew he was hooked. Damn her anyway!

The air was heavy with September heat and with silence. Hunter had looked angry when Maxie told him that Cynthia was not feeling well enough to go. She had hoped he would call the whole outing off. To her surprise, he hadn't, but from the time they climbed into the buggy until now, at least five miles out of Motherlode, he hadn't said a word.

"It's a nice day," she began.

"It's damned hot."

So much for polite conversation. She didn't deserve this, Maxie decided. What had she ever done to Hunter besides save his rotten life? *He* was the one who had betrayed his former comrades. *He* was the one who had barged in and ruined her life, called her names, mocked her, and on top of that, taken intimate liberties with her "person," as Cynthia called it. And here he was, acting as if she were some sort of scum that had risen to the top of a slimy pond.

"It wasn't my fault that Cyn got hurt," she said suddenly into the silence.

"I never said it was."

"You did. You said, 'Are you satisfied?' just before you walked out of the bank that day. Just as though I had pulled the trigger on the pistol that shot Cynthia. It was a nasty thing to say. It was unfair."

"I was mad."

"You didn't have any reason to be mad at me!"

"Like hell! Tell me you weren't cheering for those scum bags that were shooting up the bank!"

Maxie felt a momentary flash of guilt. She had been cheering for the bandits, but that had been before she saw the results. How could he believe that she could still be cheering after what those men did to Cynthia? Guilt turned to indignation.

"Stop the buggy."

"What?"

"Stop . . . the . . . buggy." She enunciated each word, as if speaking to a particularly slow child.

Hunter hauled back on the lines; the buggy rumbled to a halt. Chin lifted in ladylike disdain, Maxie stepped out.

"What the hell are you doing?"

She gave him a withering look, one she had practiced long and hard under Cynthia's tutelage. "I don't have to tolerate this. No gentleman speaks to a lady the way you've been talking. You're not a gentleman, Hunter, no matter what you want people to think."

He looked as though he couldn't decide whether to laugh or curse. "And you think you're a lady?"

"I damned well . . . I certainly am! Haven't you been telling me all along to mend my ways and become civilized? Well, I'm learning to be a lady. And you still call me names and treat me like some dirty-nosed little kid in britches." She lifted her nose higher in the air. "I'm not going to put up with it."

He gave her a long, thorough look, then smiled. "What do you think you're going to do, Miss High-and-Mighty Lady? Walk back to town?"

"Watch me!" Chin still high, she started back toward

town. After three strides her feet hurt, and with each stride walking like a lady became increasingly difficult. The high-heeled, tightly laced shoes Cynthia had forced upon her feet that morning were not meant for hikes.

Maxie heard the buggy creak as Hunter jumped down to follow, but she didn't deign to turn around until his hand landed on her shoulder.

"Maxie! Dammit! I mean . . . I'm sorry." He turned her toward him. "You're right. I've been treating you badly, and I had no call. None of this is your fault."

"None of what is my fault?" His face almost made her heart want to stop. He looked like a man torn apart inside. "Hunter, you've got me so confused I can't spit. Will you tell me why you hate me so much? I know why I ought to hate you, but I can't figure why you've got it in for me."

"I don't hate you, Maxie. Lord knows, I don't nearly hate you."

She still didn't like the look on his face.

"Let's drive down to the river and have lunch," he suggested. "Mrs. Pruitt's cook packed us a basket. It would be a shame to waste it."

They had been following the little creek that flowed through Motherlode. In the town it was a mere trickle, but out here it widened to several feet across where it flowed into the Santa Cruz. In another mile they reached the confluence, then turned north to follow a mostly overgrown wagon trace that paralleled the banks of the larger river.

Not until he pulled up the team in the shade of a cottonwood tree did Hunter speak again.

"This looks like a good place to eat."

Maxie was still mad at him, so she made no more attempts at conversation. She wasn't going to get down on her knees and beg him to like her. Why should she?

"Maxie, I'm sorry you think I hate you. I don't."

In silence Maxie got the lunch basket out of the buggy, spread a cloth, and set out the food that Georgia Pruitt's cook had packed—slices of cold ham and chicken, sourdough bread, and apple pie. Cynthia said that a lady always set out the food for the gentlemen, as if the toads were helpless or something. She reasoned that she might as well practice, even if Hunter wasn't a gentleman and didn't believe she could be a lady.

"Will you sit down and listen!"

"I thought you wanted to eat."

"Maxie. I'm trying to explain something."

"What?"

"Dammit! Hell, I'm sorry. I know, I know," he said as her eyes narrowed. "You're a lady now." His eyes softened. "I do admire your guts, Maxie. Life's handed you nothing but a hard time, and you always make the best of it, don't you."

"Do you really not hate me, Hunter?"

"I . . . I really don't hate you, kid."

"I'm not a kid."

His eyes, which had been clinging to her, slid away uneasily. "No. You're not. I should know that by now, shouldn't I?"

He ignored the ham and chicken, and even the apple pie, which Mrs. Pruitt had said was his favorite. Instead of eating, he went to the cottonwood tree and leaned his broad back against its trunk. When he spoke, he appeared to be speaking to the river instead of Maxie.

"This land is all mine, you know. I bought all this river bottom parcel when I came back from the war. I was going to start a cattle ranch here."

"What happened?"

"Apaches burned me out, killed my starter stock. The road turns in another hundred feet to go behind the hill. That's where the house and barn were. The burnt-out frames are still there."

Maxie liked the thought of Hunter being a rancher better than Hunter being a vengeance-bound lawman. "You could have started over. Built a fortress house, like the Kelleys'."

"Yeah. I was going to do that. Had a girl coming out from

back East who was going to marry me. I met her in Virginia during the war."

Maxie was silent, hearing the pain in Hunter's voice. She remembered what Sophie had said about Hunter's poor lady.

"She died," he continued. "Killed by bandits on her way out."

"And you figure if you bring in every bandit in the border country, you're bound to get your licks in on whoever killed her. Is that it?"

"Yeah," he said slowly. "That's it."

"And you've been hating me and my family because you figured we might have done it?"

"I never hated you, Maxie. And I never figured you had anything to do with this. I guess you were right when you said I was running away from what I used to be. Just happens you're a reminder of those days, but as much as I wanted to hate you, I couldn't. You're not a woman a man can easily hate, Maxie. Just the same, every time I start enjoying you for . . . for just you, something happens along to remind me of who you are and where you come from." He paused, looked at the ground for a long moment, then brought his eyes up to meet hers. "Maxie, I . . ."

"Hunter!" Maxie shied away from the tone of his voice. She was sick and tired of the game she was playing. She'd wanted Hunter to make a fool of himself by admitting he wanted her, just as he'd made her unwillingly want him. But that little scheme no longer seemed fun. The whole plot had turned sour somehow, and it had already gone far beyond a simple bit of revenge. Maxie hadn't counted on becoming more involved herself, but this Aaron Hunter, sad and vulnerable and not so tough, tugged dangerously at her heart. "I'm hungry," she insisted.

"You're hungry, so I have to eat?" When he turned, his eyes looked as though something dark had been swept from their depths. He smiled, and for the first time since he'd first reappeared at Stronghold, the smile was the gentle-humored one she remembered from the boy she had rescued those many years ago.

"All right. We'll eat. But we're going to finish this conversation"—he raised a hand mockingly to ward off her scowl—"on full stomachs."

They ate in silence. Maxie picked at her food. The afternoon heat dulled her appetite, and a tension had sprung up between her and Hunter that made her feel all squirrelly inside.

"It's hot," Maxie complained. She looked out over the green Santa Cruz. The water looked inviting, and the thought of being alone for a while was equally inviting. She needed to think. "I believe I'll go into the water. This dress pinches like the . . . like anything."

Hunter cut her an odd glance. "Last time I saw you in a river you flailed around like a cat in a washtub. Don't tell me you can swim."

"I can swim!" Maxie said, automatically denying any shortcoming. Then she looked sheepish. "Okay, I can't swim—much. But the water's not deep." Her face grew warm at the memory of that river tussle. Hunter had gotten an eyeful that day, because she'd ended up naked as a molting snake. The look in his eyes suggested he might be remembering the same thing.

After a few moments that seemed a very long time, Hunter tore his eyes away from her, shook his head, and chuckled. He threw her one of his pistols, butt first. "Take that with you. Leave it on the bank where you can get to it fast."

Maxie walked only to where she was just out of Hunter's sight, to a spot where the river pooled in quiet green along one bank and rippled over a sandbar at the other. Gratefully she peeled off her sweat-dampened dress, shift, stockings, and drawers, deciding while she did so that ladies would be a lot happier if they allowed themselves to wear loose britches and cool cotton shirts.

The water was deliciously cool as she waded into the

river. Feeling brave, she inched into the pool up to her waist, dunked her head, then shook crystal droplets from her hair. Cool at last, she stretched herself out on the shallow sand bar and let the water ripple over her body and tug at the corkscrew streamers of her hair. This was heaven itself.

No sound on the bank alerted her, no movement caught her eye. But the feeling of watching eyes penetrated her languor, and an unfamiliar tension rippled through her body. She opened her eyes, sat up, and turned.

Hunter stood on the riverbank, every line of his body taut. On his face was the crooked half smile that Maxie had always thought was dangerous. Now she knew it was dangerous.

"I tried to stay away, Maxie," he said softly. "God knows I tried."

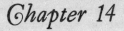

Chapter 14

$\mathcal{H}$unter unfastened his gun belt and tossed it to one side. Never taking his eyes from Maxie, unhurried and deliberate, he pulled off his boots, shirt, and pants and stood unashamed and naked at the river's edge. For a moment he just stood there, looking at her. Then he dived into the pool. In seconds he surfaced and shook the water from his hair in a spray of droplets. His eyes still clung to her face as though they had never left it.

In a panic, Maxie shot up from her seat in the shallow ripples and splashed to the far side of the pool, not stopping until the water rose above her breasts. But even with her body veiled by the swirling green water she felt completely revealed before his intense gaze—vulnerable, wanting, yet afraid.

She had watched in hypnotized fascination as he stripped. Lean hard muscles; broad shoulders; narrow hips; straight, strong legs. Every movement was supple and smooth, the play of muscles under bronzed skin like a physical melody, compelling, irresistible, exciting a resonant chord in her own body that made every nerve vibrate. The fire in his eyes drew her while at the same time it frightened her.

Now he stood there, water cascading from his hard body, giving her a stare that reminded her of a coyote looking at a fat hen. He started forward, the water swirling around his hips.

Maxie's eyes narrowed. "Don't you come any closer, you son of a bitch."

He grinned—an expression that heated and chilled her at the same time.

"Ladies don't call gentlemen such names."

"Gentlemen don't peek at ladies when they're taking a bath."

"I'm not peeking, Maxie. I'm out-and-out staring. And that's not all I'm going to do."

"Like hell."

He chuckled, then held out a hand. "Come here, Maxie."

The play of muscles in his arm nearly mesmerized her once again. The temptation to slip into his embrace was almost more than she could resist. But she managed. "Eat worms, Hunter."

"We both need this. You and me both. Maxie girl, there's a pull between us that a team of mules couldn't fight."

"I . . ." She tried to deny it, but couldn't. All she could force out was a puny squeak: "Don't come any closer! Yikes!"

He dived toward her, disappearing under the dark green water. Maxie jumped at the same time, splashing in panic, trying to see where he was.

"Stay away from me, dammit!" She turned in a circle, her heart racing. Then hard, callused hands circled her bare waist and his body surged against hers.

She screamed, twisted, kicked, and broke free. Desperately she dived for the bank. Every corner of her mind babbled with a different voice, one in panicky terror, another chortling in ribald excitement, and still another laughing at how foolish they both must look. Panic won out, and she plowed through the pool toward the bank, completely unaware that her body had suddenly discovered how to swim.

But her escape was too late. Fingers closed in a vise around her ankle and pulled her back into the pool.

"Come here and settle down," Hunter ordered. He hauled her toward him, grasped her waist, and held her at arm's length. "Ease up, Maxie. I'm not going to do anything you don't want me to do."

Maxie's flight had taken them into shallower water. Hunter's eyes slipped from her face downward to her exposed breasts, which were fetchingly accentuated by curving streams of water that cascaded from her hair. He raised his hand and gently, almost reverently cupped one small mound.

"You want me." His voice was hoarse, almost unrecognizable.

She closed her eyes. Something inside her melted at the feel of his hard hand on her flesh. Every nerve seemed to stand on end, and a sharp, almost painful, longing began to swell deep in her gut.

"No. Don't stop," she whispered as his hand slid down over her ribs, her stomach, her hips.

"I'm not going to stop," he assured her.

Every part of her body that his hand touched seemed to glow with an inner heat. In her mind's eye she could see the trail of fire blazed by his caress. Each little fire grew, spread, joined with others, became a blaze that burned every doubt, every question, every shred of caution from her soul. To hell with what she ought to do or feel. Maxie wanted Aaron Hunter. She wanted him so badly that she thought she would die if he took his hand away.

"Come over here," he whispered. He slipped his arm around her waist and guided her toward the sandbar. Gently he pushed her down onto the clean sand. Her body made a dam for the inch-deep water that rippled over the bar. It splashed against her hips and swirled around the slim length of her thighs. Maxie laughed at the cool fingers of water that tickled her skin, then Hunter lowered himself upon her. His kiss drowned her laughter, and she forgot about the sand beneath her and the playful water. She forgot who she was, who he was. She forgot about the sorry past and the doubtful future, forgot everything in the world except the feel of his mouth caressing hers, his hard thigh pressing between her legs, his fingers combing slowly, sensuously through her hair.

"God you're beautiful, Maxie. How did you ever get to be so beautiful?"

Who cared if she was beautiful? Maxie wanted him to stop talking, stop fooling around, and get down to the business of showing her where all these lovely feelings were leading. In innocent enthusiasm she lifted herself against him. She clutched at his lean hips and pressed him more tightly against her.

"Please!" she begged.

"And impatient," he continued with a grin. "I should have guessed you wouldn't be one to lie around and be courted."

She squirmed against his thigh, then groaned with pleasure when his hand slipped between her legs and began to caress, slowly, light and delicate as an elusive, torturing feather. The ache became an agony that was both joy and pain.

"Hunter! Please!"

His slow smile looked almost malicious. "You could call me by my first name."

"Aaron!" She would call him by God's first name if that was what it took for him to give her what she needed. Lordy! Who knew a man could have such power over a woman!

His fingers pushed inside her. One finger, then two, gently, rhythmically diving into untraveled territory. Maxie gasped with the delicious shock of it.

"Easy, sweet girl. We have all the time in the world."

She didn't believe him. They had only a moment. Something, someone would take this away from them. They were stealing this pleasure from a stingy fate, and she wanted to have all she could before reality swooped down and made her pay the price. She pulled him down for another kiss. He complied. The demand of his lips turned her whole body to sweet warm syrup.

Adrift in sensation, Maxie allowed her hands to wander. They slid over his broad shoulders, traveled the smooth, muscled expanse of his back, explored his ribs, slipped between their wet, straining bodies to caress his muscle-corded belly and . . . Lordy! What was that?

Their kiss broke and she drew back slightly, the fire of her passion sputtering. Maxie knew what that was. She was no prissy drawing-room miss, after all. But who knew it could get so big?

Aaron laughed at the expression on her face. His hand closed around hers, pressuring her fingers to circle that very male part of him.

"Maxie, girl. You know that I won't hurt you."

Maxie knew no such thing. Suddenly she doubted she was built for this sort of thing. Maybe she was supposed to be bigger, or maybe women came in different sizes—just as boots came in different sizes for different-size feet.

"Hunter, I . . ."

"Aaron. Last names are for . . . well, they're not for lovers."

"Aaron. I think . . ."

"Don't think, Maxie." His hand moved again between her legs, and the ecstasy washed over her in a new wave. "We've both done too much thinking."

She lay back on the sand and let the feeling take her. One last protest. "I . . . I think . . . maybe this isn't . . . a good . . . a good idea."

"It probably isn't." His voice had a strange quality that was oddly exciting—husky, rough, the voice of a man almost out of control. And she had made him that way. "But you're not going to ask me to stop, are you?"

She sighed and arched up against him. "No. Nooo."

His hand abandoned its magical work. Before she could protest the loss, he was above her, blocking the sky from view. His hips wedged between her legs, pressing them apart, while he lowered his mouth to hers and claimed her lips. "You belong to me, you know," he whispered against her mouth.

He pushed inside her, embedded himself in her flesh before she could even put up a token struggle. She was virgin no longer.

"You're beautiful, Maxie."

Horseshit. "It hurts," she complained in surprise.

"I know. Only this first time, sweet girl. Never again." He grinned down at her. "I'll make it up to you."

He did. He made up for that small hurt and then some. When he moved the earth moved with him, the heavens and the whole universe turned around him, and she was at their center. Maxie had never guessed that such sensations existed, such power, such exhilaration. She was flying, soaring among the clouds. Higher and higher she climbed, and Hunter was right there with her, lifting her, surrounding her, piercing her with a joy so sharp it hurt. They climbed until they were dancing among the stars. For an eternity they stayed there, and then the stars burst with an explosion of white fire. Hot, brilliant, blinding. Maxie thought she would die of bliss. But she didn't die. Still locked in Hunter's arms, she spiraled lazily down to earth amid glowing remnants of their passion. The earth received her—soft, warm, dark earth, lulling her peacefully, contentedly to sleep.

When Maxie woke she was lying naked in Hunter's arms, and the sun had traveled at least an hour's distance across the sky.

"Welcome back." Hunter touched a finger to her cheek and smiled.

For a moment Maxie believed she was waking from a

dream, and then the slight soreness between her legs brought home the truth. Her face promptly turned a fiery red.

"Are you all right?"

"Sure." How could she be better? She had just allowed herself to be seduced by a man who had done nothing but bring confusion and turmoil into her life. Or had she seduced him? The exact sequence of what had happened eluded her. Most of the last few hours were muddied by a flood of sensation.

"Maxie."

She looked up at him uncertainly.

"Don't look so much like a lost orphan. Everything's going to be all right."

Easy for him to say. Was he laughing under that crooked smile? Was he satisfied that Cactus Maxie was just like all the other women who came running at the crook of his finger? Was this the final mockery?

"Maxie, girl," he said softly, his fingers playing in her hair. "Together we're like a load of nitro going over a bumpy trail, whether we're fighting or loving. But there's a thing between us that won't let go, and fighting it's about as much use as pulling against a team of mules." He grinned. "I give."

"What do you mean?"

"I mean you're going to marry me, girl."

Marry Hunter! Marry him? Like hell! This scheme really *had* gotten out of control!

Maxie squirmed from beneath him as if he had suddenly become a live coal pressed against her skin. What did he think he was doing? A man didn't up and marry a girl just because she was stupid enough to let him . . . That was it! He felt sorry for her! He felt guilty about taking her virginity! That had to be it.

"You don't have to marry me! I can take care of myself!"

He smiled. The distracted look on his face reminded her

that not a single thread stood between her skin and the open air, and her clothes were across the river.

"Don't look at me like that!"

"I like to look at you."

"Well . . . hell!" She debated between retreating across the river to the safety of clothing, and standing her ground. Safety won. She turned and waded through the shallows. A splash behind her told her that Hunter was following.

"Maxie! What are you all riled up about?"

"You think I'm going to marry you?" What would he say if he knew her brothers had instructed her to get close to him so she could lead him into a trap? She'd done a pretty good job of it, hadn't she, even though she'd never intended to!

"Well, after what we just did—yeah! I think you're going to marry me!"

"Just because I let you . . . let you do . . . that to me?"

"Because we belong together, dammit!"

"Don't cuss in front of a lady!"

"Oh goddammit! Maxie! Don't try to change the subject!"

She stomped onto the grassy bank, retrieved her clothing, and retreated behind a veil of mesquite, feeling his eyes upon her back the whole way.

"It's a bit late for modesty, don't you think?"

"No! That whole . . . thing . . . was an accident."

"Like hell it was. Girl, that thing has been coming since we first saw each other."

"Well, then, it was coming. And now it's over and done with!"

"It is a long way from being over, goddammit! I want to marry you!"

She came out from behind the mesquite, clothed once again in her prim, ladylike dress with its starched cuffs and collar. "You don't want to marry me, Aaron Hunter! You think I'm a sorry-looking draggletailed ragamuffin. Sometimes you think I'm a stupid kid and other times you think I'm a whore and still other times you think I'm a low-down skunk who would side with the scum who shot my best friend. But you're so upstanding and pure that you feel guilty for suckering a stupid kid into . . . into . . ." She swallowed hard. "You don't really want to marry me. How stupid do you think I am?"

Hunter looked at her as if she had suddenly turned green and sprouted a tail. "You're nuts."

"I'm not nuts!" She huffed in indignation. "In fact, I'm the only one here who isn't loco!"

If she worked up enough anger, Maxie figured, she might forget how right his body had seemed against hers, how good it had felt when he had . . . Lordy! How had she let herself get so carried away? Aaron Hunter was her foe. He was a destroyer of freedom, of lives—of her family, given half a chance. No matter what idiocy possessed her when they touched, nothing could ever come of it. Nothing! Ever!

"Marry you, indeed!" She sat down, pulled on her lady-like shoes and fumbled angrily with the buttons. "Does a sheep marry a wolf? Does a hen cuddle up to a coyote?"

"What the HELL are you talking about?"

"I'm leaving." She stood and dusted off her skirt with determined finality, wishing she could dust him off as easily.

"The hell you're leaving!"

She ignored him and slipped one of the horses out of harness.

"Maxie, for Chrissakes stay and we'll go back in the morning. It's getting dark."

"Don't you come near me!" she warned as he stepped forward to take her horse. "I'm going back to town."

If her icy tone was not enough of a deterrent, then the pistol she pointed in his direction certainly was. The gun was his own, and it was loaded. He had checked it before giving it to her when she'd left to swim. She had picked it up when she retrieved her clothes.

"I've never seen a woman get so goddamned upset over a proposal!"

"Well, just how many proposals have you made, Hunter?

Do you propose every time you manage to get into a woman's drawers?"

"If you're so determined to go back tonight, we'll both go in the buggy."

"I don't feel like company. And besides"—she twirled the pistol around her finger a couple of times, stuck it in her belt, and swung agilely up onto the bare back of her mount —"buggies are for ladies, and I've just learned that I'm not one." She dug her heels into the horse's side. "Adios!"

Gritting his teeth, Aaron started to pull his clothes on. Damned little hellion! Damned stupid twit, riding off alone when there might be Apaches about. And with daylight almost gone. Lord save him from all women! That girl was going to be the end of him. She'd already destroyed his self-control and reason, and now she was working on his very sanity.

He shoved his shirt into his pants, wrenching a finger as he did so, and cursed out loud. What the hell did he think he was doing anyway? Cactus Maxie was everything he didn't need—a scruffy little hoyden who would take a man's peaceful, reasonable life and shatter it into a thousand chaotic pieces just for the fun of helping him put it back together. She was a dust devil in a woman's body, a thunderbolt disguised as a girl.

But he couldn't stay away from her. God knew he'd tried. He'd made a jackass of himself trying to stay away from her. But the fight was hopeless.

Her smile set him on fire. Her hair—those wild curls she tried so hard to subdue into a proper braid—begged his hands to run through its silken mass. Her incredibly blue eyes, her voice, even her sharp temper and touchy moods— everything about her drew him.

And Maxie felt the same about him, damn the stubborn little witch! She just wouldn't admit it; she hadn't given up the fight yet. Aaron could almost see the feeling shiver in the air between them. She'd made love to him with incredible abandon, yet at the mention of marriage she'd balked like a stubborn mule. All that talk about his not really wanting to marry her—she couldn't believe that. The accusations and name-calling were a disguise for her fear.

Aaron wondered who inspired Maxie's greatest fear—him, or herself?

The last remnant of daylight had fled. On the rocky uplands away from the river Maxie's trail would have been difficult to follow even in the daytime. At night the task would be impossible. She'd chosen her time of escape well, but the little she-wolf would be lucky if she didn't outsmart herself and break her fool neck in the dark.

Aaron ground his teeth, picked up a boot, started to pull it onto his foot, then threw it against the trunk of the cottonwood tree. "Shit and damnation!"

"Aaron!" Cynthia cried. "Heavens! Where have you been? I've looked and listened for you all night long, and . . ."

"Is Maxie here?" Aaron leaned wearily on the doorframe of the Pruitts' front door. He was gritty, tired, and impatient, and his voice matched his mood.

"She came in last night. But . . . but she's gone, Aaron. She borrowed Daddy's saddle horse and set out for Agua Linda. I couldn't say anything to dissuade her."

"Shit!"

"Aaron!"

He grimaced. "Sorry, Cynthia. It's been a long night. I lost a wheel on the buggy or I would've been here before Maxie."

"You come in right now and tell me what's going on." She took his arm and pulled him into the house. "Maxie wouldn't tell me a thing. All she did was mutter things that didn't make a bit of sense."

"True. That girl hasn't made any sense since I first met her."

No sooner had Cynthia put a mug of steaming coffee in Aaron's hands than a knock sounded at the door.

"There you are." Simon looked around Cynthia as she opened the door. He managed to greet Aaron without raising a brow, even though the marshal was chumming up to the town's most-sought-after lady so shortly after dawn. "Wondered where you'd taken yourself off to."

"Simon . . ." Aaron warned.

Simon's smile told Aaron he understood. No one in town would hear it from him that Hunter was in the Pruitt parlor at such an unseemly hour. "Got a couple a' agitated hombres in the office. Seems the freight wagon from Tucson was robbed early this mornin'. Two of the guards was killed. These other two want help trackin' down the bandits while the trail's still fresh. Want me to go?"

Aaron set down his coffee and ran his fingers through his hair. "No. I'll go." He was in the mood for a little bloodshed this morning. Preferably on a black-haired, blue-eyed, half-Mexican hellcat. But these poor bandits would have to do. "I have another job for you. Take a fast horse and catch up to Maxie. She's on her way to Agua Linda. Don't let her out of your sight once you catch up to her."

"She took off alone?" Simon asked. "With all a' these Apache bands roamin' around?"

"Just pity the Apaches if they run across Maxie," Aaron snorted. "Cynthia. Thanks for the coffee." He turned and gave her a quick kiss on the brow. "When I get back I'll explain everything."

"Aaron!"

But he was already gone.

The two freight wagon guards were apologetic about bothering Aaron. They knew that Motherlode's town marshal had no obligation to the freight company, they explained, but Hunter had a reputation as a good tracker and a handy fella with a gun. The freight company would be willing to pay him for his time in . . .

"You hombres want to stay here gabbing, or do you want

to hunt down some bandits?" Aaron interrupted their little speech.

"Uh . . . round up bandits."

"Let's go, then."

Hunter slung an extra belt of ammunition over his shoulder, grabbed a rifle, and walked out the door. The two guards looked at each other and shrugged. They'd found the right man, it seemed.

The outlaws' trail was easy to follow. The fools had been careless. Aaron remembered back to his years with the Maxwells. Those boys hid a trail as well as an Apache. The men Aaron followed now were certainly not Maxwells. For Maxie's sake, and for his own, he was glad they were not.

Aaron reined his horse to a halt and studied the hoofprints in the sand. "Looks like they split up here. Couple are headed toward Tucson. The others are riding for the border."

"Hell!" One of the guards spat. "They got a load of silver off the wagon. Suppose they've divided it?"

"Might have," Aaron speculated. "Or they might aim to meet later and split it then. No way to tell."

"Don't give a damn who's got the silver," the other guard said. "I jest wanna see them boys strung up for killin' Sam and Jeremiah."

"Well, then, we'd better ride," Aaron suggested. "You men head for the border. I'll take the two who're ridin' north."

"All right by us."

The bandits' trail went due north for several miles, then detoured toward the rougher country to the west. Aaron tracked them through rocky arroyos and over rugged hills studded with mesquite and Spanish dagger. Prints were hard to find in this country, and opportunities for ambush waited around every bend. Aaron began to feel the effect of a sleepless night and struggled to stay alert. These boys might be smarter than he thought.

In a sandy, dry streambed that wound between two cactus-covered hills, he found the first tracks he had seen in half a mile. A single horse had passed this way. His quarry had split yet again. One man was in front of him. Where was the other?

Aaron squinted up to the hills above, where an army of saguaro cactus marched up the slopes in ranks of prickly green. Some of the saguaro sported arms twisted into an octopus tangle. Others reached toward the sky with straight, clean limbs that could have been human arms. Too many could have been a tall, motionless man looking down into the gully, waiting until Aaron turned away to put a bullet in his back.

Weariness could play tricks with a man's imagination, Aaron decided. After double-checking the loading in his rifle and pistol, he rode on.

Five minutes later he caught a whiff of smoke on the breeze. Leaving his horse ground-reined and hidden by an outcrop of granite, he cocked his rifle and cautiously climbed above the trail. The aroma of woodsmoke soon led him to a ledge above a sheltered gully. There sat his quarry. A tall Mexican, long hair stringing down his back and greasy beard curling around his chin, squatted beside a small fire. He was skinning a ground squirrel that he'd doubtless killed with a stone. Aaron hadn't heard a shot. If the smell of smoke hadn't alerted him, he might have ridden right by this little hideaway none the wiser. No matter. This was one hombre who wouldn't be given a chance to learn from his mistakes.

Aaron rose from where he crouched and trained his rifle on the man's head. "Figure you'll be skipping your dinner tonight, compadre."

The man jumped in surprise, threw the squirrel aside, and went for his pistol. A bullet from Aaron's rifle sent the gun flying. The outlaw squawked in pain and cradled his bloodied hand.

"Next bullet's in your head," Hunter warned. "So let's be sensible from here on out."

Without taking his eyes from the whimpering bandit, Aaron slid down the slope. He pulled the saddlebags from the man's horse. They were heavy. Loaded with silver, no doubt. But before he could open them, a bullet whined past his head and plowed into the hill behind him.

Aaron dropped the saddlebags and drew his pistol in one fluid motion. His reputation with a gun was well earned; a glimpse of his attacker gave him enough of a target for his answering bullet to find its mark.

The first man took the opportunity to retrieve his pistol. Aaron caught the movement out of the corner of his eye and whirled to defend himself. Even as his finger tightened on the trigger, something kicked him in the side with the force of a mule. Gasping for breath, he thought he heard, strangely muted, the sound of gunfire. Then his world exploded.

The long-haired Mexican looked down at the lawman's unmoving body and spat. His aim with spittle wasn't as good as his aim had been with his pistol—even left-handed. The spit splatted into the sand beside the marshal's bloodied head.

The second man stumbled down the side of the gully and joined him, clutching at a wet, crimson shoulder. "He got me good, Miguel."

"Can you ride?" Miguel asked.

"*Sí.* I can ride. But shit, this hurts!"

"Quit bitchin'. Let's get out of here."

"What about him?"

Miguel looked once again at the lawman. One side of his face was coated with slowly congealing blood. His left side from armpit to hip was soaked in scarlet. Miguel nudged him with a toe. No response.

"He's dead. Let's go."

Chapter 15

*T*he morning sun had not quite risen above the eastern hills when Maxie strode through the wall gate and headed toward the hogpens, a bag of chicken feed in one hand and a basket of vegetable scraps in the other. Jake tagged along at her heels.

The hogs greeted her with their usual hungry good-morning grunts. On other mornings she had readily joined in their porcine conversation. Hogs, she had discovered, were often better listeners than people, and their comments were at least as interesting.

But this morning she wasn't in the mood for pig talk. She had other things on her mind.

Elsa came out of the barn and headed toward the pens. "There you are, Maxie."

"What are you doing out here so early?" Maxie asked.

"Gracie delivered her foal in the small hours, and I promised Mary she could watch." The German woman shook her head and smiled. "Foals are just like babies—always making an appearance in the middle of the night. But I supposed it was worth the lost sleep. Mary was happy. And Pete told her she could name the little one."

"Oh?"

"Maxie, what are you doing?"

"Just giving the hogs a few kitchen scraps."

"Chicken feed?"

Maxie paused and looked at what she had been throwing into the pen. The vegetable scraps were still in the basket, and the corn she had brought out for the chickens was almost all in the hogpen.

"Where is your head, girl? One day you've been home—only one day—and you put too much salt in the bread, try to fry tortillas without a fire, and now you think the hogs are chickens. You are walking in your sleep?"

Maxie sighed and perched herself on the top rail of the pen. "Elsa," she began hesitantly, "do you know anything about men?"

A knowing look came into the cook's eye. "Men, is it? I know a little something about men. A little. I have been a wife to a man and given birth to two sons."

"Do you think people—men and women—can hate each other and love each other at the same time?"

Elsa took the basket from Maxie's hands and began tossing the scraps into the pen. With a little smile she portioned some out to Jake, who watched her with hopeful eyes. "I have only loved one man in my life," she said. "I was married to my Frederick for ten years, and I loved him all that time. But on some days I hated him, too. Sometimes he could be so stubborn, and he wouldn't listen sometimes. . . . But I suppose men are made that way. I think if a woman loves a man and is with him night and day, it is certain she will hate him sometimes." She gave Maxie a shrewd look. "But if you really hate a man, girl, I don't think you would ever believe you loved him."

Maxie looked dissatisfied. "I don't think a woman really needs a man. Men try to push you around, tell you what to do, hurt your feelings. . . . Then they expect you to turn

around and pretend that they're . . . that they're something special."

"Yes," Elsa readily agreed. "Men are big children only.
They are seldom wise, or fair."

"And you seem to do very well without one."

Elsa gave Maxie the same look she might give an especially slow child.

"Do you think I would not have my Frederick back if I
could?"

"But . . . you haven't married again. You don't seem to
like men at all."

Elsa shook her head, tossed the last scrap to the hogs, and
propped herself against the rails of the pen. For a moment,
even though the day was just beginning, she looked very
weary. "A person can only be hit so many times before he is
dead. The Apaches tortured and killed my husband while I
watched. They held me as they bashed my little sons' heads
against a rock, and then they led me into the desert like a
mule. I didn't escape them because I was afraid, or because
I didn't want to die. I wanted to die, but only after I had
buried my husband and sons and said a proper good-bye to
their poor souls."

Staring toward the horizon, Elsa seemed to focus on nothing. Maxie wondered what dreadful scene from the past was
playing out before the German woman's eyes.

"When I watched my husband burn, I burned also. The
heart was tortured out of me, and even though I lived and
escaped, I had nothing left to give to any man."

Maxie dropped her eyes and stared at her hands. Suddenly her own troubles seemed small.

"You were the one who showed me that isn't true, girl."

"What?"

"You brought me Mary. And . . . Simon also, I think. He
told me how you nudged him in my direction." She smiled.
"I find that I do have something left to give."

Maxie's morning brightened a bit.

"You helped my life continue, little Maxie, so maybe I will

help yours start, eh? Marshal Hunter is a good man. A little rough around the edges, maybe, and he doesn't quite know what he wants. Like all men, he is easily confused." She paused. Her eyes crinkled in silent laughter. "Perhaps you should tell him what he wants, little one."

"I wasn't . . . it isn't him . . ." She gave up with a shrug and a sigh when she saw that Elsa didn't believe a word of her denial. "Maybe I should. Someone needs to take that hombre and tell him a thing or two!"

Elsa laughed. Maxie couldn't remember ever hearing her laugh before. "Let us go in and look at our new baby horse. Perhaps you can persuade Mary to come back to the house and help us tend to chores, eh?"

Maxie followed Elsa into the barn. The interior was dim, with only a few rays of the morning sun squeezing between the slats of the walls. But when Mary looked up to see them coming, her smile seemed to shine in the gloom. She squatted Apache-style in the clean straw of a stall. Next to her lay Pete's bay mare Gracie and a wet, spindly-legged little creature that was just getting its first look at the world.

Mary looked happier than Maxie had ever seen her. She almost expected the child to say something, so excited did she seem as she showed off Gracie and her newborn foal. But as always, Mary talked with her hands and face rather than with her tongue.

"Pete is going to let you name the little one?" Maxie asked.

Mary nodded happily.

Maxie knelt down beside her in the straw and whispered in a conspiratorial tone. "When the little filly gets old enough, maybe Pete will let you help train her. When I was your age, I was able to train a wild mustang that no one else could touch." She didn't add that she was only able to ride the horse after getting it loaded with whiskey she had swiped from Blackjack's lean-to. "Maybe he'll let us work with her together, you and me."

Mary looked enthralled. Her face lit up, but still she said

nothing. Almost—almost. Maxie imagined the words crowding into her mouth, trying to get out. Mary seemed ready to burst with them when a shout from outside the barn distracted them all.

"Keeee—rist!" came the voice of one of the hands. "Hunter!"

Maxie's heart jumped into her throat, and for a moment she was as mute as little Mary. Hunter had come. Had he come looking for her? Was he still angry? Did he still want to marry her? Was he going to shout to the whole ranch that she had acted like a slut and crawled all over him at the mere crook of his damned finger?

"Hunter!" she finally whispered, seeing but ignoring Elsa's knowing look.

She got up and ran out the barn door into the bright morning sunlight. She didn't want to see him. She didn't want him to see her. But she couldn't help herself.

The sight that greeted her changed her confused elation into panic. Sam Hendricks and Justin Barnhill were helping Hunter down from his horse. The left side of his face was crusted with blood, and the part of his face that was free of blood was pale as the underside of a toad. His left side, also, was spattered with blood from armpit to hip.

"Aaron! Aaron!" The name screamed through Maxie's brain as she ran forward, but it emerged from her mouth as a hoarse whisper. Even if she had screamed his name, though, he couldn't have heard her. He'd gone limp in Sam's arms.

"Hung on jest long enough," Sam said. "Don't think he even knows he's here, poor guy. I had to pry him out of that saddle."

"Take him inside, Sam," Elsa instructed. "Justin, take care of his horse."

Maxie stood unmoving, numb, unbelieving. This couldn't happen to Aaron Hunter. He was invulnerable—the fastest gun she'd ever seen, the best shot, the wiliest fighter. He was as tough as he was irritating. This couldn't happen.

Elsa took her arm. "Men are all the same, child. They get themselves ripped apart and expect a woman to piece them back together." She looked at her expectantly. "Will you leave your man for Medina to care for?"

"My man?" The words tasted strange on her tongue.

Elsa merely smiled.

"I'll take care of him," Maxie said with more certainty. "I'll take care of him."

Two weeks passed before Hunter was on his feet again. His wounds looked more deadly than they were. One bullet had creased his scalp, two others had plowed into his side. Doc Carter removed one; the other had bounced off a rib and done only superficial damage before making a bloody exit.

The most severe wound was to his pride.

"Maybe next time you'll think before taking on two gun hands by yourself," Maxie suggested one morning when her patient was well enough to be goaded.

Aaron answered with an ill-tempered growl. He was not a good patient. He did not bear well with being coddled, spoon-fed, ordered about, and lectured, all of which Maxie did with great delight. She appointed herself chief nurse, never leaving his bedside even to sleep. Medina, ignoring Aaron's accusations of plotting, ordered a cot moved into the sickroom for Maxie so she could give their patient twenty-four-hour care—or twenty-four-hour irritation, according to the point of view.

The first few days after Hunter's dramatic entrance he was beyond caring who was with him or what was done to him. Most of the time he was unconscious, suffering as much from loss of blood as from trauma. The people of Agua Linda stewed in their curiosity for three whole days before Hunter was lucid enough to tell them what had happened.

Aaron was not awake when the two guards from the freight company came to let him know that they had caught and summarily hanged all four men who had robbed the freight wagon. They never would have caught up to the slime, the guards told Pete, if Hunter hadn't tracked them through the mountains on that first day. Payment was due Hunter, just as they'd promised, and he could pick it up at the freight company headquarters in Tucson once he was back on his feet.

During those first few days when Hunter drifted between groggy consciousness and sleep, Maxie was constantly at his bedside. Nothing in particular needed to be done for him, but she couldn't drag herself away. She sat and watched him—every twitch, every moan riveting her attention. She sat and watched him until her eyes grew tired and her brain spun like a child's top from thoughts that she didn't want to think.

The young Aaron Hunter she had known as a child strode out from Maxie's memory. He was not the same man who lay on the bed. The Aaron Hunter who had plagued her since that black day at Stronghold was still cocky, but the wildness was gone. Now he was driven by forces she didn't quite understand. His passion to be lawful and civilized was a bother, but just the same, Maxie had never felt so secure with a man. Hunter had developed a tempered strength that came from maturity—something, thought Maxie ruefully, that she probably lacked.

This Aaron Hunter was much more dangerous than that green youth she had saved from dying—more of a danger to his enemies, more of a danger to her. While the youth had tugged at her heart, the man had yanked that silly organ from its very moorings. The pleasant daydreams of her girlhood had become an irresistible passion. She'd fallen for Aaron Hunter, in spite of what he'd done and what he was. Damn him to hell!

And damn him for getting himself hurt! If she hadn't had to sit and look at him hour after hour, perhaps she could have gone on pretending she hated him. If she hadn't seen him so helpless and twisted with pain, her heart might not have overwhelmed her reason. What had he been doing chasing after two armed gunmen by himself? A man just didn't take on armed enemies unless the odds were in his favor. Even brother Tom knew better than that, and as Blackjack often said, Tom wasn't quite playing with a full deck. If only Hunter hadn't been so stupid . . . !

If only . . . if only . . . ! No use gnashing her teeth over what might have been; the teeth gnashing should be directed toward what was going to be.

"What were you doing chasing down two armed men by yourself?" she queried on a day when he had recovered enough to withstand a bit of scolding. "I always knew you were a jackass, but I never figured you for a stupid jackass."

"I felt like bashing a few heads together."

From his expression, Maxie guessed that he still might like to bash someone's head. "And their heads were handier than mine?" she asked bluntly.

Had he been that angry when she refused to marry him? Why? He couldn't really want to marry her.

He shot her a look that could have frozen the hog pond in August. "I figured they might be easier to deal with."

She smiled, unable to resist. "Guess you were wrong, weren't you?"

Other times he seemed to mellow. Restlessness and boredom set his tongue speaking his thoughts aloud. He talked almost to himself, as if Maxie weren't there to listen. But she did listen. She had conceived a hunger to learn everything about Aaron Hunter that she could.

Hunter's family, she learned, lived in a place back East called Massachusetts. His father was a preacher man, and Aaron had two brothers and three sisters who had all married and settled close to their parents.

"I guess we're alike in some way, Maxie," Hunter commented one afternoon. "My ma was a real lady. Not high-class like yours, but a lady just the same. She was the only one who understood my itch to leave—told me once I needed to leave before my father and I killed each other."

Maxie's eyes grew wide. "Why'd you want to kill each other?"

Aaron shrugged, frowning as his mind dug through old memories. "Pa's a straight-arrow Methodist. He's the sort whose uprightness drives other men to drink. I was a kid with a nose for trouble. Got walloped about once a week." His mouth twitched in a wry smile. "Mostly deserved, I guess."

Maxie shook her head sympathetically. She'd had a few good wallopings from her own father, but once a week seemed a bit much. Her pa hadn't really cared enough about her to put out that kind of effort.

"I remember one Sunday when I was sixteen he hauled me up in front of his church congregation and told them in great detail about how I'd come from the Devil's seed, not his, and how I was going to burn in hell for pouring a jug of corn whiskey into the punch at the Sunday school picnic. A few months after that I left. My ma gave me some money and I managed to drift out to Arizona."

"Where you met my pa," she finished for him.

He gave her a wry smile. "Like I said, I had a nose for trouble. Your pa just helped me polish up a natural talent."

He looked so disgusted with that long-ago youthful self that Maxie had to argue.

"You weren't so bad, Hunter. You weren't vicious. Not like Pablo Seviers or Jake Gurney or . . ." Blackjack sprang into her mind. But Blackjack wasn't vicious. He was just wild. Maxwells were just naturally wild and free, but never really mean. "Remember them?" she finished lamely.

"Yeah. I remember them."

"I never saw you draw a gun on anyone who didn't deserve it, Hunter."

"You weren't along most of the time I was riding with your pa, Maxie."

That was true. But Hunter was made of different stuff than most of the men who had ridden with her father. Elsewise why would he be kicking himself over a few rob-

beries? Back then she had thought robberies were a harmless lark. Probably he'd thought the same. Now they'd both
learned better.

Through the long days of Maxie's insistent nursing and
Hunter's irritable, moody, restless recovery, Maxie felt her
doom envelope her with an ever tighter grip. She had fallen
in love with Aaron Hunter for his odd crooked smile, for the
way his hair fell in loose tousled curls over his forehead, for
the dark, mysterious depths in his eyes, and for the way he
made her feel when he touched her. But as the days
marched on and she discovered—piece by separate piece—
the Aaron Hunter she had not known before, she felt herself
slide deeper and deeper into the quicksand of love. Escape
was impossible, she finally admitted to herself. Might as well
relax and slip under with whatever dignity fate allowed.

Only one thing kept her from doing just that. The
thought of Hunter's lost love grated across newborn sensi-
tivities. Jealousy was an emotion new to Maxie, and she
didn't handle it well. She resented every moment the
woman had spent with Aaron; she resented every smile
Hunter had given her, every kiss, every—would a well-bred
lady from the East allow a man to take her before the vows
were spoken? Probably not. But if she had, then Maxie
resented every time Hunter had taken that woman in his
arms and made love to her. No doubt his highbrow ladylove
had managed to be dainty and fastidious through the whole
process, where Maxie, if memory served her correctly, had
behaved like a bitch in heat.

Most of all, Maxie resented the fact that Hunter still loved
the woman, even though she was dead. He was still hurting
so from her death that no matter how much Maxie bad-
gered him, he couldn't bring himself to talk about her. The
only information he would give her was what Maxie already
knew—she was a fancy eastern lady Aaron had met during
the war, and she was coming out west to meet him when
she was killed in a robbery of some sort. Then he would

close up tighter than a snail in its shell and refuse to say a thing more.

"You're never going to be satisfied, you know, Hunter," she told him one afternoon as he paced around his room. He was still a bit weak, but fast losing the wobble in his gait and the trembling in his hands. Only Medina's insistent cajoling had persuaded him to rest a day or two longer before riding to town—that and the fact that Medina had swiped his boots and wouldn't give them back until she was satisfied he was ready to go. "You could kill every bandit between here and Mexico City and still never be satisfied that you got the man who killed your lady. You figure to take revenge on all of us because one gang of . . . of—" She couldn't think of a word bad enough to describe men who would kill an innocent girl, at least not a word that Medina and Cynthia would approve.

He gave her a sharp look. "There's no 'us' to it. You don't have anything to do with it. And I'm not trying to kill anyone." Suddenly he seemed weary as he dropped down in a chair and looked out the window at the fading day. "After fighting my way through the war, I wanted to never see another man in my gunsights. All I wanted was to come back to Arizona and settle down to some peaceful ranching, make a home for a wife and children. But the Apaches and your bandit friends ended that."

"So you're trying to put them all in the ground. The bandits, at least."

"In prison or in the ground, it's their choice. Until these boys start paying some mind to the law, this country isn't going to be fit for anyone besides Apaches and rattlers." He turned and looked at her, and she marveled for the hundredth time how eyes sometimes so dark and cold could suddenly turn to fire. "You don't really want to go back to that life, do you, Maxie girl?"

She didn't answer. She wasn't sure she knew the answer. A body had to go where she was needed and loved, no matter if the life was good or bad. If only Hunter loved her

—really loved her . . . If only he had meant what his body said that day on the bank of the Santa Cruz River . . . If only he had proposed out of love rather than guilt . . .

Hunter caught the uncertainty in her eyes. "Son of a bitch!" he said quietly.

She looked up, startled by the intensity of his voice. He did care a little. He truly wanted her to stay. That was something.

"Sorry." He smiled that crooked smile she used to think was so irritating. "Shouldn't use such language around a lady."

Maxie shrugged. "I'm not enough of a lady that it matters. I guess I never will be."

"Why sound so downhearted? What's so important about being a lady?"

"Isn't that what you wanted me to be?"

"I don't . . ."

He scowled, stood up, walked to the window and back, then gave her a look she couldn't interpret. He had been going to say he didn't care what she became, Maxie thought. She'd heard it in his voice. And of course it was true. Why should he care?

"I don't . . . I don't know what I wanted, kid, other than to get you out of that hellhole, away from those bastards you call . . ." He trailed off at her frown. "Hell, Maxie, you don't have to be anything other than yourself." He stretched out his hand and touched her cheek with one finger. "You don't have any idea how special you are, do you?"

Maxie felt her insides turn to syrup. He thought she was special?

He moved his finger across her cheek and trailed it down her neck.

"Aaron." His name came out a warm whisper. It must have sounded like an invitation, because in the next instant she was pulled into his arms and held still while his mouth came down on hers. No more words were possible, or necessary.

Maxie hadn't known that a mere kiss could be so devastating. His mouth took possession of hers in a way that spoke of exactly what he had in mind for the rest of her. She felt engulfed, swallowed, absorbed, every part of herself intertwined with him. His tongue probed, entered, and thrust, reminding her of joys yet to come. By the time he released her, she was shuddering with desire.

"Don't move, girl. Don't move an inch."

She couldn't have moved if she'd wanted to as he went to the door and dropped the crossbar. Not until he returned to her did she feel alive again.

A real lady would've protested when Hunter started unbuttoning her bodice, and a lady certainly would never have brushed aside Hunter's trembling fingers and completed the job herself. Nor would she have willingly peeled down bodice and chemise to give him access to her eager flesh. Maxie was glad she had not been able to turn herself into a lady.

Aaron did the rest of the undressing with urgent haste—both hers and his own. Almost before Maxie knew it they were sprawled together on the bed. Neither of them needed or wanted the preliminaries. Their coupling was quick and almost violent; tensions too long held inside exploded in a flash of mindless passion. Only Hunter's hand held over her mouth prevented Maxie from screaming out the joy of her release. Her body convulsed under his at the same time she heard him growl his own satisfaction into the pillow beside her ear.

Breathing hard, sweating, drained, they lay together in silence, her legs still gripping his hips, his flesh still buried deep within her. Maxie's world had narrowed down to the man whose body was stretched so possessively over hers. They could lie there forever as far as she was concerned. She couldn't think of anything that would make her happier. Closing her eyes, Maxie floated on a wave of satiated relaxation.

"Maxie."

Aaron's finger brushed her cheek.

"Maxie. I didn't hurt you, did I, girl?"

She smiled up at him in answer. He smiled back.

"I think I can tell Medina that you've got your strength back."

Why had she ever fought so? Maxie wondered. Surrender was so much fun. She loved him. Lordy, she loved him! What's more, she liked loving him. Good sense be damned!

Gently he rolled off her. An invasion of cool air swept between them—unwelcome separation.

"You know you're probably the orneriest, most troublesome female I've ever met. Even when you were only a kid."

What kind of thing was that to say after making such glorious love? Maxie tried to feel indignant, but she couldn't quite work up the energy.

Hunter slipped a hand over her breast, tickled it across her ribs, and splayed it possessively over her abdomen. It stayed there. She could almost feel it burn into her flesh, branding her, claiming her. "But goddamned if I don't love you more than anything on this earth, Maxie."

His eyes sought hers, as if looking for the answer to an unasked question. "I love you, Maxie. Every stubborn inch of you." He grinned. "Every unladylike little bit of you."

Lethargically she lifted one hand from the sheets and brushed back the tangle of rich brown hair that had fallen across his brow. The tender look in his eyes and the confident tone of his voice left no doubt he was telling the truth. "I love you too, Hunter."

He didn't look surprised, merely touched his finger to the tip of her nose. "Do you think you're ready again to show me just how much you love me?"

She shrugged one shoulder; causing the sheet to fall away

from her breast. He was getting fairly cocky. "Medina wouldn't want her patient's strength to be drained."

"Maxie," he said, chuckling, "I haven't begun to show you drained." He raised one brow in devilish threat. "Now this might cause a strain." His mouth found her nipple, teased it, taunted it, then finally suckled it until Maxie's nails dug into his back in desperation.

"Had enough?"

Maxie tried to get a grip on her senses, unsuccessfully. "You could teach the Apaches something about torture."

"Probably," he said with a grin. "Surrender?"

"Cactus Maxie never surrenders," she breathed.

He dipped a hand between her legs, forcing them apart while his fingers searched, moving in slow, tantalizing circles until finding their target. She was moist again, ready and warm and waiting when he gently slid his fingers inside her.

She closed her eyes and floated on bliss. His thrusts grew more urgent; she began to soar.

"You couldn't possibly . . ." she whispered. "We just . . ."

". . . made love much too fast," he finished. "And I can. Believe me I can." She felt the bed move as he shifted position. The truth of his claim became apparent when he pressed himself, hard and eager, against her. She arched toward him. "Are we drained yet, sweetheart?"

Maxie opened her eyes, looked up into his face. His eyes danced with mischief and love. How had she ever thought them cold and dark? She wanted him so much it hurt.

A smile quirked her lips. "Should I give in?" she wondered aloud.

"You'd better," he advised, his voice was hoarse, "or we're both going to bust."

She ached, she burned. He grinned and rubbed against her, slipping inside enough to tantalize, not to satisfy. Tension began to stretch his smile into a grimace. He was as tormented as she.

"Now what was it you wanted?"

He growled. The animal sound sent her over the edge.

"I love you," she whispered, and rose up to meet him. Slowly he took possession of her. The haste and desperate urgency of the first mating was gone. Their passion was every bit as intense, but the climb to satisfaction was slow and deliberate. Every nuance of sensation was explored, appreciated, built upon, every ripple of feeling savored. At the end, Maxie lost herself in the man who clasped her so tightly to him. Together they exploded, one being rather than two. When their pieces fell back into place, recombined one with the other, she sensed that part of her remained with him, and part of him had somehow permanently burrowed into her.

"You're right," she told him when she could finally find the breath to speak. "I don't want to go back."

He rose on one elbow and regarded her, the beginnings of a smile curving his mouth.

"Marry me, Aaron Hunter."

His smile grew. She looked up into his face, confidence ebbing.

"Will you marry me, Hunter?"

Tenderly he kissed her. "Anything you say, sweet lady."

Chapter 16

Maxie regarded herself in the mirror. This wouldn't do, wouldn't do at all.

"There must be something else," she told Cynthia, who stood a few feet away, hands on hips, eyes twinkling. Behind Cynthia, on the bed of Agua Linda's guest room, lay the new wardrobe that the two girls had sewn up during Maxie's stay in town. All but two dresses had been tried on and discarded, Maxie finding some fault with each.

"There's the gingham and the green cotton," Cynthia suggested. "Perhaps we could dress up one of them with a bit of lace."

"Oh!" Maxie wailed. "We don't have enough time for that. These clothes seemed so beautiful when we were making them. They're still beautiful. I just . . ."

"We didn't make these gowns with an engagement party in mind," Cynthia reminded her. "But I should have known."

Cynthia had never seen her friend so nervous. Even in the worst of situations Maxie seemed to have a self-possession that spit in the face of anyone who tried to give her trouble. Now she looked nervous enough to spit at herself.

"I wish Medina hadn't insisted on giving an engagement party. I'd rather just ride out and hunt up some preacher man—though not that devil-spouting Mr. Cahill over at Motherlode, mind you—and get the thing over with."

Cynthia clucked in reproval. "You talk like getting married is a chore. Of course Medina is giving you a party. A girl only gets engaged once—usually. And besides, the folks around here need any excuse they can to get together and remind each other there's more to life than working and fighting off Apaches."

"More likely they'll be asking each other why Hunter is marrying a girl like me. I've wondered that a few times myself."

"Oh, for heaven's sake!" Cynthia's patience was nearing an end. She took Maxie by the arm and turned her back toward the full-length mirror. "Why is Aaron marrying a girl like you? Take a look at yourself."

Maxie looked. Staring back at her from the mirror was a nervous-looking girl in camisole and petticoats. No one would have mistaken her for the boy she had often pretended to be when she was younger; her shape was irredeemably female—high, rounded breasts, small waist, slender arms. Even the shapely ankles and feet that peeked out from beneath the petticoats looked feminine.

"You're beautiful, Maxie," Cynthia told her. She almost envied Maxie's Mexican heritage. Her slightly darker skin, a few freckles notwithstanding, didn't burn and blister in the sun as Cynthia's did. Her complexion looked like old ivory, smooth and flawless even when Maxie forgot to wear her bonnet outside—a frequent occurrence.

Maxie grimaced her dissatisfaction. "No, Cynthia. You're beautiful. Black hair is boring, and look at the way it curls into these stupid ringlets. And my eyes—they make a body think he's looking right through an empty head to the sky on the other side. I . . ."

"Maxie! Listen to yourself!" Cynthia chuckled. "You're just nervous. Aaron loves you." For a moment Cynthia felt a small pang of jealousy, even though she had recognized long ago that she and Aaron were destined to be friends, not lovers. She still longed to find a man of her own—someone like Aaron, a man with enough courage and strength to take care of himself and protect a wife and children in this unholy land. But Cynthia needed someone who adored her, which Aaron Hunter didn't, and someone who didn't scare her, which Aaron sometimes did.

She smiled at Maxie, who at this moment looked as if she were about to face a firing squad rather than an engagement party. "You know Aaron will think you're beautiful no matter what you wear to the party, Maxie. And what anyone else thinks . . . well, that doesn't really matter, does it?"

A knock sounded on the door, and Medina stuck her head in. "Ah, there you are, Aleta. Are you dressed yet? No? Good." She spread out a confection of white silk and Spanish lace on the bed. "This is the dress I wore at my engagement ball, dear. If it fits, I would like you to wear it tonight."

Both Maxie and Cynthia drew in long, appreciative breaths.

"It was the latest fashion at the time. Here. Let's see how it looks on you."

The dress fit perfectly, except for the length. "I can fix the hem in no time at all," Medina offered.

"Oh, no, ma'am!" Maxie demurred. "You shouldn't be sewing for me. It's enough that . . ."

Medina shook her head and shushed Maxie to silence. "We all know how you sew, Aleta. And we can't have you late to your own engagement party." She gave Maxie's wild ringlets a dubious look. "Perhaps we should ask Catalina to put up your hair. She was once a lady's maid, you know, in Mexico City."

A full hour passed before Maxie was primped to everyone's satisfaction. When she looked at the finished product in the mirror, she could scarcely believe it was Cactus Maxie who stared back at her. Cynthia was right, Maxie admitted. With her unruly cloud of black hair and jolting blue eyes, even though she wasn't the porcelain beauty that Cynthia was, she did have a certain appeal. She remembered the way Hunter had looked at her before he rode off for town that morning. The memory made her shiver and long to see that fire in his eyes again, to assure herself it was real.

"Well, now. Are you ready?" Medina asked. "The gathered guests are waiting for the bride to be." She and Cynthia both looked at Maxie expectantly. Maxie could read in their expressions that even they were surprised at how good she looked.

"I have just one thing to get from my room." Maxie whirled and sneaked one more glance at herself in the mirror. "I'll see you at the party."

The celebration already was going strong in front of the ranch house as Maxie crossed from the back door to the kitchen building and into the little room she now shared with Mary. Jake trailed after her, his flattened ears and lowered head giving him a worried look.

"Don't you worry, old boy." Maxie comforted the dog as it followed her into her room, jumped on her cot, and curled into a mournful, scraggly ball. "Once I'm married I'll take you with me. I'm not going to leave you here. Once I'm married . . ."

Married. Cactus Maxie—married. Married to—Lord in heaven—Aaron Hunter. When she lay in his arms the whole idea had seemed so reasonable, but now . . .

"I do love him, you know," she told Jake. "I do. And he loves me, believe it or not. We can build a life together with luck and a little hard work. That ranch of his is prime cattle land, and with that reward money waiting in Tucson we could build a house fortified like the Kelleys' to keep the Apaches out."

The thought of Apaches brought to mind less pleasant thoughts. Choto had also had a mind to marry her, and he would have, if her brothers hadn't ridden into Noches's camp and taken her away. She would have been Choto's wife, not Hunter's, and Choto would have crawled on top of her, just as Aaron did. Only the act would have been much less pleasant. With Hunter, one body merging with another was unequaled joy. With Choto, it would have been . . . a nightmare. Her brothers had rescued her from that. And look what she was doing in return. How they would hate her if they knew she was deserting her family to stand at Aaron Hunter's side.

"No!" Maxie pounded her closed fist against the wall, then leaned her forehead against the cool adobe. She loved Aaron Hunter. He loved her. With him she could have a decent life, children, everything that had always been beyond her reach. Hunter was right. Her family's way of life was wrong, and it was doomed. Someday soon the real law —more than an overworked town marshal and outraged citizens—would come to Arizona and the old ways would die. The old ways should die. She had seen in the last weeks that lawlessness hurt people, decent people like Cynthia and Mr. Tuttle and Hunter's betrothed—poor dead lady. Robbery and mayhem were not high-spirited games, as she had always thought. If her brothers would only realize that, perhaps they would want to change their ways and go straight.

"I'm going to be a wonderful wife." She pushed away from the wall and straightened a few mussed tendrils of hair. "Hunter's never going to be sorry that he married me."

From this night on, Maxie told herself, she belonged to Hunter. Her husband would see that she really did mean to forsake all others for him.

"This'll be a great party," she told Jake. "Everything is just hunky-dory. And I'm going to have a terrific time."

She twirled, wishing her room had a mirror, though before tonight the need had not occurred to her. Then, crossing the room to the small chest that contained her few

personal treasures, she reverently opened it and took out
her only piece of jewelry, a dainty ring with an unidentified
but obviously precious stone glittering in a pure gold setting
—one of the few things she'd taken with her that nightmarish morning Aaron had dragged her from Stronghold. Julia
—Blackjack's captive sweetheart—had given Maxie the
ring before she died. Maxie had treasured it both as a thing
of beauty and a remembrance of her brief friendship with a
real, high-class lady. Now she was almost a lady herself. And
now she had an occasion to wear the ring. Smiling, she
slipped it on her finger, closed the chest, and danced her
way out the door.

The first person that Maxie saw as she walked into the
gaily decorated yard was Hunter. He stood in a group of
men who were grinning and laughing—no doubt at the
expense of the prospective groom. But even through the
crowd, Maxie's eyes found him as unerringly as a compass
finds north. Aaron was taller than any of the others, and
handsomer too, Maxie noted with pride. There was an air
about him that set him apart from other men, a self-possession, a strength that came from more than just broad shoulders and muscular frame. She loved his strength; she loved
him. And he loved her. Unbelievable—her childhood
daydreams coming true. Only this love was no daydream; it
was solid, down-to-earth reality. Better than any daydream,
this love story was real, and it was going to last for the rest of
her life.

As if feeling her eyes upon him, Aaron turned and caught
her gaze. His smile lit up the whole yard and set Maxie's
heart to thumping. For a moment everyone in the crowd
disappeared except him.

"Aleta." Medina's voice brought Maxie out of her trance.
"You look absolutely lovely, dear." She smiled as Aaron
started to make his way through the guests in Maxie's direction. "I see you two children have found each other in the
crowd. God bless you, dear." She took Maxie's hand and

squeezed it. "In your own way, you know, you're every bit the lady your mother was. She would be proud of you."

Maxie's throat tightened so that she could scarcely speak. She grasped Medina's hand as if by pressure alone she could tell the older woman how she felt. "Doña Medina. Thank you. Not just for the party. For everything."

"You're more than welcome, dear. And you'll always be a part of Agua Linda's family. This is your home whenever you need it."

"Medina, Maxie," Hunter greeted them.

"Aaron, you scoundrel," Medina said. "You look handsome enough to turn every woman's head between here and Mexico City."

He did, Maxie thought. Instead of his usual jeans, gun belt, and broadcloth shirt, he wore a tailored suit, complete with waistcoat and watch chain. For once his unruly hair was combed back from his face in disciplined waves. Hunter looked every bit as sophisticated and civilized as Mr. Ortega, the banker. If she hadn't known him, Maxie might have thought he was one of those fancy eastern politicians who had invaded Tucson.

Hunter grinned at the amazement in Maxie's eyes. "Don't recognize me, sweetheart? Just thought I'd show you what your husband will look like once he's a big-time cattle baron."

"Are you going to take up ranching again, boy?" Pete had wandered over to join them.

"Figured I would, Pete—once Motherlode can come up with a new marshal. A family man has to do something more useful with his time than chase bandidos." He glanced at Maxie to see her reaction.

Maxie gave him a smile that stretched every freckle on her face. She couldn't believe that one night could hold so much happiness. Not only did the man she loved love her back, not only was she going to become a respectable married lady, but Hunter was going to give up lawing. Unwittingly, she had gotten him off her brothers' backs, though not quite the way they had envisioned.

"How do you feel about being a rancher's wife?" Hunter asked her.

"Oh, I think I'm going to like punching cows."

Aaron put an arm around her waist and pulled her gently to his side, where he leaned down and whispered in her ear: "I'd rather have you punch cows than punch me, querida."

Maxie felt her face grow hot. She had, a time or two in the past, landed some hefty blows on Hunter's sturdy frame—to some effect, she remembered. But from now on she would indulge in no unladylike fisticuffs. Besides, she had learned better things to do with Hunter's body than punch it.

"I think these two would like to spend some time alone together." Medina smiled and took Pete by the hand. "Don't you think you should ask your wife to dance, Señor Kelley?"

"Not a bad idea," Hunter said as Medina led her husband away. "Would you like to dance, Maxie?"

"I'm just as bad as I ever was. Even Cynthia couldn't teach me how not to step on my partner's feet."

"Maybe Cynthia isn't the right person to teach you dancing." He led her off to where old Hump MacIntosh was sawing away at his fiddle and couples were dancing everything from a jig to a waltz. What Hunter and Maxie settled on was something in between.

The rest of the evening seemed enchanted. Maxie danced, only occasionally mashing Hunter's toes. She laughed, and talked, even with some of the guests—other ranchers, a few mine owners, some businessmen and their wives from Motherlode. They all wished her well, it seemed. Maxie did miss Mother Moses and her herd of girls, but she was beginning to understand that in the society she was entering, whores were not discussed, not talked to, and certainly not welcomed as friends. Be that as it may, Maxie resolved to pay a visit to Mother Moses next time she was in town. If Hunter could be friends with Shady Sam Guenther, owner of the Shot-Hole Saloon and Gambling House, then she didn't see anything wrong in her friendship with the ladies of Mother Moses' establishment. She didn't intend to start selecting her friends from a list approved by Motherlode's prune-faced matrons.

"Are you dry yet?" Hunter asked her after a particularly lively dance.

"Dry as a gully in August," she agreed.

"I'll get us something to drink."

Maxie grinned at him. "Don't you bring me any of that sweet wine. I want a beer."

"Two beers, coming up."

She watched him walk away, admiring the fit of his fancy tailored trousers. They had better marry soon, Maxie mused, for lately she was certainly given to thoughts that were fit only for a married lady.

A tug at her sleeve distracted her. Mary stood by her side, looking nothing at all like the ragged little Loco who had been Maxie's only friend among the Apaches. Her hair, freshly washed and braided, was blond, not the dirty brown that Maxie had first seen, her eyes a clear green, and her features—more rounded now after weeks of Elsa's cooking —were almost pretty. In fact, as Mary smiled, Maxie realized that the silent little waif was going to grow up every bit as beautiful as Cynthia.

"Hey, Mary." Maxie grinned down at the girl. "Are you enjoying the party?"

Mary nodded. Her eyes sparkled. Why, Maxie wondered, was she still without a voice? Doc Carter had pronounced her healthy and said she would talk when she felt like talking. "Be patient," he'd told Elsa, who had asked him to look at the child. "She's a female. When she starts to talk no doubt you'll not be able to stop her chatter." But so far Mary hadn't said a word, though sometimes she looked as if she would fairly bust with the effort to speak.

Mary took her hand, and Maxie squeezed it. They stood together and watched the miners and ranchers and merchants and bankers jig and waltz around the floor. Pete and Medina were dancing so close a body might have thought they were lovers instead of husband and wife; but their affection no longer made Maxie envious, now that she had a love of her own. Cynthia danced by in the arms of a tall, thin man with an admirably long handlebar moustache. She'd told Maxie about him. He was a fellow who worked for the Arizona Mining Corporation, out here to investigate the Apache problem for himself. He was all right, Cynthia had confided, but not a man she would want to marry. Of course, she hadn't wanted to marry Hunter, either. There was no accounting for Cynthia's taste.

The couple of most interest to Maxie were Simon Curtis and Elsa Herrmann. Elsa was as good a dancer as she was a cook, Maxie noted, and Simon was doing his level best to keep up with her. They both looked as happy as two pigs in a puddle, and Mary seemed delighted when they danced by and Simon gave her a big wink.

Everything, positively everything, Maxie thought, was going right in her life. She watched Aaron walk back toward her, a mug of beer in either hand, and her heart swelled to the bursting point. Why had she ever fought so against loving him? She hadn't known that life could be so wonderful.

"Hullo, Mary," Hunter greeted Maxie's little companion. "You look right fetching tonight."

Mary smiled shyly and at the same time moved partway behind Maxie for cover.

"Mary still doesn't think much of men," Maxie explained. "Except for Simon. She's crazy for Simon."

Hunter winked. "You should tell her what wonderful fellows we men are."

"Not me." Maxie smiled sweetly. "I'm reformed, remember. I don't lie any more."

"You never were much good at it."

"That's not true!" Maxie denied indignantly. "I was damned . . . oops! . . . I was very good at it."

"Set your beer down, darlin'. I feel the need for a dance coming on. 'Scuse us, Mary."

Maxie allowed herself to be whirled out into the dancing. Hump was fiddling away at a lively tune that called for a jig, but Aaron pulled her close into his arms and moved to his own slow, sensuous melody.

"I like dancing better this way," he said.

Maxie sighed and rested her head against his broad chest. Dancing this close had to be sinful, but she didn't care. There were some things in life worth going to hell for.

"I talked to Preacher Cahill while I was in town. He said he would come out here the end of the week to marry us, if that sets all right with you."

"I don't like that devil-thumping old crow. He doesn't like me."

"Preacher Cahill doesn't like anybody much. But he's the only preacher between here and Tubac."

Maxie looked up at him, sank into his smiling eyes, and promptly forgot her objections to Motherlode's resident preacher man. "I suppose the important part is the marrying. Who reads the words over us doesn't really matter."

Maxie lowered her head against his shoulder. The end of the week. Saturday—only three days away. The thought was enough to make any girl nervous, and Maxie felt a flutter brush her stomach. She would feel more comfortable with the whole thing once it was over and done with, she figured. Her brothers, when they learned, would stomp and snort and call her a few names. But they would eventually accept her decision. After all, they couldn't very well do anything to Hunter when he was their brother-in-law.

"You're far away, Maxie. Where'd you go?"

"What?"

"You haven't heard a thing I said."

"I . . . I was just thinking."

"Not about me, from the look on your face."

"I can't think about you all the time."

"You could try." Hunter chuckled. "Come on, let's wake

you up." He took her hand and whirled her into a fast jig that more than kept up with the music. Maxie's mind wasn't on her dancing. She stumbled. He laughed and caught at her hand, kissed her fingers, then froze.

Maxie stumbled to a stop. Hunter had become a statue, his eyes glued to her hand.

"Where did you get this ring?" he finally asked.

Maxie didn't answer. There was a note in his voice that she'd never heard before, a deadly intensity that sent a shiver down her spine. She looked at him in confusion.

"What?"

His mouth drew into a tight, harsh line and he pulled her from the crowd of merrymakers. Not a word did he speak until he'd dragged her out of the torch-lit yard and around the wall, where the night shadows were so deep she could scarcely see his face.

"Where did you get that ring?" he repeated.

She pulled her hand away from him, looked at the ring, and frowned. "A friend gave it to me. Why? What's wrong?"

"A friend gave it to you." His voice was a quiet whisper, but the hiss of a snake would have sounded less deadly. "Tell me about your friend."

"I . . . well . . . Why? What's wrong?!"

"Tell me!"

He grasped both her wrists and held them tightly, as though she might run. She did want to run. Her world was suddenly twisting out of shape, and she had no idea why.

"Tell me!"

"Her . . . her name was Julia. My brother Blackjack . . . she was his. He took her off some freight wagon train and brought her into Stronghold. She and I . . . well, we were friends. She didn't like my brothers much, but she liked me. She gave me the ring before she died."

"Julia . . ." Hunter's voice sounded close to breaking. "I gave her this ring when I asked her to marry me."

Maxie drew in a horrified breath. Julia—Blackjack's Julia —she had been Hunter's eastern lady?

Hunter was silent, but his very silence seemed to make the night shiver around him. His grip on her wrists grew painful. "They lied," he finally said. "The wagon guard lied when he told me they'd found Julia's body and buried it. He was too much of a coward to follow and get her back, so he lied to me. All the time she was with you."

His eyes turned back to Maxie, and she flinched at the steel-bright hatred that glinted in their dark depths. "You and your goddamned stinking father and brothers took her off that wagon and into the slime of your filthy lives, and I left her there, because I thought she was dead. I left her there, and you killed her. The Maxwells aren't fit to wash the dirt off her feet, and you killed her!"

He let go of her as though her wrists were two red-hot branding irons. His fury and disgust broke over her in palpable waves.

"Hunter! You've got it wrong! Nobody killed Julia. Blackjack treated her like she was some sort of queen. He really was sweet on her, and he didn't let anyone touch her. He didn't even touch her, Hunter. Blackjack wanted to marry her, and he figured on doing it right. He never laid a hand on her. No one did!"

"No one touched her," Hunter said in disbelief. "But she's dead, isn't she!"

"I . . . well, yes. She tried to leave. Went out in the desert one day. It was July, and she didn't understand anything about the desert. When Blackjack tracked her down she was already crazy with the heat. He brought her home, and I bathed her down and sat with her. I think she could have lived if she'd wanted to, but she just slipped away."

"And she gave you that ring." His voice was taut as a bowstring.

"We were friends. She said her sweetheart gave her the ring and she didn't want it to be put under the ground . . . with her. Funny she never told me your name."

The silence that followed was leaden. Even the night seemed to get darker as Hunter stood there, unmoving. Maxie could feel his pain as if it were her own. Why had she never connected Blackjack's Julia with Hunter's lost love? Perhaps she simply hadn't wanted to. She could understand why Aaron had loved Julia so. She had been sweet and generous, and, in her own way, brave. Maxie couldn't imagine that such a fragile woman would have survived on Hunter's ranch much longer than she had survived Stronghold. Arizona wasn't kind to women who were delicate and easily crushed—like Julia. But Maxie could understand, nevertheless, why any man would want her.

"Julia was very beautiful, and kind," she told Aaron, thinking to be of some comfort. "She wasn't treated badly, and . . . and everyone liked her. They knew she was something special."

Hunter radiated such pain that Maxie reached out, wanting to comfort. But Hunter grabbed her arm in a painful grip and flung her away from him. She stumbled and fell to the ground.

"Stay away from me! All this time I've been hunting the trash who took my Julia, and here I've had one of them in my hands all along. But I can't touch you, can I! I can't wring your little neck like it deserves to be wrung, as much as I'd like to right now." His voice shook with fury. "God! And to think I almost let you seduce me into giving up the chase."

Maxie's patience—never her long suit—was nearing an end, and so was her sympathy. Hunter had a right to be furious. Maxie had never agreed with Blackjack on the subject of Julia, and she'd raked him over the coals more than once about it. Not that he paid her any mind.

On the other hand, Hunter damned well didn't have a right to act like the whole nasty incident had been Maxie's idea. Trash, he'd called her! And then accused her of seducing him away from his duty!

She picked herself up off the ground and brushed the dirt from Medina's betrothal gown. Betrothal! What a joke! "I think you'd better take back a few things you just said, Hunter. You're not thinking straight right now."

"I'm thinking straight for the first time in weeks. Go back where you belong, Maxie. And tell your brothers they'd better grow eyes in the backs of their heads. I'll be coming for them."

"You think you're good enough to kill them, do you?" She'd had enough. Aaron Hunter had been riding his high horse a bit too long. "You're not fast enough, Hunter, or smart enough."

He sent her a flat, black look that sent chills crawling down her spine. "You think not?"

"I . . . I know it!" Her voice faltered. His words, though quietly spoken, had a fierce edge that made her throat want to close in terror.

"At least my brothers don't pretend to be something they aren't!" she flung at him desperately. "But you! You strut around, so lily-white and saintlike, trying to pretend you're something more than a mongrel wolf—a gunman whose only talent lies in the gun strapped to your leg. And everybody around you has to change themselves into a posy-picking, hymn-singing do-gooder to be good enough for you."

"You don't know what you're talking about, you little fool."

"Oh, don't I? I can't believe I thought I was in love with you! I can't believe you convinced me that you were something other than a piece of horseshit! At least I am honest— or I was honest up until I met you. I've always admitted what I am—a no-good, a bandit, and now, a slut. You taught me how to be a slut!"

"Maxie . . . !"

"But the only part of my life that I'm ashamed of is being fool enough to fall for you!" With a vicious tug, she pulled Julia's ring from her finger and threw it in the dust. "There! Take your precious ring. Put it in a shrine and worship your

Julia! Let yourself shrivel and die in her honor! Now, get out of my way."

She stalked past him, shoving him aside. Head up, fists clenched, she stormed past her betrothal celebration, through the house, and across the back courtyard into her small room off the kitchen. Over the pounding of her heart she could still hear the fiddle music, still hear people laughing.

Slowly her knees gave way. She sank to her cot, where a patient Jake looked at her mournfully. She hugged the dog to her and finally gave way to tears.

"Damn, damn, damn!" she wailed into Jake's ragged coat. "Damn Hunter. Damn Blackjack. Damn Julia. And damn me. Stupid, stupid, me."

Only one thought comforted her in the bitter tumult of her despair, and that was the certainty that the whole world was full of fools just like herself.

Chapter 17

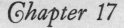

$\mathcal{T}$wo miserable days passed. Maxie told Medina that she and Aaron had argued and the wedding was off. No matter how Medina pried, she would say no more. Elsa tried her best to worm the story from her, as did Maria and Catalina. Even Pete tried his hand at getting information, but Maxie was silent and morose. All she would admit was they had quarreled.

How could she say more? How could she admit to these people that her oldest brother—hero of her childhood—had been responsible for Julia's death? The whole nasty incident had always been held in secret shame in her heart, and Hunter's fury had brought that secret shame—once so small —into the glaring spotlight of her conscience. What made the shame worse was that Maxie now had an inkling of how Julia had felt. Maxie loved the same man Julia had loved. Maxie had endured the frustration, the sick terror of captivity, and had cringed at the prospect of being made an unwilling bride. Now Maxie's shame over Julia was no longer small, and no longer secret.

Blackjack eventually would have forced the poor girl,

Maxie admitted to herself. His patience had a short fuse, and when the fuse had burned out, he would have dragged her off somewhere and taken what he wanted. Only Julia's death had saved her from that fate. Had she known that, Maxie wondered, when she gave up and died from dehydration and exposure?

Sometimes Maxie almost envied poor dead Julia. Julia, at least, had known that Hunter loved her right up until she died. Even during her ordeal she had her dreams to cherish. But what did Maxie have? Nothing. Worse than nothing. Broken hopes, a heart ripe for the plucking left to shrivel like an apple laid out in the noonday sun. Aaron hated her. She was a Maxwell, and all Maxwells were slime.

Maxie didn't blame Hunter for the way he felt. Right now she would have given anything not to be her brothers' sister. The blame belonged to Blackjack, she tried to convince herself. But painful honesty told her that she could have helped Julia escape. Julia had been kind to her, had been her friend, and yet Maxie had never even thought of defying her brother and leading the poor girl out of Stronghold.

She tried to excuse herself. The world outside of Stronghold hadn't existed for her then. She'd known nothing about kindness and respectability and decent living. Maxie had thought Julia might come to love Blackjack. What woman wouldn't love her handsome brother?

But at night when Maxie wept into her pillow, all the excuses she could invent were no comfort. She was angry, resentful, and chagrined at the same time, and she couldn't even work up a decent hatred for Hunter. Her fists itched to land a few hard blows to his midsection, and a well-placed kick or two might ease her frustration, but her fantasies of violence always ended with her in Hunter's arms, his lips brushing her ear speaking sweet words of forgiveness.

During the day she wandered from chore to chore, trying to keep up with her former routine. After a while her wall of hurt silence discouraged even the most persistent from talking to her. She didn't know quite what to do with herself.

Medina had said Agua Linda was her home, but the ranch didn't feel like home. Stronghold had once been her home, but Stronghold was destroyed. Her family had once been her home, but after what she had learned and seen, Maxie knew she would never again fit in with Blackjack and Tom and Dirty Jim. She didn't know who she was anymore. The old Cactus Maxie was gone. The new reformed Maxie had died even before she was born. And the person occupying Maxie's space in the world was . . . someone Maxie didn't know, didn't even care to know.

Then, the second night after the party, with the desert lying quietly under dim starlight and all of Agua Linda fast asleep, Blackjack came. He slipped past the wall guards with the stealth of a snake's shadow.

Jake's growl awakened Maxie only a second before a rough hand clapped over her mouth and a whisper commanded her to be silent. She struggled ineffectively for a moment until she recognized the man who held her. Then her eyes grew wide.

"Blackjack!" she whispered when her brother released her.

"Call the damned dog off."

Old Jake, hackles raised, teeth bared, advanced in stifflegged challenge. Maxie ordered him down with a wave of her hand. The dog looked uncertain for a moment, then dropped to the floor in a watchful pose.

Blackjack grinned. "Howdy, baby sister."

"Sssshhhhh!" Maxie glanced at the still sleeping Mary, who occupied the cot across the small room. "What are you doing here?" she whispered.

His grin grew wider. "Heard you was gonna get yerself hitched. Hooooee! When I give you a job, you really go at it, don'tcha, Max?"

Maxie had almost forgotten how handsome her brother was. He'd lit the candle that sat on a wooden crate beside her bed. In the dim light his hair gleamed golden, his eyes—the same cobalt blue as her own—twinkled with a wicked, irresistible light, his lips—lips that even a sister could admit were sensuous—curved back over straight, white, even teeth.

He hit her shoulder lightly with his fist. "Ya done real good, Max. Hell, I couldn'a done better myself if I was a female. The word's out that ol' Hunter's eatin' right outta your sweet little hand. Ya got 'im just where we want 'im."

"Quiet, you jackass! You'll wake Mary!"

Blackjack glanced at the still figure on the other cot. "Well, then, let's skedaddle. We'll leave a trail a kid could follow, and when Hunter chases after his lady love, he'll walk right into our little trap." He grinned, and for the first time in her life Maxie saw the grin as vicious rather than charming. "We got bigger things to come, Max. After we take care o' Hunter, we're headed down to Mexico to find Pa. I got myself a señorita in one of those fancy haciendas down there. She's goin' to make life easy for the lot of us, baby sis."

Maxie balked. She had decided when Blackjack had first proposed his scheme that she would have no part of it. "I'm not going anywhere, Jack."

"What's that?" He gave her a narrow-eyed scowl.

"I'm not going with you."

"Like hell."

"There's nothing between Hunter and me. Even if there was, it wouldn't have anything to do with you and the boys. You fight your own fights, Jack. Leave me out of it."

Blackjack's eyes turned hard, so hard and angry that Maxie wondered if this was truly the brother she had idolized and envied all her life.

"You're a Maxwell," he said flatly. "You're coming."

Maxie shook her head and thrust out her chin in stubborn denial. Blackjack smiled an unpleasant smile and glanced meaningfully toward the sleeping Mary. A chill tingled up Maxie's spine at the unspoken threat.

"I'm coming."

She hastily pulled on her old trousers and shirt, anxious to get Blackjack away from Mary, away from Agua Linda, where he might hurt someone. She wrapped her extra pair of boots, her brush, and extra socks in a scarf, then grabbed her hat. Her dresses she would leave behind; she had no more use for them. The realization made her sadder than she would have thought possible.

"I don't think Hunter will follow me, Jack," she whispered. "We had a big fight. Right now he'd rather step in pig shit than get within ten feet of me."

Her brother chuckled softly. "Better yet. The fight's a good excuse for your leavin'. He'll come, all right."

Maxie didn't like the gleam in Blackjack's eyes. "What do you aim to do, Jack?"

"Whaddya think we aim to do?" He hesitated and scowled. "You sweet on this guy?"

Maxie snorted.

"Jest squeamish, eh? You've always been squeamish. Don't worry about it, Max. You done your part, now let us do ours."

She'd done her part. The statement struck a chord of guilt. Maxie hadn't intended to be her brothers' bait, but in becoming tangled up with Hunter, she'd done just what they'd wanted her to do. Her brothers wanted Hunter dead, and Hunter, after what Maxie had told him about Julia, would surely want her brothers off the face of the earth. He'd follow them to Mexico—to hell itself if he had to. And when the Maxwells and Hunter came face to face, Maxie realized with a sickening twist of her stomach, someone would die.

Unless Maxie could somehow persuade Hunter not to follow.

"Come on, Max. We ain't got all night."

"Hold it," she said, fastening the last button on her shirt. "I'll leave a note, so the Kelleys know I'm all right."

"Since when can you write?"

"Since Mrs. Kelley taught me."

"No kiddin'! Write somethin' weepy. That's bound to get Hunter in a lather."

Hands sweating, mouth dry, Maxie picked up the little slate she had used to practice her letters. Painstakingly— she still wasn't very good at this—she wrote several lines thanking the Kelleys for their kindness and telling them she was going back to her family. Then, grateful that Blackjack couldn't read a single word, she added a caution against anyone, especially Hunter, following her. "Ef Hunter like his hide in one peece," she added as a last line, "tel him too stay away. Then his det to me is payed."

Hunter had told her he was a man who paid his debts. Was her timely rescue ten years past a fair exchange for letting her go in peace?

Maxie carefully placed the slate by Mary's hand. By the time the girl found it, she and Blackjack would be well away. Satisfied, she moved with Blackjack toward the door. Jake got up and followed.

"Leave the dog," Blackjack told her.

"Stay here, Jake," Maxie whispered sadly. "Stay."

Whining, the dog sat. Hidden by Jake's broad form, Mary's eyes slitted open as Maxie turned her back.

While Maxie had dressed and argued with her brother, Mary had awakened to the sound of their whispering. She had acquired the habit of light sleeping among the Apache, where her adoptive mother, Lazy Eyes, occasionally had trouble sleeping and decided to cure her insomnia by a bit of exercise—a good walloping of the mute, light-haired child her husband had brought into her wickiup after she had proved barren. Mary had saved herself from more than one beating by being alert enough to see Lazy Eyes coming and scramble out of the wickiup to hide. Such a habit was hard to break, and even at Agua Linda Mary had always slept with one wary eye to her surroundings.

So she had awakened to the first stirrings on the other side of the little room, though instinct told her to keep still and pretend to sleep. She didn't know who the tall man was who stood there talking to Maxie, but for some reason she didn't like him. Not until he turned toward her did she realize why. His face, lit dimly by the gleam of the one candle, was enough to set her heart to pounding. He was the same man who had taken Maxie from Noches's rancheria. But those features—the blue eyes, wheat-colored hair, square jaw—had been branded on her memory years before. His was a face that even a small child wouldn't forget.

Instantly she shut her eyes tight. Not until she heard the two of them leave the room did Mary move. The room was dark, the candle doused, but enough starlight shone through the window for Mary to see the slate beside her hand and the dim trace of the lines Maxie had written. Even had the light been brighter, she wouldn't have been able to read the writing.

Her fingers closed spasmodically around the slate as she lay back down and thought about what she should do.

Simon Curtis propped his long legs on his desk and tipped his chair back against the adobe wall of the little jail office. "Been mighty quiet the last few days," he commented. Through drowsy eyes he regarded his boss and best friend, who sat across the room idly tossing a knife so that it stuck into his desk. "Ain't even a bee buzzin' in the country hereabouts, much less a bandido. Suppose we done cleared 'em all out, amigo?"

Hunter snorted, which was one of the more articulate replies Simon had received from him during the last few days.

"I suppose they coulda just migrated south, seein' that winter's just around the corner. Not that an hombre can get much south o' here without gettin' into Mexico, and those Mexicans is just as partial to hangin' bandidos as we are. 'Course they druther hang American bandidos than their Mex compadres, but I suppose that's only fair. Whaddya think?"

Hunter sighed, stuck his knife in the desk one more time, got up, and wandered over to the rifle rack. He took a Winchester from the rack, broke down the magazine, ran a finger along the well-oiled surfaces, snapped an empty chamber home, and sighted down the barrel.

"Itchin' for someone to blast away at, eh? Figger yer trigger finger needs some exercise?"

Hunter shoved the Winchester back into the rack. "Compadre, you used to be a quiet sort of a man. Someone oil your jawbone lately?"

"Shucks, Hunter. It's just all that silence on the other side of the room. It's just sittin' there waitin' ta be filled."

Hunter didn't answer. He sat down at his desk and resumed sticking his knife.

Simon sighed and gave up. The little bit of conversation he squeezed out of Hunter wasn't worth the effort these days. He'd never known it to fail that chasing after a woman brought a man to this sort of sad state. He and Elsa were different, of course. Elsa was a sensible woman who didn't expect much from a man, and Simon no longer had the fires of youth burning in his gut like young Aaron. Not that he couldn't stoke up a fair bit of heat when the time was right, but most of the time he just simmered along peacefullike.

Hunter and that little Maxwell wildcat could start a brush fire just by looking at each other, though. Simon wasn't surprised that Hunter had got seared a bit. Whatever had happened, the boy was taking it hard. He'd been about as friendly as a rattlesnake since the Kelleys' shindig. Simon wished he'd either patch it up with the girl or go out to Agua Linda and shoot her. Either way he'd be easier to live with.

The rattle of wagon wheels turned both men's attention toward the window.

"Whaddya know," Simon drawled. "Someone in town's awake after all."

Hunter pushed himself out of his chair, went to the window, and frowned. "It's Medina Kelley with a couple of her hands riding shotgun. Wonder what brings her into town so early in the morning?"

He didn't have to wait long for his answer. As soon as Medina climbed down and hitched her wagon team to the rail she headed for the marshal's office.

"Mornin', Miz Kelley." Simon conceded to manners just enough to take his feet off his desk.

"Good morning, Simon." Her greeting was brusque, and she gave the deputy scarcely a glance. Her attention was all for Hunter.

"Aaron, Maxie's gone."

A telltale muscle twitched in Hunter's jaw, but he merely picked up his knife from where it was stuck in the top of his desk and started casually cleaning the blade. "It's a free country, Medina. I guess Maxie can take off if she wants to."

"How can you say that? She's gone off to be with those wretched Maxwell boys."

"Well, she's a Maxwell, isn't she?"

"You're the one who took her away! You're the one who said you owed her!"

"I don't owe her anymore, Medina."

Simon cleared his throat. "I b'lieve I'll just take a stroll and make sure there ain't no lawbreakers botherin' the town." Sparks were flying toward the tinder, and he would just as soon not stay for the explosion. The day promised to be warm enough as it was.

As Simon closed the door behind him, Hunter put down his knife and walked over to the window. Medina followed.

"Aaron, I know something happened between you two. What happened is none of my affair, but I can't believe you'll just sit back and let Maxie ruin her life, maybe get herself killed, just because you had a spat."

"It wasn't exactly what I'd call a spat. And Maxie's made her choice. She's a grown woman, even though half the time she acts like a kid. If she wants to run away, then there's not a thing I can do about it."

Medina turned around and folded her arms across her

chest, clasping them tightly as if an arm might decide to lash out and knock some sense into Hunter if not held firmly in check.

"She didn't run away," she declared with conviction. "Maxie's not the sort to run from anything. You know that. She may storm around like a cat with a scalded tail when things don't go her way, but the girl has good Toledo steel in her spine. There's more to this than running away from a lovers' quarrel."

"It wasn't a lovers' quarrel, Medina." Hunter sighed. Trust a woman to blame everything on love. That Maxie had left out of pure cussedness would probably never occur to Medina.

"She left a note not to come after her. More specifically, *you* were not to come after her if you wanted your hide in one piece."

Sounded like something the damned little she-wolf would say. What game was she playing? Catch-me-if-you-can? Hadn't he made it plain enough that he didn't want to catch her?

"Let her go, Medina. We're both better off without her."

Medina gave him a long, slow look. "I don't believe you mean that, Aaron Hunter."

He wished he did mean it. God, how he wished he did.

"At least come out to the ranch and talk to Pete," Medina said. Her voice softened. "You've got some responsibility for the girl, you know."

Hunter wiped his hand down his face, trying to clear his eyes of a vision he didn't want to see. Maxie. Always Maxie. Laughing. Smiling. More often scowling in a way that she no doubt thought fierce, but in reality simply made her look all the more appealing. Maxie grinning up at him as they danced. Maxie beneath him, her face lit with joy as her body catapulted his into heaven.

"I suppose I do," he sighed. "I reckon I'm never going to get away from her. Not all the way, at least."

They rode out of town in silence, Hunter's big roan stal-

lion trotting easily beside Medina's wagon. The hands had
stayed in town to take care of some business at the blacksmith's shop—and to wash the dust from their throats with
some of Sam Guenther's watered-down whiskey. Aaron
could have used some of that whiskey himself right now.

The nightmare would just not go away. It had started
when he found out about the Maxwells and Julia. He hardly
remembered what he'd said to Maxie, so blinded had he
been by his own rage. Rage and guilt—a poisonous combination. Some of the rage was for the Maxwells, but a good
part of it was directed toward himself. If he'd gone to
Stronghold right after Julia was taken, he would have found
her. But the guards on the freight wagon had said the bandits had killed her, said they'd ridden out after the villains
and found her dead along the trail. They'd buried her on
the spot, they'd claimed, the heat being what it was and
them still three days out from Tucson. No doubt the bastards hadn't taken after the Maxwells at all and were afraid
to admit it. Hunter didn't question their reason for fear.
Had he known the true story, he might have killed the
slackers with his bare hands.

Rage and guilt. How could he have sunk so low as to love a
Maxwell? He'd been going to marry her—a girl who had
helped hold his Julia prisoner, who might even have ridden
on the raid in which she was kidnapped. She was trash, dirt,
poison, about as likely to reform as a rattler. A snake might
shed its skin, even lose its rattles, but they always grew
back. And all the time the snake was changing, its fangs
never lost their venom.

Hunter shook his head and squinted at the horizon. The
sun was well up now, and the day was mighty warm for
being so close to October—almost as warm, in fact, as that
day he'd taken Maxie on their picnic to the river. The little
hussy had taken to the water like an otter, shed her clothes
with no mind of Hunter sitting just out of sight and working
up a heat that had nothing to do with the sun. Had she

known he would come after her? Had her little swim been
the hook baited to catch a sucker?

This sucker had taken the hook all right—taken it and
swallowed it. And now Maxie was yanking out his guts with
it and probably enjoying every moment.

The damned little nitwit. Her brothers would lead her
down a rugged path to hell—if she truly had gone to her
brothers. But then, where else could she go? Those vicious
brothers were all Maxie had left. Rumor had it that Harrison
Maxwell had fled south into Mexico, leaving his kids to fend
for themselves. This was no country for a woman alone,
even a tough little hoyden like Maxie.

Not that he cared. Damn her hide. One of these years
maybe he really wouldn't care.

Agua Linda, when they arrived, was the same as it always
had been. The hogs rooted in their pens. In the corral next
to the barns, the horses stood placidly in the morning sun,
heads down, ears flicking drowsily at the flies. Finished just
the week before, the wall that protected the ranch house
and yards gleamed with a new coat of whitewash.

But for Hunter the place had an empty feel to it. Since
he'd brought Maxie to stay with the Kelleys, he had uncon-
sciously strained for a glimpse of her every time he'd ridden
into the ranch. Her presence had given him a sense of
anticipation. Now that she was gone, the ranch seemed
lifeless, no matter how many people, hogs, and horses
moved among the pens and outbuildings.

Pete greeted them at the wall gate. "So, I see you've
come." He motioned toward a dark-skinned boy who sat in
the shade of the wall to take the wagon and horses to the
barn. "Have any idea where your little runaway may have
headed?"

Hunter was about to deny that Maxie was *his* runaway,
then changed his mind when he saw the accusation on
Pete's face. He supposed the little polecat was his to some
extent. He was the one who had brought her to the ranch.

"She could've headed just about anywhere if she's out to

find her brothers, Pete. They could be anywhere between Santa Fe and Mexico City."

"She's not looking for her brothers. I figger one of those boys came in and fetched her."

Hunter stared at him, unbelieving. "You mean one of the Maxwells rode into Agua Linda free as the breeze, helped her saddle a damned horse, and then they just trotted off?"

Pete sighed and rubbed at his brow with one hand. "Yeah. Seems the wall guard was more intent on catching a few winks last night than watching for Apaches and bandidos. Near as I can figger from all the tracks around this damned place, two horses left."

"Maybe she took a spare."

"Both horses were mounted. You can see that from their tracks. And there's only one horse gone from the barn—that bay mare that Maxie liked so much. The little imp left me thirty dollars for the horse. Do you believe it? Where'd you suppose she got the money?"

"Probably wormed it out of her brother. Damnation! That took nerve, I gotta admit—for a Maxwell to ride into Agua Linda bold as you please. You probably would've strung him up if you'd caught him."

"You're right about that. Damned Maxwell scum."

"Maxie's a Maxwell, yet you've been treating her like she was your daughter these past weeks."

"Maxie's a horse of a different color. The only thing Maxwell about her is her name."

Hunter chuckled bitterly. "You've got that wrong, Pete."

Pete gave him a reproachful look. "Let's go inside and talk, boy."

The house was unusually quiet as Hunter followed Pete and Medina into the front hall. Usually, the sound of Maria and Catalina chattering or Elsa scolding provided background noise for anything else going on in the house. But today a heavy silence stifled every room. Catalina came out of the dining room carrying an armful of linen. She gave

Aaron a hostile look, then marched toward the bedrooms without a word.

Medina enlightened him. "Everyone seems to think that you said something to Maxie to make her go, Aaron. I don't think you're very popular around here right now."

"Hang it! I didn't tell her to go!" Or had he? Aaron didn't rightly remember everything he'd said that night.

As they settled themselves in the parlor Elsa appeared at the doorway, her face worried. "Doña Medina, have you seen Mary?"

"No, Elsa. I haven't."

"She was supposed to be scouring out the washtub this morning, but I have not been able to find her. You . . . you don't suppose she has taken off after little Maxie?" The German cook managed to scowl at Hunter while questioning Medina.

"She was very upset when she brought me Aleta's note last night. But I'm sure she has more sense than to go running off herself."

Hunter grimaced. "I would've thought Maxie had more sense too."

Elsa gave him a "humph!", then turned back to Medina. "If you see her, please tell her to come to me. She cannot cry all the time until the marshal brings Maxie back. There is still work to do."

Medina rose to follow Elsa out. "Perhaps I'd better look for the child. I'll leave you two gentlemen to talk." She raised a brow at her husband as she left the room.

Hunter got up from his chair, walked to the window, then walked back. "Pete, I'm sorry I saddled you with this. I'm sorry I brought Maxie here." He ran his fingers through the tangle of his hair. "I don't believe this whole ranch is in an uproar over one little girl deciding to go home."

"We got right fond of the girl," Pete said, shaking his head. "Even most of the hands are sorry she's gone, in spite of her cleaning 'em out at poker at least once a week."

Hunter sighed and sat down again. "Well, she's a grown woman. I guess she can make her own decisions."

"That's not what you were saying when you first brought her here."

"Yeah. Well, that was a mistake."

Pete merely looked at him. "Aaron, boy, I want to know what happened between you and that girl." He raised a hand to ward off Hunter's objection. "I know you think it's none of my damned business, but I figger it is. You put Maxie under my care, and now she's gone. I want to know why."

"Because she's a Maxwell, I suppose."

"You want to elaborate on that?"

Hunter sighed and let his head drop down to rest in his hands. The clock in the hall ticked away long silent moments before he looked at Pete again.

"Maxie wore a ring at the party . . ." he finally began. He told Pete what he had learned, and as much as he could remember of what the two of them had said, or rather yelled, at each other.

"So you figger Maxie's to blame for taking Julia off that wagon?" Pete asked when he was done.

"No. Not exactly."

"Then she's to blame for being born a Maxwell?"

Hunter just looked at him.

"I figger you just might end up killing those Maxwell boys," Pete said. "Probably they need killing. But I don't rightly see what all this has to do with Maxie. She can't be overly fond of those skunks right now—brothers or not. She'd pine a bit if you went after 'em, no doubt. Might have some harsh words if you shot 'em down. But I expect she'd forgive you—eventually. Women can be right practical creatures."

Hunter shook his head. Maxie's forgiving him had not been a part of his plans.

"And just remember," Pete continued softly. "Blackjack Maxwell isn't the only hombre I know who once rode off with a female who didn't rightly belong to him and took her somewhere she didn't want to be."

Incredulous, Hunter glared. "You mean Maxie?!"

Pete smiled and raised a brow.

"I didn't carry her off! I rescued the damned little hellcat! And I sure as hell didn't abuse her until she killed herself trying to escape!"

"Didn't you?" Pete asked.

Hunter marched out the wall gate toward the barn, almost choking with anger. Pete Kelley had taken leave of his senses. If he was so damned fond of the girl, then let *him* drag her back from whatever hole she'd fled to. Maxie had made it plain enough in her note that she wanted to be left alone. Well, fine. He would leave her alone. He didn't care what she did with her life as long as she stayed away from him. Far away! So far away she might drop off the very edge of the earth.

Blackjack, though—he was another story. Hunter wasn't about to let that bastard drop off the edge of the earth. Blackjack Maxwell was going straight to hell, and Hunter was going to send him there. And if Maxie was anywhere near her son of a bitch brother, God help her if she got in Hunter's way!

"Goddamn it!" he snarled, slamming his fist against a rail of the corral. The little she-skunk had the nerve to refer to his "debt" in the note Pete had shown him. As if he owed her Blackjack's life! And the threat—if he wanted to keep his hide in one piece . . . Cactus Maxie needed a few of her thorns plucked, damn her hide. If he ever saw her again he'd . . . Shit! What would he do? Was Pete right? Was she an innocent caught between hell on one side and the Devil on the other?

The dusty shadows of the barn did nothing to cool Hunter's turmoil. His roan stallion whickered in greeting, and Hunter gave him a jaundiced glare. "If people had half the sense of horses, we wouldn't get ourselves into these messes," he complained.

A rustling of straw brought his attention around. "Who's there?" he demanded, drawing his pistol.

Silence. Then a muffled sneeze.

Hunter went cautiously to the empty stall from which the sneeze had come. "Come out," he ordered. "Show yourself." No doubt the intruder was some saddle bum who had holed up for the night in the Kelleys' barn. All sorts of vermin were getting past Pete's guards these days.

But the face that emerged from the stall's shadows didn't belong to a saddle bum. Hunter lowered his gun and sighed. "Mary, what the . . . the heck . . . are you doing here?"

Mary merely sniffed and wiped her nose on her sleeve. She sat down once again in the straw, and Aaron squatted so that his face was on a level with hers. "What're you doing out here, little one? Elsa and Medina have been looking for you, and I think you've set them all aworrying." He reached out and touched the dirty track of a tear that angled down her cheek—just as another tear started to overflow her eye. "Come on, sweetheart. Come with me back to the house."

He helped her up and picked a few pieces of straw from her hair. "Come on now, Mary."

She shook her head vehemently, grabbed on to his sleeve, and opened her mouth.

"It's all right, Mary. No one's going to punish you. Everyone knows you're upset over . . . over Maxie."

Mary's eyes opened wide. She began to breathe in short gasps, and still she wouldn't release Hunter's sleeve.

"Mary! Are you all right?"

The girl shook her head. Then she pressed her lips together, drew a giant breath, and spoke. "Mmmaxieee!"

For a few seconds Hunter was stunned. Then he whispered, almost afraid to say the words aloud. "Mary! You talked! Goddamnit! You talked!"

"Maxie?" Her voice was more certain on the second try. Hunter knelt beside her and took her thin arms into his hands. They were not big enough even to fill his grasp. "What about Maxie, sweetheart?"

"She . . . left."

"Yes. I know."

More tears dribbled down her cheeks. "Why did . . . why did she go?" Mary wailed. "She tol' me she liked it here. She tol' me . . ."

Like a flood bursting through a broken dam, the words spilled out. Mary sobbed out how Maxie couldn't have wanted to leave because she had told her once that she couldn't marry Choto because she was in love with a man named Hunter.

"And who was Choto?" Hunter asked.

"He's a right fine-lookin' Indian," Mary told him. "I didn't really believe Maxie when she said you was better lookin'. Not until a saw ya, anyways."

Hunter sighed. How did he explain to a child that love was not an unchanging quantity. "Maxie doesn't love me anymore, Mary. She wanted to go. We've got to let her make her own decisions."

Mary's eyes went wide and wild. "No! Bring her back!"

"Mary . . ."

"Bring her back! She went with a bad man!"

"The man was her brother, Mary. He won't hurt—"

"He'll sell her. Like he sold me! To the Indians! He'll sell her . . . !"

"Wait a minute!" Hunter put his hand gently over her mouth to stop the near hysteria. "Calm down. Who sold you?"

"That man. And two other men. They killed my ma and pa and little sister, then they took me and sold me to the Indians."

"That was a long time ago, Mary. Are you sure you're remembering right? Are you sure the Indians didn't come to your place and kill your folks?"

"I remember," she said, calmer now. Her eyes looked past him, as if seeing something other than the dim inside of

a barn. "I remember their faces. I couldn't forget. It was
. . . years and years ago. I don't remember anything else. I
don't even remember what my mother looked like. But I
remember the men's faces and I remember how tired and
sore I was and I remember them taking me to the Apaches
and leaving me there."

The tone of her voice convinced him. Goddamned Maxwells. Robbing freight wagons and mines, rustling cattle,
killing Julia—all that was enough to hang them three times
over. But murdering white settlers and selling their child to
the Apaches . . . Hanging was too good for those boys.

And Maxie was going to make her life with those stinking
pieces of snake shit. The hell she was.

Don't follow if he wanted to keep his hide in one piece,
she'd warned. Cactus Maxie had better look to her own
little hide when he caught up with her. Indeed she'd better.

Chapter 18

Maxie had been to Tucson only once before in her life. She hadn't liked the town then, and it hadn't improved much over the years.

Her first visit had been when she was twelve, right after the Confederates had retreated from Tucson and the victorious Yankee commander Carleton had declared Arizona a part of the Union. All the Maxwells—Blackjack, Tom, Dirty Jim, Maxie, and their pa—had ridden in to see what they could see. The men, of course, had been anxious to discover if they could fleece the Yanks out of anything of value, but the Yanks were war-weary and wary after a campaign fighting off both the Apaches and the Rebs. The trip had proved unprofitable except as a lark.

The bars and brothels of Tucson at that time were far better than any other entertainment the area had to offer, which wasn't saying much, considering the condition of the territory thereabouts. Still, the Maxwell men had managed to have a fine time. Even Dirty Jim was allowed to tag along on their hell-raising, while Maxie was left in a room above a saloon, where she entertained herself for three days playing poker with the whores.

Tucson hadn't exactly been jumping back in those days. Most folks—Mexican or American—didn't do much traveling in or out of town. When the federal troops pulled out of the territory to join the war in the East, the Apaches cut loose with a reign of terror. North of the Mexican border Tucson, Tubac, and Iron Pete's ranch were the only islands of safety in a sea of bloodshed. All the little mining towns, ranches, and mines that had dotted the brushy hills were either destroyed or abandoned, and venturing out on the roads was an invitation to brutal death.

Her pa hadn't given a damn, though, Maxie remembered. He'd figured that the Maxwells were tougher than any Apache ever born. By some miracle they'd gone anywhere they pleased during those years, and the Apaches had never bothered them. Maybe her pa was right, Maxie reflected. Maybe the Maxwell boys were meaner than the Apaches. She'd had experience with both, now, and, all things considered, she figured her brothers had it over the Apaches when it came to disgusting habits and senseless violence.

Now, sitting alone at a table in Tucson's most notorious saloon and gambling den, Maxie observed her brothers' antics in the same light she might have regarded the shenanigans in Agua Linda's hogpens. Blackjack was falling-down drunk; Dirty Jim was at the next table making lewd and very public advances to the girl serving up the drinks, and Tom was bragging about his exploits in an overly loud voice while playing cards at the neighboring table.

Maxie propped her elbows on the table and stared into the amber depths of a beer she'd scarcely touched. The beer was watered and weak, and it tasted as if the tobacco-chewing bartender had spit in it sometime before sending it to her table. The room stank of stale beer, smoke, sickeningly sweet perfume, and sweat. The room also smelled as if someone had butchered a herd of cattle in the back rooms and left the carcasses in the heat much too long. She figured that smell was coming from the kitchen and reminded herself not to order anything to eat.

Her life certainly had started a slide downward. Just a week ago she'd been soaring like a bird, wings outspread on breezes that were carrying her higher and higher. She'd had good friends—Pete and Medina, Cynthia and her parents, Elsa, Mary, Simon. She'd been well on her way to becoming a respectable lady, and best of all, Aaron Hunter had loved her.

And now where was she? In a smelly saloon watching her brothers stink and sweat and generally act like pigs rolling in shit.

Why was she now seeing her brothers so differently from how she had regarded them just a few months ago? Had they changed since their pa left them? Had they become wilder, more foulmouthed, more drunken, more reckless? Or was it she who had changed? Maybe, Maxie thought sadly, a little of both had occurred. The brothers she had once loved so well now seemed like shallow, swaggering, overgrown children who needed a good taste of the rod. Blackjack wasn't a hero; he was an overblown braggart whose temper was matched only by his own viciousness. And Tom, whom she had once thought so loyal, was too dumb to do anything but follow Blackjack into whatever trouble he was brewing.

But Dirty Jim was the brother who puzzled her most. He was her twin. They had spent their childhood dreaming the same dreams and fighting the same fights. Often the fights were with each other, but they had always ended up friends. They had always thought alike, just as they looked so much alike. Jim's black hair, blue eyes, and dimpled smile were duplicates of Maxie's; but the sullen expression and cynical twist of his mouth were features Maxie hoped she didn't share. Her twin almost seemed like a stranger in the past three days since Blackjack had brought her back into the family fold. Dirty Jim rode hard, talked little, and drank too much. Every move he made, every word he said seemed to quiver with barely leashed violence. Maxie hoped she wasn't around if the leash ever broke. She didn't want to see what would happen.

The heat and the smoke were making her beer look almost inviting. Maxie shook her head, sighed, and took a swig. She almost choked. It was every bit as bad as it had been ten minutes before.

"Thought you was too smart to be drinkin' poison like that!"

Maxie looked up to see a familiar face and a familiar smile.

"Hilda!" Maxie sputtered.

"In the flesh, honey. Jack said he might be bringin' you by sometime soon. It's right good to see you, babe."

"It's good to see you too. Lordy! Do I have things to tell you!"

"That's the old smile I remember. You were lookin' plum like yer best friend died. I know the beer's bad, but we both used to drink worse in ol' Hernando's cave."

"Yeah. We did." Why couldn't she think of those times as the good old days anymore?

"Say, I heard about yore pa takin' off, honey. I'm right sorry. He's a mean ol' bugger but"—she smiled, and Maxie noticed she had lost a front tooth—"he shore do have some purty kids."

"Weren't you the one who said a body wouldn't know I was female even if I stripped naked?"

"That weren't saying you ain't pretty, honey, just that you didn't look like no real live female. Ya still don't."

In her trousers and dirty shirt, with her hair pulled back and tightly braided, Maxie admitted that Hilda was right. She didn't look any more like a woman than she had a year ago when she was still scruffing around Stronghold. But she felt more like a woman, and it was the feeling that hurt.

"Now what's got ya so sad, Max?"

"Maybe I just don't like sitting here and watching my brothers act like jackasses."

"Honey, that's never made ya sad before, and they always been jackasses. 'Ceptin' maybe Jim. Use'ta be I suspected that boy had some class, but turns out I was mistook." She gave Maxie a canny look. "Besides, I don't think that's your problem. You got a man in your eyes, honey. Could be that our Max has grown up a bit?"

Maxie snorted. "There's no man in my eyes, or my mind, either."

"You're a lyin' sack o' shit, Max. He's there plain as can be for an old hand like Hilda to see. Come on. Tell me all about it."

"There ain't . . . isn't . . . ain't—shit! There isn't any man, Hilda!"

"You ain't foolin' me, honey. I just hope he ain't that good-lookin' son of a bitch who turned his gun on Stronghold. Not that I was in love with that rathole or the rats who lived there, ya understand. But your brothers don't much take to any man givin' 'em that kinda trouble."

"My brothers!" Maxie snorted, looking at Tom, who was dealing cards to three other poker players at a neighboring table. She watched his hands as he dealt, shaking her head. "My brothers don't much take to anything other than getting drunk and raising hell. That's all they've been doing since we got together again."

Hilda shrugged. "Well, they're men. Whaddya expect? They're only good for one thing, and most of 'em ain't much good at that."

"At what?"

Hilda smiled and lifted one painted brow.

"Oh, that." Maxie had to smile in return. "Hilda, you haven't changed at all."

"You want that man o' yours, Max, then you go after him. You don't let those brothers o' yours drag ya to the lockup with 'em. Because that's where they're headed, honey."

"You don't worry about me, Hilda. I can—"

"What the HELL do you think you're doing, Simmons?

You think I was born yesterday, man?" came a roar from several tables away.

Maxie jumped, startled by Tom's drunken voice.

"You think you can cheat Tom Maxwell and get away with it?" he slurred.

The rest of the saloon fell silent. Every head turned toward the potential fight, eyes gleaming with anticipation of excitement to liven a dull day.

"I weren't cheatin' and you know it, you big dumb coyote. You just cain't stand the sight of a big pot being pulled in by anybody but yer own self. Quit squawkin' and sit down."

Maxie hoped that Tom would do as Simmons ordered. She was good enough at cards to know that Tom himself had been cheating. Probably Simmons had cheated too, but that just brought the game back to being fair.

"You callin' me a liar?" Tom narrowed his eyes, but succeeded only in looking drunk, not fearsome.

"I'll be callin' you worse if you don't sit down and play. Now just pass the deck to Angelo there and we'll play another hand."

"The hell we will!"

Tom lunged across the table, grabbed Simmons by the neck, and dragged him to the floor. Everyone in the saloon, including the bartender, jostled for position to get a good view of the fight as the two men scuffled. Maxie didn't bother. She knew Tom well enough to know what would happen. If he was lucky enough to down his opponent quickly, he'd crow for three days about what a fighter he was. If he lost, which was much more likely, he'd find a hundred excuses for the fight not going his way. Of course if he lost this one, Simmons was likely to shoot him just on principle. Nobody liked being called a cheater, even if it was true.

"Tom's gonna get himself shot one of these days." Hilda echoed Maxie's thoughts. "Just outta pure cussedness."

Not today, though. Blackjack came to his brother's rescue

and joined the fight. Together the two Maxwells beat poor
Simmons into a bloody ruin. Dirty Jim remained at his table
with his whore, watching the fracas with a look of cynical
disgust on his face. Maxie turned away, sick at heart.

Hilda looked at Maxie with sympathetic eyes. "Your boyfriend will be lucky to get off so light," she said softly. "At
least ol' Simmons there will mend in a week or so."

Maxie forgot to deny she had a boyfriend. "What do you
mean?" she demanded in a low voice.

They sat down again as Simmons was dragged out of the
room to be revived in the watering trough outside.

"I figgered maybe you was in on it, honey. Jack tol' me
you'd become a regular little sugartit and were lurin' the fly
right into the swatter."

Maxie clenched her jaw. Heat slowly built in her face.

"But I said to myself—Hilda, I said, a sweet little gal like
Maxie ain't gonna be bait for no killin'. Not even for killin'
Aaron Hunter."

Suddenly the room seemed to be full of Hunter as Maxie
caught his name on Blackjack's lips also.

"Hunter's a bigger sucker than I thought," Blackjack was
saying to Jim at the next table. Maxie strained to listen.
"Toby told me he was seen in Tubac yesterday. I figger he'll
follow our trail right to where we want the bastard. Shit!" he
chuckled. "Some hombres just never learn."

"Looks like your fish has taken the hook," Hilda said with
a grimace. She also eavesdropped.

Maxie's heart beat double time. Hunter had followed after all. The damned blockheaded fool.

"He wasn't supposed to follow!" Maxie spit out, as if the
intensity of her denial would send Hunter back where he
belonged.

She'd left a note warning him. Why did he want to follow
her, anyway? He hated her, was done with her, never
wanted to see her again. Her brother was the one he followed, no doubt. Hunter must have decided that a good
turn done ten years ago didn't merit his giving up revenge,

and now he was looking to get Blackjack in his gunsights. In truth, he would probably rather kill Julia's abductor with his bare hands, but no doubt a lead slug through the heart would give him some satisfaction.

"Maxie?" Hilda prompted.

"Huh? What did you say?"

"I said," Hilda repeated in a sour tone, "that your brothers will likely send Hunter to hell the fast way. They'll fill him so full of lead he cain't do anything but go straight down."

Maxie raked the room with desperate eyes. "I've got to get out of here! I've got to stop him from coming!"

Hilda put a restraining hand on Maxie's shoulder. "There's nothing to be done for the man now, honey. You heard what Jack said. Hunter's gone and took the bait. He'll have to take care of himself." She shook her head in sad resignation. "Men is all the same, Max. They think with what's between their legs, ya know? You'd reckon a man like Hunter would know better to fall for a fool's setup like this."

"Don't say that about Hunter. He's not coming after me!" Maxie pressed her temples with her fingers, as if putting pressure on her brain would force it to come up with a solution. "Besides, you don't know him. He . . . he's . . ."

Hilda gave her shoulder a comforting pat. "Got it bad, don'tcha, Max? I'm really sorry, hon. It's a damned rotten world."

"Damn him, anyway!" Maxie swore. "He wasn't supposed to follow."

"Men is stubborn as mules. Mules is smarter, though."

"Well," Maxie said with a sigh. "I'm just going to have to save his bacon. For the second time."

Hilda's eyes narrowed. "Max, you quit thinkin' whatever it is you're thinkin'."

"Is there a back way out of here?" Her eyes began to gleam with a wild light that Hilda hadn't seen in ten years—

the same gleam that had signaled trouble when Maxie was a dirty-faced kid with a knack for creating mayhem.

"Whaddya think you're gonna do?"

"Is there?" Maxie demanded.

Hilda pursed her lips in disapproval. "Through the kitchen, then turn right."

"Thanks, Hilda." Maxie reached out and squeezed the older woman's hand. "You're a friend."

"And you're a fool." Hilda answered. She watched as Maxie got up and casually made her way toward the kitchen, then picked up Maxie's abandoned beer and took a hefty swallow. "Sometimes," she said to no one in particular, "I figger that women ain't no smarter than men."

The smell in the kitchen made Maxie glad she hadn't eaten. Some of the odor no doubt came from the cook, who was a short, rotund little Mexican with dirty strands of hair hanging well past his shoulders and a sweat-soaked shirt clinging to his back and chest.

"Get outta my kitchen!" he growled without preliminary.

Happy to oblige, Maxie dodged around the wood stove and a greasy table and out the rear of the kitchen to the pantry. As Hilda had promised, on her right was a door that led to the back alley. She grasped the handle.

"Going somewhere?"

Maxie spun around with a guilty start. Blackjack was behind her, in the kitchen, with his butt propped against the table. The Mexican cook watched him disapprovingly.

"I figured I'd stretch my legs."

"Stretch 'em in the saloon."

"Why should I? I just want to go out and get some fresh air." She was losing her knack for lying. Blackjack could see right through her, Maxie thought with a sinking heart.

"Just do like I say, baby sister."

Maxie struck a defiant pose. "You ain't never been my boss, Blackjack. I'll do as I please." She turned back toward the door, but before she could even reach for the handle, Blackjack grasped her shoulders and whirled her around.

"Not today, you won't! And don't give me none of your sass, Max, or I'll give you a beatin' that'll make Pa's seem like a love tap."

The cook jumped in with his opinion. "You two want to fight, you do it in the saloon. This here's *my* kitchen. Get out."

A black look came to her brother's face, and for a moment Maxie thought the little cook was a goner. But Blackjack merely dragged her from under the Mexican's angry glare and pushed her back into the saloon. "That old man better watch his goddamned mouth or I'm going to shut it for him."

Maxie started to go back to her table, but Blackjack jerked her back toward him. "I think maybe you need a rest. Upstairs."

"I want another beer," Maxie pleaded. If she could stay downstairs, she might get another chance to slip away and warn Hunter.

"I'll bring you one. Come on."

Maxie couldn't escape his grasp without making a scene, so she obediently allowed Blackjack to lead her up the stairs to a stuffy room above the bar. The room wasn't much. A cornshuck mattress lay on a wooden bedframe—nothing more than two slats of rough wood with a net of rope stretched between them. Along one wall stood a crude dresser. The pitcher and bowl sitting on it were chipped and dirty.

"I'll have one of the girls bring up a beer."

"Fine." Maybe she could use the mug as a weapon if she had to. "Just what am I supposed to do up here, Jack?"

"Just rest, why don'tcha. You're actin' like the heat's got to ya."

"Bull! You don't trust me, your own sister."

Blackjack shrugged and grinned. "It's a tough town, here," he said in excuse. "You ain't got the brains to stay outta trouble."

She heard him bar the door after he closed it behind him.

The window wasn't locked. In fact, the window had no glass, just shutters, which were hanging open. But the drop to the hard dirt alley could break a neck, or a leg. She couldn't save Hunter if she couldn't ride.

"Shit and damn!" Being a lady for even a short time had ruined her. She couldn't lie worth a damn anymore, she couldn't sneak out of a saloon without being caught, and she couldn't even take much pleasure from cussing, even when the situation sorely needed cussing at.

The beer never arrived. No doubt Blackjack had forgotten about her the moment he'd gotten downstairs. He would be engrossed in his bottle or pestering one of the girls for a free ride. Blackjack had always believed that his looks entitled him to the free services of any whore he fancied.

Why had she persisted in believing that her brothers were a cut above the other scum that rode the border country? All her life she had heard their stories of mayhem, seen the pride they took in their own viciousness. She'd witnessed firsthand their disregard for the lives of anyone other than themselves.

But somehow she'd always made excuses for them, refusing to admit even to herself what they were. Living with civilized people had made her realize the enormity of her self-deception about her family, her very life. The thought of her own stupidity made her ill.

Of course, she didn't have a sole claim to being a feeble-minded dolt. Aaron Hunter was doing his dim-witted best to get himself killed—even after she'd gone to all the trouble to leave him a warning. Damn the man, anyway! Why couldn't she hate him? He deserved to be hated. But she still loved the low-down son of a snake.

Maxie didn't have long to brood. An hour later Blackjack himself appeared with her beer. "Forgot this," he said. "Sorry, baby sister."

"Can I come out now?"

He didn't answer. "We're ridin' out, Max. When we get back, you can go wherever you want. Okay?"

"You going to meet Hunter?"

"It's what we planned. You knew it all along."

"I don't want you to kill him, Jack."

Blackjack laughed. "Oh, sure, we'll just scare him a bit. I figger he'll be scared right into shittin' his pants."

"Blackjack, I mean it! If you hurt Hunter, I'll make you sorry."

"Don't be an ass!" He regarded her with disgust. "What's eatin' you anyway?"

"I don't want any killing."

Blackjack sat down on the cornshuck mattress and gave her a tolerant look. "Max, you've always been funny about killin'. Now, you did a bang-up job on Hunter. But I seen it in your eyes when we first got you away from them Injuns —seen you were sweet on the man. That's understandable, Max, you bein' a female and all. You did what I told you to do and roped us our man, but I figger you caught yourself in the same toss of the lasso. I ain't blamin' ya, 'cause, like I said, you're just a woman. But I tell ya, baby sis, that there Hunter is one man who needs killin' real bad."

Maxie turned around and stared out the window. "I never really figured you for a killer, Blackjack. I know you're wild, but I never thought you were a cold-blooded killer."

"What I am ain't really your business, kid. Before you get all holy and righteous on me, remember that we got the same daddy, girl. If we're rotten, deep inside you're just as rotten as the rest of us."

Maxie's stomach turned. "Hunter's just as likely to kill you as you to kill him," she warned. "He's got a lot of hate for Maxwells bottled up inside him. Did you know that Julia came out west to marry him?"

"Julia? Oh, yeah. Cain't rightly say as I did. Glad to hear it, though."

"He near killed me when he learned it was you who took her. It's you he's coming after, Jack. Not me."

"I don't care who Hunter's after, Max, as long as he's comin'."

Maxie turned to face him, her little jaw set with determination. "Leave him alone, Jack. We could get away—go to Mexico like you planned. Forget Hunter. He's part of the past."

Blackjack grunted. "Not yet he ain't. But he will be soon."

He said these last words with a finality that brooked no argument, and when the door closed behind him, the bar dropped with a loud, decisive thunk.

Ten minutes later, Maxie had just about decided to risk the drop to the alley when the door crashed open. Tom walked into the room, a beer in one hand and a bottle of whiskey in the other.

"What're you doing here?"

"Makin' sure you don't get no ideas about breakin' down the door and runnin' out to warn Hunter," Tom answered. "Jack says you're sweet on the guy."

"I'm not."

"Jack says . . ."

"I don't give a damn what Jack says!"

"Listen, Max. I ain't too happy about bein' left here to watch my own stupid sister, so don't gimme any of your lip. Here," he said, handing her the beer. "I brought sumpthin' for you to drink."

"I already have a beer."

"You can drink two."

"Blackjack and Jim rode out?"

"Yeah. Hunter's a dead man. If you wasn't actin' so strange, I'd be in on the fun." He gave her a sheepish look. "You ain't really sweet on 'im, are ya?"

"Naw."

"Didn't think you could be. I told Jack, but he wouldn't listen. Said you was to stay in the saloon till he gets back. Then we're all goin' to Mexico." Tom beamed proudly. He didn't often have the call to string four sentences together and get the whole thing right.

Mexico might be the wisest course, Maxie reflected. She didn't have to stay with her brothers—or with her father, for that matter. Her grandfather was somewhere a couple of days' ride north of Mexico City, though she didn't know anything about her mother's father other than his name. And there she could be far away from Hunter—perhaps far enough away to forget him.

Then Maxie remembered. She didn't need to travel to Mexico to get away from Hunter. In a few hours he would be dead and about as far away from her as a man could get.

"Let's go downstairs," she said sourly.

Tom wasn't quick in the mind, but he stuck to a job like a tick stuck to a dog.

"Huh-uh. Jack said to stay here."

"He said to stay in the saloon, shitbrain. Downstairs is in the saloon."

"Oh. Yeah." His face brightened. "We could play a few hands of poker. Ain't nuthin' else to do."

Maxie smiled. Now why hadn't she thought of that?

A half hour later, Tom's share of the last Maxwell heist, his horse, his saddle, the silver belt buckle he'd won in a poker game six years ago, and his boots all belonged to Maxie.

"Hell, Max, you stripped me clean. Who taught you to play poker that way?"

"Same person who taught you—Blackjack. You just ain't got the talent," Maxie told him, slipping back into her brother's vernacular. "I've been beating you at poker since I was ten."

"Yeah. But this time you're out fer blood."

That wasn't quite what she was out for, but Maxie didn't argue. Lordy but she was glad that coming so close to re-spectability hadn't undermined her talent for cheating at cards. Not that she had to cheat much to beat Tom.

"Ante up," she said. "It's my deal."

"I ain't got nuthin' left to ante with, Max. 'Lessin' ya want my shirt and pants too."

"Don't want your stinkin' clothes. The boots I figger I can

sell, but I'd have to burn the rest." She smiled wickedly. "Guess I take it all, big brother."

"Come on, Max. Ya gotta gimme a chance to win sumpthin' back!"

She shrugged. "What'cha got?"

"I'll owe ya."

"Bull."

"I'll put up my bridle."

"Already mine. It went with the saddle. Remember?"

"No. Not that one—the silver-plated one I took off that ol' Mex rancher we raided last spring."

"Against all this?" She gestured to her winnings. "Not enough. But I'll give you a chance, since you're my brother. Throw in your pistol and your cut of the next job you ride out on and we'll call it even. One hand wins it all."

Tom thought hard, furrowing his brow with the effort. "Jack'd beat me bloody if I gave you my gun. I'm supposed to be standing guard here, ya know."

"Dope," Maxie said in mild amusement. Her tone contrasted sharply with the nervous beating of her heart. "Empty it. Then throw it in the pot."

Tom looked at her suspiciously, and Maxie prayed that this game would not be one of the rare occasions when he demonstrated a flash of intelligence.

"Or don't throw it in," she added casually. "I don't care. I've got me enough winnings here to keep me awhile."

"Hell. What harm can an unloaded pistol do?"

He found out five minutes later when Maxie collected her prize and promptly knocked him over the head with it. The bartender and few other patrons in the saloon scarcely turned an eye their way when Tom slumped over the table, sending the whiskey bottle and a stack of poker chips crashing to the plank floor.

"Sorry, Tom," Maxie apologized as she stripped him of his ammunition belt and slung it over her own shoulder. She had stacked the deck, but it was in a good cause. She loaded the pistol, hefted its weight once in her hand, and stuck it in her belt.

Then she scraped a fair amount of her winnings from the table into her spread bandana and tied it tightly. She would need the money. After she saved Hunter's bacon this one more time, she would truly be on her own—no family, no friends. She could live with that, she decided, if Hunter was alive and she could think of him ranching his land down on the river bottom, or even riding for the law and making life risky for her brothers. But if she wasn't in time . . .

She refused to think of that possibility. She would get to him before her brothers did if she had to ride three horses into the ground.

Chapter 19

$\mathcal{T}$he bay mare that Maxie had "bought" from Pete Kelley was deep chested, long-legged, and had enough strength and wind to gallop all day, if necessary. But now the mare was lathered and heaving. Maxie had ridden fast and hard over country that might well have broken a horse with less agility and heart. She had circled well beyond the spot where she knew Blackjack and Jim would be waiting and then doubled back, hoping to intercept Hunter before her brothers did. She had no plan, only a desperate knowledge that if Hunter died a vital spark would go out of her life. If Hunter died because of her own stupidity . . . The thought didn't bear thinking on, it was so horrible.

She finally drew rein at the rim of a sandy arroyo. A few hundred yards farther along the arroyo deepened into a rugged canyon. She and her brothers had left a trail as plain as the stripes on a skunk's back when they'd ridden into the canyon the day before. That alone should make Hunter suspicious. But Maxie had the feeling that Hunter knew he was being played for a sucker. He was a man who didn't miss much. Maybe he figured he was good enough to gun down the Maxwells even with the odds against him. Or maybe he was just so angry he didn't care about the odds.

Maxie had to agree with Hilda. Men were absolute blockheads from the age when they started to grow whiskers to the very day they died. Hunter was no exception.

She tied her mare to a juniper bush and clambered through the rocks to the lip of the wash. Her timing was right—just barely. A distant rider was coming toward her, a mere speck against the gray-green backdrop of mesquite-covered hills. Maxie had no doubt the speck was Hunter. He had left some part of himself inside her, and that part sprang to life when he was anywhere within sight. Right now it was singing with joy.

Maxie waited until Hunter was a hundred yards from her perch, then cocked the rifle she'd taken off Tom's saddle. Very carefully she took aim and squeezed the trigger. Hunter's mount shied violently as the lead ball whined past it and plowed into the sand ten feet to the rear. In a flash Hunter was off the horse and running for cover, pistol in hand, firing as he ran. A slug ricocheted off a boulder beside her, sending shards of rock flying toward her face.

Maxie clapped her hand to one cheek. It came away bloody. "Shit!" she cussed aloud. Hunter was the only man she knew who could even come close to hitting a target while he was on the run. He'd missed her by only a hair, and unlike hers, his miss hadn't been deliberate!

She fired again, wide of the mark but close enough to convince the mule-headed toad that she meant business. "Get outta here, Hunter, you shit-brained jackass! You damned well weren't invited to this party." Medina and Cynthia would have been appalled at her language, Maxie reflected with a twinge of guilt. But then she figured that ladylike manners weren't going to play a big part in her future.

"Maxie?"

At the sound of his voice Maxie's heart leaped. She had to remind herself sternly that she'd come to drive the man away, not run into his arms. She fired again, not even close enough to worry him. But the gesture relieved some of her frustration. "Go back, Hunter! If you're following me, forget it! If you're following my brothers, forget that too."

"Come down, Maxie. I want to talk to you." He moved out from behind the rock where he'd sought shelter, his arms spread wide to leave his chest vulnerable to any shot she might send his way. "And quit pretending you're going to shoot me. We both know better."

She stood up, rifle in hand. "Don't think I wouldn't, Hunter."

Even at that distance she could see his answering smile. Damn the man! He knew her much too well.

"Come on down, Maxie."

Slowly she climbed down into the arroyo, all the while feeling forces pulling her in opposite directions. She hadn't planned to talk to him, just scare him away. One part of her was singing at the thought of just being close to him again, and another part was quivering, fearful that the closer she got, the more dangerous was his power over her. He had the power. She could feel it pulling at her as surely as Pete Kelley roped and pulled his hogs to the butchering rack.

"This is as close as I come, Hunter." She raised her rifle and pointed it his way. "Throw your pistol over there in the sand, out of reach. You can fetch it back when you leave."

He did as she ordered, raising one dark brow. "I'm not any more likely to shoot you than you are to shoot me, Maxie."

"Then it's a good thing your gun's over there in the sand," she answered bitingly. "What do you think you're doing, following us?"

"It's a free country. A man can ride wherever he wants."

"Horseshit." How had she ever thought she could do anything but love him? He could hate her and call her names until hell froze, but she would still love him so much it hurt. And it did hurt. Lordy, but it hurt! "You're following us, Hunter. You've got no business sticking your nose where it doesn't belong. Get outta here and leave us alone. Leave *me* alone."

"I don't think I can leave you alone, Maxie."

Now what the hell did he mean by that? "Don't you understand English, Hunter? Leave. Vamoose. Adios. Get on your horse and head back where you belong."

"I don't think so."

"I'll shoot, dammit."

He just smiled that irritating, infuriating, absolutely devastating smile.

She fired. A bullet plowed the sand between his boots. He didn't move, didn't even flinch. She fired again, closer. Same result.

"You're not going to shoot me, Maxie."

"You've got a helluva lot of faith in my aim."

He just looked at her. She felt like crying, damn the man.

"What're you doing just standing there, dammit! Get on your horse and ride out of here!"

"Without my gun?"

With a sigh that was almost a sob, Maxie walked to the spot his pistol had landed, picked it up out of the sand, and emptied all six chambers onto the ground. She tossed the empty gun in Hunter's direction. He caught it and spun it into his holster in one deft motion.

"Now you have your gun. Go."

He grinned and shook his head. "Without you?"

"Damned right, without me."

The man was stubborn as a mule and possessed just about as much sense. No doubt if she told him her brothers lay in ambush up the trail his damned male pride would goad him to meet their challenge. If Hunter got hurt she would never forgive herself. On the other hand, if he managed to gun down her brothers—well, disgusting as they were, they were still the only family she had.

"Come back to Agua Linda with me, Maxie. You've got friends waiting for you there—friends who are worried sick about you. Little Mary's crying her eyes out. She's in such a bother about you leaving that she got that mouth of hers to work. Talked a blue streak about you and her in that Apache camp."

"What do I have to do to get you gone? Shoot you?"

Hunter stood his ground, ignoring the rifle that swung in his direction. "I'm sorry about what I said to you. You took me by surprise with that ring of Julia's. I said a lot of stupid things I didn't mean. You were making a good life for yourself, Maxie. Don't let a hotheaded idiot like me spoil it for you."

"You are an idiot!" Somehow she had to be nasty enough, mean enough, disgusting enough to make him want to ride away. "You think I want to come back to you?" she sneered. "You think I liked all that prancing and prissing about at the Kelleys' ranch? Lordy, Hunter! Do you really think I enjoyed myself anytime you touched me? I didn't. I wanted to puke whenever you touched me. It was all a setup, and you fell for it like a kid who hasn't outgrown short britches. My brothers wanted you to follow me into a trap, and look what a sucker you turned out to be."

"Yeah," Hunter agreed affably. "I'm a sucker, all right." The look he gave her tore right through her defenses. His eyes ripped through her heart and made her very soul bleed. How she wanted to cry out for forgiveness, to shout that she didn't want the wild life anymore! She wanted a life with him. But even if he really wanted her, she couldn't go. Her brothers would always find a way to use her to get at him, just as they had this time. She hadn't intended to lead Hunter into this trap, but she'd done it just the same—just as Blackjack had planned.

Hunter took a step toward her. A little seed of panic began to blossom in her gut.

"So you hate me, do you, Maxie?" he asked. He took another step. Then another.

"You keep away from me, you son of a bitch!" She raised her rifle. Her stomach twisted in an odd sort of fear that was half anticipation.

"Your language has gone down to the level of the company you keep. But then, I figure your brothers don't expect much in the way of feminine behavior. Not like me." He chuckled, a deep, throaty sound that set her nerves to tingling at the same time it spurred her fear. "Are you going to shoot me, Maxie? Go ahead. Pull that trigger. Fire."

She stood paralyzed as he came toward her. The rifle was a dead weight in her arms. Her breath came in short painful gasps and her heart pounded so hard that it hurt. The situation was out of control. She either had to shoot or flee, but she couldn't force herself to do either.

And then the time for fleeing was past. He stood right in front of her, so close she could feel the heat of his body reach out to hers. He took the rifle from her numb grasp.

"You don't need this," he told her as he threw the weapon to the ground. "You have more potent weapons, don't you, Maxie girl." He touched her cheek, ran his finger down her neck. "I wonder just how much you do hate me."

"Don't," Maxie managed to say. She couldn't move, helpless as a rabbit in the jaws of a wolf.

"Don't what? I haven't done anything—yet."

"Don't touch me like that."

He ignored her demand. "Why didn't you shoot me, Maxie?"

Silence.

"Why did you bother to warn me about your brothers' trap?" he asked quietly.

She couldn't answer, not with her heart clogging her throat.

"Maybe you don't hate me as much as you say you do, little Maxie."

Slowly, as in a dream, his mouth descended to take hers, his hand slipped around the back of her head with fingers threaded through her hair to keep her still. The kiss was deliberately seductive. It probed every vulnerable nerve to suck her under his spell. Hunter had learned to play her well during their few times together, and he left her breathless with need and on fire with longing.

"I could take you back with me right now," he whispered against her lips. "I could make you happy whether or not you wanted to be."

He kissed her again and she felt her insides turn to warm, sweet honey. "You don't hate me, sweetheart. And my touch certainly doesn't make you want to puke."

Maxie dredged up her last reserves of courage. She pictured Hunter with her brothers' bullets slamming into his body, the hard muscle pressed against her breasts exploding in bloody tatters. The nightmare vision would come true unless she got Hunter away from the Maxwells—all the Maxwells.

She twisted out of his grasp, hardening her heart against the terrible feeling of loss. "You want to know why I'm warning you, Hunter? You think I'm lying when I say I hate you?" She sneered and wiped her mouth on the back of her hand as if to rid herself of the last trace of his kiss. "You men! None of you can believe that you don't set a woman's heart to quivering. I'll tell you why I'm warning you, you piece of donkey shit. I decided that you're not worth the lead it would take to kill you. Or the risk. We're headed to Mexico, my brothers and I. I want them in one piece for the trip down there. Getting back at you isn't worth risking their lives."

"You don't have much confidence in their ability to jump a man."

"Depends on the man," she answered. "You're better with a gun than most."

Hunter sighed and gazed down at the sand. When he lifted his face he didn't appear nearly as mad as he should have, Maxie thought, considering the things she had just said. In fact, he looked as though he hadn't heard a single one of her words. "Maxie girl—I didn't really want to tell you this. But I guess you're going to make me let loose with both barrels, aren't you?"

"What do you mean?"

"I think you don't really know what kind of men you're riding to Mexico with."

"I told you that Julia's death was . . ."

"I'm not talking about Julia, Maxie. I'm talking about Mary."

"Mary? What do my brothers have to do with Mary?"

"Mary wasn't kidnapped by the Apaches. She was sold to them. By Harrison and Blackjack Maxwell."

"That's a lie!" she gasped, a reflexive retort she had used all her life when someone had bad-mouthed the Maxwells. "That's a goddamned, shit-brained, snake-pukin' lie."

"Mary recognized Blackjack, Maxie. She was so afraid for you when you left with him that she managed to break through that silence of hers and tell me. They robbed her folks' ranch, killed her parents, and rode off with her. She doesn't remember much, but she remembers being sold, and she remembers Blackjack."

"What does she know about who took her? She was a kid, and she's crazy. Why do you think the Indians called her 'Loco'?"

"You know better than that."

Maxie's own voice echoed in her head. She had almost screamed that last denial, as if volume alone would drown out the bitter ring of truth in Hunter's accusation. A wave of nausea pushed her stomach up into her throat. Robbing mines and rustling cattle were one thing, but killing innocent settlers and selling their children to the Apaches was something entirely worse. The tale had to be a lie, or a mistake. It had to be.

She met Hunter's gaze, and immediately her eyes darted away from his. She didn't like the look there. He wasn't gloating as a man might when telling such an awful lie. His brow was puckered with concern, his mouth a tight line of worry.

The Maxwells had done business with Noches's band before. Blackjack had admitted as much when they'd ridden out of the Apache rancheria. Noches had known him and welcomed him into the camp. And Mary, Maxie remembered, had been petrified the moment she saw him. The details all fell together too well.

Hunter took advantage of her distraction to close the small distance she'd put between them. He put out his hand and touched her cheek, not a seductive touch this time, but a gentle one. Maxie flinched, but something in his eyes kept her from moving away.

"Come home now, Maxie."

"I am home," she replied bitterly. The reasons she couldn't go with him hadn't changed. He had simply made it impossible to stay as well as impossible to go. She wanted to lash out and hit something, kick something. Hunter was the likeliest target, but she couldn't do that either. She felt paralyzed, helpless, dead. "Get out of here."

"Maxie . . ."

"Get out of here!"

She was screeching again, but Maxie didn't care. Why wouldn't he go and leave her alone? Hadn't he done enough?

A muscle in Hunter's jaw twitched. When Maxie met his gaze, his eyes were black flint—hard, blank, unreadable. "I'm going." He turned, walked toward his mount, then stopped. "Think about what kind of men you're claiming as family, Maxie." His back was toward her, and his voice was as blank as his eyes had been. "You're not like them, kid. You're not like them at all. Not yet, at least."

Maxie didn't move as he mounted and rode away. For a long time she stood perfectly still in the bottom of the little arroyo, as if frozen in place, and when she finally moved it was to sink down into a heap of misery upon the sand.

Up the trail Blackjack and Jim lounged in the shade of a granite boulder while they kept watch on the little canyon below them. The canyon wasn't much as canyons go, but it was an adequate trap for a lone rider passing between its brush-covered walls. Or at least it would be an adequate trap if Aaron Hunter would quit lallygagging and ride into it.

"Where the hell is he?" Blackjack complained, as much to himself as to his brother Jim, who was leaning back against the boulder, his hat covering his face. "What'd the son of a bitch do—stop along the way to have a picnic? Hell. If he started from Tubac at sunup he should have been here an hour ago."

Jim grunted, lifted his hat, and yawned. "Mebbe he slept late. Or found himself a señorita to spend some time with."

"His señorita is locked up in a bar in Tucson," Blackjack growled. "That's why he's ridin' this way."

"Shit. That's only Maxie. Hard to believe a man like Hunter would go to all this trouble just for Max."

"Women ain't so common out here that a man can afford to be choosy. Besides, little sister's quite a looker when she gets prissed up. She's filled out right like she should. Could be she'll make us a good pile of money in Mexico."

"Who, Max?" Jim scoffed. "She wouldn't whore for all the gold in Mexico City. And she's stubborn as a mule. Might as well forget makin' money off of her."

"There's other ways of fleecin' those rich señors. Look at what Max did to Hunter. The son of a bitch is a double-dealer and a deserter, but he used to be smart as a wolf and twice as tough. Look at him now, sniffin' after a woman like a randy stud followin' a hotted-up mare—not paying any mind to the rope that's about to slip around his fool neck. She's turned him to damned mush."

Jim snorted. "I don't see him comin' up no trail, Jack."

"He'll come. Like you say, maybe he had some business in Tubac. But he'll be along. And when he comes"—Blackjack looked down the trail through the sights of his rifle—"no more Mr. Smart Ass Lawman."

"You know Max ain't gonna be pleased about that."

"Max'll do as she's told. She'll forget about the bastard

quick enough when she sees all those rich rancheros where we're headed."

"Yeah? Well, I've never knowed Max to . . ."

Blackjack held up his hand for silence. "Shut up. I hear something."

They both sat still. Slowly the sound grew louder, rising above the small animal and insect noises that always populated the desert silence. Hoofbeats were drumming along the plain to the north, coming steadily closer.

"He's coming," Jim said, a slight quaver betraying his nervousness.

"Shitbrain. It ain't Hunter. Wrong direction."

"He circled around."

"Like hell he did."

"Then who the devil is it?"

"Shit if I know. Don't be gettin' wild on me, boy. Just keep your damn gun cocked and your eyes peeled."

Jim did as he was told. But his lips pressed into a tight line and his knuckles grew white on the hand that gripped his gun. The hoofbeats faded for a moment, then grew loud again.

Finally, the oncoming rider appeared above the ridge to the north. Even at that distance Jim recognized the bulky figure. Brother Tom.

"Hell," Jim muttered.

"What the shit is he doing here?" Blackjack spat.

They found out soon enough. Five minutes later Tom pulled his lathered horse to a stop and slid to the ground.

"Is Max here?" he asked as soon as his feet hit the ground.

"No she ain't here!" Blackjack answered. "You idiot. What'd you do? Let her slip through your fingers?"

"Dammit! The little she-skunk won all my money, then hit me with my own damned gun. I figgered she just wanted to come join the fun."

Blackjack spat into the sand and let loose a string of curses that impressed even his brothers. "You got maggots for brains, you stupid son of a bitch. I leave you to guard one undergrowed girl and you let her give you the slip."

Tom looked offended. "Max may be on the small side, but she's shifty as an Injun. Besides, a man's sister ain't oughtta be cheatin' 'im at cards and hittin' 'im over the head."

"Won all your money, huh?" Jim noted with a grin. "She probably didn't even have to cheat to do it."

"Yeah," Tom admitted, shamefaced. "My horse, too. She set it loose, the little varmint. This here pony belongs to Jed Baker at the livery."

Blackjack didn't see the humor that prompted Dirty Jim's grin. "Goddamn it, Tom. One of these days I'm goin' to give your head to ol' Noches to hang his scalps on. That's about the only thing it's good for. Come on. We might as well git."

"Whaddya mean?" Jim asked. "Hunter might be comin' any minute. We can track down Max anytime. She won't be hard to find."

"Max can go to hell for all I care." Blackjack yanked his mount's reins loose from the branch where they were tied and swung into the saddle. "But for sure the little slut warned Hunter. He won't be coming this way anytime soon."

Jim scowled. He wasn't sure he liked hearing Blackjack call Maxie a slut. She was their sister, after all. And though she might be a prickly little troublemaker, she wasn't a slut.

"Where we goin'?" Tom asked, eager as always to do anything Blackjack asked.

"We're goin' to Motherlode to show Aaron Hunter he's bit off more than he can chew. The middle of a town ain't where I would choose to do the job, but just let anybody try to stand in my way." Blackjack smiled a smile that would have made a rattlesnake pause. "I'm in the mood for a little action, boys. Whaddya say?"

Maxie sat in the wash, staring at the dirt. Time passed— moments or hours, she didn't know which. Nor did she care. All the energy, determination, and fire had left her. She

could dredge up no will to get on with her life, no will to
even move. A dreadful lassitude kept her sitting in the sand,
numb, shaking, and more alone than ever before in her life.

In the course of a few days she had lost both a lover and a
family. Hunter's revelation had snapped the last tie that
bound her to her father and brothers. All her life she'd
made excuses both for them and herself. Since going to
Agua Linda she had experienced things that made her wonder about her old ideas. Slowly but surely the wrongness of
how the Maxwells lived was pounded into her brain. She
might still try to make excuses for them. Maxie had gotten
good at making excuses over the years.

But murdering settlers and selling their children to the
Apaches was beyond her capacity to understand. Settlers
had no gold, no silver—nothing but their lives, and their
children. Her pa and brothers—her purely vicious family—
had taken even those.

For a moment Maxie felt like lying down in the warm
sand and dying. She felt soiled by the very blood that ran in
her veins. Running Woman had told her one day about a
Chiricahua *di-yin* who could cleanse a person of polluted
blood. How she wished that she could find that Apache
sorcerer. He could make her into a new person—maybe a
Kelley, or a Pruitt, or a . . . a Hunter. Hunter . . .

Tears came in a flood. Maxie put her head between her
drawn-up knees and let them flow. No Apache magic could
restore the friendships she had come to value, or the love
she had learned to crave. The world was only what it was.
And that was that. Her family was slime. Aaron Hunter and
her friends on the other side of the law were lost to her.
Maxie was alone, so she'd better make the best of it.

She pushed herself up off the sand, wiped her eyes with
the back of her hand, and started to climb up to the lip of
the wash, where she'd left her horse. Jake the dog at least
would stick by her. She would swing by Agua Linda, pick
him up, and pack the few personal items she had left behind. At the ranch she could say a proper good-bye to the

life she'd almost had. Maybe then she would feel better. Proper good-byes were important.

As she mounted the bay mare, Maxie looked back to where the arroyo deepened into a gorge. Let her brothers stew in their own vicious juices while they waited for a man who wasn't going to come. She didn't owe them an explanation. Cactus Maxie wasn't a Maxwell anymore.

Around a blind bend of the wash, Aaron Hunter watched, frowning ominously, as Maxie spurred her horse south toward Agua Linda. The itch to kill Blackjack still raged, but sometime during his confrontation with Maxie, the need to keep her within reach of his hand—and his protection—had grown to paramount importance. Pulled in two directions at once, he waited, a muscle in his jaw pulsing as furiously as his thoughts. Down the canyon, Blackjack—and sweet revenge—waited; and in the other direction, Maxie was headed out of his life, exactly as he had wished not too many hours earlier. Hunter snorted with self-contempt. He'd been a fool not to realize which Maxwell had the greater claim on him.

When Maxie was well hidden in her own dust, he nudged his horse to follow.

Maxie reached the Agua Linda compound just as the sun was setting. She reined in her horse atop a little hill and looked down upon the ranch. The cattle grazed peacefully on the grassy floodplain of the creek; the hogs grunted in their pens; the horses dozed in the corral. She could hear one of the dogs barking—one of the feisty cattle dogs, not Jake. Jake would be in the kitchen under Elsa's feet, hoping to catch a morsel or two that might fall to the floor.

Nothing had changed—except the wall. The wall that surrounded the house and courtyard was finally finished. No more Apaches would come bursting through the gap as they had during the attack in early summer, when she and Medina had fought for their lives against two Apache warriors. Both women would have lost their hair that day had

328   *Emily Bradshaw*

Medina not been such an expert shot with a rifle. What a surprise to Maxie that such a ladylike female knew her way around the business end of a Winchester. She remembered being more impressed by La Doña's cool head and marksmanship than by the fact that they were both still alive.

That incident had convinced Maxie that she just might have something more to learn, even though at the time she had thought herself as close to perfect as a female could possibly get. She smiled ruefully, remembering how hard Medina had worked to turn her into a lady. Cynthia, too, had taken a good shot at the task. And they had both failed, bless them. Maxie figured she was as much a hoyden now as she ever had been. The only difference was that she was no longer proud of the fact.

The last sliver of the sun was bathing the desert grass and mesquite in a soft red glow. Elsa came out of the compound to throw scraps to the hogs. Jake was at her heels. A ranch hand tipped his hat as the cook walked by. Two other hands, saddles slung over their shoulders, walked out of the tack shed toward the corral.

The scene below was so ordinary, so peaceful, and so desirable that a painful lump grew in Maxie's throat. When she had been twelve her pa had taken the family to Tucson. Maxie remembered looking into a bin of hard candy in a mercantile store. She had wanted that candy so badly that the wanting became a physical pain in her belly, but it was as far beyond her reach as the moon. Her pa wouldn't have bought her any. He wouldn't have minded if she had swiped a handful—as long as she didn't get caught, but the storekeeper had too watchful an eye. So she had just stood there, her mouth watering and her stomach gurgling, wanting those sweets but knowing they weren't for her.

Sitting atop the hill looking down on Agua Linda was just like looking into that forbidden candy bin—with one difference. If she had wanted the candy badly enough she could have stolen it. She couldn't steal Agua Linda or the life it represented. The peaceful, decent life simply was not for her. She was what she was—a Maxwell. Not all her desiring could change that gloomy fact.

So she'd best collect her things, say her good-byes, and get on with her life, whatever it was going to be. With a resigned sigh, she nudged her horse with her heels and headed down the hill.

The wall guard was the first to see her. He hallooed at the ranch house, and within moments Medina, Catalina, Mary, and Maria had appeared at the wall gate. Elsa looked up from feeding the hogs and gave her a wide grin as she rode in.

"I told them you would come back," the cook said to Maxie as she rode past, nodding as if confirming to herself how right she had been.

Medina and the two Mexican house girls swarmed around her, pelting her with questions, while Mary stood by silently, tears dribbling down her cheeks. Finally, Medina silenced the other women with a glare. "You must be tired," she said, holding her own questions in reserve. "We were about to have supper. You can go wash up around back. I'll see that your horse is taken care of."

"No, ma'am." Maxie shook her head. "I can't stay. I've come to collect my things—and take Jake, if you don't mind."

Medina frowned. "Aleta, dear. Look around you. In a few minutes it will be full dark. You will at least stay the night."

"I can't. I really can't."

Medina regarded her with narrowed eyes. "Is the law chasing you?"

Maxie shook her head. Not likely that the only law in this part of Arizona Territory would ever chase her again.

"Your brothers?"

"No," she mumbled.

"Then give me one good reason why you can't stay?"

Because the longer she was here the more she would want to stay. But she couldn't say that to Medina, who

wouldn't understand why Cactus Maxie Maxwell could
never fit into this world.

"I thought so," Medina said in a satisfied tone. "Come
along, now. Sam will take care of your horse, won't you,
Sam. You look as if you could use a good meal and a bath.
Then you can tell us everything that's happened."

Then came the shout from a wall guard. "Rider comin'
in!" shouted a wall guard.

They all turned. No rider was in sight, but a column of
dust marked the path of someone headed their way. A horse
topped the hill on the other side of the creek—the same hill
where Maxie had sat to watch Agua Linda and daydream.
The rider was silhouetted against the dark purple sky. Even
in the near dark and at such a distance, Maxie couldn't
mistake him. Her stomach lurched into her throat.

Medina frowned. "Who is it?"

"Hunter," Maxie choked out.

"Well, good." La Doña looked inordinately pleased. "Catalina, go set two more places at the table. Good thing we
cooked up enough chili to feed the whole ranch."

"I gotta go," Maxie said.

Medina took her arm in a firm grip. "Now, Aleta, we
already discussed that."

"You don't understand!"

"I think I do," she said with a smile. "Now come wash up
and we'll all have a very entertaining supper, I'm sure. Sam,
tell Hunter to wash up around back and come in for supper.
We'll be waiting for him."

Maxie had no choice but go with Medina. The Spanish
doña was almost as small as she was, but her grip was like an
iron vise.

When Hunter made his entrance into the dining room, a
place had been set for him at the table. The spicy fragrance
of Elsa's chili—one of Hunter's favorites—filled the room,
but he didn't seem to notice.

"Sit down, Aaron," Medina invited. "You're just in time to
eat. And to tell Aleta good-bye. She's leaving, you know."

"That's what she thinks." His tone brought a smile to Medina's face. Maria and Catalina looked at each other and giggled. Mary smiled in relief.

"Quiet, girls," Medina instructed. "You sound perturbed, Aaron. Is something wrong?"

Hunter looked at Maxie, his eyes as black as his scowl, and Maxie gripped the sides of her chair seat until her knuckles were white.

"I'm here on business." His words were addressed to Medina, but he still looked at Maxie. "I came to arrest our little friend here."

Chapter 20

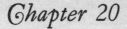

"*A*rrest me?" Maxie exclaimed, rising halfway out of her seat. "For what?"

"Attempted murder will do," Hunter said in a solemn, official voice. "I could probably come up with other charges if I tried."

"He's loco!" Maxie cried, looking around the table for support. "I've never done any such thing!"

Hunter raised a dark brow. "Then who ambushed me in a draw just south of Tucson this afternoon? Or maybe those rifle slugs were just your way of saying a friendly hello." He gave her a quizzical smile.

"You know damn . . . very well what that was!" Maxie slammed her fist down onto the table, making the dishes jump. "Besides," she said, eyes narrowing to angry slits, "I hit what I aim at. If I'd been aiming at you—you jackass!—you'd be a meal for the buzzards right now."

Maria and Catalina giggled as Maxie and Hunter exchanged glares. Mary's eyes were wide, and Medina raised a disapproving brow. "Perhaps we should have this discussion someplace other than the supper table. Catalina, take the chili back to the kitchen and keep it warm over the fire. Maria, take Mary and help Cat."

The girls cleared away the chili and bowls as slowly as they dared, no doubt reluctant to miss such a promising bit of drama. Not until La Doña sent a frown their way did they disappear through the doorway.

"Now, children. Continue."

Hunter's brows drew together in a harsh line. "Medina, may I talk to Maxie in private?"

"No." Medina refused with a smile. "I think not. From the look of her, you need someone here to protect you. Aleta, dear, did you really lay an ambush for our upstanding lawman friend?"

"I most certainly did not! Well . . . I did. But it wasn't really . . . oh . . . oh, pooh!" Sometimes Cynthia's pet word did come in handy when a body couldn't let loose with a proper cuss. She turned on Aaron, her eyes the electric blue of crackling lightning. "You liar. You . . . you . . . !"

"Ah, ah!" Hunter cautioned. "Remember you're in civilized company."

"Medina is the only civilized person I see here, you belly-slinking snake-nosed son of a skunk." She could think of no description nasty enough that she could speak in La Doña's presence. "You know damn well I wasn't trying to kill you. I was trying to save your rotten, worthless hide. Why are you doing this?"

He smiled innocently, as if he weren't acting like the lowest villain in the territory. "I've decided that jail might be the best place for you right now."

"There isn't a jail built that I can't get out of."

"I think mine might do the job," he answered softly. "Medina, do you have a sturdy room that has a bar on the door?"

Medina's brow puckered uneasily. "Aaron, do you know what you're doing?"

"Trust me."

She looked at the seething Maxie, then back to Hunter.

"I'll have one of the boys put a bar on the door of Aleta's room. It's off the kitchen. Will that do?"

"Just fine. Thanks."

Maxie couldn't believe her ears. She had thought Medina was her friend. This whole scene was a nightmare. She was almost tempted to think she would awaken at any moment and find that all of the summer's adventures had simply been a terrible dream.

"Let's go, Maxie," Hunter said in a voice that, to Maxie's ears, was insufferably smug. "You're going to jail."

Maxie sat on her cot and fumed. The door to her room was securely barred, and the slit of a window that looked out upon the yard was much too small for even her slender body to slip through. Given enough time she would have thought of a way to escape, but she had only this one night before Hunter would drag her off to the lockup. Even if she could have gotten out of her room, every hand on the ranch had his eye peeled to make sure she didn't make a run for it. No doubt they thought it was a rare joke that Cactus Maxie, who had given more than one of them a comeuppance or two, was finally being penned and hog-tied.

Maxie sat and scowled at the adobe walls. Right then she couldn't think of any torture quite painful enough to make Aaron Hunter pay for this villainy, but she would come up with something eventually.

She was still sitting on her cot, scowling and plotting, when a knock sounded on her door. Hell and damn! Who had the nerve to bother her now? The sky outside her window had been black as pitch for hours. The time had to be midnight or later.

"Go away!" she growled.

"Maxie, may I come in?"

The voice belonged to Hunter. Maxie had to give him credit for guts. No brains, but guts.

"Go away, you slime-sucking son of a bitch. You come in here, I'll rip your damned face off."

The newly installed bar squeaked as it was removed. Hunter opened the door and stepped in, looking not at all daunted by her threat. Maxie's heart jumped. Even now, after all that had happened, the sight of Hunter's broad shoulders, the familiar curve of his mouth, and the deep timbre of his voice sent a quiver down her spine.

"You can just turn around and get out, Hunter. I'm not speaking to you. You're lucky I don't cut your lying tongue right out of your head."

"Rip my face off? Cut my tongue out? Maxie, you haven't become civilized at all, have you?" He made himself at home on the cot with his shoulders propped against the wall and his long legs stretched out in front of him.

"Civilized ladies don't go to jail," she sneered.

"That's what I'd like to talk about."

"Well, I don't want to talk. I don't want to look at your ugly face or listen to your lying mouth. I'm so mad at you I could spit."

He smiled. "I know you are. But you still love me."

Maxie's mouth dropped open in astonishment, then closed with an angry snap. "Don't be a stupid jackass."

"I can't help being a stupid jackass at times. That's the way I'm made. The way I figure it, we're made for each other, since you can't lay claim to a full load of smarts yourself."

For once in her life, Maxie was speechless.

"Come sit here beside me." He didn't wait for her to comply, but reached out and pulled her down on the cot. "I'll tell you the truth, Maxie. No more lies between us. You've got more thorns than a jumping cactus, but I love you. And you love me. You never would have been in that draw to warn me away from your brothers if you didn't love me."

"Like hell! You've got a pretty high opinion of yourself if—"

"Just shut that overworked mouth of yours and listen to me. Like you say, I've made a jackass of myself more than once over the past few weeks. I figure I've loved you since the day you punched my gut in Hernando's bar. But I kept thinking that you were part of a past I didn't want to be reminded of. *I* wanted to be civilized and law-abiding. So I needed a civilized, law-abiding lady—which you aren't."

Maxie snorted indignantly.

"But there are some things a man just can't fight, Maxie. I don't want some civilized, tea-sipping lady anymore. You're not my past. You're my future. I want you. I love you. I don't care what your brothers are or what they've done, or what you've done. Marry me, Maxie, and we'll just start fresh from this day on—all our jackass mistakes forgotten."

Maxie's heart twisted with longing. Sometimes doing what was right and good and sensible was harder than hitting a snake with a pistol shot at fifty feet. She dredged up all the anger she could find.

"You love me," she said sourly. "You want to marry me. So you're going to throw me in jail. That makes a lot of sense."

"More sense than letting you ride off on your own. That jail of mine can hold you for as long as it takes you to admit that we belong together."

"There's not a jail built that can hold a Maxwell."

Hunter reached up and drew a finger along the side of her neck. She shivered. "It'll be my pleasure to convince you that you want to be held, then."

She sprang up from the cot and moved out of his reach. But the heat from his fingers still burned her skin. "I'm not going to marry you, Hunter. How stupid do you think I am, anyway? Do you think I want to stick around this territory while you and my brothers tear at each others' throats?"

Hunter stood up and walked over to her. His hands closed on her shoulders in a gentle grip. "I don't give a damn about your brothers, Max. They can find their own way to hell. The only Maxwell I want is you."

Maxie slapped his hands away. "You think you can just call off the fight, then? Lordy, Hunter! You've gotten my brothers good and riled, and now you figure you can back off?"

She laughed unpleasantly. "Think again, lawman. You may have started the war, but they surely aim to finish it. One of these days they're going to fill you full of holes, or you're going to do the same to them. Either way I'm the loser, aren't I? My brothers may be slime, but they're Maxwell slime. And as for you—well, there was a time when I was fairly attached to you."

He smiled. "You do love me."

"Oh, I love you, all right." The admission sounded like anything but an endearment. "But I'm not sticking around to dig your grave—or graves for my idiot brothers, either."

"Maybe no graves will be required."

"Yeah. And it snows in July, too."

"In some places, it does."

"You're as stupid as you are stubborn."

"Woman," Hunter said with a shake of his head. "Didn't anyone ever teach you when to stop talking?"

Maxie was so engrossed in her own frustration that she didn't notice how close he had drawn. He had only to reach out his hand to touch her, and he did. Tentative touches—first on her chin, then on her cheek. He moved closer still and his arms went around her.

Her spine stiffened. "Get away from me, or I'll scream my damned head off."

"I don't think you're the screaming kind, Maxie."

He pulled her against him and buried his face in the mass of her hair. She wanted to scream, but she couldn't. All her determination couldn't hold against the unreasoning desire that flooded her veins.

"You haven't heard a word I've said."

"Yes, I have," he murmured between nuzzles. Then he sighed, set her a few inches away from him, and looked at her. Maxie decided she would have to be colder than a January freeze to resist thawing in the heat of that gaze. "Under all those cactus thorns you're the very devil of a woman, sweetheart. I love you, Max. I love you so damned much it hurts. But I love us—together—more than I love you. If that's selfish, then all right, it's selfish. One way or another, you and I are going to be together." He grinned. "And we're going to be happy, dammit, if it kills us both."

Maxie resisted the urge to giggle at how ridiculous Hunter sounded. Damn the man! He was doing his level best to ignore the dreadful seriousness of his situation.

"I think you're the only person I've met who's more stubborn than I am," she admitted.

"That's mighty stubborn."

"I don't hold a candle to you."

He merely smiled and kissed her hair. His mouth moved to her brow, then the tip of her nose, then her neck.

"This is getting awkward," he murmured in complaint. "How did you get to be so short? Come over to the cot."

Maxie allowed herself to be pushed gently down onto the mattress. Surely yielding this one more time could do no harm. She deserved one more time with Hunter, one more time of sinking into the pleasure of his embrace, surrendering to the heat that was rushing through her veins. One passionate good-bye would have to last her a lifetime. The future stretched out in her mind's eye like a barren plain. How could she resist a last stop at this oasis before setting out on such a joyless journey?

"I do love you, Hunter," she whispered against his chest as he lay down beside her. The chest was naked. By some trick of magic he had rid both of them of their clothing.

"Of course you do," he answered warmly. "How could you not love me when I'm so crazy about you?" He slipped his hand over her breast, tantalized the nipple, then followed with his mouth.

Shivers crawled down her spine and exploded in roiling heat between her legs. She arched against him. "Hunter, I don't think I'm in the mood for doing this slow."

"Patience," he whispered. "We have all the time in the world, all the years of the future, time and time again."

Stubborn and crazy, that was what he was. But now was not the time to convince him. They had only one time, this one last time. A lifetime's worth of loving had to be packed into a single final encounter.

"Now, Hunter." She wrapped her legs around him and pulled him down into her waiting softness.

Hunter groaned hoarsely when he felt the warm readiness of her offering. "Whatever you say, love." He plunged inside her, sending them both into spiraling rapture.

Before the night was over, one time turned into two, then three. Finally calm, Maxie drifted on the border of sleep, Hunter's hard body pressed against hers and exhaustion waiting to claim her. Still she felt the need to set Hunter straight—now, while the sharp edge of their passion was dulled with satiation.

"I do love you Hunter," she murmured sleepily into his chest. "But I'm still not going to marry you."

Hunter lifted her hand from the mattress, where their fingers were interlaced, and raised it to his lips. She felt his mouth curve into a smile. "That's what I figured, Max," he whispered in answer. "And that's why you're still going to jail."

Cynthia stood on the wooden plank walkway in front of her father's dry goods store. Both of her parents were inside the store, staunchly determined to defend their merchandise if need be, though the town's intruders so far had shown no interest in anything besides whiskey and loose women.

Yesterday evening they had ridden in. As on most Tuesday nights, the town had been quiet. A few prospectors had gotten drunk—one snoring peacefully outside the Shot-Hole Saloon, two others thrown out of Mother Moses' house for unseemly behavior (though what was deemed unseemly behavior in a house of that sort Cynthia couldn't imagine). But on the whole the night had been peaceful until the Maxwells had ridden into town.

Now, with most of the morning gone, the town was quiet again. But the stillness was unnatural, born of fear, not peace. Deputy Marshal Simon Curtis had been unceremoniously locked in his own jail, and with much hooting and rib jabbing the Maxwells had tossed the key into the latrine in back of the marshal's office. Curtis would play a leading role, they'd promised, in the double execution planned for when the marshal returned.

The citizens of Motherlode were all shuttered in their houses, like ostriches with their heads in the sand, trying to pretend this day was like any other day—business as usual. Of course, it wasn't a normal day; it was a day for killing. Everyone in town knew it, but no one had the guts to do anything about it. The Maxwells had made no secret about the purpose of their visit. The citizens of Motherlode had best find a new lawman, they had yelled from the streets. Because Aaron Hunter was a dead man.

The only person in the whole town who'd had the fortitude to stand up to the outlaws was Mother Moses. She had stood in front of the door of her establishment, a shotgun in her hands, and refused them entrance. Her ladies didn't cater to scum, she told them. They laughed in her face, ugly-sounding laughs, until she peppered the street around them with buckshot. Then their tune changed. The Maxwells told her in great detail what they would do to her once they got her without the shotgun, but in the end they backed off. The youngest of them had balked at attacking a woman, it seemed, and he had talked his brothers down from their fury.

That one youngest Maxwell might have a shred of decency somewhere deep inside him, Cynthia thought bitterly, but the older brothers were slime. Any relationship they bore to little Maxie was hard to fathom. Maxie was a bit wild, true, and at times she could even be crude by civilized standards. But at her core she was gentle as could be—a gem, uncut, unpolished, but a gem just the same. How she could share common blood with the scum who now sat in the saloon across the street was beyond Cynthia's understanding.

She paced up and down the walkway, eyes focused on the wagon road out of town. Sooner or later Aaron would be riding in. If she could spot him before the Maxwells did, then at least she could give him some warning.

Thirty minutes later she did spot him, riding along the dusty road with someone else riding at his side. She stepped out into the road, determined to give him a sign that all was not well, but the sight of a leering face staring at her from above the swinging doors into the saloon froze her motion. Blackjack Maxwell smiled at her as he rested his arms on the doors. The smile was an evil one, straight from the devil himself. He shook his head no. The message was clear.

Cynthia's heart did a quick kathump within her chest. For a moment she hesitated, toying with the idea of defying the outlaw. But only for a moment. The man would kill her with no more thought than he would swat a fly. Good sense won out, and she retreated carefully through the doorway into her father's store.

"Aaron's coming," she told her father, who stood behind the counter dusting his apothecary bottles.

Mr. Pruitt shook his head. "God help him."

"I should hope so! No one else in this town will." Cynthia's skirts swished angrily as she swept behind the counter. She took the feather duster from her father and pointed it at him like an accusing finger. "I can't believe that not one man in this craven town will help him! There are only three Maxwells, and at least a hundred men are cowering behind the walls of this town."

Her father shrugged. "How many would be killed trying to take those devils down? Why should the men of this town risk their lives? They hired Aaron Hunter to protect Motherlode. I guess they think he should be able to protect himself as well. After all, the Maxwells haven't bothered any of the shops or the bank."

Cynthia gave a ladylike snort. "They will! As soon as they get Aaron, they'll turn this town upside down."

Mr. Pruitt shook his head sadly. Cynthia huffed and slammed the duster onto the counter.

"Mercy, I wish I were a man!"

When Hunter rode into town with Maxie, he was unsuspecting. If his mind hadn't been so focused on the girl riding beside him, he might have sensed the danger that awaited. But he had ridden all morning with one eye on Maxie's every move. She'd made it no secret that she still intended to elude him, and he had the feeling that if he made a single misstep he would lose the best thing that had ever come into his life. Damned stubborn woman. He didn't dare underestimate her. She was quick and wily as a skittish rabbit. Too bad she didn't have half as much common sense.

Hunter was looking for trouble from Maxie, not from the direction of his town. When trouble came, he was caught off guard. He and Maxie had just passed the Shot-Hole Saloon when Aaron found himself suddenly surrounded by two cocked pistols and one rifle, each with a Maxwell behind the sights. Caught with his hand too far from his gun, Aaron halted as the Maxwells closed into a deadly circle around Maxie and him in the middle of the dusty street.

"Howdy, Hunter," Blackjack greeted him from behind his rifle. "You're right disappointin'. Here I thought you was smarter than to walk into a trap so easy. Thought we might have to do some work chasin' ya down. You're dumber than I thought."

"Blackjack. Tom. Jim." Hunter's voice was calm, but Maxie heard the undertone of tension. The sudden sight of her brothers had startled her own nerves to attention, and now they were stretched so tight they were ready to snap.

"Get down, lawman." Blackjack motioned with his rifle. "Shootin' you is gonna be a pure pleasure, but I'd hate to miss my aim and hit that fine horse of yours." He grinned. "I might have some use for it once you're dead."

"Blackjack!" Maxie blurted. "This is crazy! Why don't you just—"

"Shut up, Max. You done your part. Now git!"

"I didn't!" She looked at Hunter helplessly.

"I know you didn't," he comforted her with a brief smile.

He trusted her. After everything she had done and said, he trusted her, the idiot.

"Get outta here, Max," Dirty Jim ordered.

"Maxie, go." Hunter's fierce tone left no room for disobedience. Her heart pounded, a painful hammer in her chest. Her teeth clenched, grinding in angry, helpless frustration.

"Go," Aaron repeated.

She met his eyes for one last time and wished she could say so many things to him that now she would never get to say. Then she gave her brothers a venomous look, turned, and spurred her mare into a startled gallop down the street.

"Get down, Hunter," Blackjack said with a smile, "and toss away that gun of yours."

Hunter obeyed, moving slowly.

"Take his horse, Jim. That's a mighty fine-looking rifle on the saddle. Figure that alone's worth killin' a man."

If Blackjack had hoped to goad Hunter into a display of fear, then he was disappointed. Aaron didn't flinch as the oldest Maxwell brother's rifle swung in his direction.

"Wonder how it feels to get your head blowed off," Tom speculated with a chuckle.

"My guess is that you'll find out someday," Hunter answered.

Tom's grin collapsed. "Come on, Jack. Let's get this done and celebrate. There's a gal waitin' for me over to the saloon."

"Not so fast, Tom. You'll take all the fun out of it. Killin' a pest like Hunter—now that's a thing that should be drawed out, so's a body can appreciate how good it feels. I think we should take some time to have some fun. Whadda ya say, lawman?"

Hunter didn't answer, just fastened his eyes on Blackjack. Tom and Jim he ignored.

"Maybe I'll start by puttin' a slug through your knees. Or

. . . if ya wanna be organized about it, I could begin by shootin' holes in your feet and work my way up." Blackjack's eyes gleamed maliciously as he watched for a reaction from his victim. "Even better, I could start in the middle, blow your dick off, and then work down from there. That might be entertainin'."

Not a flicker of emotion crossed Hunter's face. He simply stared at his tormentor with black eyes as feral as a wolf's.

"Jim," Blackjack said with a grin. "Go shoot the lock off the jail and fetch Curtis. We wouldn't want to leave Hunter's deputy out of our little celebration."

"Aw, Jack! Send Tom."

Blackjack glanced toward his sullen brother. Hunter took advantage of the opportunity. In the small moment that Blackjack's attention was diverted he crouched, scooped up a handful of dust from the road, flung it into Blackjack's face, and ran toward the nearest alley. Jack cursed, spit dirt, and fired blindly. He missed. Never quick on the uptake, Tom gaped for a moment, then sprayed lead in a wide fan along the street as Jim looked on in bored disgust.

Hunter zigzagged, seeming to dodge the slugs that whined past him and puffed up grouts of dust from the road. Blackjack's curses followed him as he ducked into a dim alleyway that led between the empty theater house and Herrera's Hardware, Leather, and Harness Supply.

"We're gonna fetch a rope, Hunter!" Blackjack roared. "And when we catch you we're gonna hang both you and that deputy of yours. Shootin's too good for you. You're gonna die slow, you yella-bellied son of a bitch. I'll make sure you dance on the end of that rope a long time before you die!" Blackjack turned toward his brothers and snarled. "Jim! Go find a rope! Tom! Don't stand there gaping. Get after Hunter, dammit! That alley don't have but one way out between the harnessry barn and the theater. I'll circle around and cut 'im off so he can't get out."

Hunter plastered himself against the wall of Herrera's Hardware and smiled grimly. Three to one odds. Not good, but he had faced greater odds and come out the victor. First he had to find a better place to fight.

He turned to flee—and tripped. The obstacle under his feet let out an indignant squawk. Nearly blinded by the change from bright sunlight to shadow, Hunter hadn't noticed old One-Eye Dugget, who had relocated his drunken nap from the front of the saloon to the more restful shadows of the alley.

"Dammit, One-Eye!" Hunter shook the old man from his stupor. "You get outta here now. There's hombres coming who . . ." He didn't have time to finish the sentence before Tom Maxwell rounded the corner, pistol in hand. "Lay low," Aaron warned the drunk. He pushed the oldster deeper into the shadows, then took off at a run toward the harnessry barn, an add-on to the back of Herrera's shop where the old man did harness repair work.

"Yiiiyiiee!" Tom gave a poor imitation of an Apache war cry and set off in chase. He suffered the same fate as Hunter, and poor One-Eye grunted again as yet another pair of boots stumbled into his ribs. Tom landed on his backside and cursed. "Stupid old man! I oughtta . . . !"

Before Tom could raise his pistol, One-Eye raised his favorite weapon—his whiskey bottle—and brought it down over Tom's head. Tom fell facedown in the dirt. Old One-Eye had had enough of these clumsy oafs disturbing his well-earned slumber.

When he heard Tom's curse, Hunter spun around. He'd thought even Maxwells were above murdering a helpless old drunk, but for a moment he feared he was wrong. But no sooner did he start back to Dugget's rescue than the old man took the law into his own hands. Dust puffed up in little spurts as Tom hit the ground.

Hunter chuckled and saluted the old man. Maybe luck was with him after all. One down and two to go. He ran to where Tom lay and tied the man with his own kerchief—not a very effective restraint, but from the look of Tom's noggin, he was going to be out for a long time. One-Eye muttered at him as he worked. If the old man had had another whiskey bottle, Hunter would have gotten the same treatment as Tom. As it was, Hunter merely told him to continue his nap in another alleyway, and promised him a bottle of Shady Sam Guenther's best whiskey for his help.

As One-Eye ambled off, still muttering, Hunter took Tom's pistol—a new-style cartridge Colt whose chambers held sleek brass bullets instead of powder and a lead ball. All six chambers were loaded. He hefted the weapon in his hand a few times, spun the cylinder, settled it in his own holster, and smiled. Things were looking better and better.

He headed once again for the harnessry barn—the best spot he could think of that could tip the odds in his favor. It was dimly lighted with numerous dark nooks and corners for a lone gunman to lie in wait for a victim. He couldn't get careless now. Two Maxwells were still after his blood, and a third Maxwell was no doubt waiting to get in a few licks if he hurt one single hair on her brothers' heads. Maxie sidled into his mind, and he promptly tossed her out on her shapely little backside. Her brothers were more than capable of killing him on their own without the distraction of her image to help them.

Blackjack, circling around back of the harness shop toward the alley, sighted Aaron even before he reached the barn. Motherlode was a small town without many alleyways or buildings to afford cover—not many places for a man to run without being seen. "It's about over now, lawman," he shouted as he cocked his rifle and followed.

The barn was even dimmer than the alleyway. Light filtered in only from between the slats of the walls and through a small window set high up at one end. But Aaron knew his way around well. He slipped into the shadows and wedged himself into a corner where he was mostly hidden by two harnesses that had been hung up to await repair. A few seconds after he was settled, the barn door opened, allowing a bright shaft of light to cut through the gloom and cast the corners in even greater relative darkness.

"I know you're in here, Hunter." Blackjack chuckled. "My brother's lookin' for rope—one that's kinda worn, with the stretch gone out of it. I figger that's about what you rate. And we aim to tie a right sloppy noose. Wouldn't want you to get off easy with a quick broken neck. You're gonna dance on that rope till your face turns black, lawman. Then maybe we'll let you hang there for a while, just so everyone can see what happens to a man who messes with the Maxwells."

Blackjack stepped out of the light, but his silhouette was etched plainly against the open doorway. "Come out, Hunter," he called. "It don't do you no good to hide like the rat you are."

Blackjack's eyes reflected the dim light. He was like a wolf, Hunter thought, then amended his analogy, for he'd always been partial to wolves. A wolf had a wild nobility that Blackjack lacked. Snake was a more apt description—cold-blooded, a killing machine with no thought for its prey. But then, maybe he was doing an injustice to the snake.

Hunter could think of no reason not to end the man's life here and now. He was an easy target, and Hunter's pistol was cocked and ready. With Tom out of the action and Blackjack dead, the third brother would be easy to handle.

Then Maxie pushed into his mind again. "Sooner or later either they'll fill you full of holes or you'll do the same to them. Either way, I'll be the loser." Those had been her words. Blackjack might be a piece of human trash, but he was Maxie's brother.

Hunter raised the aim of his pistol and fired.

The citizens of Motherlode had trickled out of their doors to watch the goings-on from the storefronts and walkways. The women looked horrified and indignant, the men a bit sheepish.

Among the indignant women were Mother Moses and Cynthia Pruitt, who stood in front of Pruitt's Dry Goods. Between them they restrained a grim-faced Maxie, each grasping one arm. Their prisoner looked ready to hiss and spit at the same time, but neither woman would release her. They'd caught her charging toward the fracas from the livery, where she'd shoved her horse into a stall and unsuccessfully tried to talk the blacksmith out of a gun.

"You just stay right exactly where you are," Mother Moses instructed Maxie.

"You'd just make things worse for Aaron," Cynthia said. She had joined with Mother Moses to restrain her friend without quite being able to meet the eyes of Motherlode's notorious madam. But that didn't hamper her efficiency. Maxie fumed in their grip, but she couldn't go anywhere.

Maxie felt her temper reach the boiling point. As soon as they'd seen her, these two female leeches had grabbed onto her, as if they could read her intentions of swiping a gun from someone's holster and saving Aaron Hunter's bacon once again.

"Let him save himself this time," Mother Moses advised. "Men like to do that every once in a while."

Maxie hadn't even gotten a chance to snatch a pistol. "Let me go! You don't understand! I could help!"

"I do understand," Moses replied. "Hunter can take care of himself. He's a hard man to kill."

"You don't know my brothers," Maxie told her gloomily.

"No. But I know Hunter."

"Look!" Cynthia cried.

Several of Motherlode's bolder citizens, taking advantage of the Maxwells' preoccupation with Hunter, had liberated Simon Curtis by shooting out the jail cell lock. The deputy had followed the sounds of mayhem in the alley and now stepped out of that shadowed passage pushing a groggy Tom Maxwell in front of him.

"That one's not going to give Hunter any more trouble," Moses said with satisfaction.

Maxie didn't have the heart to tell them that of all her brothers, Tom was the easiest to corral.

"See, Maxie," Cynthia added with a relieved smile. "You

didn't need to worry. Simon's going to hand—what's his name?"

"Tom," Maxie supplied, her voice sad.

"Tom—he's going to hand Tom to Doc Carter and go back to help Aaron."

"He won't need to," Mother Moses told them. "Look who's comin'."

Maxie's heart leaped. Emerging from the alley was Hunter himself. A body was slung over his shoulder. Blackjack . . .

"Blackjack!" Her voice echoed the pain that was in her heart. Blackjack. Bold, handsome, with the conscience of a rattlesnake. How could she still love him, even though he was no good?

"Don't look so tragic," Hunter said to Maxie as he eased the body to the street in front of her. He motioned Simon to take Tom on to the jail. "He's just got a lump on his head."

He spoke the truth. Blackjack was still breathing. Maxie looked at Hunter with joy brimming in her eyes. He smiled his irresistible, endearing, crooked smile.

"Jackass here obliged by standing right under a kerosene lamp that was hanging on a rafter. I shot it down on top of him."

"Oh, Hunter! I . . . !"

"Drop the pistol, Hunter!" Dirty Jim's voice rang down the street. "Everybody back off," he ordered as he came out of the saloon, where he had been preparing for a hanging. "You too, Max. Get away from him. I don't want you to get hurt."

"Jim," Maxie said. "Don't be a fool. It's over. Finished."

"Like hell it is. Drop the gun, Hunter, or I'm going to drop a couple of innocent citizens while I'm waiting."

The innocent citizens in question made a hasty retreat back through the doorways from which they had emerged —all except Maxie, Moses, Cynthia, and Simon, who'd handed off his prisoner to a retreating onlooker and reached for his gun.

"Don't do it, Curtis!" Jim warned. He swung the pistol briefly in the deputy's direction, then immediately brought it back to bear on Hunter. "Throw your gun over here."

Simon obeyed. His pistol landed at Jim's feet.

Hunter held his hand out from his holstered gun. "I'm not going to throw mine down, Maxwell. Do you think you can kill me before I can kill you?"

The wild look on Dirty Jim's face frightened Maxie. Was this her twin, her childhood playmate and fellow mischief-maker? Did she know him at all?

"My gun's in my hand, Hunter," Jim reminded him. "You can't beat a man with a gun already in his hand."

"You want to bet your life on that?"

Hunter's eyes were steady, his hand didn't show a trace of tremor. Jim's cheek twitched, his grin faded.

"Jim!" Maxie pleaded. "Don't!"

"Get out of here, Max!" both men ordered at the same time.

She surprised them both by obeying. Eyes wet with tears, she fled into Pruitt's Dry Goods. Moses and Cynthia looked at each other warily and followed.

"Give it up, Jim." Hunter kept his voice soft, calm. He could see the heady excitement in the boy's eyes—eyes of pure cobalt-blue, eyes that could have belonged to Maxie.

"You're a dead man, Hunter." His finger tightened on the trigger of his gun. With an unholy smile stretching his lips, he fired.

Hunter dived aside. His bluff hadn't worked, but a flicker in the boy's eyes just before he fired gave a split second's warning. An undignified double time crawl brought him to shelter behind a horse trough.

Jim fired again. The trough splintered. A stream of water began to trickle onto the street and run in rivulets through the dust.

"Come out, you son of a bitch!" Jim shouted. He fired again and again, until the pistol's hammer clicked down upon an empty chamber.

Hunter stood. All he had to do was draw his gun and fire while Jim was groping for his second pistol—an easy task for a man who was one of the fastest guns in the border country. But Hunter's hand froze. Looking at Dirty Jim was too much like looking at Maxie. The boy had her eyes, her mouth, her sweet, stubborn chin. He even had her hair. For a moment Hunter couldn't bring himself to draw his gun.

The moment of hesitation almost proved fatal. Hunter saw Jim grab his second pistol and thumb back the hammer —in slow motion, it seemed. A shot thundered in his ears. He jolted, expecting the impact of hot lead.

But it was Jim who fell, a look of surprise on his face. Hunter turned, finally realizing the shot had come from behind him, where Maxie stood with a smoking gun in her hand—a sleek new cartridge pistol from Pruitt's gun case.

Maxie swayed, stunned. She let the pistol drop from her fingers and clatter onto the wooden walkway.

"Maxie!" Hunter said softly. "My God!" He stared at her, disbelief and wonder battling in his eyes.

She stared back. For a moment she felt her body go cold and her vision begin to swim.

"Maxie!" Hunter started toward her, holding out his arms as she tottered.

Then Dirty Jim groaned. The groan ended with an obscene curse as he reached for the pistol he'd dropped. In one smooth motion Hunter turned, drew, and shot the pistol out of reach of Jim's hand.

A new jolt of adrenaline brought Maxie back to life. Her breathing steadied as she focused on her cursing brother. "I see my aim is as good as ever," she said with a satisfied grin. "You're not hurt nearly as bad as you deserve, you chickenshit horse's ass."

She suddenly felt as if the weight of two worlds had been lifted from her shoulders. At last she knew which world she belonged in. Still shivering, she hugged herself as Hunter came close, then gave herself over to his embrace as he took her in his arms. "And he once told me I'd never be able to shoot a real person because I was chicken. He was always calling me chicken."

Hunter smiled and dropped a quick kiss on the top of Maxie's head. People were streaming into the street, crowding around, staring. Simon had stepped forward to take care of Dirty Jim, and Doc Carter was instructing two boys to lift Blackjack and cart him away to his surgery.

"Show's over, folks," Hunter said. "For now." He brushed errant, curling tendrils of hair back from Maxie's face and watched a smile steal over her face as she looked up into his. "But stick around, people. There'll be a better show tonight. We're going to have the loudest, rowdiest wedding you ever did see."

His words were for the crowd, but his eyes were for Maxie only. "Come on, Maxie girl," he said quietly. "I know a place where we can get something cool to drink and something warm to wash in. And then . . . I'm going to make you glad you shoot like a man instead of like a lady."

"Hell, Hunter." Maxie smiled up at him and slipped her arm through his. "From now on I'm gonna be the damnedest lady you ever did see."

Mother Moses and Cynthia stood together on the walk in front of Pruitt's store. Maxie gave them a knowing wink as she and Hunter slipped away from the crowd and made their way down the street.

Epilogue

*D*irty Jim Maxwell kneed his horse into a canter. Aaron Hunter was not going to be pleased to hear that twenty-five head of his newfangled Hereford cattle had been rustled the night before. That herd of white-faced cows was the thing closest to Hunter's heart—next to his wife and daughter. Jim found it hard to believe an ex-gunman could get so wrapped up in a ranch, or in a woman either.

When Jim brought news of the missing cattle, Hunter was going to have a hell of a fight on his hands—not so much with the rustlers as with Maxie. For all that she was a proper married lady now, she could still give Hunter the devil of a time when she wanted, and Jim would bet his last nickel in wages that she would be itching to ride after those rustlers along with her husband. Hunter would object, of course, as any sensible husband would, and Max would argue and stomp about until Aaron was madder at her than at the rustlers.

Jim figured Hunter would win this one. When Maxie's safety was at stake he generally wouldn't budge, no matter how his wife fussed and fumed. Jim had never seen anyone handle his hot-tempered sister as Hunter could. Aaron would give her a lopsided grin and cock one brow and she'd gentle down like a well-broke filly.

Six years of marriage hadn't changed Max, Jim mused. She might wear skirts now instead of britches and an apron instead of a gun belt, but she still had the same talent for mischief. Most times Hunter didn't even try to keep a lid on Maxie's spirit. He seemed to enjoy having a wife who could outshoot and outride most of the C C Ranch hands.

"Hold up there, Jim!" Jim reined in as Pancho Galvan rode up beside him. "How many head you count gone from the west range?"

"Twenty-five. Any more missing from your bunch?"

"Not today. The boss man's gonna be plenty mad. Plenty mad! General Crook comes and whips the Apaches so we can raise cattle in peace, and now we gotta put up with these damned rustlers."

Jim grinned as they rode together along Chiricahua Creek, from which the Chiricahua Creek Ranch—abbreviated by almost everyone to the C C—took its name. "Don't bother feelin' sorry for Hunter, Pancho. More like you should feel sorry for those rustlers. Aaron Hunter ain't exactly a body to trifle with. And my sister ain't, either, for that matter."

And didn't Dirty Jim Maxwell just know it! He still bore the scar from where she'd shot him.

"Apaches tried to throw 'em off this ranch, bandits tried to run 'em off, and now this bunch of rustlers. If you ask me, both of 'em enjoy the fightin'."

Pancho grinned. "You oughtta know."

Jim's stint in prison was no secret from any of the ranch hands, nor the fact that his two brothers were still rotting away in Yuma's "Hell-Hole," as everyone in the territory called it. Few of the men gave him much grief over his messy past, though. If Maxie had seen fit to forgive him and put him to work after he got out of prison, the ranch hands saw no reason to make trouble over it.

Jim was grateful for a second chance. Prison had been a nightmarish cure for a disease worse than a nightmare, but it had worked. Sometimes, as Hunter had once told him, a man needs a good stiff jerk to move him from the wrong side of the road to the right one.

The ranch house—a walled adobe compound built in the same fashion as Pete Kelley's Agua Linda—came into sight around a bend in the creek. "Why don't you take in the news," Pancho offered. "I'll get together some of the hands. I figure the boss'll wanna to start out after 'em right away."

"You do that," Jim agreed.

He rode into the compound and swung down from his saddle. His feet were scarcely on the ground when a little dust devil with braids and freckles tackled him at the knees.

"Uncle Dirt! Uncle Dirt!"

Knees were about as high as Theresa Medina Hunter could reach at the age of five, but when she grew a bit she was going to do real damage by unleashing that kind of energy, Jim mused. Still, he gave her his best unclelike grin. "How's my girl?" he asked.

She looked up with a wide smile that stretched the freckles on her face. "I'm fine, Uncle Dirt. Will you talk to Ma for me?"

"Now why else would I be here in the middle of the morning if not to talk to your ma—and your pa. They inside?"

"Ma's inside. Pa's over at the horse corral. No, wait!" She bounced alongside him as he started walking in the direction of the corral. "Will you tell Ma I could ride Duster?"

Jim chuckled, picturing his tiny niece trying to ride the half-broken stud that Aaron himself could scarcely handle.

He slowed his walk so that her five-year-old legs could keep pace. "You're not nearly big enough to ride Duster, kiddo."

Her lower lip shot out. "I rode him, and I only got throwed twice. But Ma beat my butt."

"She should've beat more than your little butt. You shouldn't go anywhere near that horse." He grinned as a memory intruded: Maxie riding a stallion at Stronghold that no one else could ride—but after pouring a bottle of whiskey down its throat. Not that he would dare tell Theresa that story. She would likely try the same thing herself.

"Why don't you hop up and take a ride on me?" he invited.

Gleefully she held her arms out. He swung her up onto his shoulders. "Now point me in the direction of your pa. I've got some news for him."

"That way. He's puttin' shoes on horses with Charlie."

"Good."

Theresa grabbed two handfuls of Jim's hair as he set out at a fast walk. "Uncle Simon and Aunt Elsa are coming to visit today," she told him happily. "And they're bringing Mary. Mary has a new boyfriend."

"Mary always has a new boyfriend," Jim said with a chuckle.

"He's teaching Mary how to shoot a gun," she hinted.

"Is that so?"

"It's true," she answered solemnly.

"Did I ever tell you about the time your ma almost shot me in the foot when we were kids trying to learn how to draw a gun?"

"I wouldn't hit your foot, Uncle Dirt. Will you teach me to shoot?"

He reached up and swung her from his shoulders to the upper rail of the corral. "You better ask your ma about that."

"But will you?"

Jim didn't answer. He could hear the clanging of the ferrier's hammer around the corner of the barn. The business of the day awaited, and he had no time for dawdling with a kid. But he couldn't resist touching her cheek and giving her a smile. She reminded him so much of a grubby, freckle-faced girl with whom he used to squabble, play, and run wild over a country that now was well on the way to becoming civilized. Little sable-haired Theresa was the very image of her mother in both looks and temperament.

"You run back to the house and tell your ma I'm here," he told her, lifting her from the railing. "I've got to talk to your pa. And if Marshal Curtis comes, you tell him to come on out here. We got some work to do." She pouted, and Jim relented. "Later I'll talk to your ma about those shootin' lessons."

Mollified, Theresa scampered off. Jim watched her go, and wondered. General Crook had gentled down most of the Apaches. Aaron Hunter and men like him put a real cramp in the style of rustlers and bandits. Sometimes Jim figured that the once wild frontier was becoming hopelessly civilized—until he looked at little Theresa Medina Hunter. He hoped Arizona was ready for another hellion Maxwell to be loosed upon the territory.